THE NANNY

An absolutely breathtaking psychological thriller
with a stunning final twist

ELEONOR SAMUEL

Joffe Books, London
www.joffebooks.com

First published in Great Britain in 2023

© Eleonor Samuel

Cover art by Nick Castle

ISBN: 978-1-80405-975-3

To our little Bluebird, who taught me never to give up hope.

PROLOGUE

A montage of photographs. Picture on picture. Memory on memory, blowing off the dust as each one found its unceremonious home in a cardboard box. Freshers' week, clubs, house parties, birthdays, graduation. The images muffled by the darkness of a closed lid. An empty shelf, room, house. An end, and a beginning. Like a whole era's hangover, a heavy head and leaden stomach. The sick feeling hadn't subsided, and the silence was still too loud.

Dear Hope.
Hope . . .
To Hope.
No.
My dearest Hope.
No. Not now. Not like that.
I screwed up the sheet of paper.

CHAPTER 1: RIFWAY

Outside the car windows, the world was turning grey. The clouds had arrived, a swarm of foreboding on the swelling wind, and now the sky was darkening. I had been in the car for nearly three hours, having stopped twice at dull and noisy motorway services, before embarking on these last few miles to nowhere.

I glanced in the mirror at the stack of scrawled-on suitcases in the back seat, *India McKenzie* four times over. My world packed into four bags. The thought was depressing. Out of the windscreen, the weather had got the wrong season; all there was to see over the wind-buffeted August fields and swelling dark green hills was unbroken cloud. It seemed that perhaps I'd left the sun in my old room, with my confidence, when I set off in the early morning light.

Too late to change my mind. I was committed now. They had only interviewed me four days ago: John and Julia Maine, a surgeon and his wife. And Alicia. Although I'd never met Alicia . . . which seemed strange, the more I thought about it, given that I was going to spend every moment of my waking time with her for the undetermined future. I wasn't a nanny. Just some poor graduate with an excuse for a degree, and no plan.

It was starting to rain.

Rifway. Even the sign was dark, splattered with mud. The road gleamed wet under the beam of the headlights as I switched on the windscreen wipers and turned down the distracting babble of the radio.

I was nearly there.

The streets were strangely empty, devoid of traffic. Buildings passed in a blur of stone and pebbledash and very little colour. On the road ahead of me, a traffic light went from green to red and then back again, its glow refracted into sharp shards of light by the ceaseless movement of the rain.

I sped up a little through the signals, an open stretch of road leaving the other side of the village. I glanced out of the window at a group of teenagers on the pavement, laughing, running in the rain. It was as if I already knew what was going to happen.

The girl stumbled out without a second glance. I slammed my foot onto the brake, the breath catching in my throat, a sudden hot flush of adrenaline racing through my blood.

Everything slowed down. I saw the girl turn, not laughing anymore, not even smiling.

I wanted to close my eyes.

It was like a dream, unreal; I watched from the pavement as the car didn't stop, didn't even slow, heard the sickening clash of metal unmatched by the resistance of flesh and bone. Saw the body rise, jerk, twist strangely, as if it had thrown itself onto the bonnet with a will of its own, until the glossy dark head contacted the windscreen with another deadly thud, and cracks spidered across the glass. I saw the limp figure, suddenly so young and childlike, slide with a smear of blood down the bonnet and onto the wet road, under the wheels, only a shape in the glow of the dirty headlights . . .

Bile rose in my throat as I brought the car to a halt. I blinked hard, gripped the wheel tightly with one hand and changed back into first gear. The girl paused, twirled on the spot, a startled pirouette as she found herself trapped in the beam of my headlights. For just a moment she caught my eye through the windscreen, embarrassed, before tossing back her hair and running the rest of the way. Her friends were still laughing.

The ringing in my ears receded, and the world returned from slow motion. My cases had all slid off the back seat into the footwells; the contents of my handbag strewn over the front of the car, Hope's brown eyes gazing up at me from the back cover of my purse.

I watched the figure of the girl recede along the pavement in the mirror as I pulled away. My heart rate hadn't slowed by the time I finally reached the end of the village, and left the thirty limit for a narrow, high-hedged country lane. My hands were sweating on the wheel. Nearly there. I would need to be calm when I arrived. The near miss hadn't helped.

Drizzle clung to the windscreen as I turned a sharp corner and found myself face to face with it: the Manor. My new home.

Perhaps I hadn't processed how intimidating it was when I came for the interview. Built high on the hillside, it was as grey and bleak as the craggy hill and the sky above that now threatened storms.

I'm not sure what made me think coming here was a good idea. Perhaps it was the already severed ties. The loneliness, at home, or in the empty Leeds student house where my last month's rent had nearly run out. I was out of options. The possibility of a new beginning was all that was left.

The two storeys of age-dulled stone faced out over sloping green grounds, a blurred distinction between parkland and garden. The windows were framed with dark wood that seemed, somehow, to throw the glass into shadow. I wasn't sure why looking at it made me shiver.

The entrance to the drive was half-hidden by shrubs, and I had to stand on the brakes to pull in through the stone pillars onto a driveway lined with dense rhododendron bushes. I was suddenly reluctant to switch off the engine.

Rifway was a very long way from home. Uni had been a long way from home, but it had been full of boarding-school-esque familiarity and a sense of the temporary. And Hope. It had been full of Hope.

I glanced in the wing-mirror as I climbed out of the car, suddenly exhausted. I was a mess, my skin pale, my grey-green eyes staring back at me dark-ringed as I dragged my fingers hastily through my hopeless, black-streaked blonde tangles. My jacket had spent the day hanging on the back of my seat, but I pulled it on now; I needed to at least try to look smart.

They wouldn't have employed me if they didn't like me, I told myself as I approached the heavy-pillared porch, found the doorbell and rang it with shaking fingers.

Or perhaps they were as short on options as I was.

The elbows of my jacket felt uncomfortably tight. I tugged the sleeves further down over my hands to hide the chipped nail varnish that I had forgotten to take off.

"Hello, India." The door was opened by Julia Maine, a slim, middle-aged woman dressed immaculately in a designer two-piece with flawless makeup and elegantly knotted black hair. Her blue eyes were piercing.

"Hi." My voice sounded oddly strangled. Not much like my voice. It wasn't only the house that intimidated me. I reached out a hand, forgetting about the nail varnish. She took it and shook it firmly.

"You're right on time. John's upstairs; I think he wanted to say hello to you before he had to go back into the General. Alicia's upstairs too. Follow me."

* * *

Dear Hope,

I'm starting this letter at home, but by the time I get the chance to finish it, I'll be somewhere else. Somewhere miles away. So far from you that the thought itself hurts.

But I have no choice now. When Angela recommended me for the job I leapt at the chance. I guess now isn't a good time to actually start thinking it through.

I know I could have messaged you. To ask how you were. To tell you I'm here safely. But you always used to say how exciting it was to receive an actual letter once in a while. And anyway, what's a message? Anyone could be writing it, and you'd never know.

So yeah. I'm here safely. I don't know what else to write — I'm trying to fill the page because I want to make it last longer. You know that, too. I'm crap at saying bye. Really why I'm writing, I think, is because I want you to wish me luck. But as that's rude, I'll wish you luck instead, with your new beginning.

What else is there to say?

Oh yes.

I miss you.

CHAPTER 2: PROBLEMS

"Alicia." The call was too considered to be a yell. We were at the bottom of a wide wooden staircase with scrolled banister rails and perilously smooth boards.

I looked around, bewildered, at the sturdy hat and coat stand, shelf of perfectly lined-up shoes and exotic potted plant at the foot of the stairs, trying not to feel lost.

"I'll show you around." Mrs Maine's smile wasn't exactly warm; more business-like. "There's a lot to get to know. We can go upstairs first. You'll want to meet Alicia. Then I'll show you where everything is and run through the routine." Her eyes travelled unmistakably from my scruffy nails back to my face. "We did go through it before, but just so we're absolutely clear."

I nodded, unnerved by her scrutiny. "Um yeah . . . yes. That would be . . . really helpful."

"Alicia!" She raised her voice again, only a little. I couldn't imagine her actually shouting. "Alicia, India's here." She turned back to me. "If you wouldn't mind taking off your shoes before we go up. It's a rule, no shoes upstairs." The fierceness of her stare unsettled me further as I removed my Converse. "And I'd prefer it if you call me Mrs Maine, in front of Alicia."

I nodded again and followed her up the creaking wooden stairs in silence.

"Alicia! Could you come when I call you, please! I thought you wanted to give India the tour."

She turned back to me, voice lowered confidentially. "While it's still the holidays the rules are slightly different, obviously. Alicia can stay in the house or go outside, you don't have to stay with her if she's just in the garden." She shooed a cat from our path as we reached the top of the stairs, and dusted her hands together with distaste. "She needs to practise the piano for at least half an hour every day; she works better in the afternoons, so usually four o'clock. She has piano lessons twice a week; Mr Trevers comes in for them. She's only allowed to watch TV for an hour on holiday days and half an hour on other days. Unless she's ill. You need to give her tea at five, after homework and piano — not before, because otherwise you'll never get her to practise — and then give her a bath. Bedtime is half past seven, strictly lights out at quarter to eight. She gets very difficult when she's over-tired. And the cats need to be in before then, otherwise she doesn't sleep."

Mrs Maine pulled her sleeves up and pushed the door on our left open with an impatient gesture. "Alicia!"

I looked past her into a huge room, carpeted in magenta and painted baby pink. There were teddy bears, dolls, a million toys cast carelessly on the floor, a fish tank and a hamster cage. The furniture was all painted white: a wardrobe, a chest of drawers, a desk. The four-poster bed was made up with pink and white too, with a bookcase of colourful books, perfectly ordered and arranged, against the wall beside it.

"Oh, she's not here. I'm sorry. Her room's a frightful mess." Mrs Maine closed the door quickly. "It's because the cleaner hasn't been in this week. It would be good if you could keep an eye on it, just a quick tidy round every night. Hang her clothes up, otherwise they get ruined. Oh, and the hamster needs food and fresh water every evening, and cleaning twice a week. The last lady used to do it while Alicia was at piano." She glanced around the landing and I followed her gaze from closed door to closed door, endeavouring to walk quietly on the creaking floorboards in my socks and desperately attempting to memorise every instruction as we went.

"Alicia! She must be in the playroom." Mrs Maine strode quickly to the other end of the landing and pushed open another door, next to a narrow staircase which appeared to lead to an upper storey. I peered through into a vast room with cushions and rugs strewn across the wooden floor. A small girl with glossy chestnut curls was sitting cross-legged right in front of a wall-mounted television, her eyes fixed avidly on the screen.

"Alicia. There you are. Didn't you hear me calling you?" Her mother crossed the floor to stand next to the television, in the hope of attracting the child's attention.

Alicia didn't look round. She nodded, unworried. "I heard you. But this is my favourite show." Her voice was sharp; crisp BBC English that mirrored her mother's every intonation.

"Well okay, darling. But India's here. Don't you want to say hello and show her around?"

"When it's finished. Ssh." Alicia still didn't turn from the screen.

I took a deep breath.

"We'll wait outside then, sweetheart. Or I'll show India a few things and you can come and join us when you're ready. You could show India your pets, couldn't you? I'm sure she'd love that."

"I have thirteen pets." Alicia glanced backwards at me for the first time, tossing her hair over her shoulder, full childish lips pouting beneath wide, innocent blue eyes. "Four cats, two rabbits, two guinea pigs, a hamster, three fish and a tortoise."

"Wow." I smiled, somehow. "You'll have to introduce me to all of them."

"Later." Alicia waved her hand in a very majestic dismissal. "You'll meet them all anyway."

"Okay." I fought the urge to turn and run away; Julia Maine had disappeared somewhere, and I knew I'd be completely lost if I didn't find her. "Well, I'll see you in a minute, Alicia."

I found Julia on the landing, and started as a door at the other end flew open suddenly. The man in the doorway was noticeably older than his wife, in his late fifties and plump, with thinning silver hair and a pair of steel-rimmed glasses that were sliding down his nose as he finished tying his tie.

"Oh. Hello, India." He gave a vague, scholarly smile as we approached, and held out a hand. "It's nice to meet you again. You can call me John." His palm felt sticky as I shook it. I let go quickly.

With a final tug on his tie knot, he turned to his wife and gave her a peck on the cheek. "I'm sorry, darling, but I'll probably be late tonight. This surgery's already been rescheduled three times, so unless there's any change in the next hour, I think we're going to have to press on and do it anyway."

"Okay. Well I'll probably have left by the time you get back, as long as India seems to have—"

The crash from upstairs cut her off mid-sentence, and almost made me lose my footing on the slick oak boards.

"Alex!" John Maine's roar made me flinch. He strode to the foot of the narrow second-storey staircase as I watched in bewilderment.

Julia's face tightened with disapproval. She turned back to me. "Why don't we go downstairs? I can show you the kitchen and utility. When Alicia catches us up, she can show you to your room."

I cleared my throat. "Um . . ." I didn't want to ask a question out of place. But it seemed a big thing to have missed. "Who's Alex?"

Silence. As if no one had spoken.

I took a deep breath and followed Julia Maine, retracing our steps back downstairs into the hall, and into the dimmer light of a corridor that I had somehow failed to notice before.

"That's the sitting room and dining room." The next two doorways only warranted a nod of the head. "And John's office is at the end."

There were pictures on the corridor walls. Portraits and photographs. Of children, a family, a younger Alicia and a sketch of a young, dark-haired choirboy. But I didn't have time to do anything more than scan them. Julia Maine marched abruptly back the way we had come, along the corridor to the foot of the stairs.

"The kitchen's in here." She opened the door on our right, to a huge kitchen with high-gloss white tiles and marble-topped surfaces. A vast table was littered with pieces of paper and used wax crayons; the fridge was covered in scribbled pictures, lists of spellings, school timetables and phone numbers held up with alphabet magnets.

"Alicia's quite a fussy eater, but she does like pasta and fish or chicken. Don't let her snack in between meals. She can have a bowl of cereal before bed, though, if she's hungry. I assume you're okay cooking pasta, macaroni cheese . . . She quite likes omelettes too, but don't use fat, use sunflower oil . . ."

I tried my best to listen as my eyes travelled over the room, establishing an impression and then running back for details. Expensive-looking kitchen units and cupboards lined the walls; the sink was in front of a window next to what was presumably the back door; sturdy oak with a latch and an old lock.

"This door's the larder." Julia Maine pulled a door open and closed it again before I managed to catch up and look inside. "And this is the utility room. Really there's a proper utility on the east side of the house, but it's more convenient to have it here next to the kitchen, so Alicia keeps her pets there now. I'm sure she'll show you that. Right. What else do I need to show you? The drawing room, for piano lessons, the visitors' sitting room. That's on the east side. Let me think . . ."

I spun to follow her flawless figure and its small prim steps out of the kitchen and back along the corridor, my eyes lingering on the pictures. It was the pencil portrait that struck me, the young boy with the dark hair and strangely piercing eyes . . .

I could barely keep up as she crossed the hall. There was the heavy sound of footsteps on the stairs above us.

"Alicia?" Julia sounded hopeful as she opened a door and held it, waiting to see if she'd join us.

I spun, and took a step back.

Not Alicia.

There on the stairs, paused halfway down, was the boy from the picture. Unmistakable, except for one thing. He wasn't a boy anymore. He was tall, easily over six foot, perhaps in his mid-twenties. There was no doubt that he had his mother's handsome features: the same powerful, stubborn jaw, the black-brown hair that curled a little at the back of his neck, untidy on top and too long at the front. And blue eyes. Frighteningly fierce, angry blue eyes. He was staring at me.

I was staring back.

I suddenly realised, and dropped my gaze, not sure whether to speak to him.

"Is that Alicia?" Julia's voice was as light and airy as before.

"Um . . ." I hesitated. I didn't know what to do. His eyes were still on me, unabashedly, uncomfortably perceptive. Then suddenly he turned on his heel and started back up the stairs.

I gawped at the empty steps.

"No . . . uh . . . no it wasn't." I still couldn't quite look away, even though he had gone.

"Oh." There was a pause. "Then it must have been . . ."

"Alex?" I finished for her softly. Julia Maine's expression had hardened.

"Alex is our son," she told me coldly. "He's staying with us temporarily while some things are sorted out. His room's on the top floor. I don't suppose you'll see much of him. None of us do."

"Oh." I couldn't help noticing that she sounded relieved at the fact.

Mrs Maine sighed. "He had to move back from London four months ago. There had been . . . issues. Alex is very bright. He was supposed to be going into medicine, like John. He'd finished his degree at Oxford. Six years of medical school . . . But he gave up on all that and then—" Suddenly she stopped, her lips pursing tightly. "Well, anyway. I'm sure he won't disturb you."

"Well I guess Alicia and I wouldn't mind if he did," I offered nervously. "He—"

"He won't."

There was silence. Neither of us moved. I felt my cheeks start to burn. Julia Maine's eyes were fixed on my face.

"My car's arriving in an hour and a half," she told me suddenly. "I fly at ten to midnight. I won't be home until next weekend. My PA's number is on the fridge in case . . ." Her eyes travelled once more from my dusty socks to my nail varnish and then back to my face. "In case you have any problems."

CHAPTER 3: BURNING

"Mum doesn't do it like that!" Alicia's voice was indignant. "You're meant to put the pasta in first! Do you even know what you're doing?"

I let out my breath slowly. "Yes. It's okay." I forced a smile. "Thanks."

"Are you my new babysitter? I mean, are you going to stay? Our last babysitter didn't stay. The one after Sara. Mum didn't like her. Mum didn't like Sara, either."

"Oh." I tore at the top of the bag of pasta and it split suddenly, fusilli raining loudly onto the surface. "Yes, I am."

"You're called India, aren't you?"

"Yes." I picked up the pasta, cheeks starting to burn. "That's right."

"How old are you?"

"I'm twenty-one." I finally managed to pour an over-generous serving of pasta into the pan of boiling water. "You're seven, aren't you?"

"Seven and a half." Alicia was staring at me. "Did you know, you're kind of small for a babysitter? You're smaller than Mum and Sara, my old babysitter. And kind of young. Sara was thirty-five. She was fat. You're not fat. You're really skinny. Like the girl that Alex used to bring back. I didn't like her. She was mean. She didn't even like Alex, anyway. No one likes Alex. He's always bad, but Mum told me not to talk about it. Dad says Alex will never turn out any good because he never tries. By the way, Mum *never* does it like that."

I snatched up the saucepan as the water boiled over, pouring white foam onto the hob and dripping sullenly to the floor. "Oops. Got it." I could see that Alicia wasn't fooled. I lowered the spitting saucepan back onto the hob.

"Surely you like Alex *really*?" I mopped up the water and glanced back at Alicia's nonplussed face.

She raised her eyebrows. "Duh. No. *No one* likes Alex."

"Oh." I went back to the pasta, a little perturbed. "That's not very nice for him."

"So what?" Alicia sat down at the table and started scribbling on a piece of paper with a red wax crayon. "He doesn't care."

There was silence for a few stretching minutes, broken only by Alicia's wild scribbling. I burned my tongue on a piece of chewy half-cooked pasta. More water splashed onto the hob and hissed.

"I don't want pasta," Alicia announced suddenly.

"It's a bit late now, I'm afraid." I did my best to keep my voice light. "The pasta's cooked."

Alicia shrugged. "Well I'm not going to eat it." She slammed the wax crayon down on the table and regarded me with distaste. "Eat it yourself. I'm going to watch TV."

She got up from the table and ran out through the door into the corridor. In a split second's panic I started after her, but then stopped again, despair sinking heavily in the pit of my stomach.

"Alicia!" I tried to sound friendly, unconcerned. "Come on, Alicia, you'll be really hungry!"

"No I won't!" The voice was distant now. I heard a door slam.

There was silence. I swallowed and looked around at the kitchen, at the steam still rising from the pan. I couldn't give in that easily. I drained the pasta reluctantly and tipped it into a bowl. Really. I couldn't be outwitted by a seven-year-old. The kitchen door banged open suddenly. I spun, relieved.

"Alicia . . ."

Alex stopped dead, apparently expecting to find me about as much as I was expecting him. For a moment we simply stood and faced each other. His gaze travelled over me, and a helpless shiver ran through me; it was hard not to feel scared by the intensity of his eyes, so darkly blue, so bitter. I imagined he would have some idea of his mother's less than favourable portrayal of him. How old was he? Old enough to have finished six years at Oxford. And yet she talked in terms of an errant child.

"Hi," I offered finally. "You must be Alex. I'm India."

"Hi," he muttered. His eyes were still on my face. They were difficult to read, beyond their darkness.

"Um, I'm just getting Alicia's tea," I ventured, unreasonably nervous. "Can I get you anything?"

For a moment, Alex looked surprised at the question. His eyes flicked from me to the plate of food. He shook his head.

"I'm fine. Thanks." Then he turned on his heel and walked away, his footsteps echoing on the tiled floor.

Once again, I was left alone in the silence. I walked to the table, letting my gaze drift over the colours, crayons, Alicia's scribbles. A normal family mess. I picked up the top piece of paper, the one Alicia had been drawing on while I was getting tea. An angry figure scrawled in red, childishly cruel, named underneath in case it wasn't recognisable. I couldn't help wondering whether Alex had seen it. Whether, if he had, he had paid it any heed. Whether the coldness and the distance really bothered him at all.

Possibly not. After all, I didn't know him. I didn't know Alicia or John Maine or his wife, or what she had been going to say at the end of her hastily bitten-off sentence.

I stared at the picture for a moment, at the zig-zag mouth and burning red eyes. Alicia had been right about one thing. Alex's eyes did burn. They saw through everything. It scared me.

Like this house and its silence. Like John Maine's sudden roaring voice. Like his wife's tight lips and tighter-bound hair. Like the feeling of helplessness when faced with Alicia's scorn.

Who was supposed to be in charge here? I gritted my teeth. I was a grown woman, for heaven's sake. I'd survived far worse than this.

"Alicia!" The shout was becoming familiar now. The way the name played on my lips. "Alicia, can you come and eat your tea, please?" I made my way uncertainly into the hall. "Come on!"

"You'll have to find me first!" The voice echoed around the corridors and rooms, impossible to place. I started to walk without direction.

"Come on, Alicia! I'm not playing games with you!"

Yes you are, a corner of my mind reproached me.

I found her by accident, on the verge of giving up and waiting for her to get bored. It was either bad memory or good luck that made me open the cleaner's cupboard instead of the door into the drawing room.

"*No!*" Alicia didn't look startled for long before her pout returned. "That's not fair!" She jumped to her feet, tried to duck under my arm to escape, but failed. "That's not *fair*! Get *off* me!"

I stood still for a moment, struggling not to give way as her weight hit me full force. I tried to think of something stern to say, but failed.

"Alicia . . ." It sounded far too much like pleading.

"NO!" Alicia grabbed the door and tried to pull it closed. Automatically, I put my foot in it.

"Go away! I hate you!" Alicia shoved at the door again, only succeeding in jarring my foot. Her pout wavered, lips trembling with anger, frustration . . . defeat? Suddenly, she had started to cry.

Crap.

"I hate you! I want Mum to come home!" Her voice came in hiccupping sobs, her cheeks becoming even redder, her jaw more stubbornly set. "Go away!"

I let go of the door to reach out to her, feeling horribly guilty and utterly useless. Great. Just great. I'd been here for less than two hours, and I'd already made her cry.

"Hey, come on . . . Alicia!"

She smacked my hand away.

"Leave me alone! Don't think you can be my friend just like that!"

I bit my lip. "I'm sorry. I'll go if you want me to. Do you want me to?"

Alicia hesitated, apparently not expecting passivity.

I shrugged. "Although I was kind of hoping you'd show me your pets. But if not, I guess you could show me some other time."

There was silence for a moment. Alicia sniffed. "Do you actually want to see them?" Her eyes travelled from the door to my hopeful face, almost as scrutinising, just for a moment, as her brother's had been. "Or are you just saying it to make me do what you want?"

I smiled slowly. "I do want to see them. I used to have a cat at home. I really miss her."

Alicia's frown lightened a little. "What was her name? Your cat."

"Womble." I laughed despite myself. "After a programme I used to watch when I was little."

A smile had broken out on Alicia's face too, tears gone. "Womble? That's really cute! My cats are called Pepper, Tiger, Shelley and Byron. I know Byron's a stupid name, but Alex named him. And it's bad luck to change a cat's name." Her eyes met mine earnestly. "I hope you never changed your cat's name."

I tried not to look amused and shook my head. "Is it really bad luck?"

Alicia nodded seriously and wiped her wet cheeks as if nothing had happened. "Very bad luck. I'll show you them.

If they're not out. Come on." She seized my hand suddenly. "You probably don't know the way."

"No." I wasn't sure whether to feel relieved yet or not. "I probably don't."

Alicia led me out across the hall. "Remember: Pepper, Tiger, Shelley and Byron."

"Right."

"Shall I show you your room before we go and look?"

"That sounds like a good idea, Alicia." I glanced down at her earnestness. "I'll have to go and get my stuff in a minute."

"What stuff?" Alicia's hand was sticky in mine, her eyes inquisitive as she looked up.

"Oh, nothing very exciting." I shook my head and followed her up the stairs. "Just clothes and books. You know."

"That's kind of boring. Although I bet you're not as boring as Sara. She was the boringest person I *ever* met." Alicia had paused outside a door by the attic staircase. "This one's your room. It's the only one with a bolt. You can lock it from the inside, I think, so you can stop people coming in. I'm not allowed in there anyway, though. Even Mum and Dad don't go in there. I wish my room had a lock."

I pushed the door open slowly. It was an oddly shaped room, wide at one end and narrow at the other, with strangely angled walls that made extra corners; it had its own fireplace and leaded lights in the window. The furniture smelt old.

"Wow." I smiled. "It's bigger than my room at home. It's really nice."

"Is your room really *that* small?" Alicia looked horrified.

I bit my lip. "Well, my house isn't as big as your house, Alicia. Do you want to introduce me to all these pets now? Then it's bath time."

My heart leapt as I said it. The end was slowly coming into sight. And suddenly, despite the loneliness I had fled to come here, I needed to be alone.

* * *

Well here I am. And here's the rest of your letter, like I promised.

It's hard to believe I'm so far away from you. That I'm not going to see you for longer than I can even imagine.

I still remember the day you started at school with me. You had no front teeth, do you remember? You were the new girl and everyone else wanted to be your friend, be your skipping partner, lend you their pop-a-point pencil. But I won, in the end. You chose me. I bought you a pop-a-point pencil for your birthday and we had our first ever sleepover.

Strange to think that that new beginning is over, and so is the next, and this is the first beginning I have ever made since then without you.

I got my pictures back from the grad ball yesterday, at last. I thought I'd get some printed — they're just not the same on Insta . . . I can't believe I moved out of Leeds nearly 2 weeks ago now. But it was just too weird being there with it empty.

It could be ok here, I guess. This place is nothing like I expected. Alicia is going to be hard work. The Maines scare me a little. And they have a son they never told me about, Alex. He must be our age, perhaps a bit older. He scares me more, I think.

I really didn't expect it to be this difficult. I can't remember why I wanted to get away so badly. I can't understand how I ended up this alone.

At least I still have you. I don't have anyone else. No one else understands me like you do.

I'd better go. I guess I have to sleep. I wish I didn't.
I'll write again soon,
Still miss you.
Love, India.

* * *

I sat down heavily on the edge of the pristine white bed and hauled one of my suitcases up beside me, starting to shiver.

I hadn't realised how cold I was; my clothes were still damp from trying to bath Alicia. It had taken at least three attempts to get her into bed; I had been getting desperate, afraid that John Maine would come home and find me failing, and think I was floundering already. Even if it was true.

My throat ached. I unzipped the case and tugged a pair of pyjamas from the top, too tired to unpack properly. The envelope I had forgotten tucking in on top of them fell out, a hoard of glossy photos raining to the floor and cascading over each other. I bent down to pick them up.

It was too late now to decide I wanted to go back. Back to the friendly faces, yellow roses, perfect smiles. I pushed the photos back into their envelope and tucked it in the top of the suitcase again, remembering something. I sought out my purse from my jacket pocket instead, and held it in both hands to look. The picture in the back still surprised me every time I saw it: my own, younger, shy smile and messy hair, the careless arm slung confidently around my shoulders, the perfect shiny hair and the teasing brown eyes I knew so well, the glitter of the infinity ring on the slim, pale finger.

A newspaper cutting; I fiddled with it and drew it gently out. The card slipped in behind it was bent and battered, the corners becoming tatty. I looked at the reassuringly familiar handwriting, and took a long, slow breath in.

New beginnings. That was what mattered. I blinked away my tears fiercely and closed my eyes.

CHAPTER 4: THEN

The photos were on the wall, stuck up with Blu Tack. The sky was grey. I'd woken at dawn, trying to remember the smiles. But the clouds were all I'd seen when I'd opened the curtains, and the flood of early daylight only seemed to wash out the colour from every picture, until I fled my solitude to wake Alicia and start again.

The walk to the village was much further than I had anticipated. It was starting to rain by the time the two of us reached the first signs of civilisation, and Alicia broke her hand free of mine to dance off along the pavement. I had to quicken my pace to keep her in sight, the flash of her shiny black patent leather shoes gleaming wet in the rain.

"Look at the kitten!" Alicia stopped suddenly and bent over to fuss a frightened-looking tabby that had appeared from beneath a parked car. I caught her up.

"Yeah, he's cute," I conceded. "But please don't go too far ahead, Alicia."

She looked up into my eyes questioningly. "Why?"

"I'd prefer if you'd stay with me."

"But *why*?"

"It's just safer, that's all. Especially by the road."

"I'm not going to get *run over* or anything." Alicia looked scornful. "I'm not stupid."

I shook my head. "Most people who get run over aren't stupid," I told her softly. "But it doesn't stop them getting run over."

Alicia rolled her eyes. "*Whatever*. What do we have to buy?"

"We need bread, milk and some more pasta." I glanced down at the list that had been left for me, with the prepaid card, on the kitchen table. "And you can choose a breakfast cereal."

"I'll see you at the baker's, then." She looked me straight in the eye. "Bye."

"Alicia!" I reached out to try and catch her sleeve, but she was too fast. She ducked to safety and broke into a run, glancing back over her shoulder at me with a smug smile.

"Alicia!" I sped up too, to an awkward semi-jog. People passing were starting to turn and stare at us. "Alicia, come back!"

She started to run faster, towards the zebra crossing. I clenched my fists.

"Okay . . . Alicia, wait at the crossing please!" I sped to a run. "I said *wait*!"

She wasn't waiting. She didn't even get as far as the crossing. A quick glance both ways and she was out into the road. I felt my breath catch. What if—

Alicia spun to face me as she reached the other side.

"I'm waiting." Her pert smile was daring me to argue.

"Alicia!" My hands shook with the effort of suppressing my anger.

"Don't get all huffy." Alicia pouted up at me, unimpressed. "I don't like strict babysitters."

"It doesn't make a difference what you like!" I took a deep breath. "We need to get a few things straight. I'll be nice to you only if you're nice to me. I ask you to do things for your own safety, or your own good, not mine, okay?"

Alicia huffed a sigh worthy of a fifteen-year-old. "Whatever."

"No." I took her firmly by the shoulders. "Not whatever. I want you to listen to me." I lowered my voice. "I want us to be friends, don't you? I want us to have fun. When you do things like that it doesn't make it easy. Don't you want us to be friends?"

Alicia's pout softened. "I suppose."

"Come on then." I held out my hand. "Now I want you to stay with me. And *no* crossing roads without me."

Alicia took my hand. "Okay. Do I still get to choose my cereal?"

"I guess so. You'll have to show me where to go."

"Don't you know?" Alicia shook her head, despairing. "Mum usually gets the bread from the baker's and everything else from the supermarket, but it'd be quicker if we just bought everything at the supermarket, wouldn't it?" She looked hopeful.

I laughed. "Show me the way."

Alicia started to pull me along faster. "Let's be quick. I hate shopping. You see that sign?" She pointed. "That's where Alex's piano teacher lived. The one Mum didn't like."

I looked for a moment at the boarded-up windows.

"Is Alex good at music?" I held open the door as Alicia gestured me into the small supermarket.

"He's really good. But he's not meant to play. Dad won't let him. He was meant to study. There was loads of trouble. He went to university to be a doctor, and he used to come and visit in the holidays. But then he went to London, and *then* he did something *really bad* and—" Alicia broke off suddenly, oddly, reminiscent of her mother.

"And?" I prompted, despite myself.

Alicia glanced conspiratorially around the racks of fruit and vegetables.

"I'll tell you later," she whispered, too loudly.

"So Alex plays the piano then, like you?" I tried to backtrack.

Alicia pulled a face. "Not now. You weren't listening. Mum and Dad don't like him to play anymore. I don't really get it. Because they *always* make me play and I don't like it and I'm no good anyway. I wish I could never have a piano lesson again. I hate Mr Trevers. He's boring. I liked the other teacher better. He did lessons at school. But Mum wouldn't let me have him." She picked up a box of cereal from one of the shelves and inspected the advert for the toy inside. "I mean the one that died." She put the cereal back on the shelf and picked up another box. "Can I have this one? It has Skellytombs cards. Limited edition leading up to Halloween. I could collect *all* of them by then."

But I wasn't really listening. I was thinking about the choirboy in the picture. *He did something really bad—*

I sighed. "Let's go find some bread. You can choose a loaf, if you want."

"Whatever." Alicia seized the nearest one and dropped it into the trolley. "Can we watch Netflix when we get home? Oh no!" Her gaze had fallen on the windows at the other side of the checkouts. "Look at the rain! We have to walk home! We're going to get soaking!"

She was right. By the time we reached the driveway back to the Manor, my hair was hanging in sodden locks that were hard to keep out of my eyes. Alicia's white tights were mud-splattered, and her buoyancy flattened. Thunder rumbled distantly as I flung open the kitchen door and let Alicia in first, watching as she kicked off her shoes and danced uncomfortably in her wet tights on the tiles. I slammed the door and shook the waterlogged hair back off my face, gasping.

"You'd better get changed!" The noise of the rain striking the window almost drowned me out. "Take your tights off down here, I'll put them straight in to wash. You're soaked through!"

Alicia sat down on the floor with a bump.

"Do *you* like Alex?"

"I . . . don't know him."

"I guess you won't, then." She bounded to her feet with an unconcerned shrug and skipped out through the door, leaving damp footprints on the tiles. I picked up the tights and hung them over the radiator. One of the cats was winding around my legs.

"Hello, puss." I bent down to rub its back. "Hello."

I couldn't remember its name. It did another circuit of my legs, then froze, ears flattened. The crack on the outside air echoed once, distantly, before it faded. Like a firework being let off. I strained to see out of the side window. The rain was easing off. For a moment I couldn't see where the noise had come from. Then I made out the figure on the other side of the wooden fence that separated a stretching area of paddock from the gardens. Alex was reloading the rifle. I watched as he lifted it again, took careful aim, and fired at the target pinned to a hay bale at the other end of the field.

"Did you know that Daddy has a gun?"

I jumped.

"I don't know where he keeps it. Locked in the garage, I think." Alicia had returned stealthily. She jumped up to the windowsill to look out past me. "Alex has a gun too, but it's not a proper one. Daddy's is a proper one. He likes shooting. He used to take Alex and his friend shooting, a long time ago before I was born, but Alex and Daddy don't really talk to each other anymore."

I turned slowly away from the window, not keen on Alicia seeing me watching. "Oh."

"Alex doesn't really talk to *any*one." Alicia pulled at her tangled hair and followed me away from the window.

For just a moment, I glanced back over my shoulder at the figure in the falling rain. It was hard, not having anyone to talk to. Or maybe it wasn't, for him. I watched Alicia run ahead, out through the doorway. It was hard to imagine he had been like her once, small and feisty and cheerful.

My eyes fell on the picture of the choirboy again as I followed Alicia into the corridor. So many things were lost, between then and now. And it was strange, how you didn't notice them going until they were all gone. Strange, how you never knew, until it was too late.

* * *

Dear Hope,

Beyond the circle of lamplight on the desk, it was dark. I shivered. I hadn't been expecting it to be dark. The merciless fluorescent attack of the lights in my dream was still too vivid.

It was my first proper day here today. Just me and Alicia. It was hard. But it's getting easier. It seems that some things do get easier. Some things don't. Being without you doesn't get easier.

The sweat was evaporating from my face now, leaving it cold and tingling. I needed to stay awake until the nightmare was gone. I knew that from when I was little, when I would wake up from a bad dream, and know my mother would be angry if I disturbed her.

I shivered harder. Stared at the letter and tried to read it.

I shouldn't complain. Things here aren't bad. I have my room. I have our pictures. I've saved you some. You've got to see them. They'd make you laugh. Or cry, perhaps, if you're anything like me. You always told me I was an emotional wreck. I guess you were right.

Anyway. Back to Rifway and Alicia. Alicia, Alicia, Alicia. I must have said it a hundred times today. I'm pretty sure that she's running rings around me. You know, in some ways, she reminds me of you. So pert, so quick with a retort, so full of life and backchat . . .

I screwed my eyes tightly closed. My head was starting to ache, and for some reason a painful lump had fought its way into my throat. I tried to dispel it. But the dream came back instead – suddenly, and with breathtaking force. I gripped the edge of the table.

"No," I whispered. "*No*. Stop! Go away . . ."

But it was still there, insistent, as if it wanted me to look. As if I had no choice but to see.

Dreams. They were always the same. And the blood was always so vividly crimson. My fist clenched so hard on the table that my knuckles turned white.

Please . . .

I started to sob.

Please, no . . .

* * *

Hope

I just wanted to write a quick addendum. I needed to ask you something.

I need to know what your thoughts are about telling the truth. The whole truth. At what point does an omission become a lie? And at what point does wishful thinking become deception?

I wish we could meet up. Just once more. So that I could explain to you. So that I could ask you in person. So that I could tell you the truth. The whole truth. Nothing but the truth. All the things I should have said, and didn't.

I'm sorry.

India

CHAPTER 5: NICE

"India!"

"Mm?"

I punched another series of buttons on the indecipherable front panel of the washing machine and breathed an inner sigh of relief as it finally condescended to hum into life.

Rainy days were exhausting. Especially after disturbed nights. I barely seemed to have closed my eyes before the seeping grey summer light forewarned me of Alicia's waking. I had dressed hurriedly, unprepared and lethargic, and greeted my small companion with a distinct lack of vigour. We had eaten toast in the cold kitchen, and I'd tried to tackle Julia Maine's never-ending job list as Alicia followed me impatiently from room to room.

"Indiaa!"

In the kitchen behind me, her footsteps crescendoed across the floor.

"In here." I stood back, racking my brains for an idea to save us from another day of cabin fever and chores, and failed miserably. I had already exhausted my reserves. Yesterday we ran races outside in the wet grass, built a den in the playroom out of duvets and dining chairs, and argued about the one-hour television restriction before I ran out of impetus.

Monopoly had brought fleeting relief, but quickly ended in tears when Mr Trevers arrived and I realised I had forgotten about the piano lesson.

"INDIA!" Alicia appeared at a run. "Can Lily come round?"

Oh, God. A sudden image of two Alicias instead of one rampaging through the house made my stomach contract with dread. I definitely hadn't established play-date rules with Julia Maine. I noticed, too late, the cordless phone clasped in Alicia's fist.

"Here you go! Lily, this is India, my new babysitter. The one who forgot my piano lesson!"

Before I had realised what was happening, she thrust the phone into my hand.

"See you!"

Thankfully, after a brief negotiation, I ended up on the line to Lily's mother, who evidently had as much confidence in me as I did, and offered to take Alicia off my hands for the afternoon. So, an hour later, the tyres of the Betton-Worthings' Range Rover were ploughing through the gravel, and I was pushing the front door closed.

The house was oddly empty without Alicia. I shivered, and tried to remind myself that my mother's house was equally desolate, and that I had managed perfectly well there for the two weeks before I came here, right up until the day that I'd signed the contract with the letting agent and packed my childhood into storage cases.

My mother. I breathed out through my teeth. I really should have phoned by now. I pushed the thought from my mind.

Somewhere behind me, the washing machine screeched distantly to a conclusion. Laundry. Pets. I set off in the direction that I thought the utility was in. Ridiculous, to have a house so big you could lose whole rooms in it, just for three people.

Four people. I found the door, and eased it open, making the guinea pigs blunder from one end of their cage to the other in a tumult of noise and alarm. I tiptoed past their run uneasily. I could see why Julia Maine didn't use this room. From here, I would have no idea if something happened in the rest of the house. If Alicia called. If someone was there—

"Hello?"

Holy shit.

I froze, flattening myself against the cupboards. Someone *was* there.

"*Hello?*"

I opened my mouth to reply, but no sound emerged. And then the figure appeared in the doorway.

She was ageless, gaunt, and she looked like death. If I hadn't been rooted to the spot, my first reaction would probably have been to run. But then I noticed the maroon cleaner's tabard over her loose-hanging clothes, and the very real, very pink elastic hairband in her shock-white hair. Her hand was on her chest, as she apparently recovered from a burst of palpitations as shocking as those she had given me.

"Oh, duck!" Her smoker's voice grated with relief. "You did give me a scare."

I gaped at her, speechless.

"Vee," she croaked. "Lavinia. You must be the new nanny. I bet she didn't tell you to expect me."

She. Julia Maine. I was staring unabashedly at the new-comer's brittle-thin frame and protruding cheekbones.

"India." I gulped. "Yes. No . . . She didn't."

"I do Tuesdays, duck, and Fridays alternate weeks. Don't you mind me." Vee reached behind the creaking door to retrieve a mop and bucket. "I won't disturb you or the little girl."

"She . . . she's out." I wasn't sure why I needed to explain. "Everyone's out."

For a moment, there was silence. Searching, weighty silence. Our eyes met through the dim light of the utility.

At last, Vee nodded. "You'll get used to it, duck." There was an unexpected note of kindness in her voice. "I've seen people come and go. This building's full of ghosts and bad memories. Makes settling in hard. But you'll get used to it." The door groaned as she made her way back out through it. "If you need anything, just ask me, duck."

I nodded, mute. She smiled a wry, nicotine-yellowed smile. Then she vanished, her footsteps soundless on the tiles.

"Thanks," I whispered to the empty air.

I was still shaking as I set to work on the guinea-pig hutch. I wasn't sure if it made me feel worse or better that Vee was elsewhere in the house, as I dutifully repeated my trips back through the kitchen and outside to the coal shed where the Maines kept the straw. Every now and again, I could hear the roar of the hoover or the clatter of wheels and brushes on the wooden floor.

I didn't encounter her again that day. By five, the animals were clean, Alicia's laundry was hung, and I sat in my room, alone. The sound of the kitchen door latch dropping sounded dully in the silence, and I watched from the window as Vee's frail figure dwindled into the distance.

I wrapped my arms around my chest. I couldn't help wondering what she had meant by bad memories.

Alicia would be back soon. I stirred myself into life and made my way to the playroom to tidy up. I straightened the duvet-roof over the tops of the den and paused, blinking hard. Blinking away the glossy little brunette head that had ducked back inside, the pull of a teasing smile. The echo of bygone laughter.

Indie's it! Den's home, no return!

Whose bad memories?

I swallowed. My hair had dropped out of its braid; I pushed it back with one hand, suddenly exhausted. Then I started back out onto the landing – and stopped.

Alex had come to a halt, too. The light from the landing window fell directly over his face, illuminating every detail of his improbably beautiful features and guarded eyes, and I realised that he must have been here all day; his car had never left the drive. I faltered, wrong-footed by the full force of his stare. For a split second, neither of us moved.

The tuneless shrill of the doorbell jarred up the stairwell as if on cue. I descended the stairs quickly, heart pounding, and tugged open the door.

"*INDIA!*" Alicia greeted me like a long-lost friend. She charged in, depositing wellingtons and swimming costume in a puddle at my feet, then doubled back on herself to stand, panting, in the doorway.

"BYE!" she yelled at the top of her voice. I gestured an awkward 'thank you' in the direction of the tinted windscreen.

"Hi, Alicia." I shepherded her in through the front door as the car disappeared. "Did you have a good afternoon? Are you hungry?"

"Yes. And yes. What's for tea?"

The answer was not much. Julia's menu instructions hadn't allowed for a great deal of variety. Maybe that was something to work on. Alicia vanished upstairs, and I bent down to retrieve her swimming costume as the powerful engine of John Maine's car drew to a halt on the drive.

I moved through to the kitchen, an unbidden shiver running the length of my spine. The back door was ajar. For a split second, Alex Maine's backwards glance alighted on my face, so dark — so hauntingly, bitterly blue — that it stole my breath. Then he pulled the door closed behind him, the latch falling heavily in the silence. I watched through the window as he felt in his pocket for a cigarette and lit it slowly, leaning backwards against the wall and staring into the iron-grey sky.

"Oh, hello, India"

I gave a violent start. John Maine's scholarly-soft voice seemed to have come out of nowhere. He put down his briefcase on the kitchen table and picked up a copy of the *Times* as I spun to face him.

"Hi." I flashed him an awkward smile. Was the timing of his arrival coincidental? I couldn't help noticing that his eyes had darted to the back door.

"I hope you and Alicia have had a good day?" He tucked the paper under his arm.

"Oh." I hesitated. "Yes, we have, thank you."

"I wanted to let you know I'm going to be at home this evening. I'm not on call, so when you're done with Alicia's tea you could take the evening off. I'll do her bath and get her to bed. Just send her through to my study when you're ready. You can escape, if you like."

Escape? Really?

If only. If only I really *could* escape.

The truth. The whole truth. *And nothing but the truth.*

I swallowed.

"Thanks," I managed. "That would be . . . nice."

But as he turned away, I was unable to stop myself from chancing one last look towards the window, and the curl of cigarette smoke in the damp air.

* * *

Hope. What now? I'm on my own. An evening off. I have to leave the house. Go somewhere. Do something. Meet people. You know, I have no idea how. I'm twenty-one years old, and I've never done this — I've never had to — I've always had you. In fourteen years, I don't think I once went somewhere new without you. You always talked enough for both of us. People were always so dazzled by you, Hope, I never had to try.

God, I wish you were here. I wish you were with me this time. So much. So, so very much. That things hadn't turned out the way they did. Tell me it won't be long, that it won't be much longer without you. Even a word would do. Even to hear your voice.

Okay. I'm going. I'll try and do it how you'd do it. Don't laugh, okay?

I'll write more later,
All my love,
Indie xox

I didn't want to drive. I was too tired; when I blinked I saw cracks across the windscreen, and I couldn't face it. So I walked, even though there was nowhere to go. One pub at the end of the long main street, the only option beside a customerless Chinese takeaway.

Having reached the pub, I spent a long time checking the bar-snack menu in the doorway, plucking up the courage to go in by myself. Friday night. It should have been busy, but it wasn't. A monotone of conversation hovered over the spitting protests of a burned-down log fire and the subdued roar of ultra-high-definition Sky Sports. The girl behind the bar was my age and bored, and the other three or four customers were only there for the football. There was a woman, who didn't seem to be with them, perched on the one remaining barstool, and I wondered briefly how long she had been propping herself up with her glass of wine. She didn't look like she was going to last much longer.

I hovered, eyeing up the door, until the barman noticed me and it was too late to walk out again. I panicked and ordered lemonade – because it was the first thing that came into my head – and glanced around uncomfortably as the man filled the glass from the pump.

The place was a far cry from Leeds, and the rowdy student crowds that had made being inconspicuous so much easier. I paid for the lemonade and drank it much faster than I'd intended to. I didn't have a back-up plan. Half an hour wouldn't be enough, would it? I couldn't go back to the Manor yet. It would be churlish to decline John's invitation to go out for the evening, even though I would a hundred times rather have stayed in my room with my notebook and my headphones in my ears.

I made myself put the drink down, and let my attention wander over the pub: the fire, the tables at the back, the bar . . .

I froze. An inexplicable prickle of nerves ran up the back of my neck as my gaze fell on someone familiar. Or almost familiar. Dark, dishevelled hair, curling a little at the nape of his neck, hands thrust moodily into the pockets of his jeans . . .

Shit. I stared, paralysed, at the back of Alex Maine's shoulders, torn between the desire to speak to him and the urge to run out of the pub.

"Hi."

I nearly knocked over my drink.

He had turned around, and he wasn't Alex at all. Pale blue eyes alighted meaningfully on my face and paused.

Shit. He must have seen me looking at him. No, not looking, staring. Hot colour flooded my cheeks. I dropped my gaze.

"Did you lose someone?" He grinned and moved away from the flickering flat-screen TV to lean against the bar beside me instead.

I swallowed.

"No. Sorry." Forget blushing. It was a raging inferno in my face. "I thought you were someone else."

He was straightforwardly attractive, in calm possession of an easy smile, and oozing the kind of quiet confidence that I had spent years trying unsuccessfully to learn from Hope. His eyebrows lifted.

"Then maybe you came to catch the end of the match?"

"Uh . . ." I shook my head, mute.

"No, I figured as much." He grinned again. There was a loaded pause. I picked up my drink, mortified.

"So." He half nodded towards the screen, where the three remaining spectators were frozen in various stages of drink-to-mouth tension. "You're not here for the match — which is good, because I hate football — and you didn't lose anyone."

"No," I affirmed. I resisted the temptation to press the cool glass to my flaming cheeks.

"So, I must have missed something." He was digging in his pocket for a card. "Because that would mean you're by yourself. And no one goes for a night out in Rifway. So what are you drinking?"

"Oh . . ." I cleared my throat. "I'm okay. I haven't finished this one."

"Oh, come on."

"Lemonade." I took another sip of it to hide my smile, but he saw anyway. I hovered, chewing my lip, as he ordered and turned back. "Brett." He held out his hand and, after slight hesitation, I shook it.

"India," I mumbled, blushing.

"I'm sure there's some kind of well-worded pick-up line in there." He raised his eyebrows, a calculating smile in his light eyes. "But I've never been to India, and I'm shit at pick-up lines. So a drink will have to do."

"Oh." I was smiling too, despite myself. A pick-up line? "I've never been, either."

"So what brings you to the Manor, India?"

"What?" I glanced up sharply, surprised out of my self-consciousness. "How did . . ." I trailed off.

Brett slouched against the bar, amused.

"I saw you walking down." His gaze travelled over the damp sleeves of my jacket. I frowned at him.

"Then you *knew* I was by myself."

He grinned guiltily. "Maybe."

"I'm working there. Just started."

"*Working* there?"

I didn't miss his intake of breath. Suddenly, my mouth was dry.

"Shouldn't I be?" I whispered.

"You're not from here." Brett stood up straighter, pushing my empty glass carefully aside to rest one arm on the bar. "Are you?"

"Why?"

"You don't know much about the Maines?"

"Um." I hesitated. "Not really. Why?"

"It doesn't matter. In fact, it's probably a good thing." Brett shook his head. There was an awkward silence. Then he shrugged.

"So what are you doing there? Workwise."

"I'm looking after Alicia. Their little girl."

"You're living there?"

"Mm." I hesitated again, but curiosity got the better of me. "So what don't I know about the Maines? Do *you* know them?"

Brett laughed under his breath. I watched as he glanced out of the window at the rain falling in the Rifway darkness.

"I used to. They're quite infamous in their own way. Especially since Alex was sentenced. There were bets on whether he'd do time."

Sentenced? I faltered. So that was what everybody had been avoiding saying. I stared at the rain too, absorbing the revelation.

"I'm guessing you must have come across Alex?" Brett continued, unperturbed. "Their son? The last thing I heard was that he was living back at the Manor."

I nodded slowly, preoccupied. "Yeah. He is."

Sentenced. For what? And, if it was common knowledge, how had the Maines thought I wouldn't find out?

I jumped as a roar of triumph erupted from the huddled figures around the TV, then fell abruptly silent. I suddenly noticed that no one around us really seemed to be talking. The woman on the barstool had almost finished her wine. The bartender had gone.

"Crazy, the way people turn out," Brett sighed. "Alex and I were friends, way back. Before he went to Oxford. Seems ages ago now. I don't really know what happened to him, but rumour holds that it was John Maine who kept him out of prison, and it wasn't the first time he'd paid to bail him out."

Issues. I remembered Julia Maine and her tightly pursed lips.

"It's amazing how much people can change." Brett finished his drink and pushed a hand loosely into his pocket. "But anyway." He smiled. "Enough of that. I don't want to scare you away. I'm sure you'll be fine at the Manor."

I nodded, wordless, and contemplated my second glass of lemonade, the warmth in his voice not quite enough to dispel my discomfort.

"Don't look like that." He laughed softly and pushed the glass towards me. "Maybe you need a shot in this? You'll be fine. They're probably nuts, but you seem pretty switched on. I'm sorry, I need to get this." He held up his phone. "Give me a second?"

I nodded again, silently, and he moved around me, getting closer than was really necessary, his hand touching my waist as he brushed past.

"Don't go anywhere."

He vanished through a door beside the bar, and I blushed and looked down, dazed. This wasn't me. The one getting the compliments. This was Hope.

But Hope wasn't here.

Brett. I slipped my phone from my pocket and fiddled with it, playing the name in my head a couple of times, a private smile breaking slowly across my face. *Brett.* I imagined what Hope would say and flushed scarlet at the thought.

"India, is it?"

The woman with the wine — now without wine — was on her feet. There was an unsteady wobble in her voice that could have expressed one of a thousand things.

"Yes." I laid down the phone quickly. "I'm sorry . . . um . . . who . . . ?"

She held out a fleshy hand, which I shook.

"Sara." Her slightly unfocused eyes travelled from my tatty canvas pumps to my face. "So, you're the new girl at the Manor. Oh, I can just see it." She was laughing, but it wasn't a pleasant sound. "I *so* see it."

"I'm sorry?" I withdrew my hand quickly.

"Oh, isn't that just them? Keeping up appearances . . . just like them. You're bloody perfect aren't you? All public-schooled and skinny and sporty with your posh accent and pretty face and red cheeks. What the fuck do you know about kids? You're barely older than Alicia! And Alex . . . Alex must be older than you. Oh, no." Her lip curled. "Don't look at me like that, as if you don't know what I'm talking about. They've only taken you because you look good, and we both know it. When *I* deserved that job more than *anyone.*"

A firework fizzled and popped dully in my brain.

Sara. *Mum didn't like Sara . . .*

"Two whole years! Two fucking years I gave to that family." She didn't seem to have noticed that people were staring. "And they didn't appreciate a second of it! A week's notice, no references, nothing."

My heartbeat was thundering in my ears. Tiny flecks of her saliva were landing on my clothes.

"India?"

I might only have known him for ten minutes, but at that moment I'd never been as glad of anything in the world as the sound of Brett's voice.

"Are you okay?"

Sara's tirade ended abruptly. Her reddened eyes flickered to Brett's face. Then, without another word, she turned and walked out, the pub door banging behind her.

The silence was absolute. The football had finished. If anyone had been talking before, no one was now.

"Yeah." I cleared my throat and turned to Brett. I was shaking from head to toe. "Yeah. I should probably be going."

"Right." He regarded me for a moment. Thankfully, he didn't try to ask me what had happened with Sara. Just handed me my phone and my jacket, and followed me to the door. Outside, the sky was dark and rivulets of water were cascading along the edges of the road. The relief of escape soaked through me as I paused, trying to remember which way to turn.

Brett spoke suddenly. "Do you want me to walk you back?"

I glanced back at him. "No, I'm okay. Thanks." My voice sounded uncharacteristically husky.

"Are you sure?" He nodded into the blackness beyond the reach of the last streetlight. "It's quite a way. And there're no street lights once you get outside the village."

"No. Thanks." I tightened my grip on my bag firmly. "I'll be fine."

This time, it felt like my blush must be radiating through the darkness. I told myself there was no way he could see. One of his hands brushed my waist again, only lightly.

"I'm sure you will." He leaned close, his voice low. "You can handle the Maines. You'd better. I'd like to see you again."

"Oh." I drew a tremulous breath in. He stepped back.

"It was nice to meet you, India. Be careful on the road."

"I will." I turned away, not daring to look back at his face.

"Oh," His voice followed me the last few paces to the end of the street. "And call me. If you want to."

I defied him and didn't turn, just kept walking. I didn't let myself waver until I knew that I was well out of sight, far beyond the dim glow that was Rifway's last orange streetlamp.

Call him?

Something occurred to me, and I felt in my pocket for my phone. Sure enough, the backlight hadn't timed out yet. He'd done something with it. I stared at it for a moment, confused. He couldn't have unlocked it – could he? What did he mean?

My head was aching harder than ever. I had so many questions, and this was probably the least of them. But as my blush receded, and I started uphill towards the unforgiving glare of the Manor, a definite thrill ran along my spine.

CHAPTER 6: ALL FUCKED UP

Dear Hope,

September already. It's impossible to believe. It's been over a month since I came here. Two months since everything changed, so utterly and completely. Sixteen hours, and everything will change again. Because tomorrow, Alicia goes back to school.

I'm sorry there haven't been as many letters as I intended. I thought I'd write every day, but the days have gone so quickly that they've overtaken me. Lots of things seem to have overtaken me lately. It's this place. There's something about it. I don't know.

Anyway, I can steal ten minutes now. Alicia is having afternoon tea with her parents and one of Julia Maine's colleagues. I don't envy her.

Things here aren't as perfect as they appear from the outside. Nothing ever is, I guess. A house is only a house if there's no love in it. Beauty is often only skin deep.

That said, Alicia isn't a bad kid, Hope. Despite everything I wrote before. I'm starting to realise that below the surface there's a different child. An affectionate, lonely little girl who craves approval. I remember what that's like. I remember what it was like before I met you.

And then there's Alex . . .

You know, I think Alex is hiding someone else beneath the surface, too. But that's a different story. One, perhaps, that's best not told. Whatever he did, it was bad. It must have been. He almost went to prison. I was wrong, before; when I said he scared me a little. He scares me a lot. The look in his eyes scares me. The way that I feel when I'm near him scares me more. I want to run. Or at least, I think I do. But I can't. Because when he looks at me, I can't see anything except his darkness, and something about the darkness just seems to draw me in.

Let's not talk about being afraid. You hate it when I get deep and melancholy, I know. (I'm sorry, it always made me a terrible drunk, didn't it?)

I found out a secret the other day. I don't know what to make of it. Alicia has piano lessons twice a week — her teacher, Iain Trevers, comes to the house. Afterwards, he always stays for a while, half an hour sometimes, to play the piano. He has always asked, and I've always said yes — the Maines have an amazingly nice piano (of course they do), and I couldn't see anything wrong with him enjoying it. But last Wednesday, I went back through to offer him a drink, and they were both there — him and Alex — poring over something, so serious and absorbed . . . I've never seen someone so instantaneously changed, Hope. For a moment, I couldn't believe it was Alex at all. He was different. Completely different.

It's four o'clock. I'd better go. Before someone comes and finds me slacking (I'm meant to be bag-packing. And stitching name labels — name labels, Hope . . . the dizzy heights of domesticity.) I'll finish this later.

Oh, and I still haven't figured out what he meant about his number. The boy from the bar, I mean. I'll tell you if I do. I guess I haven't really tried.

The trouble is, Hope, no one could ever live up to you.
Miss you, so much,
All my love,
India xxx

* * *

43

"And how's Regina?"

"Regina's very well, Julia. Had you heard she's in Highgate now?"

"I hadn't, no."

"Yes, she is. *Everyone's* in Highgate, darling. Really, I don't know why you and John don't just move back. All these years! You'd be *much* more at home. And just think of the opportunities for Alicia! The pre-prep Regina's daughter goes to is rated exceptional in *every* area. She must be Alicia's age, and she's learning *two* foreign languages."

"Well, Alicia's French is already very good, isn't it, darling? Say something, so Hester can hear how well you can speak French to her."

"I don't want to."

"Alicia . . ."

"No."

"*Alicia.*"

"I hate French."

A pause. A tinkle of laughter over the delicate chink of spoons on bone china.

"Perhaps she's going to be a scientist, like her father. Stuart says he saw your paper in the *Lancet*, John. Did I tell you he's a consultant at Barts now? Which reminds me, is your son still at Oxford?"

Icy silence. I could practically hear Julia stiffen. A cup lowered carefully into a saucer.

"Not just at the moment." John's voice, mild, unreadable. "Can I get you another drink, Hester?"

The corridor seemed to amplify the voices from behind the sitting room door. I retrieved Alicia's trainers from the shelf of shoes and tiptoed back in the direction of the drawing room, trying not to listen.

"Oh no, thank you, John. I mustn't have another after this one. I need to get back, really. What's he doing these days then? He must have graduated?"

"He's taking some time out." Julia's voice was sharp. "Alicia, don't touch the sugar bowl. Go and wash your hands. Now."

"But *Mum*—"

"Do as you're told."

"Alicia," John tried. "Please wash your hands. Perhaps you'd like to say goodbye to Hester, and go and find India."

"But—"

"Now please."

Oh. I snapped back to reality at the sound of my name. *Dismissed.* Poor Alicia. I heard the shuffle of her feet on the polished floor..

"Susan Cliffe tells me *her* daughter's got a place at . . ."

Alicia was pink-faced and frowning as she emerged into the hall. I touched her shoulder gently.

"It's not *fair*," she growled. "I don't *want* to wash my hands. And I don't *want* to go back to stupid school."

"I know." I held out a hand to examine her fingers. "Come on. You *are* a bit sticky I didn't know you could speak French."

She turned to glare at me as we started up the stairs. "I can't."

"Your mum said you could."

"*She* can. *I* can't." She poked out her tongue and made a gargoyle face at me. "Speak it yourself."

"I can't, either." I stuck my tongue out in return. Alicia stopped in the bathroom doorway, astonished. Then she started to giggle.

"Can you *really* not?" The question came as I sought out the soap.

"A tiny bit. *Je m'appelle India.* There you go. Shall we go and finish packing your bag?"

"Huh." Alicia waved her hands in the vague direction of the towel and started back towards the stairs. "I hate school."

Nonetheless, she accompanied me back to the drawing room, and watched as I resumed my tagging and folding, ticking the items off the kit-list as I went. *Airtex shirt, white with gold trim. Netball skirt, navy blue.*

Her patience didn't last long. By the time the crash of the front door marked Hester's departure, Alicia had already moved on. For the next few minutes her company, and my progress, were intermittent as she buzzed back and forth, indiscriminately seizing items from the freshly packed bag and holding them up to admire them or hate them in turns.

"Have you ever played hockey?" she wanted to know, as *Lycra shorts, black,* and *Hockey boots, black, soft studs* came back out of the bag and started their journey across the hall floor towards the stairs. "Hockey is the stupidest game *ever*."

"I played it at school. I was rubbish at it, but I'm sure other people had fun."

"I don't have fun," Alicia told me bleakly. "I'm rubbish at it, too."

"It doesn't matter. No one's good at everything. And you're good at lots of other things instead. I bet no one else is as good at writing stories as you."

She grinned, consoled. "No. I think I'm probably the best. In my whole class. Mrs Folger said she loves my stories and that I should be an author."

"Well, there you go." I stuffed *Trainers, white with coloured flash* into the end pocket of the bag. "Can I have the boots back please, Alicia?"

She was headed for the stairs, but she dropped them over the banister at my request, and they landed with a thud and skitter of studs on the hall floor.

"And the shorts—"

I was too late. She was gone again, flitting off like a butterfly between flowers.

I decided not to go after her. There wasn't really any need. She would gravitate back to me eventually, plus or minus shinpads. I smiled to myself. The feeling of her hot hand slipping into mine was one that I had got used to recently. Even the prospect of piano practice wasn't as terrifying as it used to be. If we took it in turns to play, then her protests were quickly forgotten. I was no pianist, but Alicia wasn't born to it either; and perhaps sensing my ineptitude made her feel more confident.

I don't mind doing things with you that I hate doing with Mum, she had said, one night over dinner. *Because Mum makes everything hard. But you make everything fun.*

I glowed inside for days, after that.

I stuffed the boots back into the end pocket and struggled with the zip. Five o'clock. Where had the day gone? I blinked. Between staring, cross-eyed, at the name labels, and John and Julia's incessant behind-closed-doors bickering, I had another headache.

A thud upstairs interrupted my reverie, and I looked up from the fully-packed schoolbag. Shouting, again. I toyed with the zip, uncomfortable. Full-on, vehement shouting this time. And feet. Running feet, light feet.

Alicia's feet.

"No! I'm *not*! I don't *need* a bath anyway! My hair isn't dirty!"

"Alicia, come *back*! Right now!" Julia Maine's voice was high-pitched and stressed. "If you're not in that bath in two minutes, then—"

"I don't care what you say! You'll never remember it tomorrow anyway! I'm *not* having a bath and that's it!"

"You're grounded and *that's* it!"

I cringed at the empty threat. It would be me enforcing it. Until Julia came home from work in five days' time and instantly contradicted herself. With a sinking feeling of obligation, I started up the stairs.

"You don't even mean that!"

"Well, you can tell India why you're grounded, then!"

I rounded the banister.

Tears were swelling in Alicia's large eyes and sticking to her lashes. There was also a giveaway tremble of her chin beneath the pout.

"Alicia, why is it that you're grounded?" I thought this was better than openly opposing Julia Maine.

She didn't reply, didn't even look round, simply kept staring at her mother, the pout beginning to waver.

"Is it because of the bath? Because I know you want to go to Lily's for tea on Thursday, and I'm sure she'll be really sad if you can't."

Momentary silence. Alicia turned to me.

"I don't want a bath. It's not fair. Mum said yesterday I wouldn't have to have another one today."

I nodded. "I know, but you want your hair to look nice for school tomorrow, don't you? And if you have a wash really quickly while I wash your hair, we could be done in five minutes. Then maybe you could still go to Lily's." I glanced at Julia, who nodded stiffly.

Alicia looked from me to her mother and then back again.

"Just five minutes then." The frown softened. Her hand caught hold of mine. "Will you plait my hair though?"

"I can plait it tonight *and* tomorrow for school, if you want."

"Okay." She still looked doubtful, but she seemed to accept the escape; she ran through to the bathroom leaving Julia silent in her wake. I paused for a moment before I followed her. Julia didn't utter a word. But she did manage a tight smile before she turned away and walked, upright and perfect, down the stairs.

Alicia's bath was more of an all-over scrub than a bath, but she was out, tousled and red-faced, in four minutes and thirty-six seconds as timed by her watch. I was exhausted in every way as I descended the stairs, trying not to think about French class and pencil cases, and the smattering of freckles that always dusted Hope's nose after the summer holiday.

It was only as I reached the bottom that the shouting in the kitchen became apparent to me. I faltered, uneasy, not sure whether to go in. The last thing I wanted was to stumble in on a row. But the decision was inconsequential. As I wavered on the last step, it exploded into the hall. Or rather, Alex did.

"Fuck that! The only reason you got me back here was to save your own face — to patch up your own reputation! Because everyone knows you couldn't even fix your own son!

Well, I don't give a fuck if you're ashamed of me! I'll leave tomorrow if that makes you happy. I'd rather sleep in a doorway than be indebted to you!"

John Maine was in close pursuit, his round face creased with rage. "So the fine wasn't enough? You want to talk about debts—"

"I don't know why you made me come back here. To wave it in my face every day, how much of a disappointment I am? Like I don't know that already. That's not a debt."

"We brought you back here because, despite everything, we wanted to help you. Because you're *supposedly* our son—"

"Like fuck I am."

"Alex!"

"Forget it!"

For a moment, Alex and John just stood and stared at each other. Then John shook his head and walked away. I hovered by the stairs, uncertain.

Alex wasn't looking at me; he was looking out of the window, assuming indifference. But I could see the emotion there, in his tense shoulders, in his stillness. The pain in the silence. I swallowed. Suddenly, I couldn't stop myself from wondering just what it was he had done. Just how bad it could be.

How bad *could* it be?

"Alex?" I whispered.

He spun to face me, startled. And instantly, I regretted my action. His suspicious, burning eyes fell on my face, darker than ever; his brows lowered in a frown so bitter that I took a step back, terrified.

"Sorry." The word seemed to stick in my throat. I could hear the hammering of my heartbeat. "I . . . I didn't mean to intrude."

Silence. I should have moved. But I couldn't. I was rooted to the spot, trapped in his scrutiny.

I made myself breathe a slow, measured breath out.

"And . . . and I know I'm nobody. But I just wanted . . ." Suddenly my throat was ridiculously dry. I cleared it. "I just wanted to tell you that . . ." I trailed off. Alex's gaze was still on my face. Forbidding, unmoving. Waiting.

I took a deep breath.

"That it doesn't matter to me." I held my ground. "I wanted to tell you it doesn't matter to me. I don't know you. I don't know about . . ." I floundered for the right words. "About *this*. But I do know things aren't always as hopeless as they look from the inside. And if you ever wanted to talk . . ."

Scorn flickered in his eyes for just a second.

"Yeah. Sure." His voice bit into the silence. "Let's talk about how things are never as bad as they look." He turned away in disgust. "Let's talk about your clouds with silver linings. Then maybe, after we've thoroughly dissected my failings, we could move onto discussing why it is that *you* cry?"

I froze.

"What?" I whispered.

"I've heard you. Every night. You can pack in the facade."

And suddenly he was facing me, the rage still bright in his startlingly blue eyes.

"What kind of hypocrisy do you call that? There you are, trying to make things better and make everybody smile again, all fucking sweetness and light. Well open your eyes, India. We're all fucked up. There's pills for that if you want them — ask my dad — pills that stop you feeling. Problem is, they don't stop you having fucked up."

"I . . ."

Silence.

I couldn't speak. What could I say? The first conversation we had ever had, and it was this. A spilling of resentment and derision so frank and bitter that in an instant I was at his mercy, powerless in the face of his scorn.

"Why don't you get out?" There was disbelief in his frown; a dark conflict played out across his handsome face. "You know as well as I do that this place is hell, and that you wish you'd never come here. If there was a choice, I'd be out. Fuck it, I'd be long gone." He shook his head. "I don't understand why you're still here."

At last he fell silent and looked away. I glanced down at my shaking hands, and at Hope's infinity ring on my middle finger.

"I . . ." I hesitated, and looked out of the window instead, to where he was looking: at the rain falling on the beds of dying roses.

"You're wrong," I told him softly. "I don't think this place is . . ."

I faltered.

Didn't I?

"I don't wish I'd never come."

There was a pause. Alex didn't reply. He lifted the catch on the window and pushed it open, letting the rain whisk in. I turned on my heel, and silently walked away.

* * *

It was a photo. A screenshot of the emergency call screen — the one you get when you don't unlock the phone properly — with his number in it. I found it by accident, when I was looking for the picture I'd taken of the school gate code. I clearly wasn't as smart as he had thought I was. And now here I was, staring in panic at my ringing phone as though it was a ticking bomb.

I'd been so miserable, I hadn't really thought the idea through when I texted him. I swallowed hard and picked up.

"Hi."

"India?" There was a smile in his voice.

"Yeah." I scuffed my toe on the flagstones, glancing awkwardly around the collection of flowerpots and tangled, dying tomato plants. I hadn't imagined he'd call straight back, or I'd have found somewhere more private than the kitchen courtyard.

"How are you? I was starting to think you'd bailed."

"I'm okay. Still here." I shot a glance toward the mist-ed-up kitchen window, from where Alicia's background prattle was faintly audible through the glass.

51

"Look, when are you free? The White Lion's a shithole. We should go somewhere decent."

"Um. Okay." What had I been expecting when I picked up the phone? "Friday? John's taking Alicia to see a play, so they won't need me."

"Sounds good."

The prattle was gaining in volume. And urgency. *"Indiaa."* I could hear the shout through the closed door. *"INDIA?"*

"I have to go."

"I'll pick you up at seven. At the Manor?"

The idea of John Maine seeing that sent a jolt of alarm through me.

"No, the village is fine."

"I'll see you outside the Co-op."

"INDIIAAA!"

"Bye," I whispered.

I slipped back into the kitchen, a film of drizzle clinging to my sleeves.

"I didn't *mean* to do it." Alicia was right inside the door. I almost fell over her. It took me a moment to process what was going on.

"Mean to do . . . what?" I had a sinking feeling.

"I know I'm not meant to play in there, but I was just . . ."

"In where?" I could see from her hot red face that it was bad.

"Mum and Dad's room." She waved it off. "That's not the point. The point is, I was only *looking* at the ring — I definitely wasn't *touching* it — and it went down the back."

I stared. "Down the back . . ."

"Into that stupid gap behind the mantlepiece. How should I know there was a stupid gap?"

"A ring," I repeated stupidly.

"Mum's special one." She nodded gravely. "The one with the big jewel from when Dad asked her to marry him."

It felt beyond wrong for me to be tiptoeing across the luxurious silver carpet of the master bedroom. I tried not to look at the bedcovers, or the face creams and jewellery cast

52

off on the dressing table. The fireplace was a Victorian affair, mercifully unused, and decorated with an expensive spray of faux foliage that stood in the grate.

There was no way anyone's fingers, even Alicia's, would get into the gap. If I shone the light from my phone, I could see the glint of metal wedged in a sliver of space between the cast iron mantel and the wall. By some stroke of providence, it had stuck on a folded envelope that had clearly been lost there a long time before, judging by the amount of accrued grey fluff, rather than disappearing into the oblivion beyond. I tried a bent coat-hanger first – terrified of knocking the ring off and losing it forever, and even more terrified of someone arriving home and finding me in Julia Maine's bedroom – but it wouldn't fit.

"Alicia, can you get me some paper from the playroom?"

She was back in seconds. I stood her to the side and made my sweep with trembling hands. At first, nothing moved. I was starting to sweat. On the second attempt . . .

"Yessss!" Alicia's hiss echoed in my head as the envelope pivoted ninety degrees to protrude, easily grabbable, from the edge of the mantelpiece.

"Wait, Alicia . . ." I began. "Don't—"

But it was too late. My heart plummeted with the ring as it struck the skirting board and rolled.

I dropped to my knees.

"Did it come out?" I scrambled around the thick carpet, cold sweat breaking on my lip. But Alicia wasn't looking.

"Al-ex-an-der." She peered at the writing on the dislodged envelope. "I think this was for Alex."

"Alicia!" I hissed.

"What? Oh!" She crouched with an exclamation of glee. "You got it out! Thanks, India!"

I did?

I did. I almost snatched it from her, along with the envelope. I didn't even want to imagine what the ring was worth.

"Where did it come from? We need to put it back." I replaced it carefully where she was pointing. "Now, let's get out of here."

"Okay!" She didn't need telling twice. She scarpered off along the landing, as I looked down at the torn envelope in my hands. I had no intention of reading it, but it was ripped across the back and the paragraph inside caught my eye.

It is my sincerest pleasure to write to you to inform you of Alexander's appointment as Head Chorister, and accordingly to congratulate him on his offer of a full scholarship to the Minster specialist music school, commencing in September.

The choir boy. I frowned, and pushed the letter into my pocket.

* * *

Dear Hope,

I haven't got long, but I had to start this letter now, because I remembered I have a promise to keep.

I found his number. Brett. The boy from the bar. I promised I'd tell you, didn't I? Well, I texted him. As if that would remedy everyone else thinking I'm an idiot, as if it would validate me. He called back, and now he's picking me up in the village in forty minutes, which is why I haven't got long.

Ugh. I am an idiot. You'd think it, too. There's no point in arguing. Because for some reason, Hope, it entered my head to try and befriend Alex. So, that conversation went well . . . something along the lines of 'we're all fucked up, India — you should leave'. Okay, maybe not word for word, but I think it's a fair summary.

And if that wasn't enough, I got a call from the Shelgate Unit on Tuesday, about Mum. They had to section her and sedate her, Monday night. It's never been that bad before. They asked if I wanted to go down and see her. I told them I don't know. Because I don't. I don't know. What difference would seeing her make? She doesn't remember me.

She'll never remember me — I'm wiped, like a video tape from the '90s; there's nothing left but static and snow. So why should I go there, just to torture myself? And her? My being there only confuses her. I haven't seen her since we went together, before graduation.

But then I feel so guilty. So confused.

I don't know. I know you understand, at least; you always did. And it's enough just to tell you. I'm all alone here, except Alicia, and I can't exactly tell Alicia.

I always could tell you everything. I'm sorry that things are so hard now. I'm sorry, so sorry, that I let you down.

I'm trying not to let it change things. It's bound to get easier again, isn't it? I keep telling myself that.

Oh, Hope. I have to go. Twenty minutes, and I have to get into the village in the pouring rain. What am I doing? You were always the one who was good at this kind of thing, not me. And don't pull that face at me either, it's not going to be anything like that. Definitely not tonight. Not even soon. Probably not ever. Okay?

I have to go. I'll finish writing later.

x I x

"India, seriously." Brett leaned over with a smile to take my dripping coat, and threw it into the back seat. "I could have picked you up at the Manor."

"I like rain," I muttered.

"Right." Brett shook his head. It was hot in his car. He glanced over at me as we pulled away.

"How's life with the Maines?"

I pulled a face. "Fabulous."

"I don't believe you." He laughed. "Not for a second."

"It's fine." I shrugged.

"Lonely?" He glanced back.

"I . . . I hadn't thought of it that way." I frowned, unnerved by how close he had come to the truth. "But yeah, I guess. It can get a little lonely when all your conversations are with a seven-year-old."

"Do you see much of Alex Maine?" Brett asked, off-hand.. "What's he doing these days?"

I glanced around sharply, very conscious of the sudden ache in my jaw. The memory of dead roses.

"No." I shrugged. "No, I don't really see him."

"Fair enough." Brett shrugged too. We rode in silence for a few minutes, bar the faint babble of the radio.

"Did you say you and he were friends, once?" I couldn't quite stop myself from asking. I knew I shouldn't be so curious.

"Once." Brett shook his head. "Last time I saw him, we . . . weren't on such good terms, shall we say."

"Oh?" This was doing nothing to curb my curiosity.

"Let's not talk about Alex. Sorry, I know I brought him up. But really. You'd better ask him about it."

"Hah." It came out more bitterly than I'd meant it to. "I wouldn't exactly say that we're on talking terms, either."

"Ah." Brett's eyebrows raised a fraction.

"You're right." I made an effort to recover my smile. "Let's not talk about him."

It took forty minutes to reach the city. The multi-storey where we parked was brightly lit with unflattering harsh fluorescent tube lighting; I waited as Brett paid for a ticket, looking out over the neck-high railings at the jagged outline of the buildings below. The sky was dark, but the clouds had dissolved in places to leave one or two struggling pin-prick stars.

"Ready?" The car door slammed, and I turned to find Brett standing close behind me. For the first time, in the unforgiving light, I was able to make him out in more detail.

It was easy to understand why I mistook him for Alex at first glance; he was the same height and build exactly, and even his dark, deliberately dishevelled hair was similar. But on closer inspection, I didn't think he looked like Alex at all. There was a hint of dry humour in the slight curve at the corners of his mouth, a confidence in the relaxed posture of his broad shoulders, and his pale blue eyes were a startlingly light colour, a complete contrast to Alex's darkness.

Right now, those eyes were on me. I felt his gaze travel over my body and my blush returned instantly – then I reminded myself that I was the one who had been staring first.

"Shall we?" He smiled.

* * *

The restaurant was small and intimate, and made it difficult to avoid Brett's direct scrutiny. He sat across from me, frustratingly at ease, as I wrapped my hands around a vast glass of white wine and pored over the menu. It took a long time for our food to arrive, but as I made it onto my second and third glasses of wine, the conversation finally began to flow more freely.

I found out that Brett had moved to Rifway from East Haringey when he was twelve. That now he worked as a software engineer for a finance company, a job he despised, and that until a year ago he had been successfully running a business from home designing apps. That his father had been a musician, but that Brett had never taken to it.

"So how about you, India?" Brett toyed with his napkin absently, folding all four corners inwards to make an octagon. "You haven't told me much about yourself."

"There's not much to tell, really." I shook my head. "You already know most of it."

"Where did you grow up? Not Leeds, I'm guessing, from that accent."

"Oh," I shrugged. "No. I went to boarding school, near Cambridge."

"That explains it."

"My father moved to the States and remarried when I was little. My mother was chief of a county police force. She was at work a lot, so I lived at school during the week."

"Was?" Brett gestured to pour me more wine, but I stopped him. My thoughts were starting to feel clouded enough already. "What does she do now?"

"Oh." I twiddled the edge of the tablecloth between my fingers. "She had to . . . um . . . retire." I glanced up quickly, not sure why I was telling him. "She has Wernicke-Korsakoff syndrome. A kind of dementia. From drinking. She lives in a residential unit near our old house."

"I'm sorry to hear that, India." Brett's voice had softened. "Really sorry."

"It's okay," I found myself saying. "I don't see her much. She can't remember the last twenty years at all. As far as she's concerned, she never even had kids."

"That must be very hard." The sympathy in Brett's glance wrong-footed me. I turned my attention quickly back to my half-eaten plate of food, no longer hungry.

"I lost my father six months ago," he continued quietly. "So I do have an idea."

"I'm sorry." It was my turn to look up.

Brett shrugged. "Life goes on, India." His eyes were on mine, level and calm. "You have to focus on the good things. The new things." For a fraction of a second his gaze flickered downwards over me, keen and appraising, and I felt my pulse quicken.

I took a sip of water to counter my dry mouth, trying not to think about what Hope would say. The thought made me blush again.

Brett smiled. "You're very evasive, India. You don't say much of what you're thinking."

"I like to be careful." I smiled back hesitantly, in spite of myself. "Otherwise, I have a surprising ability to put my foot in my mouth."

Brett's smile twitched, as if he was going to say something and stopped himself.

"What?" I didn't miss the lift of his eyebrows.

Brett shook his head, enigmatically. "I'll tell you later. I hope."

I regarded him across the table, perplexed, still very conscious of the unsteady rhythm of my pulse.

"Have you finished?" He eyed my plate and empty glass. I nodded.

He paid the bill, despite my brief but vehement protest. It was dark outside as we set off along an unfamiliar city street. I found myself watching the road, my eyes drawn to the smooth glint of tramlines winking in a graceful line along its length. A bell sounded in the distance. It had stopped raining, and we walked side by side in silence for a long time, until I started to shiver and Brett stopped suddenly.

"You know we're walking the opposite way to the car park, right?" The teasing, enigmatic look hadn't gone.

I frowned. "*You* know I haven't got a clue," I chided him.

"Mmm." He flashed me a guilty grin. "Sorry."

"Where are we going?" I had stopped too, and faced him, hands on hips, assuming more confidence than I felt.

Brett cocked an eyebrow at me. "I was hoping you'd tell me that." He took a very deliberate step closer, so that I had to look up to keep meeting his eye, so that he was near enough for one of his hands to lightly brush the hair back from my face. I paused, my throat suddenly very dry.

"I'm not sure I have an answer, yet," I whispered.

Brett smiled. His hands brushed my waist.

"I like the word *yet*."

"We should go home." I steeled myself. It was hard not to betray my lack of conviction. Brett laughed under his breath.

"If you say so, India." His voice was soft, and very close. I tried not to notice the creases in his shirt, or the smell of his body wash, or the warm roughness of his thumb as it brushed my cheek. He let go of my hair slowly, and I focused on making my breathing return to normal.

"Come on, then." Brett nodded back the way we had come.

I hesitated. He started to walk, and I had to run a few steps to catch him up. This time, the silence was more expectant than natural as we followed the tramlines back to the multi-storey; his fingers found my palm and explored it lightly before they slipped through mine.

The stairs in the car park made me more breathless than usual. My eyes felt slow to focus, and a glow of alcohol-induced confidence was slowly starting to seep into my extremities. I caught myself looking at him again; muscled arms, easy stride, lingering self-assured smile. As we reached his car, he followed me to the passenger door.

"No central locking." He held up the key, as if in explanation. But he didn't really look bothered about explaining. He didn't unlock the door, either.

I suddenly remembered something.

"What were you about to say earlier?" I frowned up at him. The confidence had gained momentum. "What was it? You said you'd tell me later, *you hoped*."

Brett raised his eyebrows again, a playful grin tugging at his lips.

"Oh I don't know if I can answer that, India." His voice was low. "*Yet.*"

I bit my lip.

"You said you'd tell me." I held my ground. "And I've drunk too much, which is your fault, so I want you to."

Brett leaned close, to whisper, "Well, from what I remember, *you* were talking about your ability to put your foot in your mouth. But I thought better of saying what I wanted to say."

"Which was?" My tipsiness, and the thought of Hope's reaction, were egging me on.

Brett's gaze flickered downward knowingly. "Which was that I can think of much better things to do with your mouth, India."

His lips on mine were cool; he tasted of white wine and night air as his tongue tested mine and his hands slipped into my back pockets to pull me tantalisingly close.

"You're drunk, India." His breath was hot against my ear. "And I like it. But you were actually right. As much as I hate to admit it, I probably should take you home."

"To the Manor, you mean." I found myself frowning again.

"If that's what you want," he murmured.

"Yes," I nodded, before either of us could change our mind. "I think that would be a good idea."

* * *

Hope,

I wish you were here. How much longer is it going to be? There's so much I need to talk to you about. But I sit here and I can't — I just can't — write it.

I want to know if you still think about what happened, like I do. I need to know you miss me too, Hope. I know you must. But I need you to say it.

I'd better finish this — I hear Alicia on the stairs. I guess it's time to go.

Yours (forever),
India
xXx

* * *

It was a glorious September Sunday: summer-hot and cloudless. Saturday had passed in a headachey blur; fortunately Julia had taken Alicia into town to choose new school shoes. Meanwhile, I trudged delicately around the house, washing my clothes and putting away Alicia's clean ones, in possession of a hangover that I wasn't sure I deserved.

It had been back to the norm that morning: breakfast, battle stations, cajoling Alicia into her best clothes ready to leave the house by half past eight. By nine I sat in church, sticky and overdressed, watching Alicia colouring in in the transept from my uncomfortable vantage point squashed beside John Maine. My presence was expected; we sat silently in one of the rearmost pews, and for an hour I fumbled through the hymnbook, too awkward to look up from the pages. I wasn't alone in my reticence. No one seemed eager to associate with the Maines. I couldn't help noticing that there was a two-pew exclusion zone around us, and I wasn't quite sure that I could explain why.

For the first time I could remember, the Maines cooked when we returned to the Manor. I let Alicia direct me to a seat in the dining room as food smells permeated the house, and squirmed with embarrassment as John politely declined my help in carrying the steaming dishes to the table.

"Alicia." John addressed his daughter. "Would you please say grace?"

"Thankyoufortheworldsosweet, thankyouforthefoodweeat," Alicia gulped. The words emerged garbled. "Thankyouforthebirdsthatsing, thankyouGod foreverything."

Silence. At last, John picked up a serving spoon, catching one of the dishes with a chink that echoed around the dining room. Alicia grabbed a Yorkshire pudding with her fingers and then withered in her mother's stare. I busied myself with helping her to fill her plate as John carved.

Nobody spoke. I cut up Alicia's meat for her, then concentrated on forcing forkful after forkful of roast beef and all its trimmings into my mouth.

"Mrs Bosworth says you can go and play with Charlotte and Alfie at the Grange this afternoon, Alicia, and they'd like it if you would stay for tea." Julia Maine replaced her knife and fork on her plate with a muted clink. She barely seemed to have eaten either. The dishes in the middle of the table were still full of cooling food and congealing gravy.

"India will take you." She turned to me. "Charlotte and Alfie's nanny is about your age. Mrs Bosworth thought it might be nice if you were acquainted."

I nodded dumbly. Alicia spoke before I had a chance to.

"Lotty and Alfie are *weird*," she protested. "And their nanny is a *looney*."

"Alicia, don't be rude please." John put his knife and fork down on his plate carefully. "It's very kind of them to invite you for tea."

Alicia pulled a face. "Lotty is the weirdest girl in the class. She always wears her duffle coat, and she never has a pencil case and at break time she makes you pretend you're a *fairy* and she won't let you play with *anyone* else and—"

"Thank you, Alicia. Have you had enough to eat?" The meaning in John's voice was gently plain. Alicia fell silent and nodded. Her mother began to gather together the plates. I helped her carry the leftovers back through to the kitchen, relieved at the chance to do something and duck out of the uncomfortable scrutiny of the dining table.

* * *

It was two-thirty by the time we arrived at the Grange. Alicia was sulky, and I was nervous, so the car journey was uncharacteristically quiet. The house was very unlike the Manor; full of rambling chocolate-box charm, painted white and covered in Virginia creeper that was starting to light the walls with a glow of autumnal colour. Outside the door, two figures were waiting on the stone drive. I opened the car door as Alicia reluctantly undid her seatbelt.

Lotty was a waif of a girl, imp-thin with long, very straight, dull brown hair. She looked impatient and unimpressed. A match for Alicia, perhaps, in *princess potential*, as my mother would have called it. And the second figure must be . . .

"Maeve." The girl beamed at me, freckled face creased, eyes full of interest.

Julia Maine had been right; Maeve was the same age as me, sturdily built and eccentrically dressed.

"India, I take it." Maeve grabbed my hand and shook it hard. "Off you go, Lotty, Alicia. Alfie is in the garden; be sure not to leave him out now, go on."

Lotty grasped Alicia firmly by the wrist. With not much more than a second's hesitation, Alicia skipped along with her on one of the gravelled paths that wove its way among the shrubs.

"Ah, you have no *idea* how excited I am that you're here, India. I can just *tell* that we're going to get on fabulously." Maeve engulfed me in a terrifying hemp hug. "How are you getting on? How are the Maines? You have to tell me *all* about them — I've heard all kinds! Come on inside — tea?"

I nodded wordlessly. She ushered me in through the trellis-framed front door and along a smooth-tiled hallway to the kitchen, a large open-plan room with a leather sofa and a dining table laid for five. I found myself looking again at Maeve's folded arms and bush of red hair, beginning to feel intimidated.

"How are you finding it, India? How long have you been there now? Is it your first place? Andrea — Mrs Bosworth — says you've come from university?"

I nodded again, not quite sure which of the barrage of questions to answer first.

"Where did you go?" She put a kettle on the electric hob to heat, a strange arrangement, but I didn't dare comment.

"Leeds." I smiled and took down two cups from the cup-hooks beside me. "These?"

She nodded. "Thanks. I'm from Belfast, myself. But I know Leeds. Did a job in Harrogate before I came here. Always looked after kids . . . five brothers at home, you see." She threw teabags into the cups and produced a gallon of full-fat milk from the vast refrigerator, beaming. "All younger. I looked after every one of them. Colm's at secondary school now, back home. Twelve, unbelievable." She poured hot water into the two cups so quickly that it was surprising it didn't splash. "He would've killed for some of Alfie's toys when he was little, even a tenth of them. It's a different world, don't you think, how the other half live? Well, you must have seen *that* working at the Manor . . . How is it?"

"It's okay." I nodded lightly, forced a smile. "It's not bad. Alicia's sweet and—"

"Oh, isn't she!" Maeve enthused across me. "She's beautiful. Mind you," she leaned nearer, conspiratorial. "Some of the rumours I've heard about that family . . . well, you'll have to tell me if there's any substance to them. But some of the things Andrea — Mrs Bosworth — says . . . goodness." She shook her head, disbelieving. "Lotty's been over there to play a few times. Comes back *full* of stories. Might just be made up to scare her brother, mind. Poor little soul."

"How old's Alfie?" I tried to change the subject. For some reason, I didn't want to hear about the rumours. The image of Alex's stormy frown and piercing blue eyes was unwelcomely fresh in my mind.

"He's five, bless him." Maeve sipped her tea loudly. "But India, tell me about *you*! Andrea — Mrs Bosworth — said you *must* come over. The Manor's an awful place — everybody thinks it. She knows John Maine from way back, you know. Before he knew his wife. Met in London, Andrea says. While John was a house officer. Proposed to her out of the blue. Changed him forever, Andrea says. He came back a different man. And their son . . . *well*. Have you met him?"

"Once or twice." I wrapped my hands around my cup carefully. "Not really."

"No, well. Probably just as well, from what Andrea says."

I let the tea go cold and stared out of the window, the babble of Maeve's voice and *what Andrea said* washing around me like a stream. In the back garden all three children were bouncing violently on the trampoline. The sky beyond them was cornflower blue, the colour of Alex Maine's eyes. Lotty and Alicia were holding hands, apparently best friends, despite Alicia's previous complaints.

Seven years old. They were the same age now as I was when I first met Hope. Had we really been so young? Had we *ever* been so young?

I swallowed, and tried to tune back into what Maeve was saying. If we had been young — Hope, Maeve, Alex, me — had we been like them? Carefree and careless? Before the scars, inside and out, before the experiences and opinions, bitterness and mistakes. What had we been like? I tried to picture myself at seven – and couldn't. It's strange, the way that you forget how to be a child.

With one last lingering look at the sky and the promise of fresh air and youthful weekend enthusiasm, I turned back to Maeve, and told myself that the afternoon couldn't last forever.

CHAPTER 7: DIFFERENCE

The concept of insanity was strange, I pondered, as I drove the car back from the other side of Rifway in silence. Some people would say I was mad, most people would say the Maines were mad, and after a further four hours of monologue, Alicia and I were clearly in agreement that Maeve was mad. I was exhausted; almost as exhausted as Alicia, who had fallen asleep in the back of the car.

The drive gleamed wet with drizzle that had started during tea, as my tyres crunched over the last few feet to swing into my parking spot next to Alex's shiny black Volkswagen. I turned off the engine and sat in momentary stillness, the looming shape of the Manor behind me filling me with a sudden feeling of unease. I climbed out of the car and opened the back door.

"Wakey-wakey, sleepy-head," I chided gently, undoing the seatbelt and pushing back a lock or two of chestnut hair from Alicia's soft white forehead.

Maeve was right, I reflected. Alicia was beautiful. But the most beautiful thing of all was the fact that she didn't know it yet. The thought gave me an unprecedented feeling of sisterly pride. Her long dark lashes brushed her cheeks as she stirred, then fluttered open to reveal bewildered eyes.

"Come on." I moved backwards a step so that she could get out of the car. "Let's find those pussycats and get you to bed, huh?"

Alicia nodded and clambered out, letting me slam the car door behind her. She gave an almighty yawn, and I stifled my own, as we went in through the front door. It seemed like a long time since I had arrived here, nervous and tongue-tied, to be let in by Julia Maine for the first time.

Alicia yawned again as we reached the stairs, and turned round, swinging on the banister rail. Her voice was soft and sleepy.

"I *told* you their nanny was a *weirdo*."

"Mmmm." I tried not to let my wholehearted agreement come across in my voice.

"I can't imagine she would *ever* have a boyfriend."

I smiled, amused by the judgement. "What would you know about it?"

"Well, it's obvious, duh." Alicia slipped her thumb into her mouth and looked up at me sideways. "Do *you* have a boyfriend?"

I gawked at her.

"Um, no," I said at last. "Should I?"

Alicia considered this for a moment, regarding me from beneath heavy lids.

"Yes," she told me finally. "I think you should, really."

"Okay." I couldn't think of a better reply.

The house was silent, and the sitting-room door was closed, light seeping sullenly from beneath the two inches of forbiddingly latched oak. Neither of the Maines came out to greet their daughter. I dithered over filling Alicia a glass of milk in the expectation that one or other of them would put in an appearance; it was a rare occasion that either, much less both, of them were home for bedtime. But it became quickly apparent that no one was coming. Alicia didn't bat an eyelid at the lack of interest as she gulped down her drink and wiped her mouth on her sleeve. Both of our feet dragged as I cajoled her upstairs and into her bath. I helped her into her pyjamas and dried her hair, then sat on the edge of her bed as she finished cleaning her teeth at the sink in the corner of her bedroom.

"India?" Her voice was small, as she got into bed with uncharacteristic compliance.

"Mmm?" I realised I had been drifting. Alicia had climbed under the covers but hadn't snuggled down. She sat cross-legged, her fingers closed tightly around her tatty, careworn toy rabbit.

"You know Mummy and Daddy?" She looked up at me from beneath lowered brows that were startlingly reminiscent of her brother's.

"Mmm." I moved a little bit closer to her, detecting the slightest wobble in her voice.

"Well, you know I told you Alex doesn't really talk to Daddy anymore. Well . . ." Alicia faltered. "Well, Mummy doesn't really talk to Daddy anymore, either. Except when they're cross at each other, when they think I can't hear."

There was a pregnant pause.

"That's okay, Alicia." I took her hot hand in mine and held it, trying to sound reassuring. "I'm sure she *does* talk to him. And everyone argues sometimes. You and I argue sometimes, don't we? And sometimes you don't want to talk to me."

"Mm." Alicia didn't seem convinced. She stroked Tatty Rabbit's ear thoughtfully. "India, is a divorce the thing when a mum and dad don't love each other anymore?"

"Um . . ."

How could I reply? What could I say? Suddenly, in that moment, the carefree child and the cornflower sky were gone. Alicia was waiting for my answer.

I swallowed the lump in my throat.

"Sometimes it's just what happens when people love each other in a different way than they used to, Alicia," I whispered at last.

"Oh." Alicia lay down slowly, pulling the duvet up to her chin. "But Lotty said . . ." She paused, thinking.

"My mum and dad got a divorce, Alicia. And it turned out to be . . . okay." I touched her hair gently. "But all mums and dads have arguments sometimes, you know. It doesn't mean they don't love each other."

"Oh." Alicia seemed to relax slightly. For a moment there was silence. Then, unexpectedly, her hand slid out from underneath the duvet and found mine again.

"Didn't *your* mum and dad love each other anymore?"

Jesus Christ. I blinked fiercely.

"I don't really remember," I said. But I couldn't quite meet her eyes.

"Did they still love *you*?"

I sucked in a deep breath through my teeth. "Of course they did," I told her firmly.

Alicia sighed. "You know, when I argue with you, I don't hate you. Even if I say I do, by accident."

"I know," I whispered.

* * *

Dear Hope,

Where do I begin tonight? I'm not sure. It's 11 pm, and I've finally left Alicia's room. I stayed with her until she fell asleep. Which took a long time, because she couldn't sleep.

I know that feeling.

She told me I need a boyfriend this evening. What's with that? Dating advice from a seven-year-old. Amazing. Then she asked me if her parents were going to get divorced.

How could I answer that? She's seven years old. Seven years old, and she needs her mum to talk to her. Or her dad. Or her big brother. But not me, a nobody, with nothing but bad experience to draw on.

John and Julia are both here tonight, not that you'd know it — I don't think they've come out of the sitting room at all since Alicia and I got back. They didn't even come to say goodnight.

I can't help noticing that they're hardly ever here together. I mean, really, they're hardly ever here at all. Julia is never at home during the week — more often than not, she's not even in the country . . . She works for the Foreign Office, or at least, I think that's what Angela said. She's usually only back for weekends. Which, strangely enough, usually seem to coincide with John being on call. Most weekdays he's back either at four, or at eight. Very occasionally, he'll put Alicia to bed. But at weekends . . . well . . .

Anyway, I guess my point is, it's a shock when they're both here. And now, like a coward, I'm hiding in the playroom. Thankfully, they're both at work tomorrow. I just have to get through tonight.

At least Alex is out. I don't think I could have coped with running into him again tonight. I don't think I could bear the way he looks at me. The way he despises me, and I don't even know why. He doesn't have to say it. It's there, in his eyes.

So why can't I stop thinking about him?

It doesn't make sense, Hope. The more I find out, the more I realise something awful must have happened. Truly awful. There's every reason on Earth to stay away from him. And yet, I can't reconcile it. I can't get the thought out of my head. I wish I knew something more about him. Anything. I can't help thinking about him. I can't help wondering . . .

If I knew what they know, maybe it would change my mind. Maybe he would turn out to be right — that we're all fucked up.

Maybe, truly, he knows more than any of us.

Oh, Hope, I'm so tired. My eyes are closing. I feel like there should be more news for you, but there isn't. You're probably bored hearing all about Alex and the Maines. Actually, I am too.

Don't look so accusing. I know . . . I know. I should put this away and go and try to sleep.

But when I fall asleep, I dream.

And I don't like dreaming.

Okay. I'm going. I might write some more tomorrow, if there's anything else to write. Or maybe, I might send you that picture. One from the grad ball with the yellow roses, when they were fresh and we'd just tied them into our hair. Before they wilted. Before everyone was drunk, and our hair came down and things descended into disarray.

I'm still sorry things descended into disarray.

Love you, as much as ever.

Sleep well,

Always,

India

Xxxxxxxxx

* * *

The crunch was sickening; an adrenaline surge jerked all my limbs at once. I opened my mouth to cry out.

But then I had sat up, and the cry was silent, and I was in bed, my face cold and damp with sweat, semi-darkness surrounding me like fog. There were voices on the landing.

". . . out all night! And then you turn up like this, with your sister in the house . . . But what ever changes?!"

I slumped back under the covers and rolled over with a groan to look at the clock. Five to six. Some time to be shouting.

". . . living under this roof . . . some sense of decency! But you don't!"

The shouting hadn't stopped. I sat up quickly, heart thudding as I caught the dangerous edge in the voice. John's voice.

"I'm a fucking adult." It was Alex. "It's none of your fucking business what I do." His voice was slurred.

"It's entirely *my fucking business* what you do. You can stop right there and—"

"Fuck that! Seriously, what do you think, you're going to fucking ground me? Get out of my way."

"I *said*, stop!"

71

"John!" Julia's voice was shrill and lacked its normal force. Perhaps she wasn't properly awake, either.

"*Alex!* Stop right now!"

There was a heavy crash. I sat absolutely still, tense, listening even though I didn't want to.

"Ow! What're you doing? Get the fuck off me!" Alex's voice rose again.

"What's this? What the hell is this?!"

Violent movement vibrated the wooden floorboards. Something smashed resoundingly on the stairs: the unmistakable shattering of glass.

"Get the fuck off me!"

"You can't be *serious!*"

"Just fuck off already — don't pretend like *you* never went there! You're no fucking saint—"

"*Don't you*—"

"Ow! *Fuck* you! You want to fucking try it?! Get off me, get off—"

Then a resounding, tumbling crash had me out of bed in an instant, snatching my dressing gown around me, my palms sticky with panic. Surely someone had fallen . . . or worse? I stood frozen in the middle of my bedroom floor, straining my ears to listen, the taste of dread sharp in my mouth.

"John! *Alex!* Let him go!" Julia's voice had risen to another pitch. "Let him go, Alex! John, are you—"

"I'm fine." The banister rail creaked in protest. "Go downstairs. Alicia will have woken up."

"Now get the fuck away from me." Alex's voice was terrifyingly low. I tried desperately to stop hearing.

"Next time, I call the police." John was barely restraining himself from shouting. "Next time, *I'm* calling them, and I'll *let* them put you away. I don't know why I ever brought you back here! For what? For this?! To ruin my home? If I ever thought I could help you turn around, I was sorely wrong!"

"Don't pretend you did it for me! You know what? All of it, all of it was only ever because *you* wanted me to be someone else. Because you wanted me to be *you*. Well, suck it up — I'm not. I'm a fucking waste of your time. You know what, I'd *rather* be in prison than in your house! At least it would only have been a three-month sentence, not a whole-life term!"

There was another crash, a nauseating smack of flesh hitting flesh, more thundering feet on stairs. I hoped they were feet.

"Alex!" Julia was back. "Stop it! Stop it now! Leave it! *John*! *Leave* it! Alex, *no*!"

A crack, splintering wood. I fought the urge to clamp my hands over my ears.

"Get the fuck off me! *You fucking*—"

"*Alex*!"

"That's *it*! Enough!"

More noise; John, on the stairs. Heavy feet hurried past my door.

"Julia, this is it! One more time and he's out! It'll be the police again next time, you know that! I'm not having it! He's had his warnings! He's had more final chances than I can count! You hear me, Alex? You're out!"

"*I fucking wish*!" I heard Alex's footsteps pound arrhythmically on the stairs.

And then, suddenly, there was silence.

I waited for fifteen long minutes before I sought out my towel and clean clothes, desperate to avoid bumping into John or Julia, even though it was obvious that I must have overheard. Hopefully, by some miracle, Alicia had slept through it. I threw my towel and clothes over my arm ready to shower, shivering a little as I tentatively opened my bedroom door and stepped out onto the landing. Everyone seemed to have gone. I started towards the bathroom slightly more confidently and pushed the door open.

Alex was bent double over the toilet, retching. He coughed and spat, then looked round as he realised there was somebody there.

I stopped, immobilised.

He looked terrible. I'd never seen a face so pale, or such dark circles under anyone's eyes. There was a slow trickle of blood running from his nose and crusting on his upper lip. In my shock, I was openly staring.

"I, I'm so sorry," I stammered at last. "I . . ."

Alex raised his eyes. And with a jolt, I realised what I was really seeing. Because in his gaze it wasn't anger, it was despair; it wasn't hatred, it was a hunted look that wrenched at something deep inside me, even though I barely knew him.

He yanked the chain on the toilet with force and strode past me without another word, out through the doorway, leaving me motionless in the flood of sunlight that illuminated the water stains on the green bathmat.

I wanted to turn back after him, to say something. Anything. But I couldn't.

What kind of hypocrisy do you call that?

Instead, I locked the door and undressed, watching my distorted reflection in the gleaming white tiles. The harsh prickle of the water on my face as I showered was a distraction. I slid to sit under the merciless torrent, watching the water cascade over my skin.

I touched the tattoo on the inside of my ankle. A yellow rose. For friendship. It had been Hope's idea. Hers was on her wrist. She always had been the flamboyant one.

I turned off the shower and stepped out. The memory of the altercation was still resoundingly fresh as I dried myself and dressed in jeans and a camisole that suddenly felt insubstantial against the chill air. I rubbed my hair roughly dry and braided it, a few damp curls breaking free to tickle the exposed skin of my neck as I stooped to put on my socks.

I'm not sure why I noticed it. It was poking out of the bin beside the toilet. A crumpled envelope, and a balled-up piece of paper with a logo that I recognised. *The Minster School.* I fought the urge to take it out. How had it got there? It had been in my jeans pocket. And it wasn't mine to lose.

Uncomfortable, I unlocked the door. The landing seemed dark, in comparison, my towel clammy against my arm as I tiptoed back towards my room. The house was silent. I hoped that meant that they had gone out, that I was left alone to wake Alicia without facing everyone else and their problems.

The creak of a floorboard made me jump. I paused. Looked up.

He was there, on the attic stairs. As my eyes adjusted to the dim light, suddenly I could see.

There was paper everywhere. On the stairs, on the floor, scattered like oversized snowflakes and saturated with the smell of cheap spirits. Alex descended another step, broken glass crunching under the sole of his trainer, and halted, his gaze travelling slowly from the fraying hems of my jeans to the wisps of disobedient hair that had escaped my hair tie. His face was a contrast of frowning, seductive darkness and bright blue eyes that made me think, suddenly and inappropriately, of Brett's kiss three nights before. There was blood on the collar of his shirt, a remaining tell-tale trail on his lip that hadn't been wiped away. I looked down, flushing horribly. His sleeves were rolled above the elbow, revealing surprisingly muscular forearms. He uncurled his fists.

I swallowed. Alex descended the rest of the way without a word. He pushed the fractured base of the glass bottle aside with his foot, and stooped to pick something up from amongst its remnants.

My breath seemed to have stuck in my throat, choking off my words. I lowered the bundle of towel and pyjamas cautiously and crossed the floor to join him, picking my way through the shards of glass.

It was manuscript paper. At least a dozen sheets of manuscript paper, all drenched and radiating the pervasive fumes of evaporating alcohol. I raised my eyes to his face.

"Let me help you," I offered quietly.

"I don't need help."

"That doesn't mean you wouldn't appreciate it."

One of his dark brows flickered upwards. He didn't reply. Just retrieved an old towel from the end of the splintered banister rail and used it to start sweeping together the glass.

Wordless, I set to work too. A sheet of paper at a time, limp and sodden. I held them in my hands, looked at them for long seconds, at the ink that had bled through their fibres, blurred, indistinguishable. Whatever had been written on them was gone forever. I bit my lip.

"I wouldn't worry about it." Alex spoke suddenly, making me jump. "It was shit anyway."

I looked up, startled. His eyes were still on my face, hard and unreadable.

I smiled wryly at him. "'Thanks' would do."

He shrugged. Silence again. I scooped together a few more sodden sheets, and he moved measuredly beside me, treading the towel into the wooden boards to soak away the last of the spilled spirits and gather up the shards of glass. Neither of us spoke another word. Beside the bottom step, his phone glinted dully in the light from the landing window, its screen cracked from side to side. I bent down to pick it up, wiping it clean with my thumb.

I felt, rather than saw, him watching. My mouth was unnervingly dry as I reached out and put the phone in his hand. For a fleeting fraction of a second, my fingers contacted his.

Alex didn't move. The silence shifted from hesitant to awkward.

"You don't have to try this hard," he said.

I let go of the phone quickly. His voice was very quiet.

"It's really best for you if you *don't* try so hard to win me round. My parents like you. They won't, if you start associating with me."

I glanced up at him, uncertain. "I'm not trying to win anyone round."

He raised his eyebrows.

"Then why are you helping me?"

I faltered, uncomfortable. Why *was* I helping him? Because I felt sorry for him? I couldn't say that. And it wasn't true; it wasn't because of that.

76

It was much worse than that.

"Because I wanted to," I told him.

He shook his head. Crouched down to pick up the towel, glass grating as he screwed it tightly into a ball and straightened. "Right."

"Does that make a difference?" I asked softly. "To you?"

For just a second, Alex held the gaze.

"What *I* think doesn't make a difference, India." His eyes were sharp, ascertaining. Hard to meet. "I guess what matters is whether it makes a difference to *you*."

CHAPTER 8: YELLOW ROSES

The hospital foyer was cool and smelt of disinfectant. I was alone, bar the tired-eyed security guard. One of the automatic sliding doors shuddered intermittently open, admitting blustering spirals of wet summer leaves and cigarette ends. An empty Coke bottle rolled in, bouncing over the threshold and skidding in a lopsided arc across the foyer, and I wrapped my hands around the cold, full bottle I had just bought, my fingers sliding in the condensation.

Two seventeen. I stared, without sense of time or context, down the deserted corridor I had arrived from.

I had said I would be ten minutes, and it had taken me most of that just to walk here and find a vending machine. The coffee shop and convenience store were shuttered and in darkness.

I took a swig of my Coke, the fizz making my eyes water, and gave up on it, screwing the lid back on as I started to retrace my steps past a row of empty trolleys and cages full of nightgowns. There was already a lift waiting as I reached the lobby. As the doors closed behind me, everything was abruptly muted, and I slid my head against the mirrored wall panel, exhausted. I pulled my phone from my pocket, but it had no signal.

The lift slowed.

Level four. Mind the doors.

I stumbled out and along the next corridor: a path that my feet had come to know too well. I pressed the button outside the double doors and waited.

Nothing.

I pressed again, dazed with tiredness. The intercom crackled into life.

"Hello?"

"India McKenzie." My voice sounded gruff with underuse.

A low buzz accompanied the permissive click of the door unlocking. But before I had a chance to pull it, it opened outwards, a blue uniform mostly obscuring the chaos within. Dimly, my mind registered someone hastily pulling across a screen.

"India." The nurse's voice was very gentle. "Would you come down to the quiet room?"

"No." Suddenly everything was sharp, painfully over-focused. I heard the panic rising in my own throat. "No—"

* * *

I gasped awake, the early daylight a shock to my system. The faded face of my alarm clock read six fifteen. For a while I lay still, orientating myself, closing my fingers around the cold brass bed frame.

The screen had lit up on my phone. I fumbled with it, squinting to read it in the half-light. *University of Leeds Alumni*. Delete. I slumped back in my pillows.

Six twenty-five. I watched the minutes pass on the screen. Six thirty. I dialled on impulse, staring at the numbers until someone picked up.

"Good morning," the answering voice was end-of-night-shift bleary. "Shelgate Unit, Sister Lee speaking, can I help?"

"Hi. It's India McKenzie."

"Oh, hi India. She's had a settled night. Let me pass you to Sheneen. She's been looking after her."

"Okay."

"Hi, Sheneen speaking."

"Hi, it's India." I slipped from my bed and moved to the window, twitching back the curtains to reveal a world of unbroken grey. "How's Mum?"

"She's been fine, India." I remembered Sheneen from the beginning. I could picture her kind, placid smile and immaculate silvery eye shadow. "She's had a really good night. We had a long chat before she went to bed and went through some of her photos. They said at handover that she's been much more settled since last Tuesday."

"Good." I traced my fingers over the scars in the old windowsill. "That's good."

"Do you know when you're next going to visit?"

"Um, not really." I scratched at a mark on the bottom pane of the window. "I, um . . . actually can't talk now. I have to go. I just wanted to make sure she was okay."

"Sure. She's fine, India. It's good to hear from you. I'll tell her you called."

"No. It's okay." I gritted my teeth. "Don't. Don't . . . bother her with it. Unless she asks."

She had never asked. Not once, in two years. I knew that Sheneen knew that, too.

"No problem, India. We'll call you if anything changes."

"Thanks." I felt churlish, useless. Some daughter. "Thanks for the update."

"You're welcome, India. Bye now."

"Bye." I exhaled.

Downstairs, the cats were prowling hungrily. I shooed Byron off the kitchen table and prepared the breakfast things on autopilot. The bin was full, and I hauled it out, manhandling it across the floor. To my surprise, the kitchen door was already unlocked. I navigated the bin-bag outside and across the rectangular kitchen courtyard.

Julia Maine wasn't working today. That had only occurred to me, with a slow sinking feeling of dread, last night after she got back from London, when the usual routine of car-booking and online check-in hadn't unfolded as expected. The idea of spending the day home alone with her fell some way short of appealing. I had lain awake for several hours in the vain hope that I could construct an escape plan. But nothing was forthcoming.

I walked briskly back inside. The house was silent. No suggestion that anyone else was up yet. I wrapped my arms around myself with a shiver, relieved that I was still alone, and tiptoed out into the hallway. The front door was locked. As I opened it to collect the milk from the doorstep, I realised that Alex's car was missing from the drive. I envied him his strategy. Somehow, he never spent the day at home when one or other of his parents were there.

I took the milk through to the breakfast table and went upstairs. Ten minutes and I'd need to wake Alicia. I pushed open my bedroom door, then paused.

"You wouldn't thank me if I *did*!"

The voices were filtering not-so-indistinctly through the door of the master bedroom.

"I'd thank you to take some *interest*!"

"You've barely slept in this house for seven years!"

"You've barely *lived* in it for twenty!"

"I have a career. You knew that when you married me."

"*You* knew ab . . ."

"India?"

I let go of the door hastily.

". . . when *you* married *me*. It hasn't stopped you turning it back on me every single minute since—"

"India!"

I spun. My bedroom door crashed closed. Alicia padded over to join me, a frown furrowing between her eyes.

"Why's Mum shouting?" She rubbed at her face with the back of her pyjama sleeve. "Why isn't she at work?"

I glanced along the landing. The voices had stopped, perhaps at the bang of the door. I rested a hand on the top of Alicia's tangled hair with an unconvincing attempt at cheerfulness.

"She's got the day off, Alicia." I smiled. "You'll probably be able to have breakfast with her. And your dad, too, I think, before he goes to work." I ushered her in the direction of her room. "Is your uniform ready? Look at your hair! We'd better get brushing!"

"Why were they shouting?" She obediently found me her hairbrush from the sea of crayons and storybooks on the dressing table. Obedience always alarmed me.

"I . . ." I copped out. "I'm not sure. I didn't hear. Maybe it was something on the TV." I started to brush, teasing the bristles through her matted chestnut curls.

Alicia's lips pursed. "Mum doesn't *have* a TV in her room."

"Oh."

By the time I managed to get her dressed, correct and present at the breakfast table, Julia Maine was already there, primly eating granola. I perched awkwardly beside Alicia until she had successfully poured herself cereal, milk and juice, and then retreated to a safe position in the pseudo-utility with her school shoes and a tin of black polish.

"Good morning, Alicia." The kitchen door opened and closed. John's quiet doctor-voice traversed the length of the room as he clicked the switch on the kettle and filled a cafetière with boiling water. One of the wooden chairs scraped on the tiles. There was a brief, frosty, silence.

"Alicia, would you please pass me the milk?" John spoke pointedly.

"Here you go." Alicia's voice was muffled through a mouthful of cereal.

"Mind your sleeve, Alicia!" Julia snapped. "It's in the — now *look*."

"It's only butter."

"Don't speak with your mouth full please, Alicia."

"Sorry."

"How did your spelling test go yesterday?"

"Spellings, smellings."

"Alicia. Answer your father properly."

"It was okay. I got seven out of ten."

"Seven?"

"Yeah. Seven. Please may I get down?"

"Have you finished? Well put your spoon down properly then. No . . . don't be silly."

My wrist was aching. I glanced down at the polished-to-oblivion shoes and tried to think of something else to do. I was going to need to stay busy today. Really, really busy. Julia was still eating as I made for the back door, and I could hear the exchange of John and Alicia's voices in the hall. Animal cleaning. I would be able fill at least an hour with sorting out Alicia's menagerie.

The courtyard was quiet. Too quiet. I paused on the step, unnerved by the silence from the treetops. The absence of birdsong felt wrong. There wasn't even a breath of wind. It was almost like the garden was holding its breath. Watching me. I wet my lips, trying not to think about Vee's ghosts and Andrea Bosworth's rumours.

The tangle of thick bushes around the old metal oil-tank was in need of Roy the gardener's attention, encroaching awkwardly onto the hinges of the coal shed as I opened its lockless latch and ducked inside. Beyond the rectangle of daylight from the door, the depths of the shed were too dark to make out. A shudder ran down my spine. I quickly lifted the lid of the straw bin to check whether there was enough left. My sleeve caught on the nail inside the top of the bin, rending a hole.

"Ow, shit." I fumbled to free myself, the silence buzzing loudly in my ears. What a place to keep a spare key. I must have knocked it off. It wasn't there. I pulled the sack of straw out to look.

Something clanged outside. The door let out a low creak. I glanced up sharply.

Then the door banged closed, plunging me into darkness.

I collided with the bin in panic, dropping the straw and slamming my fingers in the lid.

"*Shit*," I gasped.

I couldn't see a thing. My skin crawled with cobwebs, spider-legs . . . I blundered to the door. There was no latch on the inside. How would I get out? Who had shut it? I scrabbled at the wood. *Shit.*

"Alicia?" I croaked. "*Alicia*?!"

It gave suddenly and before I could register the tang of terror in my mouth, I was stumbling in the courtyard, dusty and sweating, spider-webs clinging to my sleeves.

"Ali—"

There was no one there.

I stood for a moment, fighting to get my breath back. "Alicia?"

I was shaking from head to foot as I pushed open the kitchen door. By a stroke of luck, both John and Julia appeared to have gone. Alicia sat innocently on the floor, buckling up her shoes.

"Alicia!" her mother's voice echoed through from the hall. Not gone, after all. "Are you ready, darling? Is India ready? Oh, there you are." She had re-materialised in the doorway. "Alicia needs to go into school five minutes early. She tells me that she lost her trainers in the changing room last Thursday. I want her to find them before school. You'd better get going."

"Oh." I dashed the sweat from my upper lip and glanced up at the clock. "Sure. Um . . . Alicia, have you got everything?"

"Yep!" Alicia jumped to her feet and Julia thrust her schoolbag into her hands.

"Come on then." My hands were still shaking as I shepherded her down the hallway and outside to my car. How? She couldn't have been in the courtyard and got back into the kitchen that fast.

"See you later!" Alicia hollered to her mother as I pulled the door shut behind us.

I spent most of the school run trying to rationalise events. The wind. A latch that hadn't latched . . . whichever way you looked at it, I'd had a lucky escape. My phone had been in the utility room; I couldn't even have called for help. Although spending a whole day in a dark shed full of spiders and mouse-droppings might actually have been less terrifying than calling one of the Maines for help.

It was only on my return an hour later that I realised I'd left in such a state that I'd gone without my keys. Even before a futile root through my bag, the dread was heavy in my stomach. Knocking really would convince Julia Maine that I was a complete imbecile.

I made my way through the stone arch at the side of the house. John's Porsche was gone from the drive. As I had feared, the kitchen door was locked. I started, with a distinct feeling of unease, for the coal shed, my pulse bounding hard in my throat. This time, I kept my foot in the door.

I opened the straw bin and stared in relief. It was there. The key. Hanging on its nail where it belonged. I was too thankful to question it. I snatched it up and slunk back to the kitchen to let myself in.

"India? Is that you?"

Oh, God. I slumped against the door.

"Could you spare a moment?" Julia Maine's voice reverberated through the hall.

And so it begins. I composed myself and tracked her down to the sitting room, where she was tapping impatiently at a tablet, a cup of coffee steaming on the table beside her.

"Hi." I put my head round the door awkwardly. "Yes?"

Julia looked up with a brusque smile. "Oh, good. I need you to do me a favour. The dry cleaners have called to say Alicia's spare blazer is ready, and needs picking up. And she needs some new school blouses. Oh, and I need you to— *Hello?*"

She whipped her phone from her pocket before I had even registered that it was ringing. She covered the mouthpiece, her pale blue gaze still trained on my face.

"I've written a list," she mouthed.

I nodded dumbly.

Once I'd located her instructions, I didn't waste any time in leaving. I double and triple checked that I had my keys and Julia Maine's prepaid card in the back pocket of my jeans, then headed for town.

The motorway was at a standstill. I fiddled with the radio impatiently, half-listening to the inane adverts. My phone buzzed somewhere in my bag, and I reached over to the passenger seat to find it, just as the queue started to move.

Typical. I fumbled with the bag for a second or two longer than I should have, unloading everything onto the seat: purse, headphones, the last two letters to Hope. I really needed to buy some envelopes. I seized the phone, triumphant, as the traffic started to accelerate around me, and chanced a look at the screen.

Brett: 10:02
Are you free lunchtime?

What were the chances?

I didn't reply until I'd parked. The multi-storey was full, and I ended up abandoning my car in a dodgy, unevenly surfaced car park half a mile from the city centre. I shoved everything back into my bag and swung myself out into the sunshine, suddenly desperate for respite from the rumours and ghosts.

Yes, I typed.

* * *

"Hey."

The heaving crush of September-sunshine shoppers parted as I fought my way through. The café was Italian, and busy. I could already smell the strength of the coffee.

"How are you, India?"

Without even pausing for my answer, Brett relieved me of my armful of weighty shopping bags, and before I knew it we were inside. A waiter ushered us to a table, and I sat down as Brett stowed the bags between our feet.

"I'm good, thanks," I murmured, inexplicably shy.

"Good." His voice was warm. "You were already in town?"

I nodded. "Julia Maine's shopping errands."

"Your enthusiasm's killing me," Brett laughed.

I toyed with one of the oversized wine glasses, and drew in a deep breath, remembering Friday evening. Was it really only Tuesday, now? I hadn't noticed it happening, but in just three days something had changed— something subtle — an infinitesimal sideways shift. The recollection of white wine and tramlines seemed oddly distant. Or maybe it was just the fade of alcohol on memories, washing them out, like ink from manuscript paper.

We ordered antipasti to share, and I picked at the focaccia and olives as Brett recounted stories of Rifway and its various occupants.

"Tell me about Cambridge, India." He picked up a piece of bread and tore it decisively down the middle. "It must be pretty different there, compared to up here. What made you decide to leave?"

"Oh." I glanced up at him. "I don't know, really. University. And I just sort of never—"

At our feet my phone began to ring, rescuing me from the question.

"Here." Brett reached under the table for my bag and handed it to me. I got to the phone just as it stopped ringing. *The Manor.* Crap. I didn't particularly want Julia Maine to realise I was accepting lunch dates instead of picking up her dry cleaning. I stared at it for a moment in indecision.

"Julia Maine's trying to call me," I muttered.

Brett took the phone from my hand. With one steady finger, he pressed and held the off switch. We both watched as the screen went black. He slipped it into my bag, which he lowered back under the table.

"You can call her back." His light blue eyes were calm. I nodded, speechless. His fingertips brushed mine across the table. "Relax, India," he told me softly.

We were interrupted by the arrival of our main course. I withdrew my hand quickly from his to let the waiter put the food down, my cheeks still hot.

The food was good, but I was by no means hungry. Instead of eating, I found myself studying Brett, listening to him talk.

There was an honesty about his smile, the occasional shake of his head, the open invitation in his laughing eyes. I was a fool. He was attractive in every sense of the word. Attractive and uncomplicated – and I'd told him I didn't have an answer.

Brett caught a waiter for the bill, then turned back to me. "Are you free this weekend? I've got a few days off. If you can get away, we should do something."

I hesitated, something knotting unexpectedly in my stomach. A memory, uninvited and unwelcome. A bloodied nose and sodden paper.

"I'm not sure."

Brett's eyes were on my face. Then he nodded. "Okay."

It was warm, so unassuming, that I immediately wanted to change my mind. To tell him yes. But I didn't. This time, he didn't let me argue about the bill. I scooped up my assortment of carrier bags from under the table, and we walked together to the door.

"Call me, India." He stopped me just inside, before the city crowd could sweep us away, catching my wrist with one careful finger. "When you *are* sure."

Sunshine was streaming into my eyes. I squinted to look up at him.

"I will," I promised, uncertainly.

Brett laughed, unconvinced. And then he was gone, striding out easily into the chaos.

The trouble is, Hope, no one could ever live up to you.

I slumped against the terrace with a sigh.

* * *

It took half an hour to walk back to the dry cleaners with my pile of shopping, the carrier bag handles cutting into the soft skin of my palms. By the time I had Alicia's blazer, I was sweating. The September sun was burning on the tramlines.

God, I wanted to go home.

I blinked hard, angry at myself. I should have told him yes. Brett. I felt for my phone. I should have said—

It wasn't in my pocket. I juggled the shopping and came to a sudden stop.

Not in my pocket. It was in my bag. I stood paralysed on the pavement and a man with a briefcase nearly walked into the back of me.

Oh, no no no . . . I dropped the shopping in a heap on the flagstones, tearing each bag open in turn to rifle through it. I didn't have my bag. I didn't even remember when I'd last *had* my bag. My hands had been so full that I hadn't noticed I wasn't carrying it.

I felt my jeans again, as if my memory might have misled me. But no. The car keys were there, the key to the Manor. The prepaid card – I'd kept it separate, in my pocket, to do Julia's shopping. Nothing else. Everything else was in my bag. Purse, phone, driving licence, bank cards. Everything.

I knew, somehow. As I deposited the shopping in the car boot with unsteady hands. As I jogged back across town. It wasn't at Carluccio's. It wasn't at the dry cleaners where I must have last had it. It was gone.

Gone, forever, with the newspaper-print reproduction of shiny hair and teasing brown eyes. With the winning smile, and the alcohol-washed memories. Gone, untraceably, with the tattered remains of my resilience.

* * *

Oh, Hope. I've lost the card you wrote. I'm so sorry. I was keeping it in my purse. The one from when we moved into the Leeds house. The one about forever. Forever seems like such a long time now.

Ugh. What am I doing here? How am I supposed to withstand days like this? Sometimes I feel like such a failure.

I've got to go. It's school run time. I'm going to be late (again).

I'll finish later. I'll try and cheer up before then.

Love you, I x

* * *

I wasn't late. Thankfully, the doors hadn't even opened when I arrived at the top of the school drive, and even when they did, Alicia was last out, wandering absently through the crush of impatient parents and fractious children. She barely seemed to notice me, until I stepped forwards to relieve her of her weighty book bag.

"Hello, daydream." I greeted her with a smile.

"Oh." Alicia came to an abrupt stop. "Hi."

"Penny for your thoughts." I took her coat, too, as she pulled off her navy jumper and tied it around her waist.

Alicia looked up, sceptical. "You're a weirdo."

"That's not very nice." I was laughing despite myself. "You can't really say that to people, Alicia."

"Not to people, no," she agreed. "But I can to you."

"You can?"

"Well, yes." Alicia tugged the jumper from her waist and threw it into the back of the car as I unloaded her schoolbag and coat into the boot. "Because you and me are friends."

"I hope you remember that when I tell you that it's piano this evening."

"Oh, what? No!" Alicia kicked the dashboard as we pulled out of the car park, and to an immediate halt in a traffic jam. "Oh no, *please*! I don't want piano! Is Mum still at home?"

"Yep. Well, no, she was out. But I expect she'll be back before we are. Look at this traffic."

Alicia's face brightened. "Maybe we'll miss piano?"

I shook my head, struggling to suppress my smile.

"We'll see."

"'We'll see' *always* means no," Alicia huffed.

We didn't miss piano. To Alicia's disappointment and my enormous relief, neither Julia Maine or Mr Trevers had arrived when we blustered in through the door, hot and bothered. It was a surprisingly warm day. I sent Alicia running to get changed out of her school uniform as I sought out her piano notebook and music and arranged it in readiness.

Iain Trevers was a quiet man, reserved and pleasant, perhaps in his late thirties. Everything he did seemed to be understated, his shoes politely left on the doormat beside Alicia's, his voice soft, his smile mild. By the time Alicia was changed and ready, he had arrived and installed himself at the piano, and I was left to my own devices. I heard Alicia's fingers make a wobbly start on a C-major arpeggio and went to fetch the menagerie-cleaning equipment. It suddenly seemed to have been a very long day.

"Hello? India?"

"Oh . . . hi."

It was about to get longer. Dutifully, I staggered through to the kitchen with my armful to greet Julia Maine as the door slammed behind her.

"Ah, brilliant." She gave a terse smile and a nod, as the C-major scale followed immediately and arrhythmically from the drawing room. "Iain has already started."

She offloaded her designer handbag and matching briefcase onto the kitchen table.

"He's such a nice man, very polite." She perched on the edge of the table, apparently not noticing the way my grip was slipping on the bucket of cloths and sprays and the weighty bag of dried pet food.

"Mmmm."

As if she was in the mood for chatting. Julia Maine, who had barely had three words to string together in my honour since I had come here. Now, of all times. I readjusted my grip, hoping that my exasperation didn't show in my face.

"Alicia's school took him on properly about a year ago, to replace their old teacher, who died suddenly. Frightful." She drummed well-manicured nails against the table. "But Iain couldn't offer hour-long slots at school, due to the number of children he's tutoring. So we had him start coming here, for Alicia. She needs to be stretched."

I gave up on the bundle of pet supplies, and lowered them carefully to the tiled floor, trying desperately not to let them spill.

"Don't get me wrong," I was unsure whether Julia was still talking to me, or just musing aloud. "It was terrible what happened to the old teacher Jim Egan, absolutely tragic. But I didn't like the man." Her face clouded suddenly, and all at once I felt awkward, as if I was witnessing some thought process that really should have been private.

"I never really trusted him. I wouldn't have had him any-where near Alicia. Word gets around. One shouldn't speak ill of the dead, I know, but . . ." Her lips pursed tightly. "Well. He taught Alex. But I found out, goodness knows, months, perhaps *years* down the line, that Alex had started going to his house to have private lessons. Without even asking us!"

She shook her head, disbelieving, one of her high-heeled shoes tapping on the floor in agitation.

"We had no idea. John was incandescent. We'd never even set eyes on the man at that point, knew barely anything of him! Can you imagine?"

Could I imagine? I thought of Alex and Iain Trevers col-luding over the piano; serious, absorbed.

"Alex was extremely difficult, very strong-willed. I should have put a stop to it sooner. It wasn't appropriate at all. In the end I met with the man, and we pulled Alex out."

Julia's lips pressed more tightly together. "There was clearly something not quite right with him. About half a year ago — yes it must have been, because it wasn't long after Alex finished his exams—"

Her eyes hardened at the thought, and I suddenly couldn't help wondering why she was feeling the need to spill so much information to me when neither of us wanted it.

"Well, anyway, about half a year ago he very suddenly killed himself. Tragic."

"Oh, goodness." I hadn't expected such an abrupt or dis-turbing ending. Another tiny clue about Alex, another piece of the intricate, mysterious puzzle, failed to fall into place.

"Well," Julia stood up quickly, snapping back to her usual abrupt self in an instant, "I wanted to go and listen to Alicia's lesson. I'll let you get on."

"Sure." I nodded, not quite able to squeeze out a smile. Julia seized her briefcase from the table and disappeared in the direction of the drawing room. I let out my breath in a rush.

Why was I suddenly so uncomfortable? I stood still and listened until I heard Alicia greet her mother, and waited for the playing to resume. A faltering first verse of 'au Clair de la Lune' wavered on the air. I stooped to take some plastic gloves from the cupboard under the sink before re-embarking on my animal-cleaning mission.

Juggling the bag of nuts and seeds upright so that it wouldn't spill, I scooped up the rest of the bundle in my arms and made for the back door as Alicia blundered her way through a second rendition of 'au Clair de la Lune'. I glanced nervously over my shoulder.

The door opened suddenly, and I half fell through it. Alex stumbled, taken by surprise, and caught my arms to steady me.

Shock jolted through me. His hands were firm and strong. And suddenly, unfathomably, my heart was racing.

I blinked and looked up at him, speechless with embarrassment. For a fraction of a moment, Alex looked directly back.

I ducked away.

"Sorry," I managed.

"Don't worry." His deep voice startled me. For some reason, I hadn't been expecting him to answer.

I held the back door open with my foot as he started towards the hall, trying to regather my load, and my wits. I glanced at the clock. As a degree of sense returned to me, I realised with a lurch why Alex must have suddenly arrived home. Alicia's fumbled playing still echoed through the hallway. Piano.

He didn't know that Julia Maine was sitting in the drawing room.

"Alex," I hissed.

He turned back, dark brows lowered questioningly.

I shot a meaningful glance towards the drawing room.

"Your mother's in there," I whispered. "I'm guessing she doesn't know about . . ." I trailed off.

For a beat, Alex stared at me. There was something con-spiratorial in our silence. Something that made my mouth inexplicably dry.

"Thanks," he said.

Then he was gone, disappearing through the doorway into the hall. I heard his feet on the stairs as I slipped out through the kitchen door and stood in the courtyard.

For a moment I faltered. Then I stepped back inside, took the collection of pet supplies back to the utility and climbed the stairs, shoulders drooping. Rosy evening light was falling from the octagonal window halfway up, making a crimson stain on the wooden boards. I had left my room in such a rush earlier, when I was late to pick up Alicia, that I must have forgotten to close the door. It was ajar, and creaked as I nudged it with my foot. I closed it gently behind me and stopped mid-breath.

The dying sun through the leaded lights cast criss-cross shadows over the windowsill. And there, in the centre dia-mond, there was a rose.

I staggered a step backwards, colliding with the closed door.

Not possible.

For a moment I couldn't breathe in again.

"No . . ."

I mouthed it soundlessly; nothing would emerge from my throat. All I could do was stare, in terror. Stare at its dark stem and slightly wilted leaves, at the scattering of yellow petals, starting to wither and dry, that had fallen from its slowly opening bud.

How long had it been there? Hard to say. My fingers closed unconsciously on the door handle behind me. I could feel the sweat standing out on my top lip.

I wanted to believe I was imagining it. Really, really wanted to. But I couldn't convince myself. Couldn't per-suade myself. I had to be sure.

The thorns sank into my hand as I picked it up.

I had known all along. Deep down.

"Oh God," I whispered. The silence swallowed my words hungrily. The shadows were extending on the windowsill, reaching for my hand, stretching out to engulf me.

"Hope," I breathed. "Oh God, Hope."

* * *

Dear Hope,

I'm back. To finish the letter, like I promised.

But mainly because I need you. I just need you. Today has been awful, and I actually don't know if I'm losing my mind.

I had the dream again last night. I don't know when it will stop. Maybe never. How can I stop dreaming about it? Perhaps I never will. Sleep is exhausting. It would be easier not to sleep, not to dream at all. But what would a world without dreams be like? What would be left?

A yellow rose on my windowsill. Is that what? Perhaps I am going crazy. Oh God, Hope. I really wish I could hear your voice. So you could tell me I'm not. I'm not, am I? It's not crazy to miss you.

I told Brett I wasn't sure. He asked me to go out with him at the weekend and I said I wasn't sure. And for a moment, I thought it was about you.

But it wasn't. Because suddenly, all I could think about was Alex. All I could think about was the way he looked at me when he told me to stop trying to win him over.

What could I say to that?

He's so full of hatred, and so alone. All I wanted was to make him see I'm not like everyone else. He asked me why I helped him. I didn't have an answer. Or perhaps I was just too afraid of him to say it.

I can't help wondering what he looks like when he smiles. He's one of the most beautiful people I've ever seen. Dark and secretive, guarded, an enigma. He never gives anything away. Nothing at all. And I've never seen him smile.

I don't think I'd be afraid of him if I'd seen him smile. Just once.

There was a fight yesterday morning. A proper, full-on fight, with blood and broken glass. John, and Alex, and the shouting . . . the shouting is the worst. There's no way to shut it out. It's like when I was really small, and I would hear my parents screaming at each other through the floor when I was trying to sleep. And they always thought I couldn't hear. But I heard every word.

I never told anyone that. No one except you. You know everything about me. I need you, Hope. You're my sanity. I swear it.

But maybe I can't keep on needing you like this? Forever? Is it unfair to? You <u>would</u> tell me, right? If I was writing too much? If you wanted me to stop?

The time has gone so fast. I've had to grow up and move on more quickly than I ever thought possible. I never imagined myself grown up. I didn't even notice myself growing.

I guess that's something no one notices until after it happens. I wish you were here to laugh at me and tell me I'm turning into my mother.

But I'm okay, right? Promise me I'm okay?

I have to go, anyway. For now.

Still miss you, more than anything,

Love,

India

xxx

CHAPTER 9: TRESPASSING

No Alicia. Other than the distant hum and clatter of the hoover, the house was disarmingly quiet. Friday evening. The week had passed quickly, a repetition of school runs and maths homework. I was still terrible at maths.

Today there had been no afternoon school run, and no homework. Alicia, shocking-pink sleeping bag in tow and Tatty Rabbit hidden safely in the bottom of her backpack, was going to sleep over at the Betton-Worthings', and I would be minus her company until Saturday lunchtime.

I sat, with Julia Maine's sewing box, in the drawing room, swamped by an unbidden memory. Sleeping bags on the treehouse floor, two girls — blonde and brunette — riotous and over-excited.

I wrapped myself in one of the woollen rugs that lived on the drawing-room sofa, and picked up Alicia's blazer. Thankfully, her mother hadn't borne witness to whatever terrible playground mishap had befallen it. On the downside, I had no idea how to go about repairing it. I selected needle and thread, and a mouthful of pins, and set about trying to pin the crested pocket back on.

"Hello, duck."

I nearly inhaled the pins. Vee's skeletal frame had appeared silently in the doorway. I hadn't even noticed the noise of the hoover stop.

"Made you a drink." Vee smiled, accentuating the deep brown-paper creases in her face. I saw her gaze travel shrewdly over the blazer as she shuffled through the doorway with a mug in each hand.

"Fancied a minute's company, to tell the truth." She passed me a scaldingly hot cup of tea and perched on the other end of the ornate sofa. "Lovely room this. Sometimes come and sit in here, by myself. Catch my breath."

I gathered up the sewing box quickly to make room for her, feeling oddly shy.

"Yeah. It is lovely," I nodded. "Thank you for the tea."

"You're welcome, duck." She put her cup down carefully on the side table. "That's quite a tear." She nodded to the blazer.

"Oh," I sipped my tea and burned my lip. "Yeah."

Vee laughed softly.

"Mind you, you should've seen some of the rips and holes Alexander used to come back with." She held out one wrinkled hand for the blazer, and I passed it to her, uncertain. Vee examined my haphazard pinning with pursed lips.

"I used to help them out with the mending then. Laundry, bits and pieces like that. Didn't have a nanny back then, see." Without so much as a by-your-leave, she started to remove my pins. "*She* was at home then, of course. Julia, I mean. Not that it made much difference. Didn't lift a finger, really. I don't think she knew how." Vee shook her head. "Pass us that thread, duck. No, not the black, the blue."

I obliged wordlessly.

Vee sighed. "She wasn't much more than your age when they came here, twenty-seven. A little bit of a thing, not much bigger than you, duck. She didn't belong here, and she made that clear to everyone. Londoner through and through. I never understood why she didn't go back there. Here." She handed me the pins and plunged the needle deftly through the blazer pocket.

"She can't have been much more than a child herself when she had him. Studying for her degree. She used to take two days a week down in Leicester for it, and even when she was here, she wanted nothing to do with him. Spent hours playing by himself, poor little chap. I felt sorry for him. His father was always at work, long hours training to be a surgeon of course — had no time for him either, not really."

She tutted and shook her head, holding the blazer up to examine it.

"Can't hardly be surprised at the way he turned out — have you got those scissors, duck? The little ones, that's it — it's not no way to bring someone up, really. No love at all, except that piano. My Lord, though, if you'd ever heard him play . . ."

She smoothed the blazer over her knees. She had restored it to its former glory in less time than it would have taken me to thread the needle. I glanced, uncomfortable, at the gleaming dark wood and worn ivory. *No love at all.*

I turned back to look at Vee, unnerved and curious all at once.

"How long have you worked here?" I asked.

"Oh . . ." She reached for her tea, and I remembered mine and took another tentative sip. "Thirty years at least, duck." She shook her head again, with a distant, knowing smile. "A long, long time. Before it was owned by the Maines. It was a hotel before they bought it, I bet you didn't know that."

"No. I didn't." I accepted the blazer back from her gratefully. "Thank you for this."

"You're welcome, duck. Any time. I do hope you're starting to feel settled here now. Like I said before, the place takes some getting used to, that's all. Wouldn't want to see you give up on it too soon. It's good to have a bit of company. And I'll talk to anyone, me."

I couldn't help smiling.

"Even her." Vee shot a glance over her shoulder, back towards the hall. "Julia Maine. I tried, you know. She was

99

ever such a lonely soul when they first moved here. Failed her degree, first time, I heard. Married John and they moved here . . . had barely any contact from her family — not for years, not until the little girl was born. I felt she could've done with a friend. Someone to tell things to, when it all got a bit much. But she didn't want to know." Vee shrugged.

For a moment there was silence. I thought about loneliness, and fear, and something occurred to me. Vee was watching me astutely. She had finished her tea.

"Ah. I did need that." She drained the dregs from her cup. "I'll find you some pictures, duck. From when it was the Manor Hotel. Quite a place, back in the day. Owned by a family in the village, the Selleridges. You might've come across their daughter, Sara. I think she does clothes alterations or something these days, at a dry cleaner's in town. I lose track. For a while she was doing the school dinners. She came here to look after the little girl for a time, too. Lived in the room you're in now."

"Oh, yes. I met her." I shuddered. For some reason, that thought had never occurred to me.

"He bought it for next to nothing, you know, John Maine." Vee sighed, remembering. "It was stood empty a long time before that. Awful, really. They'd been struggling to keep the hotel going for years, but then Steven Selleridge passed away quite suddenly, and it ruined them. In the end they had no choice but to take what they could get for it. It was terribly unexpected — he only went in for a routine operation, died on the table. Sara was about fifteen. Must have been very strange for her coming back here to live, after all those years."

"Mm," I agreed, unsettled. No wonder Sara hated the Maines.

"I'd best be off, anyway." Very suddenly, Vee was getting to her feet. "You've set me talking again, what did I tell you? You'd have thought I'd have learned in seventy years when to shut my mouth. Just look at the time."

I got up quickly too, and moved to collect the tea cups, but Vee had beaten me to it, dangling each mug from a bony finger.

"No, no." She gestured to me to sit back down, and I did, awkwardly. "Don't get up. I'll put them away on my way out. See you Tuesday, duck. It was nice to chat."

I heard the wheels of the hoover skate over the floor, and the bang of the cupboard in the hallway. I sank back into the sofa, my mind more full of questions than answers.

"India?"

I jumped. Vee's throaty voice echoed through from the kitchen.

"Mmm?" I scrambled to my feet and hurried through.

"Young man at the door for you." Her eyes met mine with a twinkle. Then, with a grin and a nod at whoever was there, she disappeared into the autumn sunshine.

Slightly breathless, I stepped into the doorway.

"India."

Brett's powerful frame filled most of the doorway, one hand thrust into his pocket, the other behind his back. There was something unusually serious in his face. Almost a frown.

"Hi," I whispered.

"Hi." He paused, noticing my awkwardness. "India, look." His expression softened; his voice was level, warm. "I'm not here to hassle you. I got a call from Carluccio's. Apparently, you left your bag there? Someone handed it in."

"They did?" I stared, taken aback.

"Here." He produced it from behind him. "I haven't opened it. You'd probably better check that everything's still there."

"Oh." I took it quickly as he held it out. My heart sank. It felt suspiciously light. I could sense him watching as I tugged open the zip and tipped out the contents. Scrunched paper, receipts, a dusty two-pence coin. A half-empty bottle of water. I swallowed and gazed bitterly at the slightly tatty lining.

"That's it?" Brett's words echoed my thoughts. His eyes had narrowed. "There's stuff missing."

"Yeah," I affirmed. "Yeah. My phone. And my purse."

"Shit." The concern in his voice was tangible. "India, you ought to report it—"

I shook my head. "It's fine. I already cancelled my cards."

"That's not the point." Brett was frowning.

"Really." I bit my lip. "It doesn't matter." I looked up at his light, troubled eyes. "Thanks for bringing it back."

"Any time." His frown faded. I suddenly realised how churlish it was, leaving him on the doorstep. I blushed.

"Do you want to come in?" I stepped back into the kitchen.

Brett shook his head. A smile warmed his eyes and played on his lips.

"It's okay, India," he said. "Really. Like I said, I'm not going to hassle you."

My blush intensified; I looked down at my feet. *Not sure.* How could I have said that?

"I'm sorry." I glanced up quickly. "About Tuesday. I didn't mean to sound like . . ." I took a deep breath. "I just . . ."

"I'm still off for a few days." Brett shrugged. But the suggestion in his soft voice was meaningful. The fleeting lift of his brows. The travel of his calm blue eyes from my face to the scrunched paper in my hands. "Let me know if you turn out not to be busy."

"I . . ." I hesitated. "I'm busy tomorrow. But . . ." I heard myself saying it, before I could think it through. "I could do Monday. While Alicia's at school."

"Monday." Brett gave a lopsided grin. "Monday could work for me. Half two? Coffee at the Old Posting House?"

"I have to be on the school run at half three."

"Two, then."

"I . . ." I bit back a reticent smile. "I can't call you," I pointed out.

Brett laughed.

"Then you'll just have to show up," he said.

It was strangely silent, once he'd gone. I felt lost without Alicia's banter. The house was empty. Julia wasn't coming home tonight either. She had travelled back to Austria on Wednesday, and she was staying there for the best part of a fortnight. Next week, John would be flying out to join her for a five-day weekend. It would just be Alicia and me.

And Alex.

I exhaled slowly and crossed the kitchen, trying not to dwell on Vee's words. But they haunted me. *No love at all.* I'd never known what that was like, until I came here.

Alicia's school would be closed next Friday for teacher training. I couldn't fathom why John Maine wasn't taking her with him to Austria, why he and Julia hadn't found room for their daughter in their plans. I knew Alicia was disappointed. She hadn't sulked or stormed. But the misery in her eyes when Julia told her had spoken more than a hundred words.

I had watched from a distance. An outsider, a nobody, with nothing but bad experience to draw on. I'd watched, and I'd decided that I had to do something.

I retraced my steps back through to the drawing room, trying not to think of yellow roses, and sat silently for a while. Sunshine was streaming in through the window. One of the cats jumped up beside me, butting its way under my arm and onto my lap. I suddenly remembered the weather report on that morning's breakfast radio. An Indian summer, the forecaster had said. Two weeks of October sun.

I turned the cat off my lap gently, an idea taking root in my mind. I drifted to the window to look outside, my fingers toying with the latch. It was beautiful here. I often forgot just how beautiful, because the grey skies and darkness of the Manor seemed always to overshadow what lay beyond: hills, woodlands, bright shades of autumn. We just needed to escape the shadows. Just for a day. Alicia and me. To run, unrestrained, into the colourful leaves and crisp wind. To sleep under a blanket of stars. To breathe.

Why not? Hope and I had camped every year, with her family. We must only have been Alicia's age, at the beginning, over-excited and riotous.

The rattle of a latch startled me, the soft knock on the kitchen door.

"*Hello?*"

A knock again. I fell out of my reverie, and almost tripped over my own feet in my hurry to get through to the kitchen, unduly nervous.

103

Who? Brett had gone, hadn't he? Who would be—

I opened the door hastily, to find Iain Trevers on the doorstep.

Crap. Piano.

"Oh." My face transitioned rapidly from apprehensive pallor to beet red. "I'm so sorry!" I stumbled out of the way and gestured him awkwardly into the kitchen, mortified. "Come in, oh gosh, I'm really sorry, Alicia's not here—"

It all came out garbled. Iain looked at me, mildly surprised.

"I was supposed to phone you to cancel." I was ushering him in, trying to explain, although I realised there was really no point. "Alicia's at a friend's."

"It's fine," Iain said calmly. "Not to worry."

There was a resounding pause. I hovered anxiously.

"Can I get you a drink, at least?" I pushed my hair back off my face, flustered, and tried to recover a degree of good grace. "Tea, coffee?"

"Thanks, India. A tea would be great."

We stood in silence as the kettle boiled.

"Is Alex in?" Iain asked at last.

Alex. I hadn't thought about that.

"Yes!" I exclaimed, then realised that I must have sounded far too enthusiastic.

"Great." Iain Trevers smiled and took the proffered mug. "Do you mind if I . . ." He nodded in the direction of the drawing room. "Perhaps I could give Alex a call?"

"Of course." I nodded vigorously.

I took a scalding gulp of my tea. Iain smiled his thanks again and disappeared. I wrapped my hands around my mug, feeling like an utter fool.

The soft exchange of voices in the hall gave way to the gentle fall of fingers on piano keys. I sat down at the kitchen table, as Shostakovich's 'Piano Concerto No. 2 in F' swelled and reverberated through the house. I frowned into my drink.

There was the sound of tyres on the driveway at the front of the house, making me jump. In an instant, I was back in reality, and for some reason I felt like I had trespassed, strayed into another world. One where I wasn't welcome.

The piano stopped abruptly. I heard the drawing-room door open and close, and the soft, swift ascent of someone on the stairs. I stood up. Then John Maine's key turned in the front door.

"Hello, India." He popped his head round the kitchen door.

"Hi." I smiled bravely, quailing. Iain Trevers' car was still in the drive.

"Is Iain Trevers here?"

"Oh," I said brightly. "Yes. It's my fault, I completely forgot to tell him that Alicia's lesson was cancelled. I thought the least I could do was get him a drink. He's just in the drawing room. I was on my way through."

"Ah." John smiled absently. "Yes. Oh dear. I'd forgotten that Alicia was out, too. I'll be in the study, if you need me."

"Sure," I nodded.

I listened to his footsteps recede along the hallway. A few moments later, Iain Trevers came to wish me goodbye, and once again I found myself alone.

Until I came to Rifway, I had never been alone. Not since I was Alicia's age, when I had first met Hope. We had met at primary school, gone on to the same boarding school — an era of dormitories, communal meals, laughter, chatter, bickering — neither of us had ever been alone. Not once.

I hugged my arms around my chest and climbed the stairs.

I first noticed the chill from the landing. Seeping from around my bedroom door. Rattling it in its frame.

I felt myself stiffen. My footsteps slowed. Yellow petals. I blinked away the picture desperately. Cracks in glass . . .

I suddenly didn't want to go in.

"No." I whispered it aloud, to remind myself. "Not possible."

I pushed the door.

The breeze hit me in a blast. The window was wide open, the photos were flapping on the walls, fighting free of their Blu Tack. From every angle, she was straining to reach me. The dry petals were strewn everywhere, the rose destroyed by the gale, dismembered across the bed and the floorboards.

For long seconds, I didn't move. Then I lurched across the floor and banged the window shut, my hands almost too unsteady to flip the lock.

Vee. It must have been Vee. Airing the rooms. She must have forgotten to close it.

Except Vee never usually cleaned in my room.

I swept up the petals and put the rose in the drawer beside the bed, out of sight. Not out of mind — no matter how hard I tried.

What was I going to do? What did it mean? The rose, the open window. My head was aching, pain throbbing behind my eyes. I couldn't think straight. It couldn't mean what I thought it meant. That wasn't possible. And yet . . .

Outside, it was starting to get dark. I took out my notebook, pen and envelopes with unsteady hands. The eyes in the photos were watching me, *the truth, the whole truth*, and I couldn't bear it. I folded the front page over, slipped the notebook into my pocket, and took the letter downstairs instead, back to the safety of the drawing room, the closed lid of the piano, the cat still sleeping on the pink and gold patterned sofa.

I curled up, tucking my feet under me, and opened the notebook.

Dear Hope,
I don't know what to write. Why do I always start letters
to you that way?

I laid the pen down for a moment, staring at the envelope where I had written her address. *Hope Bryant, Ridge Farm House, 32 Cedar Walk.* The notepad had almost run out. How many pages of letters had it already provided? I had no idea.

Too many. I chewed the end of the pen, letting the words blur before my eyes, letting my gaze focus somewhere else instead. Somewhere distant. Somewhere away from slamming doors, and windows that left themselves open. Somewhere where there were colourful leaves, birds singing, where the air smelt fresh. Where Alicia would run riot, get muddy, wet, happy. Where we could both forget.

I need to get out. There's something wrong with this house. Or with me. Maybe it's just the shadows. Or the dreams.

What do I do? Who can I tell, except you?

No one. Nothing. There's nothing to say. I'm a disappointment, Hope. Too scared to face the truth. I want it to leave me alone. The truth. I thought I'd be safe from it here. But I'm not sure I am.

The Maines are away next weekend. One blessing, at least. Alicia has Friday off. I want to take her camping, but I'm not brave enough to ask John Maine.

The weather is amazing. (As if I'm writing to you about the weather.) They said on the radio we're going to have an Indian summer — yeah, I knew that would make you smile. The autumn leaves are so beautiful, I wish you could see. They remind me of you. Of us. Of half terms at Kielder Forest. You'd love it.

That's why I need to take her. Alicia. It wouldn't have to be far away. Even the grounds would do. Close enough that we could come back if she didn't like it.

Would I even need to ask the Maines, if we were only in the grounds? I wouldn't, would I? What do you think?

It only needs to be far enough away that she's out of these shadows. Far enough that I am. Otherwise, they're going to break me, Hope. The shadows. I think they're sucking me in.

I leaned my head back in the sofa cushions, tired and melancholy, and the envelopes slipped from the seat onto the floor. The darkness fell around me. I didn't bother to turn on the light. I was exhausted, but it was too early to sleep. And I really didn't want to go to sleep. I dreaded going to sleep.

Usually, I'd put my headphones in my ears. Drown out my thoughts. It hadn't occurred to me how lost I would be without my phone. I tried to fill my head with remembered music instead. With forbidden, whispered thoughts. Shostakovich. 'Piano Concerto No. 2 in F'.

I didn't hear the drawing-room door open, or the approach of footsteps on the wooden floor. It wasn't until his shadow fell over the place where I sat, cast long by the light from the hallway, that I noticed there was someone there.

I jumped and flapped the front page of the notebook over, covering what I had written.

"You don't have to stop." Alex's gaze had fallen momentarily on the envelope at my feet. He strode quickly to the piano. "I'm not staying."

"It's okay." I found my voice. "I don't mind."

He crouched to search through the box of sheet music beside the piano, flicking deftly through the books and loose papers. At last, he found what he was looking for, and straightened. He looked back at the closed notebook, then turned away.

"Really, India." His voice was soft, and utterly unreadable. "I didn't mean to interrupt you. I'm going now."

I looked down at the notebook. Alex had paused in the doorway. For a moment, I thought he was going to say something else. But he didn't. Neither did I.

As he walked away, I remembered the envelope. I stood up quickly and retrieved it from the floor with a hand that wasn't quite steady, her name blurring before my eyes.

Perhaps it wasn't only me that had trespassed.

* * *

Hope, I'm tired. But I'm trying to stay awake.

I'm doing it by remembering things. Stupid things. Like your rubbish cooking, and the Irish coffee you made for us last year with a whole bottle of whisky. I thought I was going to have to call you an ambulance.

There are so many things that could go on that list. The list my mother probably kept. You know she always had you down as a bad influence?

They were the best times. The dares and double dares. The things we really shouldn't have done. I'd do them all again in a heartbeat.

I miss you. I miss you all the time. Time is going so fast that I'm almost scared you'll get left behind, but you never do.

I'm afraid sometimes, Hope. So afraid, and I don't know why.

I dreamt about you last night. I often do. That's something that doesn't change. Although sometimes I wish everything would change. Dreams and all.

Some dreams have real fear in them, real pain. They make you wake up screaming. You cry without even knowing it.

Sometimes, I'm too afraid to sleep.

CHAPTER 10: MARTIANS

Coffee. It was only coffee. So why did I feel so bad about it?

The tearoom was a mile from Rifway, in the corner of a cramped and undiscovered art-gallery-bookshop where the views were better than the paintings, and the second-hand paperbacks were covered with a year-old film of dust. I had finished my latte and was staring speechlessly instead at a gleaming black touchscreen, while Brett regarded me over his empty glass.

"I can't," I said at last. "I can't take *this*."

Brett folded his arms on the table, reproaching. "I want you to. You can't call me without a phone, India."

"I . . ." I traced my finger over the silver apple on the back of the barely-scuffed cover, relenting a little, despite myself. It looked almost brand new. "Okay. Well, how much—"

"Nothing," he cut across me firmly. "I have a new one. I don't need it. Consider it a long-term loan, if it makes you feel better about it."

I wasn't sure it did.

"Okay," I nodded reluctantly. "But—"

"No buts." Brett slid the coffee cup aside, so that I couldn't hide behind it. I glanced up, discomfited. He was smiling, amused.

"Seriously, India." He rolled his eyes, reached to run his fingers over mine and made me let go of the phone. "You're hard work, sometimes."

"Sorry," I mumbled.

Brett leaned in close to me over the table, and slipped the phone into my pocket, his face brushing my hair. "Would you stop apologising?"

I smiled awkwardly, uncomfortably conscious of his knees touching mine under the table.

"What time did you say you needed to get back?" His voice was warm. He moved his legs very deliberately against mine.

I hesitated. "Half three."

"We'd better make a move, then. Or you're going to be late." He picked up the tab from the corner of the table.

"Wait!" I caught his wrist. "Not again. No way."

Brett raised his eyebrows. I saw him bite back a laugh.

"Fine." He let me take it, watching as I counted out the money I had, thankfully, stashed in the desk drawer in my room. My new cards still hadn't arrived. "Just try not to leave your bag behind this time, okay?" He grinned.

I meant to glare. But I couldn't quite help smiling back.

Outside, our cars were the only two in the untidy gravelled car park. We took our time, picking our way between the nettles and weeds. We reached my car first, and Brett leaned against the back bumper to face me.

"So . . . when am I going to see you?"

"I'm busy this week." I looked down and back up quickly, ashamed of my own transparent excuses. "Both the Maines are abroad, so it's just me and Alicia. For the weekend, as well. I'll have my hands full. But I'll be in touch? After they get back . . . As soon as I know . . ."

"Uh-huh." His voice was hard to gauge. I touched the phone in my pocket.

"I promise," I whispered.

Brett smiled, unconvinced. He shook his head.

"Don't make promises you can't keep, India," he said softly.

* * *

"Can I try it yet?" Alicia jumped up and down on her stool.

It was Wednesday, and she had been in startlingly high spirits since her father's departure. In fact, a feeling of release seemed to have pervaded the whole house. The biggest surprise of the evening, though, had been Alex. He had been sitting at the kitchen table when Alicia and I had returned from school, finishing a glass of orange juice and reading a weighty-looking hardback. And he hadn't left. He glanced up as we came in, and went back to his book, as if it was the most normal thing in the world. I had to restrain myself from staring in disbelief; although Alicia was doing just that, unabashedly. Judging by her face, there might as well have been a Martian at the kitchen table.

Outside, the sun was starting to sink in the sky, turning everything a surreal shade of high-definition gold. In my pocket, the phone was a guilty secret. I had texted Brett once, out of obligation, and then felt ashamed I had done it for that reason.

"Isn't it *ready* yet?" Alicia leapt back down from the stool in impatience.

"Almost." My wrist ached desperately from stirring. The mixture was gradually starting to resemble a precursor to cake. "Here." I relinquished the spoon and lowered the bowl back onto the surface. "You'd better try it. If you keel over, I'll know not to eat it."

Alicia seized the spoon and scraped a dollop of mixture from it with two fingers, frowning. "What does 'keel over' mean?"

I bit back my laugh. "It means . . . er . . . fall over. Like, if the cake mixture was so bad that it poisoned you."

Alicia thrust the spoon into her mouth. "It's not *that* bad. You're being silly."

"Not that bad?" I reiterated. "*You* can stir it next time!"

Alicia giggled. "Can I get my paper cases now?"

"Yep." I checked the temperature of the oven. "Over here, look." I showed her the tray. "You're going to need that stool. Come and put a case in each one of these little holes."

I watched as she obligingly picked up the step and brought it over. She hummed to herself as she climbed onto it and unloaded a colourful array of meticulously felt-tipped paper cases onto the side.

"India?" Alicia arranged the cases carefully, turning each one round so that the pictures she had drawn were visible from the front.

"Mm?"

"When you're sad, who makes *you* feel better?"

I halted, bowl in hand, momentarily immobilised. Alicia looked up at me, an earnest frown creasing her forehead.

"When I'm sad, *you* make *me* feel better," she continued, holding the last paper case between her fingers. "Like the other night. But you said everyone gets sad sometimes. So I was thinking, that means you must get sad, too."

"Um . . . sometimes."

There was silence. I was uncomfortably aware of it, and of the sudden ache in my chest.

"But I've got you," I carried on hastily. "And *you* cheer me up, Alicia."

"*Do* I?" Her face lit up.

"Of course you do." I smiled at her and hoped that she wouldn't see the way my fingers shook on the edge of the bowl. "Are you ready? I think we need a new spoon!"

"Oh!" Alicia jumped down from the stool to fetch me one. "Can I help you put it in?"

"It's heavy," I warned her.

As much mixture went on Alicia and the surface as made it into the paper cases. But ten minutes later the cakes were in the oven, and I sent Alicia to get changed. I ran a bowl of water to wash up. Alex was still sitting at the table reading. I glanced over my shoulder, and for a split second his eyes met mine over the top of his book.

It occurred to me that I hadn't heard him turn a single page. I frowned. Alex raised his eyebrows. There was silence.

I turned back to the washing up and plunged my hands into the hot water, deliberately obliterating the silence with the clink of crockery. Seconds turned into minutes. Outside, a mistle thrush was singing loudly from high in the top of one of the trees; Byron stalked across the courtyard in its direction, orange eyes turned upwards, tail flattened. I finished washing and shook out a tea towel from the rail.

The bell of the timer heralded the thunder of Alicia's feet on the stairs.

"They're ready!" She bounded across the kitchen. "They're ready, they're ready!"

"Steady." I shepherded her backwards so that I could open the oven door safely. "Let me get them out."

It might have been a lifetime that we had to leave the cakes to cool, if Alicia's impatience had been any measure. I persuaded her to help me dry up, to try and pass the time. Not even that mundane task seemed to quash her buoyancy; she busied herself putting away the bowls and utensils we had dirtied, clattering loudly around the cupboards and singing nursery rhymes under her breath.

A-tisket, a-tasket
A green and yellow basket
I wrote a letter to my love
And on the way I dropped it . . .

A shiver ran through me, and I wrapped my arms around myself, turning my gaze back out of the window. The cat had curled up in a sunny patch beside one of the plant pots, and the thrush had flown away.

"India." Alicia was tugging at my sleeve, and I realised that my thoughts had strayed. "India, aren't they cool enough yet?"

She let go of me and ran to inspect them.

"I think they are," she told me seriously.

I joined her, to check. "Probably," I agreed.

"Yesss!" Alicia jumped off the stool and back on again. "Can I try one?!"

I shot a fleeting glance back over my shoulder. Alex was still there, his finger and thumb toying with the corner of the page he was reading.

I crouched down to Alicia's height.

"Why don't you see if Alex wants one?" I whispered.

Alicia grinned widely and seized the nearest one. She ran across to where he sat, skidding the last bit in her socks.

"Alex!"

He looked up, startled.

Alicia held out the cake to him. "We made fairy buns! They've got fruit in. I even coloured the paper cases."

For a moment he didn't seem to know what to do. He stared at her, speechless.

"Take it, then!" Alicia thrust it into his hand. "You can try the first one. Don't you want it?"

"Thanks." Alex's voice was quiet. Fleetingly, the hint of a smile played on his lips: of surprise, of gratification. Alicia beamed.

I stood in silence, keeping my eyes deliberately fixed on the rest of the rack of cakes and counting them for no reason at all, letting the moment linger.

"If you keel over, I'll know not to eat it," Alicia said brightly.

I had a sudden overwhelming urge to bury my face in my hands.

* * *

It was seven before tea was made and not really eaten. Eight, by the time I managed to persuade Alicia into the bath. Julia Maine's rules were falling like dominoes.

"Why is your piano notebook on the towel rail?" I glanced back over at Alicia as she squeezed out an empty bubble-bath bottle vigorously, foam erupting everywhere.

"I dunno."

I smiled, not fooled.

"Come on, let's get you out before you shrivel away to nothing."

Alicia held out her wrinkled hands. "I almost have."

I handed her a towel as she slithered to her feet and clambered out.

"I'm going to take your notebook back to the drawing room while you get into your pyjamas," I told her. "Before I forget." I picked up the notebook from the top of the towel rail.

The sound of my feet on the wooden staircase echoed surprisingly around the walls in the darkness. There were no lights on in the hall. I found myself scanning the shadows, on edge, unnerved by my own imagination and how vividly it could reproduce the click of the front door latch, the tread of footsteps, the rush of the wind. A face looking in through the leaded lights. I shuddered.

The boards were cold under my feet as I started in the direction of the drawing room. I stopped.

Someone was playing the piano. Not just playing: it was the best playing I had ever heard. Too real to be a recording, but too flawless to be real; the notes echoed, reverberated, throbbed from the half-open doorway. As I listened it grew, spreading outwards like ripples on water, swelling to a haunting, hopeful climax.

In an instant, my fear had evaporated. My fingers tightened subconsciously around the notebook and I realised I was holding my breath. I tiptoed a few hesitant steps nearer. Slowly, silently, I pushed the door open far enough to see.

Alex was sitting at the piano, poised, absorbed, a silhouette in the soft white-blue light of a single lamp above the keyboard. So utterly involved in the flow of sound, song, story, that he hadn't noticed me at all.

I drew in a deep breath, watching. Watching his strong hands stretch over the keys. Watching it flood from him, uncensored and unchecked, the beautiful, harrowing account of a life unspoken. Daylight and light falling rain; fresh air, birdsong. Places that I could no longer picture but could feel — the way he felt them — somewhere deep and raw and cherished.

My hand found the edge of the door and gripped it hard. How long I stood there, I wasn't sure. A long time, long enough that the hazy air had grown darker and colder, when suddenly he stopped.

There was complete silence. He didn't look round. He picked up a pencil from the piano and leaned forwards to write on the music in front of him. Handwritten. My breath left me in a rush. It was all handwritten, a thousand pencilled notes in a small, cramped hand. I let go of the door, and the creak of its hinges ripped abruptly into the silence.

Alex jumped, visibly. The pencil jerked across the page. And suddenly he spun, and I was caught mid-transgression, exposed in the pale pool of lamplight that spilled over his shoulders.

"Did . . . did you write that?" I choked out at last.

His brows drew darkly together. For an agonisingly long moment, he didn't reply. Just stared, in slowly gathering realisation, at my face.

"I . . . I'm . . . sorry." I disintegrated under his scrutiny. My cheeks were flaming. "I . . . just came to put Alicia's notebook back. I . . ."

I stepped gingerly through the doorway and put the book down on the table. He still hadn't spoken. A tiny frown played on his forehead.

"But, I mean . . . That was . . ." I trailed off. My lashes were wet. I tried to dash a hand across them without him noticing. "It was . . ."

What? It was what? Beautiful. Heart-rending.

Soul-destroying?

"Incredible," I whispered. "I'm um . . . sorry." I retreated hastily. "Sorry I interrupted."

"Yeah." At last he spoke. I wavered in the doorway. He was watching me. His voice was very soft. "Yeah, I did write it." He rose slowly, scooped up the sheets of music and closed the piano lid with a thud. "I'm glad you like it. One day I might finish it. I don't know." His lips pressed tightly together, stifling the ghost of a painfully self-denigrating smile. He shook his head. "You don't have to leave. I'm done now, anyway. I think Alicia's calling you."

"Oh." I turned to see Alicia appear in the corridor with the Monopoly board tucked under her arm.

"India! There you are! You've been *ages*! Will you play Monopoly with me?"

"With only two people?" I smiled and took the board, unreasonably shaky. "Are you sure Monopoly's the best game?"

"Well. Alex can play too." Alicia rounded on him as he stood awkwardly in the doorway. "Can't you?"

For a split second a look of uncertainty crossed Alex's face.

"No, Alicia." He spoke under his breath. "Sorry."

Alicia sighed deeply. "I guess we'll just have to play with two people then. We did before. When you first started."

She rearranged the box under her arm and something fell out, rolling with a metallic ring on the floorboards. A tiny pewter cannon. Alicia crouched to retrieve it. I watched as Alex sourced a cigarette from his pocket and rolled it between two fingers. Alicia glared at him as she straightened.

"I'm going to get ready," she announced. "In the kitchen. Hurry up and come."

The sound of her bare feet faded on the boards. Still, I couldn't quite bring myself to move. Alex was barely a pace away.

"No doubt she'll tell my father." He crushed the cigarette and pushed it back into his pocket. I shrugged.

"I don't know why you risk it." I kept my gaze trained carefully on my hands. "Why not just play by their rules?"

Alex shook his head. "I've tried, believe me." The undertone of quiet ridicule in his voice was inescapable. "But you've met my father. There'll always be something. He likes to remind us both that I'm at his mercy."

"You can't leave?"

"Do you want me to?" His eyes met mine, his sharp gaze taking me by surprise.

"I . . ." Again, he had snatched away my power of speech. I gaped at him, momentarily. "Not for my sake," I managed at last. "But I don't know how you stand it."

A bitter smile twisted his lips. "I have nowhere else to go, India. I'm sure you've heard the story by now."

I blushed, uncomfortable. His eyebrows lifted.

"You can't tell me that you haven't?"

I looked quickly away. The silence was aching. I stared fixedly at the piano stool, fighting not to frown at the recollection.

"I was charged with assault," Alex broke the silence flatly. "Well, bodily harm, actually. If we're being specific."

It was there again. The sardonic breath of laughter, the bleak overspill of irony and loathing. I couldn't judge what he was thinking. What he was looking for in my reaction as the words sank in; as the knowledge crept through me, dark and terrifying.

"Oh," My mouth was suddenly dry.

"So you see, there aren't many options. You don't do so well getting work when you have a degree in medicine and a criminal record for violence. My parents are right, India. About me. I fucked up my life, and now I have to pay for it."

Daylight. Light falling rain. I looked intently at the chips in the old dark wood. The scrolled handles. The leather seat. Ripples in water.

"It was a mistake," I spoke suddenly, surprising even myself with my earnestness. "You're not a bad person, are you?"

Alex regarded me from beneath lowered brows, his face shadowed, cynical.

"Oh, I don't know, India." His voice was very soft, darkly captivating; his gaze didn't leave mine. "I don't know if that's true at all."

"No." I shook my head. The word emerged huskier than I'd intended it to. "I don't think you're as unsalvageable as you like to make out."

Alex laughed bleakly. "You're on dangerous ground, India. You'd be better off if you listened to them. You know that."

I nodded. "I know."

There was silence again. We looked at our feet. At our long shadows on the wooden boards.

"Alicia's right," I told him lamely. "About the smoking. It really sucks. I'd tell you the same, if I wasn't too scared."

Alex looked up quickly. His expression wavered.

"You're scared of me?"

"You just told me I should be," I pointed out quietly.

"India! Come *on*." The Doppler effect on Alicia's voice told me she was approaching along the hall. "What are you *doing*?!"

By the time she reached us, Alex had turned away. Alicia took me firmly by the hand.

"Come on. Let's go. I'm going to be the dog."

I glanced one last time at the back of his shoulders, and the bundle of paper and pencilled notes under his arm.

"You can be the hat," she insisted.

I paused. Alex had looked back. His dark brows were lowered in a perplexed frown, and his bright blue gaze was on mine.

"Don't be scared of me," he said.

CHAPTER 11: MINUET IN G

A-tisket, a-tasket. I slammed the kitchen door and kicked off my trainers, hopping inelegantly across the floor.

A green and yellow basket . . .

Alicia was horse riding with Lotty Bosworth until three. My jeans were covered in mud. And Maeve had my new number. The phone pinged in my pocket as if on cue. I ignored it and headed for the hall. I needed to get changed.

I wrote a letter to my love . . .

"Shut up!" I clamped my hands over my ears, as if I could silence the rhyme that had been repeating in my head all morning. My voice echoed up the stairwell. Thankfully, there was no one there to hear it. Alex's car wasn't in the drive. I took the stairs two at a time and crossed the landing at a run. Maeve had cornered me into staying for coffee, and it had eaten up most of my morning. I had so much to do . . .

It was my own fault. Despite every ounce of my better judgement, I had mentioned camping to Alicia. And not to her parents.

I was an idiot.

I still had a tent. It was rammed into the bottom of my wardrobe, along with everything else that had come from Leeds. Rucksack, waterproofs, repressed memories.

I reached my room, and the phone chimed again, demanding my attention. I pulled it out and dropped it before I had the chance to read it.

There was something taped to my bedroom door.

Alex?

Suddenly I was breathless.

But he'd been gone since before I took Alicia to the Bosworths'. I frowned. It hadn't been there when I left. My fingers shook as I peeled it off. Newspaper.

It couldn't be . . . could it? I faltered, nauseated. The cutting from the back of my lost purse . . .

No. It wasn't.

I stared, dry-mouthed. The image was blurred and pixelated, hard to make out. A red circle and a blue line: London Underground, slightly out of focus. A graffitied wall and a ticket barrier. A man on the ground.

I swallowed. The second figure had his back to the shot, broad-shouldered and tall, his dishevelled black-brown hair curling slightly at the nape of his neck. The small print in the corner read *Picture: Metropolitan Police.*

I opened my bedroom door with a crash and stumbled inside, unfolding the paper the rest of the way, reading, rereading.

NORTHERN LINE ATTACK: MAN CHARGED

A man has been charged following a brutal attack on a popular local Big Issue seller earlier this month.

The victim, known locally as Charlie, suffered head injuries and facial fractures during the attack. He was left unconscious for several minutes, and received aid only after passengers from an incoming Northern Line train raised the alarm. He was released from hospital the following day.

Alexander Maine, 23, will appear in court next month charged with actual bodily harm.

I wanted to stop reading, but I couldn't. His name in print was like a kick in the gut. I collapsed onto the edge of my bed and stared at the paper, sickened.

Maine, who was initially questioned about the incident after the release of CCTV footage, was later arrested following positive identification by his victim based on police video recordings of identity parades. Officers have confirmed that Maine was intoxicated at the time of the attack.

Maine has been released on bail. Scotland Yard said it was not seeking anyone else in connection with the investigation.

What had I thought? That it hadn't really happened? He'd told me himself. Warned me. And I hadn't listened. I folded the cutting in half, out of sight.

"It was a mistake." I whispered it to my empty room, as if in justification.

Suddenly, I was shivering. Alex wouldn't have put this on my door. Would he? I wrapped my arms around myself as I thought of his voice, the bitter self-mocking. The waver in his expression. *You're scared of me?*

No. I rubbed my forehead, confused. It didn't make sense. But no one else had been here. No one else had been in the house.

Had they?

Just like no one had been in the courtyard, only the wind. Just like no one but me could have opened my bedroom window, and only one person on Earth would ever have left a yellow rose beside my bed.

"Hello? Duckie?"

I slid hastily to my feet.

"It's Vee. Are you up there?"

I screwed the cutting quickly into a ball.

"Just a minute!" I called. My voice sounded not much like my voice. I scrambled out of my mud-spattered jeans and changed into clean ones hurriedly.

Vee was cleaning the kitchen when I got downstairs, even though it wasn't her alternate Friday. Apparently, she was going on holiday and wanted to get ahead. I loaded my breakfast things and Alicia's into the dishwasher and half-listened to her, preoccupied, as she updated me on the gossip and gave me a photo tour of her sister's static caravan in Mablethorpe.

Under Vee's watchful eye and ceaseless, cheerful chatter, I had almost recovered my equilibrium by three, at which point I set off to pick up Alicia. The day was deceptively warm. I rolled down the car windows as I drove, enjoying the buffeting of the surprisingly summery air on my face.

Whether it was camping-related or just weather-related, Alicia was already excited and distractible to the point of being fractious. To worsen matters, Iain Trevers arrived for piano only moments after we got home, before I had managed to drop her a gentle reminder. Alicia's face was like thunder as I abandoned them to the drawing room and fled.

I couldn't help feeling a pang of guilt, more towards Iain than her, as I carried the big wicker washing basket to the line and started to bring in the clothes. I tried to pull together the plan in my head. A late start. A picnic lunch. A corner of the grounds where we could make a campfire — Roy, the gardener had grumbled his assent when I asked him, as long as it wasn't on the lawns. Marshmallows. A two-man tent.

Nerves of steel.

The kitchen door opened unexpectedly, and I squinted over my shoulder to look, surprised. Alicia's chestnut curls bounced past hurriedly, followed a few seconds later by Iain Trevers as he paused on the doorstep to slip on his shoes.

Alicia's face was red and blotchy. She looked hot. Without so much as a word or a glance in my direction, she went running across the grass and into the trees.

I finished folding the skirt I was holding and turned around. Iain was hovering at a distance.

"Hi." I smiled politely. It was hard to say which of us was more awkward.

"Hi, India." Iain crossed the grass on tiptoe, watching where he put his feet. I stooped to put a pair of Alicia's jeans in the basket.

"I think Alicia needed some fresh air."

"Oh." Now I felt really guilty. "I'm sorry."

Iain shook his head. "No. Don't worry. It's just one of those things." He shaded his eyes to look into the trees. "She said you're taking her camping."

"Yeah." I folded the next pair of jeans, embarrassed. "Only in the garden. If the weather stays good. I think she's just a bit over-excited."

Iain laughed quietly. "I guess I have all this to look forward to."

I glanced at him, confused.

"My wife's expecting a baby." He smiled. "Our first. The start of December."

"Congratulations!" I put down the bag of pegs. "You must be thrilled!"

Iain nodded. "I'll need to take a couple of weeks off. I haven't told Julia yet."

"How long have you been teaching?" I asked, curious.

"Oh . . ." Iain calculated this for a moment. "Twelve, thirteen years, I suppose. How old is Alex now?"

"Uhm," I faltered. "Twenty-four, I think?"

"Yes, thirteen years then. Gosh." Iain shook his head. "Alex was in his last year of primary school the year that I started — at the old school in the village — when Jim left. It's closed now."

"Did you ever teach Alex?" I tried to sound impassive.

Iain shook his head. "No. Jim was still teaching there when he was at the primary, but his parents paid for him to go to Embarby Hall and they moved him there a term into year six. Jim moved over fully to peripatetic work at Embarby and the Minster around the time Alex moved, because he wanted more secondary-age experience, and that's when I took over. So we never overlapped. Although, to be honest Jim never really taught Alex at school anyway, he arranged to see him privately — the amount of time they'd get during the day for a lesson just couldn't do Alex justice. Alex was very talented. He was a better pianist at thirteen than I am now."

"Oh." I couldn't think of a better reply. All I could think of was a thousand pencilled notes in a small, cramped hand, and a man on the ground, bleeding.

"I wonder if we should call Alicia?" Iain scanned the garden, fruitlessly. "I don't want them to have paid for a lesson she didn't have."

I had to make a full circuit of the house and garden, my voice echoing hollowly through the apple trees and around the ornamental roses. There was no sign of her. I prayed that she was still in the garden somewhere, and that she hadn't decided to take off into the uncharted territory of the grounds in a fit of disobedience. The wind was picking up, whisking flurries of dry leaves from the grass.

"Alicia!" I emerged through the dark partition of conifer trees that separated the garden from the driveway at the front, and pushed through the low branches, twigs snagging in my hair.

"Alicia, come on." I was beginning to feel hot and bothered. It was a long time since our last game of defiant hide-and-seek. My feet crunched on the gravel as I crossed the drive. Beside me, Alex's Volkswagen was covered in dust, and a cat basked on the low stone wall that demarcated the edge of the expansive grounds. I stopped, and gazed out across the parkland, over the odd cluster of blundering sheep that the Maines let one of the local farmers graze there.

No Alicia. At a loss, I let myself back into the house.

The hall was silent, and the kitchen was empty. Outside, Iain and Alex were standing beside the door. Their voices carried intermittently, fading in and out. I tried not to listen.

"When?!"

"Twenty-third of December."

"That's incredible, Alex! What have you prepared?"

"I was going to . . ."

A gust of wind blasted through the open window, and rattled the door in its frame, snatching away the end of Alex's sentence. I glanced out at the excitement in Iain Trevers' face. I had never seen him so animated.

Still no Alicia. Starting to feel anxious, I went to check upstairs, and knocked on the door to her room. No answer.

I pushed the door open slowly. Her room was a tip. It seemed only five minutes since I had tidied it. I picked my way across the floor, checking that she really wasn't there. Then the bathroom, her parents' room, the guest rooms. Nothing.

In the end, I had to let Iain Trevers go home. Alex slipped back upstairs without a word. Trying to stay practical, I slid the lasagne that I'd assembled earlier into the oven, and resumed my search in the garden, growing slowly more unsettled. It wasn't the first time she had hidden from me. But she'd never disappeared quite so successfully into thin air before.

"Alicia?" I pushed open the sitting-room door, startling a cat that exploded up at me with a hiss of protest. I looked around at the plush sofa and the exotic collection of pot plants under the window, and pulled the door to again as the cat scampered across the hall.

It was the sniff that alerted me to her whereabouts. I stopped, mid-step, in disbelief.

The drawing room. Of all the possibilities, she had gone back to the drawing room. The one place it hadn't even occurred to me to look.

"Alicia!" I hurried over to her, alarmed. She was sitting on the piano stool, hunched, her arms around her knees.

"There you are." I looked at her tear-stained face. "What's the matter?"

She didn't even look up.

"Stupid piano. That's what's the stupid matter." She reached out a hand and slammed it down despondently on the keys, sending a discordant clash of notes echoing around the room. "I hate it!" Stress rose shrilly in her voice. "Mum

127

wants me to take the stupid exam. And Mr Trevers entered me! Even though I said no!" She turned to me suddenly, chin wobbling. "And now they're going to make me do it, and it's going to be awful. I won't be able to do it! I can't read the stupid music he gave me, I don't get it, and they don't believe me! It's a big waste of time!"

Suddenly she was sobbing.

"Oh, no!" I sat down beside her on the stool with a bump. "That's not true! Mr Trevers wouldn't have entered you if he didn't think you could do it. You've been doing really well with piano."

"*Don't* say that!" She rounded on me. "That's just what he said! *And* what Mum said! They have no idea! I'm *terrible* at piano!"

"Oh, Alicia." I hugged her. "You're not terrible. You'll get there, with practice."

"But I *hate* practising!"

"I know. I hate making you."

"Well, you'll *have* to make me," Alicia told me, hiccupping miserably. "Because I have to take the stupid exam, and otherwise I'll fail."

"You won't fail!" I took her hand off the piano gently, letting the notes fall silent. "You won't fail. I'll help you. We can learn the pieces together."

Alicia looked at me, despairing. "*I* can't understand the music. And *you* can't play it. So really, we're doomed."

I fought the urge to smile at her gloomy, if logical, conclusion.

"It'll be okay," I reassured her, keeping her hand in mine. We sat for a while in silence.

I wasn't sure what made me glance up. A sudden, uncomfortable feeling of being watched. I froze.

Alex had come in without a sound, and was perched on the edge of the sofa, his expression inscrutable. I had no idea how long he had been there. I got to my feet. Alicia sniffed.

"What pieces do you have to play?" His voice was quiet, non-committal.

Alicia looked up at him, baffled. "What?"

Alex stood up and approached the piano. Beside Alicia, he was very tall. His face was full of shadows, no smiles. He took the music book from the piano and flicked through it.

"A3, B1, C3 . . ." He scanned each page for Iain Trevers' pencil marks. "You shouldn't do C3. You should do C2. Here." He sat down beside her, and Alicia shuffled sideways to sit where I had been on the edge of the stool. "Do you want me to play them?"

Alicia nodded doubtfully, round-eyed with disbelief. I watched in incredulity as Alex stood the book back on the piano and started to play. He made the minuet sound so beautifully simple, so musical, the notes ringing prettily in the still air. He reached the end and stopped. Alicia frowned down at his hands.

"You make it sound easy."

"It *is* easy. If you learn what the tune sounds like, you'll be just as good. Come on." Alex moved over and jerked his head for her to follow. "This way a bit. Can you play any of the right hand?"

Suddenly, I was surplus to requirements. I stared, speechless, at the back of his shoulders. Then, Alicia touched her hand tentatively to the keys and started to play.

I tiptoed from the room, unnoticed. My heart was hammering for a reason I couldn't explain. It was warm in the kitchen, and the smell emanating from the oven was surprisingly good. I busied myself taking out plates for myself and Alicia, and hesitated. I added a third plate to the stack, and set the table, moving her collection of drawings and colouring pencils to one side. The sound of the piano filtered softly through from the drawing room, a slow, enchanting repeat, broken intermittently as Alicia lost her place and fumbled to join back in.

They were so long that I had to turn the oven off. The sky outside grew dark, and I moved through the house closing the curtains. I went to my own room last, lingering in the darkness to look at the shapes of the pictures on the walls, taking a few deep, steadying breaths. Thinking of our strangest conversation.

You can't leave?

Do you want me to?

I shivered.

"India?"

I jumped. Alicia had appeared stealthily in the doorway behind me.

"Is tea ready?" She hung on the doorframe, craning her head to see into my room, her eyes wide as she looked around at the photos on the walls. "Is that you, in the picture?" She pointed.

I nodded. "Yes, and yes."

"Who's the other person in the picture?" Alicia turned to stare over her shoulder as I ushered her from the room, back towards the enticing smell of the kitchen.

I hesitated. "My best friend," I replied under my breath.

"What's her name?"

"Hope." My voice emerged sounding uncharacteristically husky. I closed the door hastily behind us.

"She's pretty," Alicia observed. "What's for dinner?"

"Lasagne. Sort of." I was glad to be back on safe ground.

"Sort of?" Alicia's face was priceless. Apparently, she had as much faith in my culinary abilities as I did.

"Mm. We'll see if anyone keels over," I teased as we reached the bottom of the stairs together.

Alicia giggled. I glanced up. Alex was waiting to go up the stairs. I hesitated.

"Join us?" I finally succeeded in asking. "There's plenty of food."

Alex looked from me to Alicia, and then back again.

"Thanks," he nodded.

Mercifully, the meal was passable. We ate largely in silence, Alicia's gaze travelling alternately from one to the other of us as she chewed and swallowed. Alex didn't speak at all. But he didn't leave, either. I suddenly found that I wasn't all that hungry.

"Thank you for my tea, please can I leave the table?" Alicia was on the edge of her seat, waiting for me to finish, her knife and fork lined up neatly in the middle of her cleared plate.

"Sure," I nodded, and she vanished instantly. I heard her rummaging in the other room.

Alex had finished eating, too. I expected him to get up, to make an excuse, but he didn't. He selected one of the newspapers from the table and began to flick through it. I sat motionless, not quite brave enough to take his plate. Alicia returned with an armful of board games.

"Look." She dumped them on the table. "These have been in the cupboard *forever*. Can we learn to play one of them? Alex can play too. Oh—"

Something had fallen out from amongst the dusty boxes. A paper wallet, the kind that photos used to come in. Alicia picked it up, intrigued.

"I didn't know *this* was there." She tipped the contents onto the table. "Look, are they photos?"

Alex put down the newspaper quietly. His gaze was on the pictures.

"Alex!" Alicia seized one from the cascade excitedly. "This one's of you!"

"Yeah." His voice was dubious. "Would you give it here, Alicia?"

She didn't seem to hear him, grabbing the next one from the pile.

"What are you doing in this one?" She traced a finger over it. The picture was badly focused; the four boys in it were in their teens, dressed in layers of waterproofs, and carrying rucksacks not dissimilar to the one packed in my room upstairs. The middle one — no, two — faces were familiar. I blinked.

"Are you camping?" Alicia's expression lit up.

Alex's eyes had narrowed a fraction. He took the photos from her gently and put them to one side, out of sight.

"Yeah," he said at last.

"*We're* going camping tomorrow!" At once, Alicia was bubbling over with excitement. She clambered up onto the chair beside him. "Me and India are! You should come!"

I gaped at her, too speechless to intervene. Alex froze. He stared at her, somewhere between amused and alarmed.

"I'm not sure that's a great idea, Alicia," he replied finally.

"It *is*!" Alicia knelt up on her chair, in earnest. "India wouldn't mind. You don't, do you, India? She jumped down from the chair and danced round to my side of the table to implore me instead. "India! Tell Alex he should come!"

"Uhh . . ." I was caught completely off guard. Suddenly, both of their eyes were on me. I floundered for a reply.

"Uh . . . um. I think really that's Alex's choice, Alicia."

Alex got to his feet slowly, taking the photos from the table to push them into his pocket. His eyes were on me. Piercingly bright.

"Not this time, Alicia." He shook his head: a tiny, almost imperceptible movement. But as he turned to go, I saw his fingers slip back to the pictures in his pocket.

CHAPTER 12: ONE THING

I told you that I wasn't brave enough. And maybe I'm not. I never did ask John Maine.

But I'm doing it. Today. I'm taking Alicia camping. We're going to make some memories. Some good ones.

Because good memories last, Hope. Good memories are what really matter.

Do you remember our second year in Leeds? January. We both had exams, and we were lying in your bed watching some crappy midnight film with subtitles because we'd been revising all day? We got up, and we went to the playpark, do you remember that? The one with the wobbly plank and the spiral slide. In the middle of the night, we went to the playpark in our pyjamas and played like kids. Like Alicia plays. We played like we meant it.

I miss it. Not the playpark, but the stupidness. The spontaneity. I miss having a friend. I miss nights in the kitchen with wine, I miss arguments and getting ready and borrowing eyeliner. I miss having someone who hugs me, someone who touches me, someone who takes my hand when I cry or holds my hair when I'm sick. I miss standing still and looking and knowing what you think. I miss it all. The good days <u>and</u> the bad ones.

I miss you, Hope. Every second of every minute of every day.

I need more good memories. Like your memories. I need them, and so does Alicia.

So here goes nothing.

Wish me luck.

India

* * *

Sun, as predicted. A clear autumn sky. Only the wind was a guest at our picnic, and even its company was sporadic; it would fade away entirely, bored of our childish pursuits, before whipping back in a fit of jealousy to snatch at the edges of our picnic blanket. Alicia had refused to remove her backpack when we sat down to eat. Now, as we finished and I shook out the cake crumbs from the blanket, she launched herself across the remaining short stretch of garden.

"Come on!" She was over the fence that picketed Roy's immaculate lawns from the wilder, uncultivated grounds in a nanosecond, her voice shrill and windswept. "Hurry up!"

I did my best, cautious not to tip under the weight of my ridiculously heavy bag as I clambered over the top bar and dropped with a thud onto the wiry, uneven grass beside her.

The grounds of the Manor were vast. Vaster than I'd ever realised: acres of what was once a deer park, now grazed instead by silly blundering sheep that ran in belated terror away from us as we cut downhill across the pot-holed grass. Occasional colossal oak trees frowned at us as we fashioned our escape; Alicia ran ahead of me, diverting every few seconds to exclaim over a new treasure: a clump of greasy sheep's wool, a pheasant feather, an oddly shaped rock. I followed at a distance, content to watch. Every now and then, a rabbit would dart across our path, immobilising her with glee.

Our progress was slow, but it didn't really matter. I looked back over my shoulder at the house, the sun reflecting off its upstairs windows like cats' eyes. We crossed a ditch of nettles onto a second expanse of longer, sheepless grass, and I glanced right at the low stone wall that ran a few metres parallel to our self-made path. We were still on the Maines' land. When I had pointed this meadow out to Roy, he had grunted his approval and waved a warning finger vaguely in the direction of the next hedgerow. *Not past there.* It was a shame, because the trees beyond were a multitude of inviting colour.

There was a track on the other side of the wall, ploughed-up mud and tyre tracks. I wondered where it went. Back towards the house, I imagined, somewhere near Roy's sheds. The tended gardens dwindled behind us as we walked, the Manor shrinking slowly in the distance. A mile, perhaps a little more. I looked at Alicia, plucking faded red flowers from the flattened grass. I supposed that this would do. Close enough, but far enough. *Out of the shadows.*

"Alicia," I called her away from her picking. "What do you think to here?"

She skipped over to me, posy still in hand.

"Here?" She spun on the spot to survey her territory. I nodded, letting the rucksack slip from my back. She jumped up and down, testing the ground. Sat down in the grass with a bump.

"Maybe." She held up the posy thoughtfully. "What do *you* think?"

"*Not here.*"

I gasped. Alicia dropped the posy in alarm. In slow motion, I turned.

There was a car on the track. Black, dusty and familiar. I squinted in disbelief as its door slammed.

Alex swung himself over the dry-stone wall and stopped, his gaze travelling from Alicia's open mouth to my face. I let go of the rucksack without thinking, and it fell over with a thud.

"You don't want to camp here." He crossed his legs and leaned back against the wall, dark blue eyes on mine. He was wearing hiking boots. A waterproof coat was tied around his waist.

"I'm sorry?" I finally managed to say.

"You don't want to camp here," he repeated softly.

"Don't we?"

He shook his head. "No." An undertone in his voice was challenging me. Daring me. "I know somewhere better." He pushed himself to his feet and moved to join us.

"*Alex!*" Alicia was staring at him in a mixture of awe and incredulity. "You said you wouldn't come!"

"I haven't said I will." The elusive suggestion of a smile skimmed the corner of his lips.

"Oh!" Alicia sprung upright. "But you're *here!*" She was hopping from foot to foot in excitement "Are you going to show us? Your *somewhere better?*"

"If you want me to." His voice was inscrutable.

"Yes, yes!" Alicia danced around him, jubilant. Alex's eyes were still on me, not her.

"I . . ." I hesitated. Shot an anxious look back at the suddenly not-so-close upstairs windows of the Manor, black and staring. "I wasn't going to leave the grounds. Your parents don't know that we're . . ."

"No." His murmur was low enough for Alicia not to hear, the tiniest flicker in his brows impossible to read. "I gathered."

"Is it a *secret* place?" Alicia's eyes were round. "A proper secret? Will no one be able to find us?"

"No one." It was there again. The glimmer of amusement that played, fleetingly, around his mouth. "It's in the trees."

"Oh!" Alicia turned back to me, hugging herself. "Please, India! It'll be just like when you told me about! When you and your friend went real-life camping in the woods! Will we see owls?" She tugged at my jumper in excitement. "And foxes?"

"Maybe later, once it's dark." I picked up my rucksack in wordless, slightly tremulous assent. For some reason my pulse was much too fast. My voice wasn't entirely even. "They're nocturnal, remember?"

"You'd have to be really quiet," Alex broke in. His face gave nothing away.

"I can be quiet!" Alicia told him haughtily.

"Good. Are you coming, then?"

I watched in disbelief as he reached down to rest a hand on Alicia's backpack. Alicia's eyes widened. Her face split into a broad, mischievous smile.

"*Yes!*"

I followed a pace behind them to the corner of the field, where the forbidden hedgerow convened with the stone wall. There, overgrown by brambles, was a gap in the bushes. An old rusted five-bar gate. Alicia clambered over it as Alex held out a hand to help her. I scrambled through behind them. The scrap of land beyond wasn't really big enough to call a field; it was leftover and angular, with tall tough grass. Too steep to cultivate, too small to graze, it sloped sharply downhill and ended in a dense barricade of trees, where the wind had already beaten us to ripple tantalisingly through the leaves.

"Alicia." Alex's voice was very soft. "I'll race you to the bottom!"

I couldn't believe what I was hearing. I spun, open-mouthed, to look at him, but he was already gone. Alicia gave a whoop of exhilaration and set off in close pursuit, her backpack jolting up and down as she sprinted over the irregular ground, tripping every so often on a clump of grass.

I stood and stared, speechless. Alex slowed halfway and stopped, letting her overtake him. Alicia didn't notice; she flew on, faster and faster, uncontrollably downwards, her arms flailing wildly in the air as she attempted to slow at the bottom.

I wavered, not quite daring to move. He had bent over, hands on his knees, watching her go. And there was something in his expression that made my heart skip a beat, something I had never seen before. Something warm, so fleeting and fragile, that I was scared to look at him in case he noticed and whatever it was got lost forever.

It didn't make sense. I stood, torn by the memory – *we're all fucked up, India –;* by the whisper of piano notes in the hallway, by the Alex in front of me with the light in his eyes and the sun in his dark, untidy hair.

"*India!*" Alicia's shout was barely audible, carrying on the breeze from the foot of the hill. She was standing on a huge, fallen log, waving her arms impatiently above her head to attract my attention.

At last I started to walk. Alex strode to the bottom easily, standing beside the log as Alicia balanced her way along it with her arms out, then leapt down and abandoned her backpack to bound away into the trees. He glanced back fleetingly as I approached. The wind was roaring through the branches. Then he folded his arms and turned his attention to Alicia, who was ploughing through the drifts of leaves like a hurricane.

There was a sudden, indescribable ache in my chest. I turned in a full circle, taking in the colours, the peace, the rush of the leaves. Behind us, there was nothing to see but whispering meadow grass. The Manor was gone. The remnants of the dry-stone wall crumbled into the edge of the woodland. As if he'd read my mind. As if he'd known everything I'd wanted this place to be.

I drew in a deep breath. Hesitated.

"Are you sure about this?"

Alex shrugged. His gaze was fixed on the trees. "Technically, we're still in the grounds."

"Oh." I sucked my bottom lip between my teeth. Then I lowered my rucksack. For a moment there was silence.

"Alex . . ." I started. Trailed off. He didn't look round.

"Mm?"

"What . . ." I searched for the words. "I mean, why . . ."

"Silver linings," he replied quietly. Without even waiting for the question.

I hesitated. "Something's changed. Hasn't it?"

"What makes you say that?" He was still facing the other way, watching the ripple of the wind in the coloured leaves. I looked down at my feet.

"I saw you with Iain Trevers," I admitted. "And then . . . now . . . It just . . . I mean, it . . . seems like something's different. Like something must have happened. Something good."

"I don't know, India." He shook his head. "Nothing to pin any hopes on."

"You seem happier lately." I fiddled with a loose thread on the sleeve of my jumper.

His almost-smile was enigmatic. "Perhaps," he said.

Silence again. I looked at the leaves, too.

"Sometimes it only takes one thing to change your outlook," he said softly. "Plus, once you've fought your side enough times and never made any difference, you realise it's not worth screwing yourself over about it." He turned to face me suddenly.

"It's like you can write a hundred letters, and never get a letter back. Then, I suppose, you start to think maybe there's no point in breaking your heart about it." His eyes locked with mine.

I swallowed. Suddenly my throat was hurting. I didn't know what to say.

"People move on, India. Find something new." His gaze was still on me, impossible to read, bluer than the cloudless October sky. "The thing that makes waking up worthwhile, every day."

I frowned.

"SURPRISE!"

The shower of leaves hit us both in the face simultaneously. Alex ducked and I blinked hard, trying to get the grit out of my eyes. Alicia stood up smugly from behind the log, dusting the leaf litter off her sleeves before stooping to gather another armful. She tossed it into the air, and shielded her head with her arms as it rained down, covering all three of us with twigs and debris.

"Hurry up!" Her hands were on her hips. "What were you two talking about, anyway?"

I looked back at my feet, at the scuffed toes of my boots.

"I'm not sure," I whispered.

Alicia didn't hear. And by the time I looked up, Alex was gone.

* * *

We spent a long time in the trees. I abandoned my bag beside Alicia's and went with her to explore, admiring each discovery as it was made — an owl feather to adorn my ponytail, a bright spray of berries for hers. A perfect, smooth acorn in its cup, *A for Alicia*, and an ivy leaf for India pinned proudly to the breast of my jumper. I suggested we might need wood for the fire and was instantaneously loaded down with every stick and fallen branch that was small enough to lift. Alicia even found a broken sapling, snapped off by the wind, which she insisted on dragging behind us as we circled back towards the place we'd left our bags. I stopped, surprised.

There, at the edge of the trees, there was a splash of familiar blue. The ripple and flap of windswept polyester. My tent. It was already pitched; a few colourful leaves blew against its taut sides, brushing and fluttering away like autumnal butterflies. Alex stood up and came to relieve Alicia of her burden.

"You'd better break this up." He raised his eyebrows at his sister. "You think you can do that?"

"Yep!" Alicia nodded vigorously.

Alex positioned the tree under her instruction and then sat down again at a distance, taking out his penknife to chip away at something, half-watching as Alicia leapt into the springy sapling, bouncing off one of its sturdier branches rather than breaking it. She stumbled, and tried again, stamping hard to little avail. I suppressed a smile.

"Come *on* already!" She struggled to bend one of its still-supple limbs, in significant danger of it rebounding and knocking her over. "India, help me!"

I dumped my armful and went to her aid. The wood was green, and I had a feeling it wouldn't burn, but Alicia was

140

undeterred. I held it still as she jumped, wrestled, prised bits off – a twig here, a long swishing stick there – until she was exhausted and red in the face. From time to time, I caught myself glancing over my shoulder, back at the place where Alex sat, silently occupied. I wasn't sure when I had started noticing. Noticing the unspoken words that played on his lips, at some times deadly serious, at others almost amused. Noticing the way his dark brows knitted in concentration. Noticing how, every now and then, he would be looking back.

"Here." I ushered Alicia over to our armful of drier wood, defeated by the tree. "Maybe this wood is better?"

She nodded solemnly and set to work building the twigs and sticks into a tremendous pile. I sat back, realising it was important not to laugh. Another gust of wind cavorted through the campsite, tugging at the open tent flap and making the sides billow. I moved to zip it closed, and glanced up, with the unsettling feeling that I was being observed. Alex was watching me silently, his face half-shadowed by the shifting, dancing leaves. *An enigma.*

Suddenly, I was blushing.

"India!" Alicia sat back on her heels excitedly. "It's ready! Can't we light it now?"

I jumped up.

"Don't you want to wait until it gets dark?" I checked the time on my phone and went to join her, smiling despite myself at the higgledy-piggledy fire.

"Not really," Alicia replied solemnly. "I think it would be better to get on with it."

"Okay." I slipped the phone into my pocket and crouched down beside her to inspect her handiwork. "But don't you want to explore any more first?"

"Maybe." Alicia stood up, dusting herself off. "Oh no!" She prodded the front of my jumper. "Your leaf is gone!"

It was.

"Perhaps we could find another one?" I stood up too. "Before we light the fire?"

"Yes, we need to find some more ivy," Alicia agreed, already heading back towards the trees. "Come on! Unless there's something *else* . . . What else starts with I, India?" she called.

"Indomitable." Alex's voice was too quiet for Alicia to have heard. His sideways look disarmed me. "Or insane," he shrugged.

For a moment our eyes met. There was something in his stare, something that I couldn't quite fathom. I looked quickly away.

"Alex!" Alicia's voice resounded from somewhere in the trees. "Come on! What about yours?! You have an A too! You need to find another acorn!"

Alex rose to his feet, one eyebrow raised.

"If only you knew what you'd started," he told me under his breath.

I watched him head into the trees, following Alicia's continuing exclamations. It took all of my self-control not to go after them. I walked a few paces instead, and crouched down to pluck a nettle leaf and fold it delicately in two, cradling it lightly in one hand. I turned it with my fingertips to examine it. I knew I would probably get stung. It seemed inevitable. But I couldn't help myself. A part of me wanted just to tighten my fist, as hard as I could, to incite the pain. I slipped the leaf into my pocket and started to walk again.

"India! Here!" Alicia's shout startled me out of my reverie. "Over here!"

She was sitting on Alex's shoulders, arms flailing wildly as she reached into the branches of the tree above them.

"Higher!" She clutched at his forehead with one hand, inadvertently covering his eyes. Alex stumbled.

"There." She snatched something from the nearest bough, a wide, victorious smile breaking on her face. A tiny, wizened apple. Alex lowered her carefully to the ground.

"Here you go!" She held it out to him. "Now we have yours, too!"

"Thanks." Alex's voice was soft. He caught sight of me approaching, and in an instant his expression changed. He slipped the crab-apple into his pocket.

"Can we light the fire now?" Alicia stood on tiptoe to stick a replacement ivy leaf onto my jumper. "And cook tea?"

"Are you hungry?" I reached to help her fasten the stalk through the wool. Alicia nodded. But it was Alex's scrutiny that I felt, as we made our way back to camp in expectant silence.

The matches were damp. After a brief search, I found them in the grass in front of the tent, where they must have fallen when we were setting up. Alicia hovered anxiously as I struck one after another.

"What are we going to do?" She was wide-eyed with concern. "What if the fire won't light?!"

"It will," I told her, without conviction. "I'm sure."

"*I'm* not," Alicia said glumly as the next match snapped in my hand. Alex was standing a little way back, his face unreadable. I glanced up, something occurring to me.

"Don't you have a lighter?"

He shook his head. I faltered.

"I stopped smoking," he said.

"Oh." There was a strange, anxious feeling in the pit of my stomach. I pulled out another match, feeling myself flush.

Alex held out his hand. "Let me try."

I handed him the matchbox doubtfully. He strode out into the meadow and plucked a bundle of the dry grass and weeds, cradling the downy, flyaway collection of dandelion seeds in his hand. Alicia tiptoed up behind him to peer over his shoulder as he came back and crouched beside the birds'-nest fire to rearrange the sticks and branches. Without a word he struck the damp match and plunged it into his handful of seeds and grass, and smoke curled from between his fingers.

"Yessss!" Alicia danced around him. "You've done it!"

Alex shook his head. "Not quite." He opened his hands to show her the spark, blowing gently before he lowered it into the bottom of the fire. Slowly but surely, the grass curled and the spark became a flame that licked at the dry twigs, sending a lazy plume of smoke spiralling upwards in the rapidly cooling air.

"Yes, yes, *yes!*" Alicia hugged his waist as he got to his feet. For a split second, Alex faltered.

I looked at him, incredulous at his success. He shrugged. "Scouts," he mumbled.

"Right." I couldn't help but smile to myself. Alex the boy scout? Choirboy? Precocious, bright-eyed, dark-haired child? I couldn't imagine it.

We ate a simple tea of pasta and baked beans – which tasted good merely on merit of our surroundings – scraping our portions from the pans of my old, dented camping set. Daylight finally faded into twilight, and the birds took roost in the trees, squabbling and flapping and then falling silent. The flames stretched and unfurled, hissing and crackling in the descending darkness. It was getting cold.

I left Alicia holding marshmallows on a long, scorched stick over the flames, and went to fetch her spare fleece from the tent. When I came back, they were smoking. Alicia blew on them ferociously, before testing the sticky, stringy mess with her tongue.

"Can we tell stories?" She looked up at me, marshmallow clinging to her chin and the front of her coat.

"I don't know if I have any good stories." I smiled. "Maybe you'll have to tell one."

"Alex, do *you* have a story?" Alicia held out the bag of marshmallows to him, but he shook his head.

"I don't know any with happy endings, Alicia." His wry expression made me catch my breath. I looked quickly into the growing flames.

"Maybe we should do something else." The smoke made my voice sound husky. Definitely the smoke.

"How about songs?" Alicia stood up and threw her toasting stick into the fire. She twirled on the spot like a ballerina, a whirlwind of waterproof excitement and Wellington boots, her gaze alighting expectantly on me. There was an unsettling hush. Something screeched in the distance; an owl or a startled bird. I turned to Alex for help, but he wasn't there.

"Do you know any?" I moved closer to the fire and sat down, desperate to banish the sudden chill from the back of my neck. Alicia plopped down beside me with a bump.

"*Loads*," she told me immodestly. "How about this one?"

She started to sing. I laughed as her voice crescendoed shrilly in the darkness. her face flushed with the exertion and firelight. *Because good memories last.* Suddenly I couldn't contain my smile.

"The other side of the mou-OUN-*TAIN* . . . was all that he could see!" Alicia finished with gusto, then came to an abrupt stop.

Alex's shadow was cast long by the fire as he moved past it to sit down. There was a guitar in his hand, an old acoustic, battered and scratched, its strings glinting with the flicker of the flames.

"Ohh!" Alicia gasped. "India, *look*!"

I *was* looking. Though I was trying not to. So hard that my eyes were stinging.

"Are you going to play?" Alicia's voice was shocked, reverent.

Alex shrugged. "If you want me to."

Alicia nodded, mute.

The cascade of the first few chords through the darkness sent a shiver along my spine. Alex dropped his gaze to his fingers. Very softly, he began to sing.

His voice was warm, molten; so out of keeping with the hint of the self-deprecating smile that still lingered at the corner of his lips, that at first all I could do was stare.

I blinked viciously. Tried to focus on the words instead: folk songs, for Alicia's benefit, probably. The first I'd never heard, a lively ballad about a donkey that had Alicia in fits of giggles. The second was a sailors' shanty that I was pretty sure he was having to rework as he went along to keep its content above the belt; every now and then I caught the private glimmer of some tacit joke in his bright, dark eyes and had to look away. Alicia leaned back against me and slipped her thumb into her mouth. Without really thinking, I put my arm around her small, warm shoulders.

Alex didn't look up from the strings. The darkness in his face was focused, intent. And effortlessly, out of nowhere, his pace changed. His fingers picked out a slow pattern of clear, ringing notes: harmonics that faded enchantingly into the falling darkness.

I knew the song from somewhere. Somewhere else, some other time, some other place. One that I had forgotten, or given up for lost.

"*Oh Peggy Gordon,*
You are my darling . . ."

I swallowed painfully. Alicia had taken my hand, but all I could look at was Alex, the frown of concentration on his forehead, the way his mouth formed the words. Without warning, his gaze locked mine. Abruptly, my smile faded.

"*I'm so in love,*
I can't deny it . . ."

The new verse hovered in the firelight between us. My palms were sweating. His eyes held mine. Daring me to look away, and I couldn't. I couldn't. I couldn't do anything at all. Couldn't think. Couldn't breathe.

You're on dangerous ground, India. You know that.

I'd always known that.

I gulped in a deep breath. My voice sounded small, shaky.

"*I did put my head to*
A cask of brandy . . ."

I still knew the words. Of course I knew the words. There are some things that you don't forget. Some things you will never forget.

Alex's eyes widened, taken by surprise. Painfully intense. Then he broke into a smile: broad, boyish and utterly unguarded. I caught my breath.

I don't think I'd be afraid of him if I'd seen him smile. Just once.

Alicia jumped up, glancing from one to the other of us, bewildered. Alex shook his head and looked away.

"Give me a hand up, Alicia." I stumbled to my feet as she yanked on my arm. "Let's dance."

I took her hands. Alicia started to giggle as we swayed gently around the fire. If he hadn't been singing, Alex would have been laughing too. I could see it in his eyes, in the way he shook his head at the mistakes he kept making, now that he was concentrating on the two of us and not on what he was doing.

The heat of the fire swelled over us as we circled back again. I glanced through the flames one last time to where he sat; I couldn't help myself. The firelight made his mysterious eyes look bright, and his unruly hair was tousled into disarray by the breeze. And I suddenly realised that if I could choose to keep one second forever, then it would be this one. It would be this one, and I'd never let it go.

I couldn't help a smile spreading over my lips. I turned back to Alicia, her glossy chestnut head resting against my arm.

"You look tired," I told her softly. "Maybe it's time for bed."

Alicia pulled a face. "I don't *want* to." But she didn't sound very convincing; her protest was barely more than a whisper. I squeezed her shoulders.

"Come on, then."

Alicia conceded with a slow nod. The last few notes of the guitar died away into the treetops. I took her hand. Alex stood up and re-tied his coat around his waist.

"I'm going to take a walk," he said.

I nodded, somehow lost for words. Alicia unzipped our tent and kicked off her wellies, stifling an enormous yawn. She clambered in over our sleeping bags to retrieve Tatty Rabbit, yawning again as she reached the top. I repressed a yawn too, infected by her tiredness.

"This is the best bed ever." Alicia wormed her way inside her sleeping bag. "I wish we were *always* camping."

"I think I'd miss my proper bed, after a while," I said.

"Mm." She thought for a moment. "I wish you could be my sister," she said suddenly. "Then you'd stay forever. If you were my sister, you'd never go away. I'd like that."

"Me too." I leaned over to pull the hood of her sleeping bag out from underneath her as she wriggled deeper in.

"Then you'd *never* forget me." She squeezed Tatty Rabbit to her chest. "Even when we were *both* grown up."

I smiled. "I won't forget you anyway. How could I?"

"Can I tell you a secret?" Alicia's voice was sleepy. She reached up and put her arms around my neck. I bent under her weight.

"If you want to."

She smiled coyly and pulled on my neck to bring me close, confiding.

"You can't say *any*thing." Her face was serious. "Nothing at all."

"Okay." I held her wrists to take the weight off my neck. "I won't."

She bit her lip, smiling more widely. "Don't tell." She pulled my face down nearer hers to whisper. "But I think Alex is in love with you."

I laughed out loud. Too loudly.

Alicia frowned. "No. Really he is. He must be. He's acting *really* weird. And — don't interrupt!"

I had opened my mouth to break in, but I closed it again, somehow halted by the command in her tone.

"He's never this nice. *And* he always stares at you. And tonight he *sang* to you!"

I laughed again, softly. Tried to ignore the sudden jolt of pain in my chest.

"That was just a song about someone else being in love, Alicia. He was only singing it because it was a nice song to have by the fire."

"That's what *you* think," Alicia told me darkly.

I smiled. "*You* think too much." I loosened her arms from around my neck and let her down slowly. "You should be asleep. Not trying to set me up with your brother."

Alicia wriggled again and snuggled back into the folds of her sleeping bag. "I don't even know what that means." She rubbed her eyes.

I shook my head. "Neither do I," I murmured. "Neither do I, Alicia."

"India?" She reached out as I started back towards the cold square of starry sky.

I hesitated.

"Yes?" I whispered.

Alicia slipped her thumb into her mouth.

"*I* love you, even if Alex doesn't."

It hit me like a fist to the stomach. I froze, paralysed. By the purity of it, by the reply that had stuck in my throat. To her, there was no couldn't. No rules, no need for self-defence. She was watching me, her eyelids heavy with sleep.

"Sweet dreams, Alicia."

I turned to go outside. The zip on the tent seemed startlingly loud in the darkness, alone. I paused. Swallowed the lump that had risen in my throat and the words I hadn't been able to bring myself to say. However much I might mean them.

It was cold. I pulled my sleeves down over my hands, starting to shiver, and moved a step closer to the fire. The wind changed suddenly, blowing a blast of scorching air and ash against my face, and I blinked, eyes smarting. One of the bigger logs spat and fell, crumbling in the heat; its senseless crackle and sputter filled my ears, like wordless whispers.

A secret . . . Don't tell . . .

Something snapped. A breaking branch, loud and close at hand. A shower of falling leaves. Footsteps.

I looked up, eyes blurred with smoke. Alex. Thumbs hooked into his pockets, his breath misting in the darkness as he approached. I blinked. His image moved in a haze beyond the firelight, flickering and indistinct. He noticed me looking. I saw his expression change. The cautious smouldering of a tiny, uncertain smile. He glanced down. I did too.

I think Alex is in love with you.

The ache in my chest redoubled. I raised my eyes slowly. He was still there, the slow dance of the flames all that was between us.

"It's getting late." His voice was very soft. "I should go back."

I didn't reply. Didn't know what to say. Alex didn't move. A gust of wind sent the smoke in another new direction, fragments of glowing ash spiralling high into the air. The flames skipped and guttered; I saw their reflection in his eyes as the breeze caught us. And suddenly I was shivering.

"Are you cold?" His stare was inescapable. It penetrated mine, bluer than ever in the firelight, more vivid.

I nodded. "A little."

A fleeting, unfathomable look crossed his face. I watched as he moved to the pile of firewood. Neither of us spoke. He selected an armful of branches and threw them on; I saw them catch and spark and buckle. Then, somehow, he was right beside me.

"Here." With one sharp pull, he freed the waterproof from around his waist and held it out to me. I faltered. The fabric was rough in my fingers.

"Thanks." I unfolded the coat and slipped my arms carefully into the sleeves.

"Don't." Alex spoke between his teeth. I looked up, startled.

"What?"

"Thank me." Suddenly he was very close, his voice low, black with foreboding. "You shouldn't thank me for what I'm doing here, India."

"What . . ." My throat was dry. I sucked in a deep breath of cold, smoky air. "What do you mean?"

He shook his head.

"If you do a good thing, for the wrong reasons," his whisper sent a shiver through me, "then it isn't a good thing. It's a selfish thing. It's something you should never have done . . . Something that you shouldn't ever even have thought of." His eyes were still on my face, staring, searching.

"I shouldn't have thought about this, India."

I gasped. His hand was warm as he caught my face and tipped it to his. And then his lips took mine: hot and fierce, and unrelenting.

Shouldn't have thought of it.

But hadn't I thought of it?

Shock ripped through me. My eyes flew open and were instantly imprisoned by his: darkest, forbidden blue. He broke his mouth away.

"Alex," I choked. "I don't understand . . ."

"Don't you?" he whispered.

I reached for his face, and he caught my fingers. Held them captive.

"I told you that you were on dangerous ground." His voice was softer than ever. "That you should keep away. Because this . . ." His mouth was barely an inch from mine, his other hand in the small of my back, pressing me closer to him. "*This is going to end badly.*"

I traced my fingertips over his cheek, over the line of his powerful, stubborn jaw. Felt him take a sudden jagged breath. And then his arms closed around me, and his mouth found mine again, and everything else was gone: the heat of the fire, Alicia sleeping in the tent, the shadow of the Manor waiting somewhere in the night, biding its time until the day dawned. Until the sunrise, when it would rematerialise, ready to engulf us.

I looked up slowly, terrified, at the darkness in his eyes. At his tiny, elusive, bittersweet smile.

Alex's thumb covered my lips, silencing me.

"Don't," he whispered. "*Don't.*"

CHAPTER 13: SALVAGE

"Alicia?" I sat bolt upright in shock.

The inside of the tent had an unearthly azure glow. I was alone.

"*Alicia!*" I heard the disproportionate note of panic in my own voice. I crawled to the flap and stumbled outside, blundering with my boots. The campfire was smouldering, dying embers and a languidly rising remnant of smoke that abraded the back of my throat.

"Alicia?" I whispered, afraid.

I scrambled uphill, half-blinded by the colours of the early sun in the long grass, then came to an abrupt stop. They were both there, at the side of the field, silhouetted by the colours of the rising sun. Alicia stood on top of the tumble-down wall, clinging onto Alex's rugby shirt with one hand to steady herself. A few gravid clouds were building on the horizon, dark blue and black, the alluring, threatening colours of Alex's eyes and uncertainty. Their breath misted, curling together in the early light.

I blinked. I thought he'd gone.

"India!"

Alicia's fingers closed more tightly on Alex's shirt as she looked around, wobbling on the uneven wall top.

"Morning, Alicia." I quickly found a smile.

Alicia smiled back, exhilarated. "I'd never watched a sunrise before! Have you?"

"Once or twice." I had to clear my throat.

How many sunrises? Lying on our bellies at the edge of the forest, looking down into the whispering water, Hope's fingers wound through mine. More than I could number. I'd thought it was too late. That they were lost to me, like she was. *You can write a hundred letters . . .*

And yet—

"Alex said this is the best one he's ever seen," Alicia told me solemnly. "He was sleeping by the fire! Did you know he was sleeping by the fire?!"

I shook my head. Glanced up at him, despite myself, eyes narrowed against the brightness of the dawn sky. But he was looking the other way.

* * *

Dear Hope,

I'm back. We're back. And I hardly know what to write to you. I don't know how to start, or what to say.

So much has happened that you'll never guess. That you would never even imagine.

Camping. Peggy Gordon. Watching the sunrise. Tag in the woods and campfire toast. A log-pile den, paddling in the stream. Stories with happy endings. I wish our story had had a happy ending. Oh, Hope. I wish that I could tell you. That I could put my arms around you, and whisper it all to you, because that would be so much easier than putting it down on paper . . .

It was simply perfect. A day so beautiful that I can't even begin to explain . . .

And then

Then?

I closed my eyes for a moment.

Then it had rained. A merciless, driving onslaught that flattened the grass and battered the tent out of our hands as we tried to put it down. And in just a few short minutes, it was all over; we were climbing out of Alex's car in the drive and the shape of the house had fallen back over us, blacker than any storm cloud.

I shut the notebook with a snap. From the bathroom, the sound of the taps gushed and spluttered torrentially. The door crashed open and closed again.

"India!"

I went through to find her. Alicia was sitting cross-legged on the floor, peeling off her sodden socks.

"I've never been so wet or dirty, *ever*," she told me excitedly as she deposited waterlogged fleece and leggings onto the carpet. "Mum would *kill* me."

I smiled weakly. "I guess she'll just have to not find out."

"Mmm." Alicia nodded her head. She lowered her voice. "Maybe." She frowned up at me, unnervingly perceptive. "Maybe the *whole trip* should be a secret."

There was an uneasy feeling in my stomach. "What makes you say that?" I asked.

Alicia looked at me for a moment. Then she shrugged.

"Nothing," she said.

"Are you sure you're okay doing your own bath?" I tried to change the subject. "Let me check it's not too hot."

"I'm sure." Alicia waited until I'd tested the water, and then climbed in.

"Oh." I remembered something. "And can you give me back the spare key now, Alicia? Before I forget. Is it in your pocket?"

"*What* spare key?" Alicia raised her eyebrows at me as if I was mad.

"Oh, come on, Alicia." I tried to sound unperturbed. "You let yourself into the kitchen before Alex or I had even got our bags out of the car. How else did you get in? We need to put it back in the shed or we'll lose it. And then your mum'll kill *me*."

"No she wouldn't," Alicia grinned impishly, then thought about it. "*Would* she?" Her smile faded.

I almost wanted to laugh at her sudden concern. But the unsettled feeling hadn't gone.

"Anyway, I can't," she gazed up at me, completely in earnest. "Because I didn't *take* it. The door was open already. You can check if you want to."

"Okay." I exhaled, defeated. I picked up a soggy and sorry-looking Tatty Rabbit from the floor. "Call me if you need me to wash your hair."

"I will."

The door was already open. The knot tightened in the pit of my stomach. There was no way I would have left it open.

I was exhausted as I descended into the hall, tidying our jumble of wet boots to one side, and leaning my rucksack against the foot of the stairs. There was a splatter of muddy footprints along the length of the floor.

Alex was sitting at the table as I pushed open the kitchen door. His hair was wet and tousled, his damp shirt sticking to him in a way that made my pulse quicken unreasonably. I blushed and propped Tatty Rabbit carefully on top of the radiator, turning quickly to busy myself with preparing tea. Not that I could have felt less like eating.

"Do you want anything?" I made myself ask.

Alex shook his head. "No, thanks."

I paused. The silence went from awkward to loaded: an abyss that stretched between us, waiting for one of us to fall in.

Alicia's arrival was timely. She materialised in the kitchen doorway, red-faced and tangle-haired, just as I finished doling out the food, a blob of tomato sauce slopping from her plate and splashing onto the surface like a blood spatter. She gave an almighty yawn as she picked up her fork, and I left her to it, to go and collect her wet clothes.

I couldn't have been gone for more than five minutes. When I returned, the food was half-eaten and Alex was moving her plate gently away. Alicia's head was cradled in her arms, her damp hair cascading like a waterfall over the side of the table, her small back rising and falling with the peaceful rhythm of her breathing. I hesitated.

Alex raised his eyebrows at me. Without a word, he rose to his feet, and tucked his chair quietly under the table. I moved to Alicia and touched her shoulder. She didn't stir. I stroked her hair back, tucking it gently behind her ear. She looked so young, so guileless, her skin pale, her parted lips full and red. I realised just how easy it was to forget that she was only seven years old, when she was awake and full of never-ceasing questions.

Alex came around the table to join me. I let go of Alicia's hair, painfully conscious of his scrutiny. With no real need for explanation, he stooped to pick her up, lifting her easily in his arms. Alicia murmured in her sleep, a tiny frown flitting across her forehead.

I took Tatty Rabbit from the radiator as Alex pushed open the door with his foot. I followed him upstairs.

Evening was descending, filling the hallway and the stairs with dusk so heavy that it was almost tangible. The stillness in Alicia's room was unnerving. I put Tatty Rabbit on the pillow and moved to close the curtains as Alex supported his sister with one arm to draw back the duvet. Alicia's dark lashes fluttered against her flushed cheeks. He lowered her carefully, so as not to wake her. I hung back, somehow hesitant, as he pulled the covers over her, an unreadable expression playing on his mysterious face. For a moment neither of us moved. We both looked at Alicia, at her drying chestnut hair fanned out on the pillow, at Tatty Rabbit cast off beside her.

Alex started for the door, and I followed him out without a word, pulling it softly to behind us. The empty house threw its shadows over us, motionless and expectant as we descended the stairs into the echoing hallway. I almost tripped over my rucksack at the bottom. As I stooped to move it, Alex was right behind me. I stood up, not realising that he had stopped, too.

Without warning his hands closed around my elbows. And suddenly his mouth was on mine, fierce and warm, his tongue invading, claiming. Then he broke off, leaving me bereft.

I gasped. The darkness in his face was hot and enticing, and impossible to ignore. I couldn't look away from it. Couldn't step back, even though I knew I should.

I realised with a lurch how wrong I had been. Over? That would have been far too easy.

"So. What now?" Alex spoke under his breath. His expression sent a chill through me.

I swallowed. "I don't—"

"Come on." He jerked his head towards the drawing room. "Maybe not here."

I followed him. Alex strode to the piano, and flicked on the lamp, soft, pale light spilling over the pages of Alicia's minuet and illuminating the room diffusely. Then he sat down on the edge of the ornately patterned sofa, his eyes on me as I sat gingerly beside him.

His hand was startlingly warm on my face, startlingly careful, his skin calloused and rough. He was very close to me. I could feel the rise and fall of his breathing, smell the campfire smoke and sweat and outdoor air on his clothes. I didn't quite dare to touch him.

Alex frowned. "I need to know something." He ran his thumb lightly over my lips. Adrenaline spiked through me.

"I . . ." I was distracted by his touch. "What?"

His thumb ceased its journey abruptly, his fingers lifting my chin to make me face him.

"Are you still scared of me, India?"

My pulse was racing. I shook my head.

"Good," he breathed. And fleetingly, it was there in his eyes: the hunted, lost look, exposed and vulnerable. Something constricted in my chest.

"I told you," I whispered. "I didn't think you were unsalvageable."

The tiniest, heart-breaking smile tugged at the corners of Alex's mouth. He leaned forward, his lips close against my ear.

"Oh, what wouldn't I give to be salvaged by you, India."
There was danger in his voice. I shivered. He brushed my hair
back from my face, winding a lock of it around two of his
fingers. "Or at least, to have you try."

His gaze was on my mouth, and suddenly I couldn't
speak. Another shiver ran through me; somehow, I couldn't
stop myself from remembering: *Open your eyes, India. We're all
fucked up.*

"I . . ." I faltered. "I thought you thought I was a hyp-
ocrite." I looked up to meet his stare, and regretted it. Heat
flooded through me. I cleared my throat.

"You told me not to try and win you round. You said that
I'd dissect your failings. That it's pointless, because we're all
fucked up anyway. I thought you despised me. And now—"

"Maybe we are." Alex didn't let go. His eyes were on
mine, penetrating the ineloquent protests and the confusion.
"Fucked up. Maybe we are."

His voice was very soft, his fingers still toying with my
hair, so gentle, so beguiling that I could barely think at all. I
couldn't make sense of it. The bitterness, the anger, and this
— piano notes, unguarded whispers. Alex paused.

"I never despised you." He shook his head. "Myself,
maybe. But not you."

For a moment there was silence. I looked down at my
unsteady hands, then back up. At his sincerity, wordless and
unsmiling.

"I'd like to try," I whispered.

Dear Hope,

I sat back slowly. Let the pen fall from my hand and
took a few deep, steadying breaths.

Maybe we are. All fucked up.

I slipped off the infinity ring carefully and held it in the
palm of my hand. The inscription on the inside glimmered.

Never give up. I traced one finger over it, looking at the way it shattered the lamplight into a hundred thousand reflections.

"It's okay," I whispered to it. "It's okay for things to change."

I picked up the notebook from the bed and tore it out. The very last page.

I'm sorry I haven't been writing so much, anymore. But I know you understand. You always understood me better than I understood myself.

Some things change, and some things don't. And the way I feel about you will never change. You know that. Not ever.

I love you, Hope. And I know you love me too. No matter what.

We always said we wouldn't say it. But sometimes, it's the right thing to say. And it seems right, tonight.

Goodbye, Hope.

With all my love — truly, and always.

India

CHAPTER 14: AMISS

I was walking again. Walking through the foyer, the Coke bottle in my hands cold and slippery with condensation. Walking along the dimly lit corridor, looking at the countless entrances and exits, sub-corridors, doors with nameplates. Main Pharmacy. Outpatients 3.

I must have missed a step. I felt myself fall—

I lurched upright, disorientated. My pyjamas were soaked with sweat.

I got up and dressed in the silence. The kitchen was cold as I unloaded the dishwasher and got out the breakfast things, chilled through. I moved to the fridge to take out the milk.

I N D I A

Alicia's multi-coloured alphabet magnets stared back at me brightly from the fridge door. I stopped, unnerved, a shudder running through me. Then I scolded myself. *Alicia's* magnets. The clue was in the name.

I went to wake her. She was grouchy and half-asleep as she ate her breakfast and blundered back upstairs to put on her uniform; she'd been woken at ten p.m. by her parents to open the multitude of trinkets and presents from Austria that didn't make up for not being invited.

Our journey to school was a largely silent one. I concentrated on the traffic, and Alicia stared out of the window, watching the cars whizz by on the other side of the road. Apparently, it was only our side that wasn't moving.

My phone buzzed twice in quick succession in my pocket, and Alicia looked round.

"Can I play on your phone?"

"It hasn't got any games on it, I don't think."

"Yeah, it does." She held out her hand. "Please?"

I fished in my pocket for it and passed it to her. "You can have a look. But I'm pretty sure it doesn't."

"Oh." Alicia took it from me disappointedly. "You're right. Your phone's boring. Alex's phone has games. By the way, did you know your battery's nearly flat?"

I shrugged. "I don't really play games. And I know. The battery's rubbish." At last, we rolled into motion. I changed up a gear, relieved.

"You have a message." Alicia tapped the touchscreen. "It's from Maeve. Can I read it?"

Crap. Maeve. I had conveniently forgotten she existed.

"Maeve's a weirdo. Why is she messaging you? And who's Brett?"

I glanced at her, alarmed.

"Uh, could I have my phone back?" I held out my hand hastily. "I'll read it in a minute."

"I won't read it if you don't *want* me to." Alicia raised her eyebrows. "It's fine if it's a secret. Did you know Alex had a friend called Brett?"

"Are you ready to get out?" I had never been so glad to see the school gates in my life. "I don't think there's going to be anywhere to park. You might just have to jump out and go. I don't want you to be late."

Alicia pressed my phone into my palm. She looked at me seriously.

"I think you should probably delete Maeve," she said.

She might have been right. By the time I'd called for groceries and driven back to the Manor, I had a missed call

161

and two messages. I stuffed the phone back into my jeans pocket as I unlocked the door and went inside. I'd taken my time in the hope that John Maine would have left for work by the time I got back, and I was in luck. The Porsche was gone, and the house was empty. I clattered around the kitchen, unloading the shopping. I was supposed to be meeting Maeve in town. I'd agreed ages ago. Would it be rude to cancel now? I needed to—

I came to an abrupt stop in front of the fridge. The last carrier bag split, and grapes rained out, rolling chaotically across the floor.

"What the fuck?" I whispered. "What the fuck?"

S O M E T H I N G S D 0 N T C H A N G E I N D 1 A

I dropped the bag.

"No." I pressed one cold, trembling hand to my forehead, staring dementedly at the cheerful plastic letters. "That's not possible. *It's not possible.*"

Nausea rose in my throat. Somewhere behind me, my phone vibrated on the side. I sank slowly to my knees, scrabbling to gather up the mess. Trying to pull myself together. To think of an explanation. A better explanation—

"It's not." I shoved everything back into the bag and stood up, as if it might have gone. "It's not possible."

I reached out decisively, and swiped the words from the fridge, jumbling the letters, so that one fell to the floor and cracked. I didn't bend down to pick it up.

H

I snatched up my coat and phone, and fled.

For the second time in my life, I found myself lining up my car on the end of a row of other too-late-in-the-morning shoppers in the slightly suspect car park half a mile from the city centre. I had no change and had to jog to a nearby off-licence to break a twenty on an overpriced bottle of mineral water. I had a new purse now, with a new picture of Hope at our graduation in the back. A new driver's licence with a new surly black and white photo, a new set of bank cards. A new phone.

I passed the dry cleaners, suddenly thinking of Brett. I hadn't replied to his messages. *Don't make promises you can't keep.*

I dragged my feet on the walk into town. I didn't want to meet Maeve. But I wanted to be at the Manor even less. I gritted my teeth as I sidled as inconspicuously as I could into the café. Maeve reached out to squeeze me in a rib-crunching hug.

"*India!*" She let go and pushed me to arm's length. "You look pale!" She ushered me into a seat.

"Haven't you been sleeping? Look at the rings under your eyes!" Her voice seemed to boom around the small room. The one or two other customers turned to look at us and the rings under my eyes. "You should try an organic tea."

"Oh, um, sure," I mumbled.

"How's everything going? How's beautiful Alicia? And what about *Alex*? He was at Oxford with Andrea's niece, you know. Before he almost went to prison . . . I want to hear *all* about the Manor! Are you staying for Christmas?"

Christmas? It hadn't even occurred to me. I couldn't imagine that Julia would be working. What if they *didn't* want me? Where would I go?

"I don't know," I shrugged. "I'll see what Julia wants, I guess."

"Won't your family miss you?" Maeve put down her menu.

I studied the table top carefully. "Not really."

Fortunately, Maeve didn't seem to notice my reticence. She carried on talking as the waiter came and went, and I picked at the salad.

"India, you really have to eat."

I glanced back at her in alarm.

"Just *look* at you." She reached out and grabbed my wrist tightly between her fingers and thumb. "You're skin and bones." She held up my wrist and waved it in the air threateningly.

The waiter at the next table turned to look over his shoulder. I freed myself, and very deliberately added extra milk and sugar to my tea.

"You're not looking after yourself, India." Maeve's scrutiny was, it seemed, inescapable. "You need to. The Manor's a dreadful place to work — and the Maines are infamous for how they treat their help. Even Andrea — Mrs Bosworth — says there's something amiss in that house."

Something amiss? I pulled my jacket tighter around me, despite the radiator behind my seat.

You're on dangerous ground, India. You'd be better off if you listened to them. You know that.

I know.

I had known all along.

* * *

"Where have you *been?!*" Alicia was hopping mad.

It was five past four. Escaping Maeve had been one thing. Getting out of the city in the beginnings of the rush-hour traffic had been something else. I was so late that when I arrived one of the teachers had taken Alicia back into her classroom, undoubtedly suspecting that I wasn't going to turn up at all. My phone battery was flat. I hadn't even been able to let them know.

"I went to buy your new clothes, and I got stuck with Maeve." I hoped the story would appeal to her sense of sympathy.

Alicia gaped at me in horror. "I told you that you should delete her!" She slung her schoolbag into my untidy car, and climbed in after it. "You're lucky you're still *alive*. Maeve's crazy. Did you know it's Halloween tomorrow?"

She tugged at the sleeves of her blazer, and I realised with surprise that they had become too short.

"Has your day been any better than mine?" I asked her.

"*No.*" Alicia turned to me darkly. "My day was *terrible*."

"Oh."

"It was games this afternoon. Netball," she told me gloomily. "And I'm rubbish."

"I don't think you can be rubbish, can you?" I turned to her momentarily as we stopped at a red light. "You're a really fast runner, aren't you?"

"Mm. But I can't shoot goals to save my *life*."

"You have a goal at home, don't you? On the wall in the courtyard?"

"Yeah." Alicia raised her eyebrows at me discerningly. "*That's* exactly how I know that Father Christmas exists. That netball hoop."

"Oh?" I couldn't keep the amusement from my voice. "Why's that?"

"*Well.*" Alicia folded her arms across her chest. "He brought me that netball hoop for Christmas. So . . . Lotty said that there's no Father Christmas and it's just your mum and dad who buy the presents and pretend. But she's wrong, and the netball hoop is *proof*. Because Mum and Dad *know* how terrible I am at netball. They'd *never* have bought me a netball hoop. So it *must* have been Father Christmas."

I fought to keep a straight face. Fortunately, Alicia was glowering out of the windscreen, and didn't notice.

"Well, how about when we get home we do some practice? We could get you good at shooting goals before next week. I was in the netball team, once."

"Really?" Alicia brightened.

"Really."

The Manor was deserted. I unlocked the door and let Alicia in, and she ran upstairs to get changed as I put away her schoolbag and blazer. I deliberately didn't look at the fridge. I followed Alicia upstairs instead, thinking about netball, half-time oranges and skipping after-match tea with Hope. My bedroom door was ajar, and the room was cold as I drew the bolt.

I think I knew. I must have felt its presence before I saw it; it hadn't been obvious at a glance, not like the rose had been. It was too small. Shiny. Sparkling in the evening light.

Her ring.

"Oh no." I shook my head. "No, Hope . . ."

On my pillow. It was on my pillow. But I'd put it in the drawer, last night. Out of sight, if not out of mind. I *remembered* putting it in the drawer.

Didn't I?

Suddenly I didn't want to touch it. I sat down heavily on the side of the bed, making myself take a few deep breaths.

There would be a rational answer. A reason. I tried to make myself think sensibly, and failed.

I got changed in the bathroom. Splashed my face with cold water, waited by the mirror until I looked passably calm. By the time I emerged, Alicia was waiting on the landing.

"You've been *ages*," she told me. "We can't shoot goals in the *dark*."

"It's not dark yet." I glanced out the window at the dusk all the same, and paused, reluctant to ask, but suddenly needing to know.

"Alicia?" I kept my voice even and gentle. "Have you been in my room?"

She looked at me, surprised, and shook her head.

"Definitely not?" I looked her straight in the eye. Alicia looked unabashedly back.

"*Definitely* not," she told me vehemently.

"Okay." I swallowed. "You know, I don't mind if you have. It's okay to go in there. I'd just rather you asked first, that's all."

"I *haven't* been in there." Alicia's full lips quivered in a pout. "I said I haven't. I wouldn't *lie*."

"Okay. I'm sorry. I know you wouldn't." I put a mollifying hand on her shoulder. "But for the future, it's okay."

I realised that I did know. That she was telling the truth. I shivered.

"Come on." I squeezed her shoulder fondly. "Let's go and shoot some goals."

We threw Alicia's netball until it was too dark to see; until our hands were frozen and smarting from the impact, and our breath was misting in front of us. I could barely make out Alicia's face as her last ball clanged through the hoop.

"It went in!" She turned to me in amazement. "I'm *not* rubbish."

I smiled and opened the door to go inside. "No. You're pretty good, if you ask me. I need to get your tea. It's freezing. Are you coming in?"

Silence.

Alicia's shriek in the darkness behind me was shrill and piercing, and sent a chill straight through me.

"Alicia?" I left the door open, stumbling down the step to look for her. "*Alicia?*"

Strong fingers closed around my arm. I gasped.

"Try the front door." Alex's soft voice brought a rush of colour to my cheeks. "That's where she looked like she was headed."

I blinked up at him. "You made me jump."

"Not as much as I made Alicia jump." His playful grin made something constrict inside me.

I stepped through the open door quickly. The kitchen was warm, and the burning in my cheeks redoubled as I slipped off my shoes and fleece and washed my hands to prepare Alicia's tea. Alex regarded me silently for a moment.

"My father will be home soon."

I couldn't tell if it was an observation or a warning. I glanced at the clock. Alex's fingers brushed the back of my wrist lightly as he vanished, his tread soft on the stairs.

I set to work slicing meat and peeling vegetables. One of the cats appeared and rubbed around my legs, purring; I tipped the vegetables into a pan of water and bent to fuss it. The sound of voices filtered patchily down from upstairs.

"I didn't."

"Oh, come on. Then how did . . ."

"Uh-uh."

". . . You must have . . ."

"No, I *haven't!*"

The volume rose, taut and heated. I looked up in alarm as the shouting escalated, and headed quickly for the stairs.

"What's going on?" I took the stairs two at a time, reached the landing, and stopped dead.

Alex had paused mid-word, silent and frowning. And Alicia stood opposite him, one foot coming down violently on the wooden floor in an all-out stamp, her hands balled into fists at her sides.

"Why is everyone telling me off for going in their room!"

It was a full force, ear-splitting scream, and it had apparently taken Alex as much by surprise as it had me.

"I haven't been in anyone's stupid room! Don't call me a liar! *I haven't been in your stupid room*! Why would I even *want* to go in your room, anyway? Both of you!" She turned on me as I opened my mouth to intercede. "I haven't been in your room and that's it!"

I stared after her, perplexed, as she turned and ran, her bedroom door slamming resoundingly behind her.

"What was that all about?" I whispered.

Alex shrugged. But a feeling of unease had expanded in my chest.

The hiss and sputter of vegetables boiling over necessitated my return to the kitchen. Seconds later, I heard the roar of John Maine's car pulling to a halt in the drive.

"Oh, hello, India." He shrugged off his tailored coat as he came in, barely giving me a second glance.

"Hi." I forced a smile, cutting into a piece of Alicia's chicken to check that it was cooked. "How was your day?"

John turned back. "Oh, it was reasonable. Busy. Is Alicia upstairs?"

"Yes." I nodded, serving the chicken and vegetables awkwardly onto a plate. I caught the back of my finger on the edge of one of the pans, and withdrew it sharply.

"I'll go and say hello." John headed for the door. "Would you like me to send her down for tea?"

"Oh, yes. Thanks." Why was I more flustered than normal by his presence? I swallowed and fished in the cutlery drawer for a knife and fork for Alicia.

"Why don't you finish, once you've done that?" John hadn't gone. "Julia will be home soon. We can manage Alicia between us for the evening. You should take the night off."

Manage?

"Oh. Thanks." I had to look the other way, in case my reaction manifested itself in my face. "That would be great."

Alicia was subdued and taciturn when she finally came downstairs to eat. Perhaps, I thought uncomfortably, it was best for her to be spending the evening in her parents' company, not mine. Looking at her red eyes made me feel cold and wretched. I couldn't remember the last time that she had been so upset. And I had a definite, heavy feeling that this time *I* was the guilty party.

"Alicia," I started softly.

She looked down at her plate, full lips pressing together in an expression that was strangely reminiscent of her mother.

"Alicia, I'm sorry." I reached out to touch her hand, surprised and relieved when she didn't swat me away. "I believe you. About earlier. I know you're not a liar. I believe you that you didn't go in my room."

Alicia looked up slowly. "Does Alex believe me?" She was frowning, miserable.

"I'll tell him." I met her wide blue gaze steadily across the table.

"Will he believe *you*?" Alicia raised her eyebrows.

"I think so."

My phone buzzed loudly in my pocket, making us both jump. I stood up to read the message, moving away from the table. Alicia watched me, eyes narrowed.

"Is that still Maeve?" Her voice was suspicious.

I faltered, my breath catching in my throat.

I believe you. I gather you have the evening off. Do you have plans?

I glanced around nervously. Alicia was still watching me. Careful to keep my face impassive, I typed a reply.

Where are you and how do you know that?

I switched the phone to silent.

169

For so many reasons, India, I would love to say I'm right behind you. But I'm in the drawing room, and I heard my father. And you didn't answer my question.

My mouth was unreasonably dry as I tapped a hasty response.

No plans.

"If it isn't Maeve," Alicia was still staring at me sceptically, "then who is it?"

Good. I'll meet you in the lane outside in half an hour. You'd better tell her it's Maeve.

"It's a friend from home." I wasn't sure I wanted to incur any more disapproval from Alicia.

"Yeah, *right.*" Alicia put her knife and fork together and got up from the table. "Please may I get down?"

I nodded my assent. Alicia looked at me for a moment more without speaking. Then she padded out through the doorway in her socks, and I heard her light tread recede as she headed off in the direction of the playroom.

* * *

It was drizzling in the lane as I slipped out half an hour later. I had left Alicia watching a Disney film with John. I managed not to jump this time, as Alex's hand closed momentarily around my wrist.

"This way," he bent near to me to whisper, the mist of his breath curling warmly against my ear and igniting every nerve-ending in my body. My pulse was racing.

"Where are we going?"

"For a drink?" He sounded quietly amused. "Here." He felt in his pocket, and the unmistakable electronic clunk of a car unlocking ricocheted through the darkness. The orange indicator lights reflected off his face.

The air inside the car was muted, cold. I shut the door as quietly as I could, and Alex followed suit.

"Is that a good idea?" My mouth prickled with nerves. "Won't someone recognise us . . . you?"

Alex's half-smile was guarded. "No one that matters," he said.

He started the engine and pulled away, past the lurking shape of the Manor and out of Rifway, the opposite direction along the lane. We travelled for a mile, maybe two, in loaded silence. A pale white-blue light flashed past, the old shadowed stonework of a bridge, water that gleamed like dark glass. Finally a building came into view, warm light escaping from its windows to illuminate its swinging sign, a green man framed in leaves, and a car park full of cars. We drew to a halt in the back corner and got out. I could hear the faint spill of music and laughter from inside.

"Why are we going for a drink?" Somehow the sounds of sociability had put me on edge. My hands felt unreasonably shaky.

Alex ran his thumb lightly over the back of my wrist, his fingers tightening through mine and making me shiver.

"Isn't that what normal people do?"

I looked sideways up at him. He was so hard to read.

"I wanted to get you out of the house, India." He leaned closer again, speaking into my hair, his voice so low that it was barely audible. "I wanted to see you. Without Alicia. Without my parents. Just you."

He held open the door, and I slipped inside, starting to understand. The place was busy enough that no one looked up. There was a table right at the back, tucked away behind the chimney breast, and we made our way to it under the cover of everyone else's conversation. I tried to steady my breathing.

"What do you want to drink?" Alex didn't sit down.

"Oh, um, a soft drink." Was it the place, or his presence, real and tall and imposing in the unforgiving sixty-watt light, that had turned me into such a wreck?

"Coke?"

I shuddered involuntarily. "No. Lemonade. Thanks."

There was a fire in the grate that evoked memories of camping. I wrapped my hands around my purse.

"Who's in the picture?" Alex asked, as he returned with the drinks.

I glanced down. Hope's face looked out from the clear back panel of the purse, the yellow rose in her hair catching the light.

"Oh." I turned it over quickly. "Hope. My friend."

"The one you wrote the letters to?"

I didn't look up. "Mm." I took a tentative sip of my drink.

"I wish I could make sense of you, India."

"Hm?" I raised my eyes to his face. The same half-smile lingered on his lips.

"I wish I could know what you're thinking."

I frowned. "That, coming from *you*." I raised my eyebrows.

Alex's expression flickered. "You've *seen* inside my head."

The memory swamped me: reverberating, throbbing, a thousand pencil-written notes, daylight and light falling rain, fresh air, birdsong—

I smiled. I couldn't stop myself. And Alex smiled back.

We finished our drinks. Sat for a long time with our glasses, as if keeping them might justify us staying longer. The fire burned low, and someone called last orders. We didn't move. Didn't even speak much. Didn't really need to.

Eventually we stood, in unvoiced acceptance of the inevitable, and Alex moved to take the glasses back to the bar. I sought out the ladies', pushing my way through a glass panelled door into a surprisingly cold corridor.

"Well, hi."

I jumped violently, realising I had been lost in my own dark thoughts.

"India."

Shit.

I looked up with agonising slowness: my hand drifting, without thinking, to the phone in my pocket. *Shit.*

Brett was at the other end of the narrow corridor, a friendly smile lighting up his sparkling eyes. My colour rose instantly. In the background, muffled music and voices filtered though from the bar.

"Hi," I mumbled, my cheeks brilliant red.

"You really do get everywhere, don't you?" His voice was gently teasing. "I was starting to worry that you'd lost another bag." His grin was playful. Pointed. I let go of the phone quickly.

"Or that the Maines had already finished you off." He raised his eyebrows. "That would have been disappointing."

I hesitated, utterly lost for words. What could I say? I had ignored him. Missed his calls. Kissed him in a multi-storey car park at some stupid time of night after telling him much too much about myself. I'd made a promise I couldn't keep. And now . . .

I cleared my throat. His light gaze was on me, calm and appraising as he approached.

"I'm sorry I never called." I was flushed with guilt. "Things . . . got a little . . . crazy. I mean . . ." I trailed off.

"It's fine," Brett shrugged.

In an instant, the corridor seemed narrower than ever. Brett paused as he drew level with me.

"India, it's fine." His voice was warm, close. "I'm glad they haven't driven you out. A guy can live in hope."

I looked at my feet. Jesus Christ. Could this be worse? My eyes were stinging viciously.

"I'm . . . sorry." A knot had clenched in my abdomen. "I'm sorry I said . . . I . . ."

There was a painful silence.

"Honestly, India." Brett's voice was soft. "Don't worry about it. You've got my number. I figured you knew how to call it, if you wanted to."

"I, um . . ."

"It's okay." He opened the door back through to the bar and threw me one last gut-wrenching smile. "Really. Go on. You were going somewhere. Maybe I'll speak to you later?"

"Maybe," I mumbled, feeling wretched.

Brett turned back, holding open the door, letting a burst of heat and noise through that washed over us like a wave.

"Don't be a stranger," he said. "You know where I am. As and when."

I nodded, eyes watering. Then he stepped out into the bar, and I fled for the cover of the ladies' bathroom.

Mercifully, it was empty. The cubicle door banged behind me as I paused for a moment and regarded my reflection in the mirror.

What the hell was I *doing*?

And how me? How was this happening to *me*?

I splashed cold water on my scarlet cheeks, focussing on my breathing. This wasn't me. Hope, maybe. This might have happened to Hope, and she would have handled it ten times better than this. She would never have been so stupid to start with. She would never even have come. Here, to Rifway. Because she didn't run away from things. It was only me that did that.

Some things don't change, India.

I pulled open the door and found my way back outside. The pub was emptying; there was barely anyone left. Anyone except—

I stopped dead.

No. Oh no.

They stood a short distance apart, each a mirror image of the other, exactly of a height, separated only by an empty table. At stalemate; Brett's arms were folded calmly across his chest, his light gaze level, his eyebrows slightly lifted. And Alex . . .

I could feel the fury emanating from him, suppressed and silent. His teeth were gritted, his fists clenched, and his tense muscles and the unforgiving blackness in his expression were an unwelcome reminder of the Alex before.

A new kind of fear gripped my gut as Alex half turned and caught sight of me. I saw him release his hands, saw him breathe out, a slow, measured breath.

Brett turned around, too. Momentarily, he didn't twig, didn't register. His eyes met mine.

"Here." Alex held out my jacket to me.

Brett's eyebrows flickered tellingly upwards. His gaze was still on mine, cool and blue and quizzical. For a terrible moment, I thought that he was going to say something.

But he didn't. I dropped my gaze quickly, a painful blush scalding my cheeks.

"Are you ready?" Alex's hand brushed mine. "Let's go."

I followed, wordless. Plunged out through the doorway, into the cold almost-midnight stillness. I didn't look back. Couldn't. We crossed the car park in silence. We climbed into the car, and Alex turned the key in the ignition.

"I'm sorry." At last he spoke. I glanced around. His voice was low, regretful. And startlingly alluring. The colour hadn't receded from my cheeks.

I swallowed. "It's okay."

"That didn't end quite how I'd anticipated." He looked back out of the windscreen at the deserted country lane, unreadable.

"No," I whispered.

The hedges outside the windows made impenetrable walls either side of the car. We slowed. Ahead of us, the Manor loomed, huge and waiting. He killed the engine and undid his seatbelt. My hands were shaking as I opened the car door. He walked round to join me.

"It's goodbye here," he informed me softly.

I glanced up, surprised. "You're not coming in?"

He shook his head. I couldn't tell whether the darkness in his smile signalled humour or forewarning.

"That's not a bridge I think we ought to cross," he said.

"Where are you going?" I blurted out, unchecked. Alex smiled.

"Somewhere else." He shrugged. His eyes were on mine, enticing. Daring me. I caught my breath.

His lips tasted of alcohol and temptation, and lingered, only for a second. For a moment his hands were on me, travelling possessively over my waist and into the small of my back, light and incendiary.

"Go on." His subversive murmur made my heart race. "You'd better go in, before someone looks out the window."

"Oh," I breathed. He was right. Why did he have to be right?

Because this . . . this is going to end badly.

Neither of us uttered another word. I ran across the drive, light-footed on the gravel. The house was in darkness. I listened for the sound of his car pulling away and then turned, breathless.

"You really think they won't find out?"

I gasped. Slipped and almost fell on the stone steps. The figure was blocking my path.

"You think they won't know?" Sara's hiss was acid. "And you think he'll stick by you when they do?"

"Wh . . . what?" *Shit.* I stumbled away, cold terror flooding outwards to my extremities.

"I saw you," she spat. "I saw you with him. All over him. Who wouldn't be? But you know what?" She moved a step closer to me, the spill of light from the porch throwing her into sharp relief. "He's the only thing *they*'ve ever been right about." Her voice was barely more than a whisper, menacingly soft. "Alex Maine. What? You thought you were going to change him?" The scorn in it made my heart turn cold. "Because he's pretty, and out of bounds, and he can talk the talk? I bet he's got you *right* where he wants you . . ."

"You don't know what you're talking abou—"

"Of course I know." Suddenly, Sara was laughing. "Of course I know. I've seen it for myself . . . People just don't matter to him, sweetheart. He gets what he wants, and he'll take it just the way he wants it, the same as his parents. If it's the end of you, it makes no difference to him."

It was starting to rain again, water sticking in my lashes and running down my neck. I blinked it away, breathing fast. In the distance, the church clock was chiming midnight.

"Why . . ." Suddenly, logic was returning to me. Sense. I frowned at her silhouette through the darkness. Midnight.

176

It was midnight. "Why are you here?" I demanded. "What are you even *doing* here?"

Sara ignored my question.

"Tell me what you're doing here." I took a step towards her, trembling from head to toe. "Tell me what you're *doing* here. Why are you here?! Tell me, or—"

"Or what?" Sara's lip curled, mocking me. She reached to push something further into her bag, rearranging the straps over her shoulder. "Or *what*? You'll tell *them*?" She laughed. "They *know* I'm here. Ask them, if you want. They weren't too pleased to see me. But they might be even *less* pleased to see *you*, when they find out . . ."

I inhaled sharply. "You . . . won't . . ."

"I *could*." She didn't step back. I didn't either. I faced her, light-headed with disbelief.

"No." I shook my head. "That's it." I turned on my heel, fumbling to open the door. "That's enough. Enough. I—"

"Oh yeah." Sara's voice was caustic. "Run away. Go on. You think you've got it all, don't you? But you have no place in this house. Just remember that."

"Thanks." My voice shook. "I will."

The door clicked shut. I slumped against the wall and pressed one hand to my aching forehead.

Shit.

What . . . I realised my hand was shaking. What if she was right?

She wasn't. I ran up the stairs, suddenly tearful. She wasn't. Was she?

I went straight to my room, not pausing to think, or to listen to make sure that Alicia was sleeping. I closed the door behind me and turned on the bedside light, illuminating the room so brightly that it took my eyes several seconds to adjust. I was shivering. Not just shivering; almost convulsing – with fear, confusion . . .

Oh what wouldn't I give to be salvaged by you, India . . .

I sat down on the edge of my bed shakily; touched a finger to my lips.

He can talk the talk. I pressed my lips together, trying to shut Sara's voice out of my head. She was wrong. She had to be wrong.

Are you still scared of me, India?

"No." I said it aloud. I could picture the look on his face, the surprise, the realisation. The lost, beguiling look. The tiny, heart-breaking smile.

"No."

Of myself, maybe. But not you.

CHAPTER 15: TRICK OR TREAT

"I'm going to my study to make a call." John Maine stood in the kitchen doorway. "You'll probably have left before I'm finished. Have a good day, Alicia."

"Bye!" Alicia was cramming Cheerios into her mouth as though the world was about to end. "See you later!"

"Have fun." John disappeared. Reflexively, I released my breath and moved back to the table.

"Hey." I sat down opposite Alicia. "Maybe you should slow down. You're going to choke yourself."

It was colder than usual in the kitchen. I wrapped my hands around my half-finished mug of tea and glanced up at the clock. The thirty-first of October. Halloween. It was nearly time to take Alicia to school. We had to leave early; her class was going on a school trip.

"Can I take my fangs?" Alicia's words were almost indecipherable through a mouthful of wholegrain. "I want to show Lily."

"Won't Lily see them tonight?"

"Yes, but that's not the point." Alicia picked up her bowl and drained it of milk, then leapt from her chair, before remembering and pausing hastily. "Please may I get down?"

I smiled. Stable doors, horses and bolts sprang to mind.

"Go on then. But I think maybe you shouldn't take your fangs to school. Lily will see them when you go trick-or-treating later, won't she? Wouldn't it be better if your costume's a surprise?"

"No." Alicia stared at me as if I was an idiot. "It wouldn't. I already know what *Lily*'s going as."

"What's Lily going as?" I ushered her to the sink. Alicia rinsed her bowl and put it in the dishwasher, and I seized the opportunity to take a hairbrush to her tangled chestnut locks. She ducked in objection.

"It's a *secret*."

"Oh, okay." I continued brushing, undeterred, and she was forced to stand still as I teased the out the snarls.

"Guess where we're going today?" Alicia challenged me. I looked down at her, nonplussed.

"I know where you're going today, Alicia," I pointed out. "I had to get your mum to sign the form for school to say you were allowed."

"Oh yeah." Alicia pouted. "Well, I bet *you*'ve never been on a ghost walk."

"No," I conceded. "I guess I haven't. You'll have to tell me all about it. I thought ghost walks happened at night, anyway?"

"Not this one. Have you ever been to York?"

I paused. "A few times."

A few times? The memories were painfully fresh. The rain cascading over the cobbled streets, our soaked pumps, Hope's arm linked through mine—

"Did you know Lily's mum's coming to York, too?" Alicia escaped the last stroke of the hairbrush and headed for the door. "She's going to be a helper. Why aren't you being a helper, India?"

"I don't think I'm helpful enough." I smiled. "Besides, if I came, I wouldn't have time to finish your costume."

"Oh."

I followed her into the hallway.

"Remember, Lily's mum is going to drop you home, when you get back from the trip."

"And then we're going *trick-or-treating*!" Alicia swung around the banister post excitedly. "Did *you* ever go trick-or-treating?"

"Once or twice." I picked up the bag containing her lunch and waterproof, and held it out to her. "Come on. We need to go, or you're going to be late and miss the coach."

I opened the front door, shepherding her out into the chill morning air. For the first time since the other side of summer, there was a lacing of ice on the windscreen of my car.

"Are you scared of ghosts?" Alicia wanted to know as she clambered into her seat. I turned the key in the ignition and the heaters roared to life inside the car. I stumbled back out and attempted to scrape the frost from the windows with my student union card.

"That's a *rubbish* scraper," Alicia's voice came over the noise of the engine. "We'd better not be late and miss my trip because of your rubbish scraping!"

"We won't be late." I fell back into my seat and turned the windscreen wipers on. We had timed our night of camping within a whisker, I realised. Winter had descended in the blink of an eye.

I wasn't the only one who was bleary-eyed as I stood with the collection of inadequately caffeinated parents and watched Alicia's class board their coach in the school drive. I remembered school coaches. Field trips, museum visits, netball matches. I used to get so sick that the teachers would make me move near the front, and Hope would flick sweet wrappers at me from the back seat.

The drive back to the Manor was quieter than normal, an unnerving lull in the morning traffic. I turned on the radio to try and distract myself from my thoughts: unwelcome circular contemplations and alphabet magnets. I gripped the steering wheel tightly.

It actually wasn't possible. What did I think was going on? Some kind of preternatural message? I'd been exhausted from camping and bad dreams; sleep-deprived. I must have imagined it all. In the cold light of day, I could almost make myself certain. Almost. No one could have been in the house. No one except me. I let out my breath slowly as I rounded the corner onto the gravel drive. Perhaps I was losing my mind.

John's car had gone. I went inside, not as glad as usual of the solitude, and paced the length of the kitchen. The letters on the fridge were jumbled.

I hadn't been hungry when I got Alicia's breakfast. I ate now instead, watching one of the cats devouring the remains of some unfortunate rodent in the courtyard. I wondered briefly where Alex was, before I dismissed the thought. *Somewhere else.* For months I had worked here and barely seen him. If John or Julia was around, he wasn't.

I got up and scraped the last few soggy pieces of my cereal into the bin. The cat was wailing at the door and I let it in. It ran across the kitchen with its tail on end, leaving a trail of glistening paw-prints on the tiles, and vanished somewhere into the house.

Suddenly, I wished more than anything that there was someone else at home. The floorboards creaked as I climbed the stairs to my room. I looked out across the landing, at the particles of falling dust caught in a beam of sunlight. At Alex's stairs.

I closed my bedroom door behind me and headed for Alicia's room instead, stooping to collect up discarded toys and clothes, folding and tidying absently. From her window I could see the drive, and the road beyond the hedge. I would see if anyone came.

"Don't be ridiculous," I snapped at myself aloud.

I made myself move, searching out costume components from Alicia's extensive wardrobe as noisily as I could. But masking the silence only made me more jumpy; making so much noise, I wouldn't hear *anything*. The click of a door latch. The soft tread of feet on the stairs . . .

"Enough." I let out my breath in a rush. Enough.

I took the armful of clothes and made my way downstairs, collecting Julia Maine's sewing basket and heavy rag box from the cleaner's cupboard, and shutting myself in the drawing room. There was something comforting about 'Minuet in G' and the flood of watery sunshine that cascaded through the leaded lights. I laid the clothes out on the sofa and tried not to think about Alex's thumb on my lips, the smell of campfire smoke and sweat.

I opened the rag box. The musty collection of scraps – worn, torn outfits and outgrown clothes – must have dated back decades. I lifted a bundle out onto the floor and faltered, uncomfortable. There was something overly personal about them: pieces of other people's histories. An old tux with the lining torn out. A bright yellow rugby shirt, ripped up the back. A school blazer, its elbows burnished with wear, a gold pin-badge still glinting on its lapel. I shook it out to look at it. *Embarby Hall.* Alex's school. The crest on the pocket matched the one on the breast of the rugby shirt. I ran my fingers over the embroidered detail. It was so easy to forget that part of the story had unfolded before everything went awry.

I shook my head and put the garments aside, resuming my search. The next find was a victory: a sweeping long black skirt, lined with scarlet silk and spoiled with a shiny iron-burn. Triumphant, I shoved the rest of the rags away into the box and dragged it back to the cupboard.

Upstairs somewhere, the cat ran across the landing. I paused, listening.

Definitely just a cat. I dropped the latch of the cupboard door and stood still. The back of my neck prickled. My heart was beating hard. Indistinct, but undeniable, another noise had crescendoed: repetitive tapping, accelerating . . .

The rattle and roar of the boiler powering into life in the bowels of the house made me jump violently. The tapping reached a new level as the water expanded in the pipes. I exhaled heavily.

I was alone. *Alone.* There was no one there. I shook my head, despairing of myself. Shivers were still assailing me as I ran back through to the drawing room and latched the door.

What was the matter with me? I picked up the skirt and made an incision up its length, hands trembling. Was I going insane? It was so cold. I clamped my chattering teeth together and selected a needle and thread from the sewing basket.

I made two attempts at threading the needle, and managed to get the thread through the eye more by luck than judgement on the third pass. It was Tuesday. Vee should be here by now. Where was she?

I jabbed the needle into my finger instead of the skirt, and remembered. In Mablethorpe. At her sister's. I sucked the bead of blood from my fingertip. I should have appreciated her more when she was here; I'd have given anything now for her company, a warm cup, her reassuring croaky voice. What was it she had said? Bad memories. Ghosts and bad memories. I glanced around at the cold walls, shivering so hard that I ached.

Whose ghosts?

I gritted my teeth and resumed work on the transformation — skirt to cape. Sewing had never been my strong point. Lunchtime came and went; absorbed in my work, I barely noticed my hunger pangs. It was only as the sun moved around the side of the house, and the light in the drawing room dimmed, that I realised just how long it had taken.

It did look good, I thought as I straightened stiffly and shook it out to admire it. Even *if* Vee would have despaired at the needlework. Alicia would love it.

The sound of tyres on gravel shattered my momentary serenity. I leapt to my feet, the material cascading off my lap and onto the floor. John? Julia?

Alex.

His black Volkswagen was spattered with mud as it pulled to a sharp halt on the drive. I watched out of the window as he swung himself from the driver's seat and locked the car behind him, starting across the gravel and taking the steps to the front door in one easy bound.

I heard his key in the lock, and suddenly my equilibrium had evaporated. I swept up the cape. I heard Alex traverse the hall to push open the kitchen door and pause, and I realised I was holding my breath. Then his swift, balanced footsteps receded up the stairs.

I let out my breath in a rush. Why hadn't I spoken? I stood, rooted foolishly to the spot.

I attempted to gather my wits, and took Alicia's costume up to her room, laying it out on her bed carefully. Her fangs were on her dressing table, along with a drawing. A triangular tent, an orange fire, two figures holding hands, a third, smaller one sitting on the ground—

I stared at it, horrified. Then I snatched it up and hid it quickly on her desk under a pile of old spelling sheets and pictures.

I ducked out through her door, and faltered.

"Hi." Alex's voice was soft, his half-smile perceptive.

"Hi," I breathed.

He had paused at the bottom of his stairs, one hand still resting on the banister rail. The collar of his navy polo was turned up carelessly, and his other hand was thrust loosely into the pocket of his jeans.

"Everyone's out," he observed.

I nodded, wordless.

"I wasn't sure if you were here," he added.

At last, I recovered the power of speech. "I was in the drawing room."

"Are you busy?" Alex's gaze flickered from me to Alicia's doorway.

I shook my head.

"How long before Alicia gets home?" His tone was opaque.

I bit my lip. "A little while. Half an hour, an hour maybe. The Betton-Worthings are dropping her off."

"Good." Alex's half-smile became a smile as he descended the bottom step. "We need to stop having all our conversations on the stairs."

I nodded, and smiled back, blushing. "Where do you want to go?"

Alex raised an eyebrow. "I don't know, India." His voice was still very soft. "Where do *you* want to go?"

I hesitated over the reply that had entered my head, unbidden.

"I've never seen your room," I said finally.

For a beat, Alex's eyes scoured my face, the same dark blue as his shirt.

"Does that bother you?" I couldn't tell if he was amused, or wary.

"I don't know." I shrugged. "It's weird that I've lived here for three months, and I've never been upstairs."

Alex shrugged too, but there was something appraising in his glance.

"Be my guest." He nodded lightly back the way he had come.

I ascended slowly, running my hand over the broken banister rail, a strange chill creeping along my spine as I remembered the sound. Splintering wood, pounding feet, rage.

I pushed the door open and stepped inside. I suddenly felt like a child, venturing out of bounds. I tiptoed across the carpeted floor, my pulse slightly too fast as I took in my surroundings. The tick of a clock somewhere measured out the long, lingering seconds.

"I'm not sure this is a good idea." Alex was watching me from the doorway, his expression unreadable, his thumb and forefinger pressed lightly to his lower lip.

I turned in a circle, taking in the details of his room. It wasn't at all like I had imagined it; it was another world, an untidy world of landscape paintings and manuscript paper. Only one picture was on the wall, hung beside the bed; a craggy, undulating scene of barren hills with a tiny stone cottage nestling in a valley. Others were stacked against the walls, at least a dozen of them, old and new. Two guitars were propped against a chest of drawers. The one vast desk was strewn with paper, an army of marching musical notes that crossed the borders from page to page, black and white, darkness and light. A Velux window above the bed cast a square of watered-down sunshine, rapidly fading, over the thrownback covers. I turned back to him as the door clicked closed.

"What's not?"

Alex smiled darkly, shook his head. "Never mind."

I resumed my exploration. The bookcase against the far wall was crammed full to overflowing, and a collection of tattered paperbacks cascaded rebelliously at its foot. I picked up the closest one to place it back on top of the stack. *Great Expectations* seemed to hold a certain level of irony. I put it down silently.

There was a small two-seater sofa beside the desk, and I moved to that instead, automatically stooping to pick up the woollen throw that had slid off it and drape it back over the arm. There was more manuscript paper on one of the cushions, a thick bundle of it bound at the top corner, and something about it caught my eye.

"This is what you were working on." I picked it up, running my fingers over the shiny, uneven indentation of pencil-drawn notes.

"Mmm." At last, Alex had moved away from the door. He strolled to stand nearer the skylight, reaching to press one hand to the cold glass.

"I . . ." I looked back at the title, not sure what to say.

Indian Summer. I traced the letters with my finger, too, and sat down heavily on the edge of the sofa. Something seemed to have expanded in my chest, so huge and irrepressible that it was almost impossible to breathe against.

I raised my eyes. Alex was still watching me.

"Don't." In two strides he had reached me. "Don't look at me like that." He tugged the score gently from my hands and sat down beside me. The sofa was barely wide enough for two; his long legs were squashed tightly against mine, solid, warm and disconcerting. He ran his fingers lightly over the faded blue leg of my jeans, and I shivered involuntarily.

"Like what?" My cheeks were on fire; he cupped them in his cool hands, and I caught his wrist, terrified by the bolt of desire that the simple touch sent through me.

"Oh, India." His gaze was on my mouth, distracting me hopelessly. "If only I could tell you."

I swallowed, fumbling to return to safe ground. "You . . . finished it." I picked up the score with hands that shook.

He nodded.

"But . . . where? How?" I clung desperately to my questions, determined not to fall into the trap of meeting his eyes again. "I never hear you play."

"I'll show you. Some other time." Alex took the score again firmly, and put it on the desk, out of reach.

Something in the action left my resolve in ruins. I glanced up despite myself, and before I could even draw breath, his mouth was on mine, his fingers curling themselves into my hair, my murmur of protest lost to his kiss. His weight pressed me backwards, and I clutched at the front of his shirt—

He broke his lips away, leaving both of us flushed and gasping.

"Alex—" My voice was husky.

"You still think it's a good idea?" he murmured.

His fingers were in my hair, twisting, stroking; I could still taste him on my throbbing lips. I could feel him against me, feel everything: his heart beating, his ragged breathing. I hesitated.

"I—"

"India! INDIA!"

Alex halted, motionless. Downstairs, the kitchen door rattled on its latch and then burst open with a crash.

"INDIAA!"

Sense returned in a rush. What collection of garbled words I would have managed to force between my lips, I would never know as I ducked out beneath his arm and straightened my clothes tremblingly. I couldn't even look back at him. I half fell down the attic stairs in my haste.

"INDIA!"

I was, mercifully, most of the way along the landing by the time the hurricane that was Alicia hit.

"There you are!" She frowned up at me and paused. "You look funny."

"So do you." My voice wasn't quite even.

Alicia regarded me with distrust. "What's the matter with you?"

"I was busy cleaning my room," I told her. "I'm hot. And I didn't hear Mrs Betton-Worthing's car."

"She dropped me at the top of the drive." Alicia forgot her scepticism. Suddenly she was bubbling over with excitement. "Lily wanted to come in to see my fangs, but her mum said no. Becca's mum said that everyone should meet on the green in Meresham at six. Did you finish my costume?!"

"Yep." I smiled. "Haven't you found it? It's in your room."

"Oh!" Alicia hugged my waist briefly, and then ran. I followed her through, watching as she seized the cape from the bed.

"OH!" She flung it onto her dressing table, literally hopping with glee. "*India!*" She leapt onto her bed, bouncing up and down with such force that Tatty Rabbit went flying. "It's *amazing!* It's the best thing *ever!*"

She bounded down and grabbed her fangs from underneath the heap of fabric, fitting them into her mouth.

"Looksh!" she exclaimed. "I'mfh a vfhampire!"

"You need to have your tea before you put your costume on. It's going to be hard to eat it with your fangs in."

"Ohh." Alicia gave me a toothy scowl.

"Come on." I rescued Tatty Rabbit from the floor. "Are you hungry? Will an omelette do?"

Alicia slipped the fangs from her mouth and wiped them on her sleeve. "Okay."

She sat at the table scribbling while I cooked. It only took a matter of minutes, but by the time the food was ready she was kneeling impatiently on her chair. I sat down opposite her at the table. I had never seen her eat so fast; she virtually inhaled the omelette, a feat she had never before achieved, even at breakfast, and then threw her knife and fork together in the middle of her plate.

"PleasemayIleavetable?"

I was sure she was still chewing. But before I had the chance to reprimand her, she had made a dash for the door.

"Alicia . . ." I failed to sound stern. She flung the door open.

"India, come on! Uff."

All of the wind had left her small body as she ran, headlong, into Alex's legs. He had to grab the doorframe to steady himself, startled and amused in equal measure as he looked down at her.

"Hi to you too, Alicia."

"Alex!" she scolded imperiously, then swerved around him and thundered onto the stairs. "Come on, India!"

Alex stayed in the doorway, regarding me across the table, a hint of amusement still playing enticingly at the corners of his mouth. I got to my feet, the wooden chair legs scraping loudly on the tiled floor.

"What?" I asked him, perturbed.

He shook his head.

"India, hurry up!" Alicia's chestnut head bobbed impatiently back into sight behind him.

"I'm coming, Alicia." My voice sounded uncharacteristically squeaky.

It was only as I slipped past him in the doorway that he caught hold of me, his fingers surreptitiously brushing my cheek. For just a moment, his lips were close against my ear.

"You didn't say *no*," he whispered.

My breath hitched in my throat.

Then I fled into the hall, my heart beating a drumroll against my ribs.

There was post on the hall floor. A pile of letters that had landed on the chequered doormat and skidded across the tiles. I paused. Usually I wouldn't have given it a second glance. But the top one had my name on it.

I faltered.

Alex was still in the kitchen behind me. I crossed the floor silently, to pick it up.

India McKenzie,
The Manor,
Caldwell Lane,
Rifway

190

Alicia came back down the stairs for a second time, but I barely heard her. I stood motionless, my gaze fixed on the handwriting.

"India! Look at my cape!" Alicia's exuberant babble sounded distant, beyond the ringing in my ears.

"It's so cool! India, do you think I'm going to look really like a vampire? India—"

I swallowed.

"Alicia," I cleared my throat. My voice sounded strangely calm, alien. "Would you please go and start getting changed? I'll be with you in a moment."

"Okay." Her reply seemed to fade in and out. She scrambled away in the direction of her bedroom, the door crashing closed behind her. Still I didn't move.

It's like you can write a hundred letters, and never get a letter back . . .

I ran upstairs, my tread light, my heart racing. My room was cold; I shut the door and stopped just inside it, suddenly too afraid to breathe. I eased one finger under the flap of the envelope, prising it open, almost tearing the letter as I tried to pull it out.

Dear India,

I'm so sorry it's taken me this long to write, when you've written me so much.

Why have you stopped writing now, just as things were getting interesting?

I put out one unsteady hand and clutched at the door behind me, reaching unthinkingly for the bolt and drawing it without looking. I couldn't look away from the letter. From the familiar handwriting. So familiar. My hand was shaking so violently that it was almost impossible to carry on reading; the piece of paper was quaking in my grip.

So tell me, how is Alex?

I want to hear all about it, India. I gather he has quite the reputation. You promised you would keep me updated, remember? You said you would tell me everything.

Well, now I'm going to tell you something, too.

You should have listened to what he said, India, about dangerous ground. And you know it's true.

Why have you stopped writing to me, India?

Tell me why you've stopped writing . . .

I released my fingers suddenly, and the letter slipped from my grasp, gliding to the floor with a soft swish, the words staring back up at me. My breath was coming in uneven gasps, rapid and ineffectual. The room swirled.

Write back soon, India. Please. I miss you.
Your best friend,
Hope

CHAPTER 16: REMEMBER, REMEMBER

The fifth of November. For five days I had done everything in my power to avoid being alone in the house. To avoid writing paper, and windows in the darkness. To avoid anyone else picking up the post. For five nights, my blank bedroom walls had stared down at me as I tried in vain to sleep.

It was Sunday. On Friday, Alicia had finished school for her half-term break. And tonight, Julia Maine would arrive back from Brussels for the rest of the week. A whole week. I wasn't sure how I would stand it. *Whether* I would stand it, or whether I would lose my mind completely.

I hadn't spoken with Alex about it, but the facts were glaringly obvious. For a week, I wouldn't be able to talk to him, look at him, notice him. There would be no more strange half-conversations as we walked in the grounds in the rain during Alicia's piano lessons. No more late-evening meals after Alicia had gone to bed, that neither of us really ate as we listened for John to arrive back from his call-outs. For a week, Alex would be in exile, and I would, potentially, be in hell.

I crossed the hallway, shivering. There had been no church service this morning, and Alicia was at a birthday party. It was freezing in the Manor; I wasn't sure how it seemed only to be me that felt it, going about my daily tasks with my teeth chattering. John Maine had been in his study all morning. I hadn't even dared to go and turn on the heating.

I glanced down at myself. I was filthy; there was straw all over my clothes and my hands were cold and chapped from cleaning out the animals. I needed to shower.

I paused as I walked past the door to the drawing room. The sunlight fell in criss-cross patterns over the piano. The minuet was covered in pencil marks now; Alex's untidy handwriting and scribbled directions surrounded every line. I thought of his strong fingers on the keys, of the ripple of tendons in his wrists as he played, of Alicia sitting on his lap between his arms, watching his hands like a hawk. The difference in her playing, in such a short span of time, was remarkable. Whether Iain Trevers knew, or suspected, I wasn't sure. Either way, he would know tonight, when he opened the page and saw Alex's writing all over it.

I could hear John's muted voice in his study, dictating letters. The sound was oddly comforting. I might have been scared of him, but I was much more scared of the empty house.

I went upstairs and locked myself in the bathroom, turned on the shower and watched the steam rise. I undressed quickly and let the noise of the water fill my ears, breathing a sigh of relief as I started to thaw under its prickly, scalding flow.

There were going to be fireworks on the village cricket ground tonight, and Alicia had persuaded me I should take her. I didn't have a good excuse not to.

I opened my eyes and reached for my shampoo, the hot water coursing over my face. The bathroom was filled with steam, condensing and dripping down the window, misting the glass shower screen to opacity. I dropped the shampoo bottle with a crash.

Beside me, a picture was appearing in the condensation. Emerging, undeniably; slightly blurred, but unmistakable. The rose was simple, an outline, drawn onto the glass with one finger.

Why have you stopped writing to me, India?

I gasped. Choked on the metallic-tasting water.

Tell me why you've stopped writing . . .

I flung the screen open, almost slipping as I leapt out of the bath and clutched dizzily at the towel rail, the water still roaring down, cascading over the white tiles, splashing above the side of the bath and onto the floor.

"Oh . . ." Nausea had risen, threateningly imminent, in my throat. "Oh God."

I snatched my towel and wrapped it around myself, taking a few deep breaths, trying to fight it back.

Are you scared of ghosts?

"No." I shook my head. "This is ridiculous."

It was still there. Fading again, slowly, as it succumbed to the mist and spray. I made myself reach past it and turn off the shower. Completely ridiculous. Four other people used this bathroom; one of them was seven years old and drew hearts and flowers, and stick men with zig-zag mouths, in her own breath on my car windows all the time.

Nonetheless, I didn't get back in the shower. I washed my hair over the sink and got dressed, feeling colder than ever.

The light in John's study was off by the time I went downstairs, the door closed. I wondered if he was on call again. After all, his wife was coming home. I admonished myself for the thought as I stopped in the corridor, my gaze alighting on the pictures. Photos of Alicia, of her parents, of Alicia with her parents. The one charcoal sketch of the chorister with strangely piercing eyes. I stopped to look at it. To try and understand.

Do you have a story?

I don't know any with happy endings, Alicia.

I was tired. I wrapped my arms around myself, turning my attention to the family portraits instead. One must have been taken only last year — Alicia stood as tall as her mother's elbow, and was wearing her bright red coat and beret. But there were no pictures of Alex with his family. Not anymore.

I had rung the Shelgate Unit at midnight. Sheneen hadn't been on; I had spoken to an agency nurse whom I'd never met, who told me in her gentle Filipino accent that my mother was sleeping, and that there had been no changes. I could hear her reading from the notes on the other end of the phone. I couldn't blame her. I couldn't expect more. After all, how long had it been since I'd called?

It had been two years since I'd first walked through the doors into the Shelgate Unit. It was early November, like now, my reading week; I had gone down from uni the week before, when everything got out of hand. I had left Leeds alone. But an hour later — as I was trying to persuade my mother to come in from the garden so that I could clean and bandage her cut hands, and explain the damage to our neighbours — Hope had arrived, calm and matter-of-fact. She never said that I should have told her. She knew, anyway.

I remembered the wait in Accident and Emergency. We hadn't been able to think of where else to go, what else to do, other than calling the police, which seemed like the worst possible solution. I had known for a while that it was getting bad. At first, I'd just been thankful that the drinking had stopped. But its cessation had heralded something else, something worse: the stories, the making things up, the lack of memories — little things at first, but then big things, huge things. The death of her parents, her own address . . .

The night I left her in the unit, I felt like a traitor. A deserter. Ridden with guilt at my enormous sense of relief. I went back every day, to start with. It was only a matter of weeks before she started to forget my name. Months passed, and she didn't know my face.

Now . . . ?

I shook my head and walked back through to the hall.

I hadn't heard the letterbox. Hadn't heard the postman's van, or feet on the drive. But in hindsight, I already knew. That it was there. On the doormat. Waiting.

I picked it up.

Stamped, but no postmark. Sealed with Sellotape. I peeled the tape back carefully, and stopped.

"Ridiculous," I reminded myself, out loud. "You're losing your mind."

I had wanted it. Wanted it so badly. Her handwriting. Her words. I had heard stories. Stories about people going mad. I'd witnessed them. And they all started the same way.

5 November

Dear India,

How are you? I heard that you haven't been sleeping well. I'm sorry about that. You know, if there's ever anything you need to talk about, I'm right here.

Do you know what the date is today? You should, but I put it at the top of my letter just in case. Are you familiar with the rhyme? Remember, remember . . .

Remember how you promised to write to me? You haven't written back yet, India. You haven't written back, and I'm waiting.

By the way, did Alicia like her vampire costume?

And Alex . . . What about Alex?

I'm starting to wonder whether you read my last letter properly, India. Do you <u>really</u> still think it's a good idea?

"Shut up." The hiss of my breath escaped between my teeth. I realised I had squeezed my eyes tightly closed.

"Shut up." I repeated. "Stop. Just . . . stop."

I opened them again, but the letter was still in my hand.

"You can't be," I told it. My head was aching. Not just aching; pounding, the pain hammering behind my eyes as though it was trying to get out.

"No more."

In one decisive movement, I ripped the piece of paper clean in two.

"No more," I whispered.

* * *

The major scale descended back to middle C, and paused. Then D major stumbled up the keyboard, growing slowly more confident as it went, and faltered into a broken chord at Iain Trevers' unheard direction.

I wiped my hands and moved to check the temperature of the oven, glad of the heat that emanated from its door. I still couldn't get warm. Not even after having gone to pick up Alicia and bring her back, and making us both hot chocolate. She wanted to bake fairy cakes, and I had only remembered after we poured out most of the ingredients that Iain was coming to catch up the missed piano lesson.

I tasted the cake mixture on one finger. The paper cases this time were plain and I arranged them in their trays, smiling to myself. *What does keel over mean?*

The kitchen door clicked closed. I jumped.

Alex crossed the floor silently to stand behind me. For a moment neither of us spoke, and I went back to spooning out the cake mixture, self-conscious.

His hand brushed my waist and I turned. He wasn't smiling. His gaze was level, serious.

"When you're sad," his voice was very soft, "who makes *you* feel better?"

I froze. His eyes met mine. The words that Alicia had once uttered lingered, earnest and meaningful, on his lips. Very gently, he tugged the spoon from my grasp and laid it down on the surface.

"I want to know." He caught my hands, imprisoning them in his. I looked down at our intertwined fingers. Alex released his grip slightly, and pressed his palm against my palm, his fingertips finding mine and spreading my handspan wide and helpless.

Then the bang of the front door echoed through the house and we sprang apart, guilty and subversive.

My cheeks were still too red as Julia Maine appeared from the hallway, the wheels of her suitcase rattling on the floor tiles.

"Hello? India?"

Her plane must have landed early. I snatched up the spoon from the work surface, breathless and flustered. Julia opened her mouth to address me, and then stopped dead, doing a double take as she noticed Alex sitting at the table, his face invisible behind an old copy of the *Times*.

"Oh, hi." I broke the awkward silence, hoping desperately that my voice sounded more even than it felt. "I . . . I didn't realise you were going to be back so soon. I was just baking for Alicia. She's still at piano . . . "

I was talking too much. Julia had barely looked at me. Her gaze was on the back page of the newspaper, on her son's long legs crossed nonchalantly under the table.

I cleared my throat. "How was your journey?"

"Oh." She snapped around abruptly, apparently recovering her composure much more quickly than I had.

"It was fine, India, thank you. I made an earlier flight than I was expecting, which is nice."

"Ah, that's good," I mumbled into the oven as I shoved the cakes in.

"It sounds like Alicia's finished." Julia gave me a tight smile. "I'll go and say hello. I've got some presents for her from Paris and Bruges."

"Sure." My voice sounded strangled.

"Alicia!" Julia disappeared back into the hallway, leaving her suitcase beside the kitchen table. "Alicia!"

With infuriating calmness, Alex lowered the newspaper.

"That went well, I thought," he said.

For a moment, I stared at him. He met my gaze squarely, looking up at me from beneath his brows. Something glittered in his eyes, mysterious, teasing. Tempting. I had to turn away.

"It's a shame." Alex's thumb and forefinger were pressed to his lower lip, contemplative. "My mother likes you."

I glanced back quickly. "Huh?"

"That makes things much more complicated." The slight lift of his eyebrow made my pulse quicken.

"What do you mean? What things?" My voice emerged as a whisper.

"Oh, I don't know." Alex's expression was unreadable. He didn't sound like he didn't know.

"India! Look what Mum bought me!" In the blink of an eye, Alicia was under my feet. "Look! It's a Parisian doll. That means it's from Paris. And this is real Belgian chocolate. Mum says I can eat some of it after tea. Are you getting tea? Is it ready yet?"

"Not yet. There are jacket potatoes in the oven with the cakes." I took the proffered gifts from her, examining them and trying to voice the expected admiration. "The doll's beautiful, Alicia. You'll have to decide where you're going to keep her."

"Oh, I don't know." Alicia rolled her eyes. "*Mum* bought her. So it's not like she's for *playing* with or anything. Maybe on my bookcase. I'm going outside. Can I have the chocolate back?"

"Um, maybe not." I raised my eyebrows at her. Alicia grinned at me. "I'm not that gullible," I told her.

"What does gullible mean?" Alicia tucked the bottoms of her jeans into her wellies and opened the kitchen door. "I'm going to play in the garden. Will tea be ready soon?"

"Twenty minutes."

"See you in twenty minutes then!" The door slammed behind her, and I was left with the doll in one hand, staring up at me, its painted cheeks almost as red as mine had been. Probably still were. I could feel Alex's scrutiny over the back page of the newspaper.

"You didn't answer me earlier," he observed quietly.

I took a deep breath, and turned back, my fingers pressed to the doll's rosy cheeks.

"*You* never answer *me*," I countered.

Alex smiled enigmatically. "You might not like my answers."

"Try me."

He laid down the paper again, and folded his arms on the table, looking up at me in a way that made every muscle in my abdomen clench in apprehension.

"What were the questions?"

"What do you do? Where do you go? When you're not here. Where do you write your music?" I put down the doll carefully. "And *what things*?"

"A place, in the village." His thumb rested, briefly, against his lips, and I remembered with a lurch what it had felt like on mine. "I said I'd show you. I will. I go there to practise when I can't play here." Alex lowered his voice. "As for your other question, India, I told you that you might not like the answer. But my mother likes you. Alicia idolises you. And *you* . . . you want to keep working here."

"And?" I whispered.

"That makes this complicated. It makes . . . " His eyes were on mine. "The things I think about when I'm near you, complicated."

His gaze held mine fast. Neither of us moved. Neither of us spoke. Outside, an early firework popped somewhere in the distance, sputtering faintly into silence.

At last, Alex rose to his feet. Hurriedly I retraced my steps to the oven. Fiddled with the dial of the timer. Tried, in vain, to make my breathing return to normal.

"I can't stop thinking about you, India." His voice was barely audible, not even a whisper; he had followed me, just a step away. Close enough to touch, if I reached out. I picked up the oven gloves instead, and gripped them with both hands.

"I can't stop thinking about you, and I want to know what you're thinking, too."

He didn't come any closer. Didn't step back. I twisted the gloves into a tight roll.

The back door crashed open.

"Is tea ready yet?"

Alex turned around. I didn't. I was still staring at the gloves. *The things I think about when I'm near you . . .*

Silence.

"Alicia, what's this?!"

Behind me, suddenly, he was laughing. I turned despite myself. Alicia's face was streaked with dirt, a big smear of

201

lichen-green across the middle of her forehead. She reached up and rubbed at it with surprise.

"Oh." She scrubbed her face vigorously with her sleeve, adding more smudges than she removed. "It's from the hollow tree. We were making a den."

I returned to reality with a bump.

"*Who* was making a den?" I frowned.

"Me and my friend." Alicia grinned coquettishly.

Alex was frowning too. "What friend?" He crouched down to her height.

"It's none of your business." Alicia stuck her nose in the air. "I don't have to tell you everything. It's a secret, all right?"

I hesitated, trying to ascertain from her face whether she was serious. Who could she have possibly been playing with outside? The only other person she was likely to have encountered was Roy. Which seemed somehow improbable . . .

For some reason, there was a chill in the air. I moved more calmly than I felt to take the cakes out of the oven. I left them on the side to cool, collected a block of cheese from the fridge and started to grate it.

"Were you *really* playing with someone, Alicia?" I watched for her reaction.

Of course she hadn't been. I shook my head. Things had been getting to me so easily these last few days. The drawing on the shower screen. The made-up friend. The newspaper cutting.

The yellow rose.

"Yes." Alicia folded her arms across her chest.

"Who is your friend, Alicia?" Alex persisted gently. "What's her name?"

"It's a secret." Alicia raised her eyebrows, unimpressed. "Oh *give me a break*, both of you! It's not like it's a stranger or anything!"

"Who is it?" Alex's voice was soft.

"I *told* you. It's a secret. It's *my* friend, and — don't interrupt! We promised it's a secret. Anyway, he's not even always here. So *you'll* probably *never* be able to see him."

Alex glanced at me, clearly not convinced, but relieved. "Is your friend real, Alicia?"

She looked at him as if she thought he was stupid. "Uh . . . yes! Duh."

I felt the tension evaporate. Alex smiled teasingly.

"Is he your boyfriend, Alicia?"

Alicia shook her head. "Of course not, stupid. I'm too young to have a boyfriend." She paused and looked pointedly at him. "Even if *you're her* boyfriend." She directed a meaningful finger at me.

I flushed instantaneously crimson. Alex didn't do a very good job of covering his alarm.

"What do you mean?" He spoke under his breath.

Alicia must have seen the anxiety in his face; she suddenly looked triumphant. "You can pretend if you want to. But I saw you the other day, through the window. *Kissing* . . . eurgh." She pulled a face.

Alex stood frozen. I suddenly felt light-headed.

Alicia was giggling. "I *told* you he loved you! I *told* you so. Alex and India sitting in a tree, k-i—"

"Alicia . . ." Alex started out softly. "You—"

Alicia was still glancing coyly from one to the other of us.

"Don't worry," she told him in a confiding whisper. "I won't tell anyone. India's my friend." She padded over to me, and I looked down as she caught hold of my hand. She looked back at Alex.

"You are too, I guess. Even *though* you're my brother. And like I told you, *I* can keep secrets."

I had forgotten about grating the cheese. Forgotten about the potatoes in the bottom of the roaring oven. Her words were still ringing in my ears.

"Is tea ready yet?" Alicia reiterated, hands on her hips. "I'm *starving.*"

I retrieved the food wordlessly as Alex faltered in the doorway. Alicia went and sat down, eyeing me calculatingly from her seat at the table.

"I won't tell anyone," she repeated quietly.

203

I looked round, lost for words. I saw Alex glance over his shoulder as he disappeared, his footsteps soft and measured on the stairs. My throat was dry. I cleared it.

"Here you go." I put her tea down in front of her.

"Thanks." Alicia took the plate from me, piling the cheese on top of her potato in a precarious heap. "It would be bad if Mum found out, though." She was tucking blithely into her food, as if nothing had happened. Nothing of any consequence. She sawed through the potato skin with huge exertion. "She doesn't really like Alex. That's why I didn't tell her about the camping."

"Thanks, Alicia." My voice was a croak.

"That's okay." Alicia shrugged, and spoke with her mouth full. "If I'm allowed to have secrets, and you're allowed to have secrets, then that's fair."

I paused. "I don't—"

"India, are you free?" Julia Maine's voice in the hallway sent a gush of ice down my spine.

"Sure." I shot one last uncertain look at Alicia and walked shakily into the hall.

"I was wondering whether we could catch up." Julia was standing at the mouth of the corridor, the sitting-room door half open in the dimness behind her. Perhaps it was my imagination, or possibly her severely tailored suit, but suddenly she looked older. A few strands of grey were evident at her temples and in the bundle of the smooth braided knot at the nape of her neck.

She opened the sitting-room door the rest of the way, and gestured me inside, and suddenly I felt like a child no bigger than Alicia, summoned to the school office for some undisclosed crime.

Was it undisclosed?

You won't . . .

I could.

Shit.

I sat down gingerly on the edge of the sofa: a huge, cream, feather-cushioned affair. The wooden floorboards creaked under Julia's feet as she walked around the vast coffee table and sat down on an easy chair opposite me.

I had barely spent any time in here before. It tended to be John's domain, with the immense flat-screen TV flickering the cricket at low volume, and a stack of light reading — *BMJ* and *Thorax* — accumulating on the coffee table. The room was simple but luxurious. A row of exotic plants in designer ceramic pots lined the bay window. Neither of us moved to draw the heavy Egyptian curtains.

Julia's pale blue eyes alighted on my face. I was frozen, hands folded in my lap. Then she smiled.

"How are you, India? I'm sorry we've not had the chance to catch up before." She sat back in the chair, and I tried not to stare at her, utterly thrown.

"Oh . . . uhm. I'm fine. Thank you." If I hadn't lost the ability to move, I would have been squirming.

"Good." She nodded, satisfied. "You seem to have . . . settled in. I can't even *think* where the time's gone. John and I just wanted one of us to sit down and have a chat with you, really. And to thank you."

I gaped at her, then remembered to close my mouth.

"We're very happy with the progress Alicia has made. More than happy."

I felt like I was at parents' evening. Except it was all back-to-front. I fumbled for something to say, and failed to find anything.

Julia continued, unfazed. "Neither John nor I have seen her this motivated in a very long time. She's doing well at school, in class, with sport . . ." Her eyebrows lifted. "Even with piano. Which, I must say, is a first."

I closed my eyes for a fraction of a second, images of 'Minuet in G' and Alex's handwriting dancing through my head. I opened them again quickly.

"She seems *happy*, India." Julia smiled again, and I couldn't help noticing how tired she looked. "You've done very well."

There was an awkward pause. Forget awkward. It was cavernous, yawning, a black hole of a pause. I waited for the *but*.

"We just wanted to check that everything was satisfactory from your point of view." Julia folded her hands in her immaculate navy lap. "And, while I'm at home for Alicia's half term, to see if you wanted to take the rest of this week off."

"Unh—"

The tiny surprised sound escaped my throat before I realised I had made it. In an instant, my cheeks were flaming red. Time off? I had never even considered time off. She thought I'd want to leave. To go away — *where*? I didn't *have* anywhere else.

I cleared my throat. Julia Maine was waiting, expectant.

"Uh . . . thank you." I couldn't do it. It was too rude to turn her down. And how could I tell her the only roof I had over my head was here? I made myself smile back at her. "Thanks! I hadn't . . . uhm, thought about it. But that would be . . . great."

"Good." She nodded. "That's settled, then. We thought perhaps you might want to have a few days at home. You can go tomorrow after breakfast." Julia stood up, and I had the distinct feeling that the conversation was over — aims and objectives achieved. "We'll need you back by Saturday evening, so that on Sunday you can get her ready for school."

"Sure." I was getting to my feet too, forcing myself to let go of my hands and look relaxed. "That would be great."

"Fine." Julia's smile had finally worn thin. "Thank you, India. I hope you and Alicia have a nice time at the fireworks tonight."

"Thanks," I mumbled.

* * *

Alicia was barely mobile in her bundle of jumpers and coats as I opened the front door to let her outside, two hours later. The gravel was crisp underfoot. In only a matter of days, the colours and shades of autumn were gone, and frost reigned hard. I pushed my hands into my pockets. Alicia had to turn her whole torso to look at me, her arms stuck out at forty-five degrees in her non-compliant layers of clothing.

"Remember, remember the fifth of November!" She jumped up and down impatiently on the drive as I struggled to push the door-key into the pocket of my coat. My hands were significantly lacking dexterity inside my woollen gloves.

"Gunpowder, treason and plot!" Alicia exclaimed with glee. "We made a Guy Fawkes at school! His head was a sack full of old socks! I did his face with a felt-tip!"

I smiled. "He sounds . . . interesting."

"He'll be even better once he's on *fire*. But he'll be on Meresham's bonfire, not here. And that's tomorrow. Maybe Mum will take me?" She skipped off across the gravel, chanting. "Remember, remember the fifth of November! The gunpowder treason and plot!"

I began to walk after her, my feet numb inside my wellingtons. I unwound my scarf from around my neck and rewrapped it more warmly, watching Alicia's carefree pirouette as she reached the gateway. A few more hours, and I would be driving out of that gateway. And I had no idea where I was going to go.

The sound of footsteps crunched on the gravel behind us. I turned in surprise.

Alex caught us up in a few long strides, the cloud of his breath dispelling as he reached us, his cheeks red with cold.

"Wait for me."

"Ohh!" Alicia bounded stiffly back to him. "Alex! You're coming, too! Does this have to be a secret as well?"

I avoided his gaze assiduously. I could sense his knowing smile.

"Perhaps," he murmured.

It didn't take long to reach the cricket ground. We stopped at a stall on the way in to pay and to equip Alicia with sparklers, and then fought our way to the front. The fire was already lit, a huge, blazing memorial to treason and plot . . .

It would be bad if Mum found out.

. . . oh yes — and to the subsequent, brutal execution. I looked at Guy Fawkes, his red scribbled smile still broad as the rest of him combusted in the flames.

"Here." Alex's voice cut through the chill air. I looked back. He was holding Alicia's hand in one of his, the sparkler hissing and fizzling wildly as they circled it in the air.

"Up there. Quickly — before it goes out. Now blink!"

"I can see my name!" Alicia squealed. The sparkler died and she dropped it into the mud with a sigh.

Alex grinned. "One last go." With a fizz and flare of light, he lit another one, and put it into her hand, holding onto her closed fist tightly. "Ready? Go."

I-N-D-I-A

They spelt out the letters in the darkness together, their wrists moving in unison, their fingers intertwined. My throat was tight as my gaze travelled from Alicia's glowing face to Alex's guarded one. The first firework exploded overhead with a crack that vibrated deep in my chest. Alicia squealed again, clapped her gloved hands, and leaned back against her brother's legs. And all three of us turned our gaze to the sky.

* * *

I like remembering things, India. I know you do, too. Like the day I started at school with you. And the day we got our tattoos. And graduation, I like remembering graduation — you looked so beautiful. So why have you taken down the pictures of us?

"No." I moaned and turned over. Buried my face in the covers, so that I couldn't see the blank, staring walls. Four a.m. The room was cold, but the sheets were damp with sweat. For half an hour, I had dreamt of staring eyes and flames. If you could call them dreams; I no sooner seemed to have closed my eyes than they were open again, and as I blinked away the encroaching shadows, all I could see was the shape of his lips, and his folded arms on the table top . . .

I can't stop thinking about you, India.

I inhaled and sat bolt upright, sleep gone in a second.

I couldn't. I couldn't stand it anymore. I slipped from the tangle of kicked-off covers and stood up. I'd tried everything. Reading. Washing my face in cool water from the sink. Standing in the window until my eyelids drooped. But when I listened to the silence, I heard other things instead. The soft fall of imagined footsteps on the attic stairs. The creak of a door that hadn't opened.

A chill ran over my bare arms. I pushed open the door, the wooden floorboards of the landing cool under the soles of my feet. I tiptoed downstairs into the kitchen, flinching at the icy tiles, and ran a glass of water. I sipped it slowly, staring at my pyjamas, at the shadowy shapes of the chairs around the table, at anything except the black window-glass and whatever might lurk, unseen, on the other side.

Are you scared of ghosts?

For goodness' sake. I downed the rest of the water and turned quickly. I'd never been afraid of the dark in my life. All the noises, creaks, bumps, happened every night. Nobody was there.

I gritted my teeth. The skid of something on the corridor floor as I made my way back to the stairs was a cat. So were the heavy footsteps on the landing; I heard them every night as I lay in bed. Once, when I was here alone, I had even stayed to watch, paranoid that it was Alicia.

The boards behind me let out a low creak . . .

Suddenly there was a strong hand clamped over my mouth, stifling my cry; fingers tightened around the top of my arm. My breath jammed in my throat.

"Ssh. Don't scream. It's me." Alex's whisper was hot against my ear, so soft as to be almost inaudible. "I thought I heard someone creeping around."

He'd been in bed; his hair was tousled and he was only wearing his jeans, the faded dark blue denim hanging loosely from his hips. He released my face and stepped back, half in shadow.

"I came down for water." My pulse was racing. I wasn't sure why I felt the need to explain. "I couldn't sleep."

Silence. Neither of us moved. The impenetrable darkness of the staircase loomed above us. He was standing very close. So close, that all at once I was finding it hard to breathe.

"You're going away in the morning." He spoke suddenly. I glanced up, surprised. "I want to go with you." His fingers curled into my hair, his thumb reaching to skim my cheekbone, sending helpless shivers along my spine.

"I . . . I don't even know where I'm going to go," I whispered.

"I have an idea." Alex's eyes locked mine. "If you trust me. Do you trust me?"

I exhaled tremulously. Trust him? I nodded, wordless.

"I'll send them to your phone." His lips brushed against my hair. "Directions. Follow them, in the morning. I'll come and find you."

"Okay."

He still didn't move. For stretching seconds, measured out by the heavy beat of the kitchen clock somewhere behind us, we were caught in hesitation. In a moment that could have lasted forever but was over before we realised what it meant.

"India." His voice was raw.

Adrenaline spiked through me. Then his grip closed, painfully tightly, around my wrist.

"*Ssh.*" It was determined, impulsive; he was dragging me with him across the hall, into the corridor, one of his hands covering my mouth. He shoved me into the dark sitting room and kicked the door to behind us, his lips finding mine, hot and relentless. And then his hands were on me, roaming, insatiable, and I clutched at his arms in unconvincing protest, felt the hardness of the bunched muscle under his skin, and yielded in a single breath.

His finger and thumb slipped down the waistband of my pyjamas, his other hand inverting my camisole over my head. He took my feet out from beneath me suddenly, swiftly

— I wasn't even sure how — and we both fell in a tangle of limbs to the floorboards. With a crash that seemed as though it should have roused the dead, a potted plant toppled and fell, a mutinous landslide of soil and broken china spreading across the floor.

For a split second, neither of us dared to move. Alex's warm, hard weight held me trapped, pressing me into the boards, not breathing, listening for the inevitable footsteps on the stairs.

But none came.

Outside, the edge of the moon emerged from behind its blanket of cloud, throwing a sliver of pale, ghostly light through the window and in a criss-crossed rectangle over us. And suddenly we were moving again: frenzied, desperate, our mouths meeting with such force that my lips were bruised and jarred, his tongue hungrily exploring the depths of my mouth, his knees pushing my legs further apart.

"India . . ." he growled.

His touch on my bare skin was blissful, unbearable; I writhed with longing, heard his sharp intake of breath—

And then his hand was clamped over my mouth, silencing me, stifling my cry as he claimed me; as the intoxicating shock of our union ripped through my senses.

"Fuck . . . India . . ." he groaned.

The darkness and the shadows converged, engulfing me. The inevitable, urgent conclusion to our long days of subterfuge and pretence.

"India . . ." His voice was ragged, harsh. "*Oh fuck, India—*"

A helpless utterance rose in my throat and I fought to hold it back; he pressed his hand into my mouth so hard that it must have hurt him. I clutched at his back, his shoulders, his tousled hair, held his face against my own, and kept it there until his stifled cries ceased too, sobbing, gasping—

You should keep away . . .

I opened my eyes.

The darkness suddenly seemed absolute, the stillness suffocating. Alex pushed himself up on trembling arms above

211

me, and for a moment I could see into his eyes, the burning intensity, the danger, the truth.

Then he rolled away without a word, leaving us both still and silent as we contemplated the empty ceiling, and realised what we had done.

CHAPTER 17: FOLLY

It was still dark outside as I showered. I took my time, watching the water run away, spiralling down the aged plughole into oblivion. I had wiped the shower screen. All there was to see in it was my reflection.

I leaned my head back, letting the spray run into my eyes and caress my skin. Like unrelenting fingers, lips—

I gasped and opened my eyes. There were no signs of sunrise beyond the misted window. No signs that the night was over, even though it was.

Oh, what wouldn't I give to be salvaged by you, India . . .

Why, then, was I suddenly not sure who it was that needed saving?

I washed my hair twice, the conditioner slick between my fingers as I teased out the tangles and snarls shakily. My rucksack was packed. There was a postcode in the last message on my phone. Just a postcode. No explanation. No instructions. Nothing but a collection of seven letters and numbers and his name at the top.

I dressed warmly, in tight jeans and a loosely knitted jumper over my camisole, and went to wake Alicia. It was just starting to get light as I made my way downstairs, distracted by the feeling of the smooth wooden floorboards under my feet. I touched a finger to my mouth.

"India!"

I leapt out of my skin. Julia Maine was in the hallway, looking up at me. In her hand was a dustpan full of earth and broken china.

I flushed ferociously. "Yes?"

"Sorry to startle you." Julia was shaking her head, tight-lipped. "It's just the sitting room door must have been left open last night, and one of Alicia's damned cats got in and knocked over a plant. An Evelynne Westerman pot, as well. An original! Smashed to pieces."

For a moment, I could have been combusting like Guy Fawkes, torn between an inappropriate paroxysm of laughter, and wanting to sink through the polished staircase. A strangled noise escaped from my throat.

"Oh no," I croaked. "How . . . awful."

Luckily, Julia Maine seemed not to notice.

"Can you check before bedtime from now onwards that the door is *closed*?"

"Sure." I tried to claw back my equilibrium, and descended the rest of the stairs, pushing open the kitchen door. I almost fell over my feet.

Alex sat finishing a glass of orange juice, his long legs crossed deliberately under the kitchen table, his familiar dark blue jeans slightly faded, crumpled with recent wear. And suddenly all I could think about was the unyielding press of rough denim: warm, hard, insistent . . .

He didn't speak. Didn't even look up at me. Then I realised with an icy jolt that Julia Maine was right behind me in the doorway. I stumbled gracelessly into the kitchen to get Alicia's breakfast things out of the cupboard.

"I'm going away," Alex said suddenly, addressing his mother. "To London. I'm taking the car."

Julia spun, taken aback. "Oh."

Disapproval reigned supreme. Her lips thinned.

"Not sure when I'll be back." Alex drained his glass of juice and stood up, head and broad shoulders taller than his mother. "I've got a few things to get together."

"You know what your father—"

"Yes." Alex cut across her impassively. "I'm aware."

"And the car . . ."

"I know."

"He's not going to renew the insurance."

"No." Without glancing back, Alex strode calmly out through the doorway and into the hall. "But *I* already have."

I heard him go upstairs. Julia stood, shaking her head. Then she emptied the contents of the dustpan into the bin with a clatter.

"Are *you* all set, India?" Momentarily her cool blue eyes were on me, and a wave of panic washed over me. Could she have made an association? *The* association? I stood very still, my hands closed carefully around the box of Cheerios.

"I think so." I smiled as best I could. "I just need to check some directions."

Why did I say that? Now she was going to ask me where I was going and I couldn't tell her. Literally couldn't tell her.

"Good." She dusted off her hands and threw the dustpan into the cupboard under the sink, where I was fairly sure that Vee would never find it. There was a ringing silence. I laid out the bowl and spoon for Alicia.

"Neil Warner asked John to tell you to send his and his wife's best to your mother." Julia crossed the kitchen to pour hot water into the cafetière, the heels of her shoes sounding smartly on the tiles. "Neil said he and Angela haven't seen her for a long time, and to ask whether she'll be at the constabulary Christmas meal."

I fixed my eyes on the bowl, counting its painted polka dots in my head. Angela Warner was my godmother. She had been my mother's colleague for years. It was her that had recommended me to John Maine for this job. And she didn't know. About the Shelgate Unit. No one knew.

"I'll have to ask her," I replied lightly. "I'm sure she'll be delighted to hear from them." Bullshit. "Perhaps John could pass on our regards?"

There were twenty-two polka dots on the bowl. At least if the Maines assumed I was going back to my mother's, they wouldn't think — wouldn't contemplate — anything else . . .

Wouldn't ever imagine . . .

* * *

Did I trust him?

I was in the middle of nowhere. I was in the middle of nowhere, watching branches bend and crack in the gale-force winds, watching sticks and debris torn from the trees slam into the tarmac and shatter right in front of my car. I was holding onto the steering wheel with hands that were slippery with sweat. I was in the middle of nowhere, looking up at the craggy ascending hills either side of the road, with my heart beating arrhythmically in my chest, and wondering—

"You have reached your destination."

I glowered at the satnav.

"Don't be ridiculous," I snapped. I jabbed at the touch-screen to find out what had gone wrong. The car ahead of me swerved as a huge branch fell into the road in a blizzard of old leaves and broken bark. I stamped on the brakes.

There was a gateway on the left, a track winding into a patch of remote and overgrown woodland, and I pulled in, apprehensive of the wildly dipping and groaning branches above me.

"Okay." I flicked through the satnav menu, failing to make sense of it. "Okay . . ."

I pulled the phone from my pocket and checked the postcode again.

"You have reached your destination."

Really? I punched the power button of the satnav, and turned off the car engine with a hand that shook. Was this some kind of a joke?

He hadn't been joking. I thought of his eyes locked on mine. Of his fingers, rough and careful. *I'll come and find you.*

The radio had died when I killed the engine. I switched it back on, trying to suppress the tremors that ran through me. I searched through my bag for my bottle of water and took a sip, turned up the music to drown out my thoughts. Drummed my hands on the steering wheel and checked my reflection in the sun-visor mirror again. I was a mess. I began to drag my fingers through my hair, trying to sort out the endless tangles.

Within ten minutes, the inside of the car was cold. Within fifteen, I was shivering helplessly, and my breath was making the glass mist up, bringing to life generations of Alicia's stick men on the passenger windows.

The flash of an indicator lit up the upholstery and reflected off the dashboard. I inhaled sharply, a new burst of shivers convulsing me as I punched the switch of the radio and plunged into silence.

He was driving fast. The black Volkswagen decelerated abruptly and swung into the gateway behind my car, coming to a rapid halt in the mud. And then he was climbing out . . .

The wind almost tore my car door out of his hand as he opened it.

"You're here."

There was something startled in his statement. In his intense, excruciating stare. Exhilarated disbelief. I suddenly realised that I was holding my breath.

"Yes," I whispered.

A hint of a smile played at the corner of Alex's mouth. Another gust of wind caught the door, and he grabbed it, hard.

"Good."

For a moment neither of us spoke.

"Follow me." He was struggling to hold open the door. "It's muddy. Are you okay to drive?"

I nodded, speechless.

He reached out, as if to touch me, and then changed his mind. The car door slammed. The wheels of the Volkswagen spun in the mud as he turned onto the track, and I cajoled my car into motion behind him.

It was his car that got stuck first, splatters of wet grass and mud flying up over the bonnet. I steered around him, off the track and parked as he got out, swinging a rucksack and his tattered guitar case from the passenger seat behind him.

"This way." His words were lost almost completely to the wind. I pulled my rucksack from the back seat and fought to put on my waterproof as a film of drizzle hit my face, clinging to my eyelashes. The track ascended a slope through the trees; I followed him upwards, scrambling breathlessly, watching his easy strides and the way the squalls of wind blasted through his hair. We emerged onto a ridge of moorland, a hundred colours of bracken, gorse and heather. The wind redoubled. In front of us, the track dropped away, treacherously wet, then curled into the valley below. Beyond it, the hillside reared up again, tall and barren.

I drank in a deep breath, stunned by the cold rushing air, by the colours, so vivid; unreal, a work of art. A landscape painting.

I stared, realisation dawning slowly. *A stone cottage nestling in a valley.* In a frame above the bed, looking down over the thrown-back covers and manuscript paper.

The tiny building was old and irregular, constructed of lichen-covered stone and grey slate, all corners and angles. It was charming in its dilapidation: taller at one end than the other, its roof sloping, its narrow chimneys misaligned. What used to be a waterwheel, now only a monument to a bygone time, dipped its skeletal remains into the river that crept its way along the valley floor.

I stumbled as a gust of wind caught me, whipping my hair across my face. Alex had drawn ahead and paused. He turned back to watch. I caught him up, suddenly self-conscious.

"These hills are at the edge of the Dark Peak." His eyes were on mine. "It's pretty wild. Not many people come here."

"The house. It's the one from the picture. In your room."

Something fleeting crossed his face, an expression that I couldn't name.

"Yeah," he said. "It is."

We started to descend in long, leaping strides. In just a few paces, we were out of the roaring wind, and the hush was disarming. The valley was sheltered; even the light rain had stopped. I paused.

Very faintly, on the breeze, I could hear a sound. A soft, musical clamour, waxing and waning: out of time and out of context. I squinted ahead, to where Alex had almost reached the cottage.

There was a terrace running along the far end of the building: a wooden platform and rails, roofed over with slate, the boards crisp and surprisingly new in contrast to the weathered stone. Alex took the set of steps up to it in one effortless bound.

As I approached, the sound reached me again. The faint ring of wind-chimes, somehow eerie in the otherwise total silence. Alex ducked his head as he walked between them, hanging tubes and bells of every shape and size swaying gently as he passed. I mounted the steps behind him one at a time. The senseless peal of the wind-chimes filled my ears, gentle and insistent.

"What is this place?" I raised my eyes to his face as he replaced a loose board at the corner of the house and straightened.

"It belongs to my uncle. My mother's brother." He held out his hand, and I suddenly realised that he was holding a key. "He calls it his folly."

The door was sturdy, old-fashioned but new; the key turned easily, with a soft, permissive clunk. Alex swung his bag from his back, pushed open the door, and paused, waiting. Waiting for me.

"He won't tell anyone. He and my mother don't see eye to eye. They certainly don't talk. No one has to know."

I stepped inside, damp, windswept and breathless. My heart was in my throat. My face was burning, the tops of my ears, and the back of my neck as he crossed the threshold behind me and ran a finger gently through my hair.

I turned, wordless, straight into his arms. Straight into his stare. Perhaps we were both holding our breath.

Something in his face made my insides dissolve. The conflict of expressions in his bright, dark eyes: seductive, searching . . . shy? His hesitancy made my heart miss a beat.

"What do you think?"

It was in his voice, too. A note of uncertainty. I had the sudden overwhelming urge to wrap my arms around him. Instead, I let the rucksack slip from my back to the floor, let my gaze travel over the room; the wood burner in a beautiful old stone fireplace, the one sofa, the tiny open-plan kitchen where we stood now, all quarry tiles and simple woods. The low doorway on our right, slightly ajar; another room invisible behind the age-warped beams. We weren't just an hour from Rifway. We were a lifetime away.

"Tell me." He pulled me close to him, his voice a murmur against my hair. "Tell me what you're thinking."

"I don't know." I let out a tremulous breath. Alex released me. I took off my coat and touched the back of the sofa lightly. He was still watching me as I sat down tentatively on the edge of one of the cushions.

"I don't know what I'm thinking." My voice was a whisper. "I don't know what I *should* be thinking. I don't know anything. About you. About . . ." I trailed off, suddenly nervous. Crossed my legs, gripping my foot tightly over my knee and trying not to see it: the picture, yellow petals and thorns . . .

"What is it you want to know?" Alex asked softly. The corner of his mouth quirked upwards. "There isn't much to tell. You've probably already heard everything from other people anyway." He sat down beside me. "While, on the other hand, I don't know anything about *you*. I don't even know your second name, India."

"Oh." I looked up, surprised. Somehow, even now, he had the power to leave me speechless and stumbling.

"You're a mystery." His fingers travelled over the back of my wrist to my ankle, to the rose; he traced the outline with his index finger, the hint of a frown playing between his dark brows. "A girl without a past, who just materialises one day in my parents' house, all smiles and sadness . . . and secrets. Secrets that no one else notices."

"I don't have—" I stood up again, my cheeks on fire. "I mean—"

"*I* noticed." Alex stood up too. His enigmatic smile, the danger in his downward glance, made my legs suddenly weak and my mouth unreasonably dry. There was a momentary silence.

"McKenzie," I whispered at last. "My surname's McKenzie."

He took a step closer, so close that I could look at nothing but him. His fingers curled under my chin, his thumb travelling lightly over my cheek.

"No past suits me, India McKenzie." His lips were close against my ear, sending a shiver through me. There was something haunting in his whisper. "A future would do me just fine."

"Oh." The shivers overtook me.

"You're cold." He frowned.

There were logs in a circular holder on the hearth. Alex released me, and went to stoke the wood burner. I watched for a while, paralysed by the contrast of smouldering darkness and bright blue eyes. By the memory of broken china, fingertips, lips.

Eventually I picked up my rucksack from beneath his and eased open the bedroom door instead. It was a simple room, furnished with only a pine wardrobe and bed, and an old wooden blanket chest. A window took up almost the entirety of the far wall.

I dropped my rucksack.

The view was spectacular. On the other side of the glass, the ground dropped almost vertically down to the river, its greyish water churning and swirling endlessly. The opposite bank was wild and bleak, punctuated only by patches of gorse and fading heather, and behind that the ground swept upwards, the imminent hills drawing a peaked and magnificent boundary against the sky. I pressed one hand to the glass, watching the condensation spread outwards from my fingers, staring at the vivid green grass and gathering storm clouds. At the beautiful, uninhabitable landscape beyond.

I was so absorbed that I didn't hear him come in. Didn't realise he was there, until his hand covered mine, its warmth a stark contrast to the cold glass under my palm.

"You have no idea, do you?"

Alex was frowning. I turned in the circle of his arms.

"You have no idea at all."

"No idea of . . ." I faltered. "No idea of what?"

"What you do to me." The tiniest of smiles flared, faded. He lifted a stray lock of my hair, twisted it between his finger and thumb.

"It was unbearable. Don't you see? Every day that passed, and you somehow worked your way into every thought, every *single* thing I did. And yet I knew sooner or later they'd convince you. Just like everybody else. They'd destroy me, right in front of you — teach you to hate me."

He broke off. There was something in his expression that terrified me. Passion, blackness.

"Or worse, to be afraid of me."

"I'm . . . I mean," I swallowed. "I . . ."

"Don't say it," he whispered.

"I'm not afraid of you."

He exhaled slowly. "India . . ."

His hands inside my clothes were warm, careful; I reached to help him take off my jumper, slid my cool fingers between the buttons of his shirt and felt him flinch, felt his sharp intake of breath as it fell undone and he drew me against him.

"What?" My mouth was dry.

"Nothing." The blue of his eyes was immeasurably deep. Deep enough to drown in. I reached out to touch his mouth, tracing the remnants of his smile with one finger. He caught my hand and held it there.

"Don't look at me like that."

The memory lanced through me, sweetly, agonisingly fresh.

"Like what?"

"Like that." He lowered my hand and his lips touched mine, his voice a murmur, vividly dark. "Like that, like before . . . so unsure, so full of secrets."

His fingers twined through mine, and in a single, breathless step we were pressed against the bed.

I blinked. "I . . . don't have secrets."

Alex raised his eyebrows. "I think we both have secrets, India." His voice was very soft.

Oh. *A hundred letters . . . a thousand pencil-drawn notes.* I was losing my grip, submerged in a storm of blue as he pushed me gently backwards . . .

"I'm sorry," he whispered.

"What . . . ?"

"Last night . . . wasn't how I meant it to happen." Once again, I couldn't read him, the conflict of vulnerable smiles and seductive shadows. His fingers toyed with mine. "But it seems that when it comes to you, I'm not exactly a model of self-restraint."

"Alex . . ." I reached out my free hand for him, but he caught that too.

"No." His lips touched mine, a sweet, lingering kiss that left me reeling. His mouth was hot against my ear. "This time, I'm going to do it properly." It was a breath, nothing more, and it jolted through me like electricity. "I'm going to kiss you, and then we're going to do this the way I meant to."

He let go of me, just for a moment, to slip the straps from my shoulders, to drag down my jeans, his intense gaze locked on mine, gauging my reaction. I was dizzy, incoherent.

"Alex, I—"

But his mouth was on mine, fiercely gentle, his fingers tightening through my own. Then his lips travelled downwards, over my throat, my shoulders, and I struggled to free my hands.

Alex broke off, breathing deeply, unevenly. Smiled his tiny, heart-breaking smile.

"It's strange." His whisper was ragged. "The one thing it takes. One thing, one moment, that can change everything. That can make it worthwhile waking up every day."

I froze.

"You remember?" His eyes burned into mine.

"I . . . Of course I remember."

"Good," he exhaled.

His lips resumed their course, his hands holding mine harder. If I closed my eyes, I saw autumn leaves and guttering flames. I opened them again, and looked down. Alex's lips traced my ankle, the outline of the yellow rose. A shudder ran through me.

But perhaps I didn't need them anymore. The secrets. The scars.

Alex shifted, his weight heavy on top of me, holding me down, his face above mine, all sultry shadows and sincerity. His hands circled my wrists.

"I'm not going to let go of you, India." His voice was soft, molten. "Not ever."

And then he eased into me, and I cried out into his mouth. He kissed me again, hard, his teeth tugging at my lower lip, one hand cradling my cheek as he took me, slowly. We were only need, bittersweet and perfect. Only sensation. Nothing else on Earth mattered, nothing but this . . . what we should never even have thought of, but was all I *could* think of.

Alex inhaled sharply. "You. Are." His jaw was clenched; he spoke between gritted teeth. "So. Beautiful."

I let my fingers close, painfully tightly, in his dark hair.

"Alex." It was a sob, frantic and longing. "*Alex. Please*—"

His fingertips dug into me; I felt the tremors run through him, felt the sheen of sweat on his skin as his arms slipped behind me to lift me, crushing the breath from my lungs.

"I. Want. You." His whisper rose unevenly, desperate and forceful. "So . . . *much*."

He choked back his cry, and the sound was my undoing. My thoughts spiralled, seduced by the darkness, surrendering wholly to his hold.

And he didn't let go. *Not ever.* Not as we collapsed together, spent and gasping, into the unmade covers. Not as the twilight fell around us, a thousand shades of blue and grey, rippling with the reflections of the river in the glass. And I knew that it was too late. That there was no choice to make. No safe alternative. No other way. His gaze consumed me; I was adrift in the shadows, swallowed by them. Willingly, wantonly and completely.

He reached out one hand to touch my cheek.

"Let me in, India." His eyes saw straight through me, piercing, blazing blue. "Don't have secrets. I want to know. Everything."

I opened my mouth to reply, but there were no words. The night was descending around us. And I was lost. Truly.

"I want to know. Because you're the one thing, India McKenzie."

CHAPTER 18: MOTH/FLAME

Slowed to nonsense, she almost turns, as if she might be able to hear me scream. But she doesn't. She doesn't hear. There's no sound. Someone has muted it and I can't warn her. I want to close my eyes. If I can't unmute it, I want to stop it. But I can't do that either; all I can do is watch, again. Again . . .

"India."

The voice penetrated everything. But it wasn't hers.

"India." Alex's lips were against my clammy forehead, his fingers stroking, smoothing back the locks of damp hair; I blinked, trying to dispel the image but it was still there, so vivid that I was afraid if he looked hard enough, he'd see them too: the cracks spidering across the glass.

It was dark, he was dazed, not long woken, concern etched across his lowered brows. It took me a moment to orientate myself to the buzzing silence, the warm covers, the black ripple of reflected water in glass. To the heat of his body, wrapped around mine, as though he might be able to keep it away from me, my own subconscious. His thumbs pressed my cheekbones, wiping tear after tear until I drew a shuddering breath in.

"What is it you dream about?" The tiniest shake of his head. His eyes demanded an answer I couldn't give.

"It's every night, isn't it?"

Glass. Blood. I breathed out again. In and out. What could I reply? I didn't quite nod.

"It kills me," he whispered. "When I can't come to you."

Something in my heart was hurting. I couldn't speak, still mute, like the dream.

"I want to make it stop." There was a stubbornness in his jaw, a pain in his dark eyes, that made me think of the small boy in the cassock. The boy without love.

I met his gaze, just for a second. Shook my head. Beyond the glass, there was a red rim of dawn on the horizon.

"What if no one can?" I whispered.

* * *

Perhaps we worked on the premise that if you don't sleep, you can't dream. Red became pink, and then gold. Look became touch. Want merged into need and back again, the flow of skin on skin and the rush of co-mingled breath. There was no definition to the hours between darkness and day. The room became warm, and drenched in sunlight that poured over the bed and dripped into the dislodged pillows. The sky outside was bright and hard; the breeze rushed around the folly, blowing the rocks and paths forcefully dry, rattling the slate roof-tiles and wailing in the crooked chimneys.

Alex lay watching me, arms folded across his chest, dark hair ruffled against the white pillows. I glanced up at him from the foot of the bed. He was still half entangled in the cast-off covers, motionless, and heart-stoppingly beautiful.

"What are you doing?" His voice was soft, perhaps amused.

I hauled the jumble of clothes from my rucksack.

"I need a sweater."

He slid out of bed and pulled on his jeans. "You look fine to me."

He padded round the bed to join me, his feet bare on the boards, and planted a kiss on my neck as I stood up, too.

"What's this?" He nodded to the cascading pile of clothes and toiletries at our feet. "No writing paper? No envelopes?"

"No." I extracted myself shakily.

Why have you stopped writing to me, India? Tell me why you've stopped writing . . .

He paused. I could feel his eyes on me. Their question.

Then he stepped away. I followed him to the living room.

"Are you hungry? I thought we could take food out with us, if you're not?"

"Where are we going?" I looked up, despite myself.

Alex raised an eyebrow at me. "I don't know, India." His voice was softly teasing. "Where do *you* want to go?"

The recent memory lanced through me. His words, the look in his eyes, the hint of uncertainty that hid behind the shadows. Where? Anywhere. No matter how dangerous the ground, and even if it was a mistake.

"Have you ever been climbing? I know a good place for bouldering. If you trust me." His gaze met mine. "You didn't answer me, last time."

He jerked open the cupboard in the recess beside the hearth and started unloading its contents. I closed my eyes and thought of the autumn leaves and guttering, all-consuming flames. And a moth, drawn inexorably in.

I looked down quickly at the tangle of ropes and clips and fishing rods on the floor. I picked up two carabiners, toying with them, clipping them through one another with a snap. Alex tugged them from my hand and laid them down on the table beside the sofa.

"Well?"

At last I raised my gaze to his, my blush burning bright in my cheeks.

"Did I need to say it?" I whispered.

Alex laughed, dryly.

"You really need to stop looking at me like that," he said.

* * *

The millstone grit was punishing, abrasive and hard under my brutally cold hands. My fingertips were burning, my palms scuffed and my feet numb. The afternoon sun had peaked and started slowly to decline again, pale and clear in a cloudless November sky. The wind rushed in my ears.

"Above your right knee . . ." Alex was below me, looking up. "No . . . no . . ." He was laughing. "The other right. Left hand up first."

"No way." I clutched at the rock, pulling myself close against it. Some base instinct to do with centres of gravity. "Don't be ridiculous. I can't reach that."

"Go on."

"I'll fall!"

"Go *on*. I'll catch you."

"Uh-uh." I shook my head. "No way."

"If you don't, I'll pull you off," he warned me.

"No . . ." My voice sounded slightly shriller than normal. "You wouldn't!" I glanced down at him, realising that I wasn't sure about that at all.

Alex grinned. "It was *you* who said I'm not a bad person. Not me."

"I might be changing my mind."

I took a deep breath and leapt, feet scrabbling against the rock, and my left hand missed the tiny ledge by inches. I plummeted. Alex's hands tightened firmly around my ribcage, lowering me to the ground. His lips brushed my ear.

"You have to trust me, India."

I stumbled a step backwards, away from him. He was still smiling, hot and enticing. I clenched my smarting hands.

"It's *me* I'm having trouble trusting." I unstrapped his bag of powdered chalk from around my waist and tossed it to him. Alex caught it, weaving the strap through the waistband of his loose, chalk-covered jeans and brushing his hands on the soft, worn denim. I was staring shamelessly.

"*I* trust you," he pointed out softly as he swung around the rock, blue eyes scouring the surface for a starting point.

"I don't know why." I folded my stinging hands together.

"Neither do I." His voice was gently playful, his gaze unnervingly astute. "But I do. No past and all."

He crouched, wedging his fingers into the rock under an impossibly low overhang, then pulled himself upwards, muscle rippling tantalisingly in his back and shoulders. I wet my lips.

"I . . ." I couldn't take my eyes off him, pulse racing, suddenly flushed by vivid, unprompted flashbacks. I cleared my throat.

"I do have a past. It's just . . . just in storage."

"In storage?" Alex tested his weight in a tiny niche, and reached sideways. I watched his fingers work their way upwards. One lithe stretch, one measured step through . . . He paused, clenching and unclenching his hands.

"Yeah." I scraped the toe of my borrowed climbing shoe on the floor. Had it been his? It was old and child-sized, too tight. "Since July. My father lives in Massachusetts. I don't see him. And my . . . uhm . . . my mother's an inpatient, in a psychiatric hospital near where I grew up. She has . . . a kind of dementia. We . . . I . . . let out her house, in July."

Alex shifted against the rock to balance himself, dusting his fingers with chalk as he glanced down at me.

"You don't have anyone." His tiny frown was uncomfortably perceptive. "Or anywhere else. That's why you didn't know where you were going."

I looked down, wordless. Focused on the faded colours of my second-hand shoelaces.

I have Hope. For better or worse.

Worse.

I'm starting to wonder whether you read my last letter properly, India. Do you really still think it's a good idea?

"But there was a friend." He'd read my mind. He pushed himself easily upwards and turned back, hanging on one hand. "In the pictures. Hope. So why *are* you here, with me? Why not go to her? Why all the letters?"

Jesus Christ. I avoided his gaze.

230

"I promised I'd write to her." I shrugged, tried to keep my voice light. "And I wanted to be here, with you," I added in a whisper.

Dangerous ground.

A faint smile tugged at the corner of his lips. I raised my eyes slowly. He swung around without a word and I watched as he focused on a crack right at the top, sizing up the distance.

Fear pooled in my gut. I opened my mouth: *it's too high.* But I was mute, slowed to nonsense.

I saw him spring. His fingertips struggled for purchase, closed, briefly . . .

"Jesus. *Shit.*"

His body peeled away from the rock, pivoted; his shoulder slammed into it, gritstone mauling his skin as he fell.

And then he landed, catlike, and was straightening up beside me, barely even out of breath.

"Sorry." He grinned as I gaped at him. At his chalky, slightly tatty t-shirt and at the raw physicality of his muscular shoulders as he flexed his arm to examine the damage.

"Don't look like that." He was laughing softly, the youthful, heart-breaking smile still in his eyes. "Shit, that's sore."

"Do all your ideas involve this level of danger?" I had found my voice and lost my resolve. His skin was warm, the flesh of his upper arm hard and powerful as I brushed the dirt carefully from the grazes. A gust of wind hit us suddenly, side on, making me stagger. Alex planted a soft, not entirely chaste, kiss on my lips.

"I'm not sure that's a question I should answer." His voice was low, the words spoken under his breath. "We should eat. Are you hungry?"

"I guess."

He took my hand and led me around the rock, downhill and under a jagged outcrop, out of the wind. Everything was instantly, breath-snatchingly, quiet. His eyes were on mine as we sat, our bodies jammed tightly together in the recess. For a few moments, neither of us spoke.

"I have an audition," he said at last.

Oh. My reply stuck in my throat. Realisation crept slowly along my spine.

"London?" I whispered.

"The Royal Academy."

He was going to leave. I stared at the bag of food that I suddenly didn't feel like eating.

"That's amazing." I gulped. "When?"

"The twenty-third of December." He pulled apart a bread roll in his hands.

The twenty-third of December. I'd overheard him telling Iain Trevers.

I hesitated. "Do your—"

"Of course they don't." Alex laughed, dryly. "I wasn't planning on telling them."

There was a momentary silence. I fiddled with the laces of my shoes.

"Was it . . ." I blurted out suddenly. "Was it always like it is now?"

Alex's expression flickered. He finished his mouthful and swallowed, and in an instant the guard had fallen back over his eyes, bleak and impenetrable.

I dropped my gaze. "Your parents . . . I mean. Were they . . . Or is it just since . . ."

The wind was whistling around the rocks behind us, away across the hillside, through brush and heather.

"You can say it, you know." He crumbled the last remnants of the bread decisively, letting their dust sprinkle the flat grass. But I couldn't. I couldn't say it. I stared at the grass.

"Since the assault?" His eyebrows were raised. "That's what you're asking?" He shook his head. "You've met my mother. She wasn't exactly brimming over with affection before that." He laughed under his breath, and something in the sound chilled me. "She never had been. I wasn't the shining paradigm of childhood that she needed to keep up with her social circles. She lost interest long before Oxford and London. And my father . . ." He shrugged. "I don't know."

"You were never . . . close?"

"No." Alex shook his head again and pulled an apple from the bag, enclosing it in his hand. "I don't know . . . When I was a kid, he was never there. Maybe he tried when he was? I don't really remember. It wasn't often. He took me shooting sometimes. Taught me science. Tried to get me through my exams. I guess that was when he thought he might still be able to make something of me."

The observation wrenched at my insides: it was so flat, so matter-of-fact. I pressed my lips together, recalling what Vee had said. *No love at all.*

"When I got into Oxford, he actually smiled." Another humourless laugh escaped Alex's lips. "That was when he bought me the car — he'd always found it easier to throw money at me than use words — but I guess you could almost have said he was proud. So, no. It wasn't always like it is now." He ran his thumb over the top of the apple slowly, sending a shiver through me.

"He didn't hate me when he still thought there was a chance he might save me." Alex smiled, wryly. His voice was very soft. "But *you're* the only person who still seems to think *that* might be possible."

"What happened?" I whispered. I regretted the words the second that they were out of my mouth; I felt his body grow rigid beside me. "You said no secrets." I hugged my rucksack to me. Alex shifted his weight. After a beat, he drew his knees up to his chest.

"I don't know," he said at last.

I faltered. He crushed the apple in his hand, juice running like blood between his fingers.

"You really want to know what I *do* remember?" He looked up suddenly, and the hollowness in his stare sent a chill through me. "You really want to know?"

I wasn't sure that I did.

"I remember the look on his face when I pinned him against the wall. I remember that. I remember him asking me for money. He wouldn't take no for an answer. He just wouldn't fucking leave me alone, and I didn't have any. I didn't even have enough for the fucking train. *That*'s what I remember. Is that enough?"

"Alex . . ." I choked.

"I remember the station." His teeth were gritted, he had discarded the apple, and his fingers had ground deep into the mud.

"I remember him on the floor outside. I remember checking if he still had a pulse. People pulling me off. I remember the blood. How I couldn't work it out, what had happened, or why there was so much . . ."

I was staring, sickened. His eyes were still on me, but they didn't see me.

"No," I whispered. "Alex . . ."

I reached for his hand, but he wrenched it away.

"Don't." He spoke through his teeth. "Don't."

"But you—"

"But nothing." The self-loathing in his voice cut me to the core. "What I did to him, the injuries he had . . . it could have turned out very differently. If he'd died . . . it wouldn't have been assault, India. It would have been murder. Would you have been so desperate to know me then?"

Thundering feet. Flesh hitting flesh. A splintered banister. I studied my abraded hands, trying not to remember.

"I'm still that person."

"No." I shook my head. I wanted to show him. To hand him the other pictures, etched indelibly in my mind. Him beside Alicia. 'Minuet in G'. The two figures running in the long grass, breathless and exhilarated. "No, you're not."

"I wish that was true." He shoved away the ruins of the apple with his foot. "But there are some things I just can't run away from."

Run away? No. I took a sharp breath in. No. It was only me that did that. Who was I, to be offering forgiveness? Suddenly my throat was aching.

"It doesn't make a difference to me, Alex. I—"

What? I *what*?

"Maybe it should." His voice was hard. "The CCTV made good watching."

"You watched it?" I still felt a little sick.

"My lawyer did. She told me to plead guilty. Between that, the jacket I left at the turnstile with my driving licence in it, and the fact the guy identified me from the police VIPER, there wasn't much room for doubt."

"It was a mistake." I didn't know which of us I was trying to convince. "People . . . people make mistakes."

"Yeah," he said flatly. "Sure. Tell that to the guy I nearly killed. Tell it to the GMC. Tell it to my parents."

Ohh. I heard the breath escape between my lips. I pushed myself upright and manoeuvred around so that I was facing him. This time, he didn't push me away, although I could feel the tautness of his muscles, the tension of his folded arms as I pried them apart to sit between his knees.

Alex's fingers traced over the back of my wrist lightly.

"You have an unnerving way of making me spill my soul to you." His voice was low. "With barely a word. I can't understand it."

"Sorry," I murmured.

"One day." His eyes were narrowed. "One day, India, I'll work out how to reciprocate."

"Maybe there's no soul to spill?" I suggested softly. "Maybe there's nothing worth knowing."

Alex shook his head. "I don't believe that for a moment," he said.

We left the shelter of the outcrop and walked. Swapped our climbing shoes for the hiking boots in his rucksack, and set out into the brunt of the weather. The air was already cooling. It didn't seem to take long before the sun sank below the top edge of the hilltops, bleeding red through the heather, licking at the rocks and jagged scree slopes like flames.

It was dark by the time we circled back and made the descent to the folly, both of us stumbling over the unseen obstacles in our uneven path. My hands and face were numb, my ears aching from the wind's onslaught. The chimes on the wooden walkway jangled a wild welcome. Alex turned the key in the lock.

"If you won't talk about her, will you at least tell me about you?" He held open the door.

I realised he was waiting. "What do you want to know?" I didn't quite dare move past him. Suddenly, the deafening wind and merciless weather seemed a safer option.

"Why are you here? Why my parents, Alicia, Rifway? How do you know the words to 'Peggy Gordon'? Anything." He shrugged, but the azure darkness of his gaze penetrated deeply, impossible to escape.. "No secrets," he reiterated, darkly. The shadow in his voice haunted me. And suddenly, all I wanted was to wrap my arms around him.

"No," I told him softly. "A future would do me just fine."

I heard the rush of his breath between his teeth, and it was my downfall. I reached out to touch him.

"I was running away," I whispered. "But it turns out, there are some things you just can't run away from."

He frowned.

Inside, the air was strangely still. I stood watching as he kicked off his boots and moved to flick on the lamps, illuminating our surroundings with a soft glow that cast his shadow tall and looming on the far wall.

You still think it's a good idea?

It wasn't. It wasn't a good idea. I knew that. I was like a moth circling closer and closer to a flame. I was going to end up burning, it was inevitable, and I knew it was. But I couldn't keep away. I couldn't.

I unlaced my boots and went through to the bedroom to change out of my wet clothes, half expecting him to follow, but he didn't. Perhaps I was losing the ability to think.

Perhaps I really was losing my mind?

No.

You should have listened to what he said, India . . .

"No," I breathed. I put away the rest of the clothes quickly, shoving my rucksack under the bed.

Hope wasn't here. She didn't know. *Couldn't.*

I clicked off the bedroom light and paused. It was so very dark. I took a few deep breaths, trying to steady myself, and pushed open the door.

He sat at one end of the couch, turning the carabiners over in his hands, twirling the screw-lock absently between his finger and thumb. I watched him for a moment. No matter the questions, or the answers, just looking at him made my pulse race and my knees weak.

Alex glanced over his shoulder, his expression inscrutable. The silence consumed me.

"There wasn't a reason," I said at last. "To go to Rifway. Until I got there."

He put the carabiners down on the table with a click. Still clipped together, and locked now, inseparable. I walked around the sofa to join him. Instead of sitting beside him, I climbed onto his knees, sitting astride them so that I could look into his beautiful, guarded eyes.

I realised I was holding my breath.

Without a word, he tugged me forwards onto his lap. His lips were on the base of my throat, soft and inescapable.

"How . . ." His voice was a growl; his hands travelled over me from shoulders to waist hungrily. "How do you always know the one thing to say that will undo me?"

Undo *him*? I couldn't even breathe. How could I have chosen anything other than this?

I didn't close my eyes. Not as he kissed me, fierce and hard. Not as we came together, as he possessed me, forcefully and urgently. Not once.

We fell back together, our gasps coming in unison. It was realisation, elation. The darkness seemed alive with it. I reached out one hand to trace my fingers over his lips, and he smiled again, breathless and subversive.

"You're going to be the death of me, India McKenzie." His voice was uneven. "You know that."

I shook my head, smiling back helplessly.

One of his arms snaked around me, pulling me close against his chest. I let my head rest there, over the rapid pounding of his heartbeat. Listening.

"You realise, if anyone finds out. About this." He spoke under his breath. "It could be the end of everything."

He brushed the loose hair back from my face with his thumb and forefinger as I looked up at him.

The end of everything? I closed my eyes and thought of Alicia's hot hand slipping into mine. *I wish you could be my sister. Then you'd stay forever.*

Forever . . . Was there such a thing? Didn't they say all good things had to end? Maybe forever didn't exist. Maybe it never had. And if it didn't — if we couldn't *have* forever — then what about now? Was that what it was about? Now? Could *now* ever be enough?

Would it hurt, when I lost my wings to the flames? When I made one last circle, too close?

"I know," I whispered.

CHAPTER 19: THE PIANO MAN

Dear India,

I unfolded the paper carefully, smoothing out the corners.

This is just a quick note from me. You see, I just wanted to check that you'd read my last letter, that you'd understood what I was telling you.

Perhaps I didn't word it very well. Unlike me, but possible.

So let me rephrase. So that you do understand, India. You remember when Alex told you that you should keep away from him? That it would end badly?

Well, he was right. This will end badly, if you don't stay away from him. It will end badly, and not just for you.

You never used to be a selfish person, India. I hope that hasn't changed.

Think about it.

I miss you, India. Don't forget me. Promise me that?

Write back soon. I already asked once. And I know you have a lot to tell me about the folly.

Yours,
Hope

I traced the indentation of the writing on the page. Blue biro. The lettering was small and careful. I shuddered. The kitchen floor tiles were like ice under my bare feet. I reached out distractedly to retrieve Alicia's toast from the toaster.

No one knew. *No one knew.*

I scrunched the letter into a ball quickly, as if someone might have materialised behind me to read it over my shoulder. Then I remembered that there was no one else there, no one except Alicia who was still getting dressed. That John had left at six, and Julia had flown to Zurich for three weeks, and Alex . . .

Where *was* Alex?

I spread jam on the toast, and paced the length of the kitchen, putting down Alicia's plate on the table. It was Tuesday morning. I had arrived back in Rifway on Saturday night, and he had stayed behind. It had taken us half an hour to get my car out of the mud. I had left him in the gateway by the main road, his evening-sun silhouette dwindling in my rear-view mirror. There had been no sign of him after Sunday morning Mass, no sign of him as I picked at the Maines' obligatory once-in-a-blue-moon roast. No sign of him before the school run, or as Alicia and I wrestled with maths homework, or as I sat huddled on the windowsill of the drawing room in the early hours of this morning while everyone else slept, my eyes searching the darkness until they ached, staring across the gravel, scouring the lane for headlights, until I was shivering and exhausted and couldn't stay awake to watch any longer.

Five days had gone so quickly. How was it possible for two to pass so slowly?

I hadn't dared to call him, not with Alicia by my side for her every waking moment, and her parents close enough to overhear every other moment. His signal at the folly wouldn't be good enough anyway; my phone was the only one that had worked properly all week. Instead, I spent every waking minute checking if my messages had been delivered, and slept with my phone under my pillow.

I miss you.

When will you be back?

Soon. Not soon enough. God, if only I could tell you how much I want you here, India.

No secrets.

Except we both had secrets, didn't we? Because I hadn't found the courage to tell him the truth. Five days, five days of wilderness and wind and borrowed happiness, losing ourselves on the moors and peaks. Five forbidden nights of ripples on dark water, of candle flames and sweet sedition, and although his guard seemed to have lifted, I still hadn't told him.

He hadn't pressed me. *A girl without a past.* I knew he was waiting. It was there, in the spaces between the words, in the shadows cast by the embers. *One day . . . One day, India, I'll work out how to reciprocate.*

Maybe I thought if I didn't ask more questions, then neither would he.

I stared at the balled-up paper, overcome by a sudden, urgent need to dispose of it. No one knew. How could they? For a split second I considered putting a match to it, but immediately thought better of it. I would have to go outside, Alicia was awake, and—

"India?"

I crushed the page hastily and shoved it into my pocket.

Alicia was unfairly lively as she bounded through the doorway into the kitchen, fumbling to do up the cuff buttons of her blouse, before abandoning them entirely.

"Good morning, slow coach. Your toast's getting cold." I crouched down to do up the proffered buttons, and then rose to steer her towards the table. Alicia's shrewd gaze somehow seemed to see straight through my counterfeit smile.

"Who went on your holiday with you?" She climbed onto her chair, knees tucked under her, and stuck her two slices of toast together, jam splurging out of the middle and splodging onto the table.

"Uh . . ." I moved to get a cloth, dodging her scrutiny. "Why would someone have gone with me?"

241

"You said you went for walks. And played board games. No one plays board games *alone*."

"I went with a, uh . . . friend."

"The one in the pictures?" Alicia spoke with her mouth full.

I hesitated. "No, uhm . . . the, er . . . the one that sent me the messages." I wiped the table, struggling to lie, and quickly rescued the sleeve of Alicia's school jumper from the jam's firing line. "Please can you sit properly at the table, Alicia? And finish your mouthful before you speak."

"'*Don'tspeakwithyourmouthfull*'." Alicia glared at me. "You sound like my dad."

"Well, from time to time he's right."

"Ugh." Alicia chewed her toast emphatically for several seconds and then swallowed. "You were gone for *one* week and now you're being bossy."

"I was gone for one week and now *you're* being kind of rude." I raised my eyebrows. Alicia was still glaring at me. Then her face fell.

"It was *rubbish* with you not here," she told me glumly. She dropped the crusts of her toast onto her plate and sighed. "Even Alex wasn't here, either. Where *is* Alex?"

"I don't know," I replied. "Where did he say he was going?"

"*I* don't know." Alicia frowned up at me, then padded through to the hall to collect her schoolbag and blazer. I joined her by the front door, and immediately caught myself scanning the driveway for his car.

"Mum saw my piano book." Alicia was buckling her shoes, and the apprehensive note in her voice caught my attention in an instant. She stood up slowly. "She was making me do my piano practice, and she looked at it."

"Oh." Suddenly my throat felt dry. We stared at each other for a moment, conspirators caught mid-crime.

"Did she say anything?" I asked at last. It took a lot of effort to keep my voice even.

"No," Alicia told me darkly. "I think maybe that's why Alex isn't here."

I couldn't think of a reply. I opened the door and followed Alicia out into the driveway. If Julia Maine knew. If she had seen . . .

But *what* did she know? Really? If only she really *had* seen. Seen them there together, squashed side by side on the piano stool: Alex's gentle patience, Alicia's slowly blossoming confidence.

I shook my head.

"What are you thinking about?" Alicia sucked an unnoticed blob of jam from the sleeve of her jumper as we pulled out of the drive. My car was still covered in mud.

"Nothing." I shrugged.

"Can I play on your phone?"

Oh no.

"Uh, I don't think I brought—" It buzzed mutinously in my pocket, as if on cue.

Alicia folded her arms across her chest. "You can just say no, you know."

Just say no. But I didn't, did I? *You didn't say no.*

"Did you see your Guy Fawkes?" Why the thought suddenly entered my head, I couldn't fathom.

"Oh!" Alicia forgot about the phone. "Yes! Mum and me went and saw him at Meresham. And Lily was there with her mum and dad, and Lotty and Alfie and Mrs Bosworth and Maeve. He burned to a crisp. He was the best one, though."

"Right." I glanced at her, amused. Alicia looked thoughtful. For a while she didn't speak, leaning on her elbows to watch out of the window.

"India?" she said at last.

"Mm?" I shot another look at her as we pulled into the school drive. Alicia undid her seatbelt as we drew to a halt, and paused.

"You know once I said I didn't like Alex? That no one does?"

"I think so . . ." I replied.

"You like Alex, don't you?" Her earnest gaze met mine. I nodded cautiously.

243

"Well, I do too. I like it better when you *and* Alex are here. You make things happy. You make me good at stuff. Like netball, and maths. And camping was the best thing ever. And Alex has made me good at piano. *And* he did sparklers with me. Mum never lets me have sparklers."

I frowned, not quite sure where this was going.

"You won't go away, will you?" Alicia picked up her schoolbag and held it tightly against her chest.

I swallowed.

"I wasn't planning to."

Somewhere behind us, the school bell sounded. I glanced up. The sky beyond the playing fields was heavy with clouds.

Alicia breathed out a deep sigh.

"Good." She pulled something from her blazer pocket and thrust it into my hand. An ivy leaf.

"I know you're my babysitter." Alicia gazed up at me solemnly. "But you're the best friend ever. And I don't want you to go away again."

I flattened the leaf carefully in the palm of my hand.

"If I could've picked a sister," I reached out and ruffled her already messy ponytail fondly, "I would've picked you."

Alicia smiled widely. For a moment, we sat in silence. The bell sounded again.

I stretched over to re-pin her cardboard poppy back onto the lapel of her blazer. "Go on, slowcoach," I told her gruffly. "You're going to be late for assembly."

Alicia opened the car door and hopped down.

"See you later." She plunged her hand in her pocket again as she closed the door behind her, holding something up to show me through the window.

An acorn.

I smiled.

* * *

"Do you have a story you want to share? A secret you need to clear your conscience of? We'd love to hear from you! Call or text now on 0300—"

Ugh. I stabbed at the car radio and jumped as a hundred decibels of rock music blasted through my car. I fumbled to turn the volume down as I swung into the lane, the Manor lurching into view. I scrunched to a halt on the gravel and killed the engine. There was already a car in the drive. A black Volkswagen. Shiny and clean.

I climbed out and gathered the groceries from the back seat. The kitchen was empty. I dumped the bags on the side, and tiptoed through to the hall, suddenly on edge. There was no one there.

"Well, hi."

I started. A warm hand brushed the back of my waist, sending a thrill the length of my spine. I spun. Alex's arms slipped around me, pulling me close.

"Jumpy, aren't you?" he whispered. His lips brushed my neck and I stiffened involuntarily.

"I . . . Where have you been?" At last, I had recovered my voice.

"To the car wash." His tiny smile was teasing.

I glared up at him. "Where have you *really* been?" I frowned. "Since Saturday?"

"At the folly." Suddenly, he was serious. "Achieving very little and sleeping badly. Is my father at work?"

"Yes."

"Thank fuck for that."

This time, there was nothing gentle in his grip. His hands closed in my hair, dragging my head back, tilting my face to his. His mouth locked mine, urgent and forceful; I didn't even have time to draw breath.

"Come on." His voice was rough.

I didn't ask where we were going. He kissed me again, and took me with him, half-stumbling on the stairs. I caught hold of his belt as we reached the top of the first flight, off-balance and suddenly unsure how much further we were going to get. Alex's teeth grazed my throat, his hands moving beneath my clothes. Somehow, we navigated the second flight without falling. And then his door was clicking quietly closed behind us, and I inhaled the smell of his room, familiar and intoxicating, as he swept the cascade of manuscript paper from the end of the bed, his whole weight pressing me relentlessly into the thrown-back covers.

"That," he growled, "was the longest seventy-two hours of my life."

"Oh God, Alex . . ." I reached for him, tugging at his rugby shirt until he helped me pull it off over his head, mussing his already untidy hair. Then his legs hooked around mine, he dispensed with my jumper in one easy move, his tongue possessing my mouth as one of his hands slipped behind my back—

The hammering of fists on the front door made us both jump, followed almost immediately by the discordant echoing squall of the doorbell. I jolted half upright in surprise, still pinned between his arms.

A tiny groan escaped Alex's lips.

"Fucking not *again.*"

For a brief moment, we both halted, flushed and breathless.

I flinched at the second, insistent ring.

"Fuck." Alex glowered furiously over his shoulder.

He lurched to his feet, not bothering to retrieve his shirt before he jerked the door open and disappeared, his feet thundering on the stairs. I sat up slowly, listening to the clunk of the front door as he pulled it open, the exchange of voices, the crash as he closed it again. I heard him cross the hall, start back up the stairs, his footfalls heavy and rapid. Like my breathing.

Beside me, the bedside table was untidy: a mass of paper notes, a stopped watch, a single cufflink. Old photos: two photos, the ones he had taken from Alicia, before the camping trip. I couldn't help but pick them up. The door opened and I shoved them into my pocket.

Alex raised his eyebrows.

"I think you have mail." He crossed the floor to join me as I slid from the bed to my feet, starting to shiver. He held out the package and I took it, quaking. His arms snaked around me.

"It better be fucking important." His voice smouldered against my ear. "I had to sign for it."

But I couldn't reply. I stared at Hope's writing on the white Avery labels. All I could do was stare.

"Aren't you going to open it?" His breath was warm, the shadows in his face molten, inciting. One of his fingers resumed its previous course, regardless, tracing torturously upwards along my spine. I felt his dark smile as my body arched into his.

I shook my head. Put the parcel down as steadily as I could on the bedside table.

"Not right now." My voice was shaking.

"Your choice," he murmured.

"Alex," I faltered. "I—"

But his lips were pressed to mine, hot and persuasive. And I yielded to him, shamelessly. Blocked the thought from my mind, *this will end badly, and not just for you,* and succumbed. I clutched at him, hungrily. Wrapped my legs around him as we gave in to the inevitable: to the desperate, reckless attempt to quench the flames. The inferno from a spark; the inferno that was never supposed to have been lit.

And when it was subdued — the destructive blaze slaked, if only for a moment — he pulled the covers over us, wrapping them tightly around me as I shivered helplessly.

"Why didn't you open the package?" Alex's voice was very soft.

His gaze met mine, direct and assessing.

"Why aren't you allowed to play piano?" I countered, lightly. But the tremor in my voice gave me away.

He was undeterred. "It's from her, isn't it? Why won't you talk about it? Her? Hope? Your past?"

I looked down. Away. "Why don't you talk about yours?" My gaze fell on the photos on the table beside him. I heard him exhale.

"Okay." He nodded. "Sure. Let's talk about it." I froze. *Let's talk about it . . . Let's talk about how things are never as bad as they look.* "If you want to talk about it?" He released me. Sat up. But there was no hardness in his voice, no hostility. He slid from beneath the covers to pull on his jeans.

"I . . ." Suddenly I was uncertain, shaky. "What are you doing?"

He tossed me my clothes and phone. His eyes didn't leave my face.

"I'm going to show you somewhere," he said.

Oh. Something lurched inside me. I dressed rapidly, still shivering, and tried not to notice that he had picked up the package. That it was stuffed into his back pocket. He took me by the hand.

We were both preoccupied. I had forgotten about Tuesdays, and so had Alex. It had never really occurred to me that Vee didn't drive, that there would be no warning shot of a car on the gravel, until the skid and rattle of the switched-off hoover cornered the bottom of the attic stairs and Alex halted abruptly halfway down, my hand still in his. Beyond the buzzing in my ears, I heard his whispered expletive.

Vee looked up.

She didn't miss a beat. Just carefully manoeuvred the hoover past the foot of the banister, her eyes lingering on us for only a fraction of a second longer than was customary.

"Duck." She nodded. "Alexander."

And she was gone, clattering towards the playroom, and the hoover droned into noisy life.

"Alex . . ." I couldn't hide the note of panic in my voice. His eyes had darkened, and his jaw was tightly set. I saw him swallow.

"It's probably best if you *don't* come with me right now." His gaze was still fixed on the other end of the landing, where the hoover reverberated its way around the toys I hadn't picked up.

I nodded. The white noise still hadn't quite receded from my ears. My fingers slipped from his. "I'll message you," I rasped.

He nodded. Neither of us moved. His eyes scoured my face. Then without another word, he descended the last few stairs, crossed the landing, and disappeared.

I felt as though all the breath had left my body. I slid the rest of the way down and sat on the bottom stair, the phone in my pocket cutting uncomfortably into my thigh. I prised it out with shaking fingers and laid it on the step with a click.

"I won't tell them, duckie, if that's what's eating you."

My head snapped up. The whine of the hoover had stopped and Vee was in the playroom doorway.

For a second I must have stared at her, wide-eyed. I couldn't formulate a reply. She hobbled over and lowered herself with a grunt onto the penultimate stair, next to me.

"Find out enough of people's secrets in my line of work to know when to keep my mouth shut. But if you don't mind me saying, duck, I hope you know what you're doing."

I drew in a tremulous breath. "So do I."

"He's a handsome lad, sure enough, he always has been. Like his mother. Even when he was tiny. But there's a cruel streak runs in the family. And he's a product of the life that's made him. I don't want to sound like your nana, but you want to be careful."

A cruel streak? I realised I was frowning, and raised my eyes to her creased face. How did everyone have him so wrong?

"He isn't cruel." I forced myself to unclench my teeth.

"People can be lots of things, and none of them, duck." She patted my knee. "I remember the day he brought a little dog home. Ugly mongrel of a thing. Someone had given it him. His mother nearly hit the roof. But his father said let him keep it, that it'd be good for him to learn some responsibility. Well he doted on the little thing. Kept it in the garages and down by Roy's shed. Trained it and walked it himself. First thing he'd ever showed some love for. He must have been about ten. Then one day, he turned on it. Roy found them down there by the shed, the little boy sobbing over it. Hit it round the head with a cricket bat. He was still holding it, all covered in blood. It was so close to dead they had to get the vet out and put it down."

"That isn't true." My frown had deepened. "It can't be."

"He's got a temper on him, duck, that's for sure. And it's no secret what happened in London before he came back here."

I didn't have a reply. I stared at my lap a moment longer.

"Not that I'm saying it's all his fault. No child should have to grow up without his mother's love. She has her own skeletons that's played their part enough in all this. Perhaps he'd have been different if she hadn't."

"Skeletons?" I looked up sharply.

"Not mine to share." Vee shook her head, but her wrinkled lips had pursed. "Let's just say it takes a certain sort of person to walk away from what she walked away from."

I picked up my phone from the stairs. There seemed to be an awful lot of skeletons in this place. And ghosts. I shuddered and pushed myself to my feet.

"Just be careful, duck," she reiterated. For a split second, her bony hand rested on my forearm in earnest. "Don't get hurt."

"I won't," I whispered. But as I walked away, I was fairly sure that I saw the tiniest shake of her head.

* * *

I drove in silence until I spotted his car. He was parked in a bus stop and I flashed him out. Followed him through the village, past the church, to School Lane. It had rained since I'd dropped off Alicia; the road was a dead end, riddled with potholes and puddles.

I looked out of the window at a row of terraced cottages, an old overgrown playpark with its swing seats missing, allotments, a few abandoned runner bean frames. The gardens of the former vicarage, now overrun with brambles. At the end of the street, the road became a footpath. Alex drew to a halt beside the last building and swung himself out of the car. I followed suit.

The final building in the lane was built of stone, like the Manor. It was perhaps Victorian, and crumbling slowly. It had clearly been a school once: the fence in front was broken and revealed a weed-riddled former playground, with faded red and yellow hopscotch lines still visible on the cracked tarmac. The windows facing the road had been boarded up and at the end of the building closest to us were two doors, the script above them as legible as on the day it was inscribed, but better endowed with lichen: *Boys* and *Girls*.

"This way." Alex rooted in his pocket for a key and jerked his head towards the playground. I looked up. Behind him, the boards in one window had come loose and hung at an angle, revealing the shadows of a room behind the dusty glass.

I followed him around the corner. Beyond the playground was flat, unkempt grass, and then fields of stiff, ploughed mud and bare hedges that stretched into the distance.

There was something undeniably sad about the old school's desolation. I imagined for a second the games that had been played on the now broken tarmac, and touched the photos in my pocket. Alex unlocked the door marked *Boys* and I followed him inside without a word.

We were in a tiny cloakroom, the walls lined with metal coat pegs at waist height, the names of long-grown children still written in teacher-writing on white sticky labels below each one. The faded lettering had an unnerving quality, as did the dusty nailed-down doormat and the long-dry wash basins on the far wall, stained by years of dripping water.

"This was my primary school." Alex said as he passed me, his voice echoing hollowly around the walls. I stumbled after him, lost for a reply, unable to drag my attention away from the names: *Jessica*, *Chloe C*, *Tommy*.

India.

Hope.

I fought off the memory and ran a few steps to catch Alex up. He held the next door open, and the smell washed over me in a wave — even after all this time — carpet cleaner and PVC glue. I blinked. The room must have been a classroom, judging by the stacked, much-abused MDF tables and the one or two dilapidated plastic chairs.

"It was only small. They closed it about ten years ago."

There was still sugar paper on the walls, brittle and peeling away from the cracked display boards, and pieces of work held up with drawing pins. I gazed around, unsettled, at the drawings and achievements, the pencil lines faded to invisibility.

"Through here." Alex gestured me around a corner, to another door. I found myself in a narrow foyer with two more doors off it; one painted red, with plastic safety film peeling off from its glass, the other heavy and sealed shut, a fire door, its slow-close mechanism snapped off at one end. Alex pushed the door firmly with his shoulder, and it gave with a reluctant groan.

"And this." His voice was soft, a breath, barely more. "This was the first piano I ever played."

We were standing in what had, unmistakably, been the school hall, its memories seeming to echo eerily around us. There was work on the walls in here, too: pictures, the words of a hymn printed on white paper and blanched into oblivion by too many years of daylight. The old parquet floor was split and uneven, and covered with a thick layer of dust, flecks of peeled-off paint, crumbs of plaster. There were two cupboards on the far wall, their wooden doors thrown open, their shelves emptied of everything but grit and forgotten split-pins.

An aged upright piano was right in front of us, keys gleaming dully in the low light, improbably clean and cared for in comparison to everything else. The top of the instrument was covered in paper and pencils. Scribbled notes in a small, cramped hand . . .

I realised I had been holding my breath, and let it out in a rush. I took a tentative step forward, to explore the piano with my eyes and fingers.

It was all here, in this room. The rest of him. The part that made him alive: daylight, light falling rain, birdsong .

. . I pressed my finger gently to one of the cold ivory keys, and the note rang out, pure and throbbing. I ran my palm over the tattered leather seat of the piano stool, taking it in, every detail. The pencils were all chewed at the ends. On the floor was a water bottle, half-full, and a selection of candles, mismatched and burned to various degrees.

Alex strode silently across the hall, pausing in front of the safety-filmed door that led out onto the playground: *Emergency Exit, push bar to open.* His breath misted the glass.

"This is it." I bit my lip. "All those days. I always wondered where you were. And you were here?"

He turned back. "Yeah," he said softly.

"How? How did . . . can you get—"

"Iain." Alex crossed the floor to join me by the piano.

"Iain?" I blinked up at him in surprise. "Iain Trevers?"

He nodded. "Yeah. He owns the building now. Or half of it, anyway. The other half belonged to Jim."

Jim. Jim Egan. I drew a deep breath in. The piano man.

Alex had paused. His fingers toyed with the corners of the manuscript paper.

"He planned to renovate it, to use it to teach from, turn it into a place for the community. He talked Iain into it — they bought it from the council for peanuts shortly after it closed, when they were talking about demolishing it. But it turned out the renovation costs were prohibitive. And since he . . ."

His face clouded.

"It's been abandoned." Alex righted the piece of paper, pushing it into the rickety music stand above the keyboard. "Iain can't afford to carry on with the project alone. He certainly can't afford to buy out Jim's half. And he can't sell it, because there was some kind of complication with Jim's will, or that's the last I heard."

"Poor Iain." I moved to touch the piano keys again, their shine an odd contrast to the surrounding film of dust. But I wasn't thinking about Iain. I was thinking about reverberating piano keys, and a thousand pencilled notes.

"Yeah." Alex's fingers spanned the bottom octave of the keyboard, the notes chiming in the muted air. "He's a good guy. When he found out that my parents don't let me play, he gave me a key. Told me to come here whenever I needed to. I guess that was better than it being wasted."

"Iain was close to Jim?"

"Close-ish." Alex nodded. "Not many people were close to Jim."

"But *you* were." I looked up at him. but Alex's gaze remained firmly on the keys.

"He was a talented man, India." He released the keys and let silence ring around us instead. "An unbelievably talented man. I'm sure he had his own problems. But what I knew of him was . . . that he was nothing short of a genius."

My thoughts returned fleetingly to Iain, and what he'd told me about Alex: *a better pianist at thirteen than I am now.*

"People didn't realise it. He wasn't educated — he could barely even write his own name — but musically, he was without equal. He could have been . . . I don't know." Alex shook his head. "He could have been so *much* . . . *done* so much. But he chose not to. He said he didn't need it. His success was through other people. I've never known anyone else like him, able to inspire, to impart ability and *passion*, like that."

Passion?

I tried to picture him, this man I'd never met. But a different image ingrained itself in my mind. The memory of the two of them together in the drawing room, squashed side by side on the piano stool, Alex's strong hands and Alicia's small ones. 'Minuet in G'.

"So." Alex closed the piano lid, a muted thud that ended my reverie abruptly. "You wanted to talk. Where did you want me to start?" His eyes were on me, level and inescapable. "You already know where it ends."

Where it ends . . . I slipped a hand into my pocket, suddenly nervous.

Badly. It will end badly, and not just for you . . .

I closed my fingers around the photographs. Drew them out, feeling him watching me. If he was surprised, he didn't show it. Only the trace of tension in his shoulders gave him away as he moved beside me to look at them. They were badly focused; coats, rucksacks, roll-mats, drizzle that stuck to the lens. Four teenage boys. The two in the middle had their arms slung around each other's shoulders: one younger and slighter, one older, a head taller, his eyes a paler shade of blue. I looked from Alex's dark and unsmiling teenage face to Brett's light-hearted grin, and back again.

"Brett Egan," Alex said, unprompted. "You met him. He was in the Green Man."

"Yeah." I felt myself colour.

"I wasn't expecting to run into him." Alex let out his breath between his teeth. "I hadn't seen him since my last night in London."

I stared at the photo., something dawning in my mind Egan. *Brett Egan.*

I lost my father six months ago.

He was Jim Egan's son?

"He's three years older than me. We were friends." Alex's brows drew together. "Close friends, once. I used to see him all the time, when I went to Jim's house for lessons. When we got older, he used to come to the Manor, too — my father took us shooting."

"You're not friends now," I murmured, my eyes not leaving the picture.

"No." There was a pause. Alex was looking at it, too. And at what had been lost, between then and now.

"Why?" I pressed my lips together, not completely sure that I wanted to hear his answer.

Alex shrugged. His voice was dry. "Why?" He took the photos from me. Studied them for a moment more, then scrunched them slowly into a ball. "Because of my parents." His fist closed tightly. "Because of my father, piano, Brett. It's all the same story, India. I started learning with Jim when I was eight years old. He came and watched me in the choir when neither of my parents ever did. It was his idea to apply for the scholarship to the Minster. And then, two days before the Christmas when I was ten, my parents said that was it. That it was stopping. That I'd go to Embarby. No more choir. No more piano. No Minster. They moved me in the new term. I never even said goodbye to anyone.

"But Jim was . . ." He paused. "An incredible man. He offered to keep teaching me regardless. I didn't see anything wrong with it. My parents were never home anyway. They didn't need to know. It wasn't like he was asking them to pay for it. I'd walk down after I got back from school, two or three nights a week. That's how I got to know Brett. I get, in hindsight, how it could have looked bad for him. But it was nothing like that. I don't think Jim could even have comprehended that people might perceive it that way. I carried on practising at home. They didn't seem to mind that so much. Until one day . . ."

A flash of pain, barely hidden.

"One day, my father found out about Jim." The muscles in Alex's jaw were tight. "He lost it. Put a stop to everything. Forbade me to go back there. He didn't want me in contact with Jim or Brett. When he realised Brett and I were still meeting up, he grounded me. Even cut off my mobile when he found out we were talking. We stayed friends for a while. But things drifted. When I went to Oxford, we lost touch. And then . . ."

Then? I wanted to ask. But I couldn't interrupt. Alex's gaze was fixed somewhere else entirely. Not on me. Not on the screwed-up pictures, the manuscript paper, the sorry attempt at daylight that filtered around the boarded-up windows.

"And then Jim killed himself."

"I'm sorry," I whispered.

"The truth is, I didn't cope with it. I was a fucking mess. I hated him, for not believing in me enough to carry on living. India, he was my life, as a kid. He meant everything. He was the only person who'd ever cared. I'd just finished my med school exams. I'd got a job lined up at Barts — I wasn't in a hurry to land up back with my parents. But I was spending every night looking for a way in — or a way *out*. Medicine wasn't for me, it was for *them*. I would have taken any chance to play, whether I could make a living from it or not. Jim was my inspiration. I was going to make it happen, like I'd always said I would . . . and he killed himself. He hanged himself, and all I could think was that it was because I didn't matter enough. If I didn't matter to him, then I didn't matter to anyone. Everything seemed pointless.

"I'd got mixed up in some stupid things at medical school. There were a few people there who thought they were above the law. I was caught in possession once, and spent a night in a cell because I got into a fight at a casino. I'd put all that behind me, until Jim died. After that, I guess it was self-destruction; if Jim didn't care enough to live, then why should I?"

His gaze returned abruptly to my face.

"And the whole time, I never spoke to Brett. I wasn't there for him when Jim died. I was too busy with my own pain."

I swallowed. The story had taken on a whole new meaning. All that had been left unsaid. The guilt, resentment. Futility.

"I never even contacted him, until he came to London that night." Alex took another deep breath. His frown had deepened. I could feel the tension, held back, in his shoulders. See it in his eyes.

"We threw a few punches, outside a bar. It escalated. Someone called the police, and I left before they got there. I hadn't seen him since. Until . . ."

He paused, and I remembered the night in the riverside pub, the wordless stalemate, the suppressed fury.

"It was after that that I went for the Tube." Alex let out his breath slowly. "You know the rest."

Suddenly, my heart was aching. For both of them. For the unspoken truths. The wordless, motionless stalemate. *What was lost* . . . Brett had lost his father. Alex had lost his world. And the pain — the pain was very real. I knew that. The kind of pain that couldn't be rationalised. It turned you into somebody else. Made you do things you didn't understand.

There was no blame to attribute. No side to take. After everything, the truth was just overwhelmingly sad.

"And that's it." He shrugged. "That's the story. I never went back."

The scrunched remnants of the photos fell from his hand as he drew me into his arms. For a moment, there was silence. I studied the shadows that the filtered daylight cast on the dusty floor. His index finger brushed my neck, parting my hair gently.

"So there you go, India." His voice was very soft. "I've told you more than I ever told anyone. And now it's your turn."

His finger had come to a halt. My head snapped up, apprehension seizing me abruptly, choking off my breath. Alex's eyes met mine, dark and calculating. Waiting. I sat down tremulously on the stool.

"What?" I whispered. "My turn to what?"

Unsmiling, he reached for the package. Pressed it into my hands, the brown paper creasing in my white-knuckled grip. His eyes didn't leave mine. And I realised, suddenly, that he was testing me. That he knew something. That he suspected.

Coldness flooded through me. Strangely calm. Strangely numb.

I sat up straight. Without a word, I ripped open the paper. I closed my eyes and slipped the handwritten note out from its place on top of the parcel's contents, folding it in my hand. I didn't read it. I was weakened, powerless under his scrutiny. My fingers found the edges of the package unwillingly; I tore off the rest of the wrapping, then stopped. I sucked in a deep breath, trying to stop seeing. Trying not to let the panic surface. Trying to endure.

"India?" The gentleness in his tone almost broke me.

I clung to the notebook with both hands. Brand new and unmarked, the cover never opened, not a single page missing. *Why have you stopped writing?* Two hundred sheets of paper, all decorated with the same picture as the front cover. Rose upon rose upon rose.

"*India.*"

His hands closed securely around my wrists, hauling me back to the real world. I gasped. Looked up at him, breathing hard. The letter was still in my fist. We were both staring at it.

More than I ever told anyone . . .

"I can't." I extracted myself from his grip, trying to suppress the shaking. So that he wouldn't feel it.

Who was I kidding?

Open your eyes, India. We're all fucked up.

"Sorry." I choked. "I'm sorry."

* * *

Dear India,

I wish it hadn't come to this. But here I am, writing you another letter. And you still haven't replied to me. You've got the gift I sent you. What more do you want? What more do you need? I forgave you for not writing while you were at the folly — you were busy, after all. Despite everything I told you.

You just don't seem to get it. That Alex is bad news for you. When did you stop trusting me, India? When did you stop listening?

I know everything about you, remember. I know. And I know what you've done, you and him.

But you didn't tell him our secret, did you? Perhaps you should have.

Why am I a secret, India?

Now write back. Write back and tell me how you think this is going to end.

Give my love to Alicia, won't you?

Yours (forever)

Hope

PS. Don't forget what forever means.

CHAPTER 20: JUMP

Four o'clock, and it was already virtually dark. The chill that had settled over the Manor early in November had never lifted. And now, as the days condensed and the nights expanded, it felt as though it was closing in: something worse than winter. Something colder and more inevitable.

I rubbed my arms, bracing myself for the onslaught as I opened the back door to call Alicia in from the garden.

"Alicia!" I squawked into the wind. My shout sounded tiny. Resigned to my fate, I slipped my feet into my trainers and braved my way over the doorstep into the courtyard.

"ALICIA!" I bellowed at the top of my voice.

I stood, waiting. The shapes of the courtyard were indistinct in the settling darkness. I searched the shadows for Alicia's returning figure.

"Alicia!" I yelled again. A cat appeared suddenly, blundering past my legs and into the kitchen, making me clutch at the doorframe in alarm.

"Alicia, come on." I took a few tentative steps into the courtyard, my teeth starting to chatter. "It's time for tea!"

"I'm here."

Her voice, close by my right elbow, made me start.

Alicia grinned up at me. "I made you jump!"

"Okay, smarty pants," I conceded. "Maybe a little bit."

"It's easy to make you jump these days," Alicia observed. I stared at her.

"Well, it is." She giggled. "It's funny."

Great. So I wasn't the only one who'd noticed.

"Tea's nearly ready." I shepherded her inside and closed the door behind us. Alicia kicked off her wellies and danced on the cold floor tiles.

"I'm not hungry." She shrugged out of her coat and let it drop on the floor, then drifted off towards the table.

"Please would you hang up your coat, Alicia?" I picked it up to hold out to her, with an element of despair. "Do you want beans with your sausage and mash?"

"I hate beans." Alicia collected the coat and headed for the hall.

"Peas?"

"Not hungry." I heard her feet on the stairs. There was a loud swoosh, followed by a crash. I hurried through to the hall. Alicia ran up the stairs and climbed back onto the banister rail.

"India, watch!" she exclaimed. "I can—"

I heard John Maine's study door open before I had a chance to intervene.

"Alicia—" I hissed.

"Alicia!" John stopped at the end of the corridor, his face like thunder. "Don't even *think* about doing that again! Get down. Right now. That was irresponsible and dangerous."

John shook his head, taking off his glasses to glare at his daughter.

Alicia clambered over the banister rail and ran down the stairs to take shelter beside me. I faltered, suddenly realising that I was party to the crime.

"Now, please go with India and eat your tea. I don't want to hear you playing her up anymore, okay?"

"I was only—"

"Now, please." John's stare was crushing.

261

"I was only sliding on the banister," Alicia whispered. "Like in *Mary Poppins*."

Silence.

Alicia vanished meekly into the kitchen. John's eye caught mine across the hall.

"Sorry," I mumbled.

John smiled mildly. "Not to worry."

I swallowed and started after Alicia, but John's voice halted me in my tracks.

"Oh, India. I meant to tell you that I have to go into the hospital tonight. They're short of registrar cover, so I said I'd be resident. Would you mind telling Julia, if she calls? I may not be able to answer my mobile."

I turned back hastily. "Sure."

"Thanks." He inclined his head curtly. Then he was gone, back down the corridor to his study, past the collection of family photographs, and the piercing-eyed chorister.

Alicia was sitting at the table drawing when I went through, with two spots of pink still burning in her cheeks. She glanced up at me as I came in.

"Are you scared of my dad?" she asked me.

"Er." I busied myself mashing the potatoes. "I'm not sure."

"I was only sliding down the banister. Dangerous schmangerous. Grown-ups are silly." Alicia pulled a face. "Except you, that is. But you're not a proper grown-up."

"Oh, *thanks*." I smiled wryly. "What's that supposed to mean?"

"No, it's a *good* thing. I'm glad you're not a proper grown-up. What colour is Mary Poppins's umbrella? By the way, you know Alex? Are you—"

"I'm going to work now." John's face appeared suddenly around the kitchen doorframe. I nearly dropped the pan.

"Goodnight, Alicia."

"Night," Alicia mumbled. Her father stepped through the doorway, and she stumbled to her feet to give him a reluctant hug.

John's footsteps receded along the hall, and the front door banged behind him. I let out my breath.

"That was close," Alicia observed, unperturbed.

"Yeah." I checked the peas and sat down at the table opposite her, listening to the sputter of sausage fat under the grill. Alicia went back to her drawing, and I pulled out my phone.

He's gone, I typed. Then deleted it.

"I think the umbrella's black." Alicia searched the jumble of pencils on the table, and picked one up to examine its snapped-off tip disappointedly. "Mary Poppins was a nanny too, you know."

"Mm." I stared at the empty message.

"You're prettier than Mary Poppins." Alicia discarded the pencil and picked up a red one, the end of her tongue protruding between her teeth as she concentrated on colouring neatly. "And also, she wears funny clothes. But your clothes are okay."

"Thanks." I bit back a laugh. Somehow, her comments always managed to save me from myself. I turned the phone to silent and got up to check the food.

"Have you washed your hands, Alicia? You should put your picture to one side, so it doesn't get tea on it." The phone lit up. I hid it quickly.

Alicia sighed. "I told you," she said. "I'm not hungry."

I delivered the food to her, itching to look at my phone. "Well, try at least."

"Hm." Alicia eyed the plateful with scepticism.

"I thought you liked sausages?" I turned to face the sink, so that she wouldn't be able to catch sight of the message as I read it.

Is my father at work?

"I do like sausages." Alicia stabbed at one miserably, holding it up on her fork to smell it. "But I'm *not hungry.*"

My fingers were unsteady on the touchscreen.

Yes, I typed.

Thank fuck for that.

"Why aren't you hungry?" I jammed the phone back into my pocket and moved to the table. Alicia dropped the sausage onto her plate and looked up at me coyly.

Her giggle expressed more shame than laughter. She flattened her mash with the back of her fork, avoiding my eyes.

I scrutinised her face. "What have you been eating, Alicia?"

Alicia reached into her pocket and pulled out a paper bag, as if she still stood a chance of winning me over.

"Do you want one?"

I think we both knew the attempt was doomed to failure. She handed over the mostly empty bag of bonbons.

"Where did these come from?"

"My friend." Alicia grinned at her plate, cheeks pink.

"What friend?" I stood up, in two minds as to whether just to give them back to her. It seemed a little late now for preventative action. And at least she had been honest.

"I'm sorry." Alicia looked up earnestly. "But I *promised* not to tell. It's a secret. Like you and—"

"Okay . . ." I backtracked hastily. "Okay. It doesn't matter who it was. But next time, if someone at school gives you sweets, you really need to bring them home and save them for after tea."

"Okay." She shrugged, unconcerned. "Thank you for my tea, please may I get down?"

I gazed at her, somewhere between disbelief and despair. "You haven't *eaten* it, Alicia."

Alicia knelt forwards on her chair, elbows on the table top. We stared at each other, a silent battle of wills spanning the width of the table.

The front door crashed open. I glanced in the direction of the hall, distracted. Alicia seized the opportunity and ran, her feet pounding up the stairs and into the playroom, and I was left contemplating her plateful of congealing food. I got up slowly to clear it away.

"Now, where did you pick up that kind of language?" Alex's voice was teasing. He pushed his phone into his back pocket as he reached me, and his arms slipped around my waist.

"Oh, I don't know," I murmured, cheeks alight. "I must be spending too much time in bad company."

He grinned. "You must be."

His mouth was hot on mine, insatiable. Fleetingly, his hands moved over my back. Then he paused.

"Alicia's upstairs, isn't she?"

"Yeah." I extracted myself and ducked away to put Alicia's plate in the dishwasher, concentrating on slowing down my breathing. Alex moved to the table.

"Mary Poppins?" He was amused.

"I'm not sure who that would make *you*," I muttered.

One of his eyebrows flickered. He set aside Alicia's drawing with an inscrutable smile. "I'm the bad company."

"Oh." I smiled, too. Glanced down, and then back up at him. His gaze travelled over me once, then locked mine.

"Stop," he breathed. "Looking. At me. Like that."

I froze. For a moment neither of us moved. My mouth was suddenly dry. "How . . . uhm . . ." I changed the subject quickly. "Were . . . Were you practising for the audition? Today?"

"Yeah," he said. Something in his gaze shifted, softened.

"How's it . . ." I couldn't keep up with the transition, from teasing to serious. "How's it going?"

"Good, I think." He nodded. "I've got three weeks. Should be more than enough time."

"What are you going to play?" I felt suddenly timid.

Alex regarded me for a moment.

"You want to hear?"

His shy smile made me catch my breath. I nodded without hesitation, and his smile broadened, blithe and disarming. I followed him wordlessly across the hall and into the drawing room. He closed 'Minuet in G', and sat down.

"What was it I said before, about spilling my soul to you?" he murmured.

I shrugged.

His right hand found the keys, a high C reverberating softly around the room. Then his left hand caught hold of my upper arm and pulled me onto the stool beside him with a bump.

"Oh!" I sat down heavily, taken by surprise. "Alex . . ." My protest hissed between my teeth.

He raised his eyebrows. "You *don't* want to hear?"

I couldn't tell whether he was teasing. In one swift move, he drew me onto his lap, his arms reaching around me, one hand still on the keys. I inhaled sharply.

"Is this a good idea?"

The tiniest smile reappeared at the corner of his mouth.

"I don't know," he whispered back, mock-serious. "I'm not sure if I can use the pedals."

"Alex," I murmured. "Alicia . . ."

"We can just tell her I'm giving you a piano lesson." He smirked.

He reached around me to the keyboard. The run of notes, the opening phrase, was familiar and yearning. Haunting. I'd heard it before, in this room; not just heard it — felt it. In the darkness, hidden in the shadows, hesitant and spellbound. A shiver ran along my spine.

Alex paused, his fingers lingering on the keys, his lips against my hair, bewitching and softly confiding.

"Is it wrong that I've thought about this a lot?" His voice was a whisper.

I couldn't reply, my attempt cut short by the gentle fall of notes, settling like autumn leaves in the stillness. I realised I was holding my breath. The melody surfaced, tentatively at first, then boldly, crafted by his hands. Singing into the heavy silence of the Manor like a bird singing out from a cage.

I had never heard anything like it. It was unguarded, exposed and beautiful, the counterpoint to his darkness. The explanations to his mysteries, spelt out in the diatonic scale, patterns, pictures, thoughts. I realised that for months, I had been waiting. For months, without even knowing it, all I had longed for was this.

I settled back, mesmerised, to listen. To his soul spilling in C-minor through the darkness. To the E-flat-major memory of our Indian Summer. To everything that was unsaid.

You didn't tell him our secret, did you?

* * *

"So are you coming tonight?"

"Huh?" I snapped back to real life with a jolt. Alicia was staring expectantly up at me. The rest of her class had already disappeared inside through the glass double doors, a rowdy chaos of seven- and eight-year-olds with hockey sticks.

"Weren't you listening to a thing I said?" She was scolding me, her breath misting in front of her red nose, her schoolbag sagging from her back, her hands lost in the sleeves of her duffle coat. "I told you last week. And the week before!"

"Told me what?" I rubbed my forehead, trying to pick up the thread of the conversation. Lack of sleep was catching up with me. I blinked hard, the December sun assaulting my tired eyes, and tried desperately to repress a sudden and inappropriate flashback to the night before.

"The Advent concert!" Alicia pouted. "I told you *a million times*. You practised 'Away in a Manger' with me! How can you *not remember*?"

Oh crap, December. Advent. I stared down at her, dismayed. Already?

"And." Alicia's face was like thunder, her voice dangerously low. "*You forgot the Advent calendar*. And . . . Don't pretend!"

I had opened my mouth to reply, but she held up a hand imperiously and carried on across me.

"Because I *know* you did. Because I found it this morning in the cupboard with the sewing box where Mum keeps it. And it's *empty*."

"I *am* coming tonight." I tried to placate her. "Definitely. Of course I hadn't forgotten about 'Away in a Manger'. I just hadn't realised it was today, because we didn't practise it yesterday. We probably should have."

"And the *Advent calendar*?" Alicia glared up at me murderously from under her eyebrows, in a way startlingly reminiscent of her brother. I swallowed.

"I'll get some chocolate to put in it today," I told her. "Where do you usually put it?"

Alicia rolled her eyes. "Never mind. *I'll* do it. When I get home. The concert's at four thirty. After school. Don't be late." She looked at me accusingly.

"Okay." I rested a hand on the shoulder of her duffle coat for a moment, starting to shiver.

"*Four thirty.*" Her eyebrows lifted.

"Four thirty," I reassured her. "You'd better get inside, you're going to miss register. See you later, Alicia."

"See you later." She was still looking at me, not at where she was going, as she pulled open the glass door and shuffled her feet on the doormat. "Four thirty, remember."

"Bye, Alicia." I smiled.

She rolled her eyes again. I watched as her small, bundled-up figure disappeared along the corridor, swinging her backpack carelessly from one hand.

I drove home in silence, imagining piano music. Imagining him in my room, closing the door quietly behind him, sliding across the bolt. Remembering his finger against my lips.

He had left my room at seven, when I went to get Alicia up, taken his score and a thermos and gone into the village. We had snatched a few last seconds together on the doorstep, the mist of our breath mingling in the icy beginnings of another day.

It was at the end of the lane that the blue lights caught up with me. Perhaps they felt less urgent for having featured in too many of my dreams, because for a moment, as I pulled aside to let them pass, I didn't process it.

Until they swung into the driveway of the Manor.

I suddenly felt as though I might vomit. The ringing in my ears was her voice, as clear as the last night I had heard it.

I wish it hadn't come to this.

"*No* . . ." It was a moan, from deep in my gut. "What have you done? *What have you done?*"

* * *

There were already three cars in the driveway. And the ambulance, pulling to a halt by the open front door. Three cars. A paramedic, Iain Trevers' dented Peugeot, and Alex.

Alex.

Panic tightened around my throat. I stumbled over the doorstep, sweat breaking on my palms as they came into view. Two, three green figures around the corner at the bottom of the stairs. Iain, hovering in the hallway, phone still in hand. And—

And he was there. Kneeling on the floor, each hand holding one side of her head to keep it still, like they did in TV dramas – and in my nightmares – a bloody streak across his forehead.

"*Vee?*" I whispered. It didn't compute.

"India . . ." Iain Trevers' face was ghost white. "Oh, thank goodness Alicia wasn't here. She . . . she's fallen."

"Fallen," I repeated stupidly. There were spray bottles scattered across the floor. Something smashed. The hoover; I could see a pipe. I didn't want to see any more.

"Alex got here just before I did. Thank God, because he knew what to do. It looks . . . it looks bad."

"I . . . need to go outside." Somehow, I made it back over the step, my stomach rolling.

"Do you have John's number? I can't get hold of Julia."

"She's in Zurich." I put out a hand to steady myself against the stone pillar. "John's at work."

"I thought they'd want to know." Iain was holding onto the pillar, too. I'd never seen someone look so ill. Then again, I couldn't see my own face.

"Yeah," I rasped.

Vee. My insides were in turmoil. Vee. This was my fault. She'd befriended me. Tried to look out for me, and now . . .

"They're going to need to get out with the stretcher." Iain sidestepped away from the door, his haste mirroring my own. We plunged through the stone archway and into the silent safety of the courtyard.

"Should I try Julia again?" I noticed his hands were shaking. I shook my head.

"No." I wanted to close my eyes and ears, to block out the sounds, voices — *one, two, three, roll* — ambulance doors.

"No it's okay. I can try John."

"Thanks, India." He exhaled. "God. What an awful, awful . . ." He rubbed his forehead. "Will you let me know when you hear if she's okay?"

If? I could barely let the word sink in. *If* she's okay?

"Yeah."

"I guess . . . will you still make the concert this afternoon? After . . . Or do you want me to—"

"It's okay." My voice sounded strangled, not like my voice at all. "I can't let Alicia down. I'll be there. It's not like I can do anything here."

"No." He nodded. "You're right. I'll see you later, then."

I saw him rub his stubbled chin again as he started away through the archway. I'd never seen him with stubble. Come to think of it, pallor aside, Iain Trevers didn't look like his normal mild self at all. He looked strained, unkempt. Almost haggard.

Which made two of us, probably. I slumped against the kitchen wall for a moment, trying to gather the strength to go back inside.

I wasn't brave enough to see if they were still in the drive. Or to walk back into the hall. I let myself in through the kitchen door instead. Then stopped, and looked at the reassuring normality of the breakfast things I'd left on the table. There was condensation dripping down the half-empty bottle of milk.

I started forwards again and then froze. There, on the worktop, there was an envelope propped against the toaster.

I put a hand out to steady myself.

Dear India,

You still haven't written back. Do you have any idea how that makes me feel?

Maybe you do.

It's just you made me a promise. You promised you would tell me everything. But you're not telling me everything, are you?

Why haven't you written to me? What's the matter? You think you're losing your mind? Is that the problem? I'm sorry, India. But we promised once to be honest with each other. And I think we both know that it's a possibility.

I could help you. Don't forget that.

You know, sometimes, when you lose your mind, people start to get hurt. People that matter.

Don't let anyone else get hurt, India.

It's like I said before. You need to stay away from Alex. Stay away from him, or it will end badly, and not just for you.

I'm your best friend, India. Remember? Forever. In aeternum. I have to warn you. I already tried, but now I'm warning you again.

Stay away from Alex . . .

People start to get hurt . . . I stared, unseeing. There was blood on the paper. *People start to get hurt.*

"No, Hope," I whispered. Begged. "Please. Please, no . . ."

What's the matter? You think you're losing your mind?

"No!" I sat down with a bump. "No . . ."

I drew my knees up to my chest, tightened my arms over my head, suddenly dizzy. And cold. So, so cold . . .

"Not true." I realised that the words were coming from my own lips; I was whispering to myself, half-witted and irrational. "It's not true."

What was I going to do?

"India."

I jumped. Scrambled to my feet.

"They've gone. Are you okay?" Concern darkened Alex's eyes. He looked drained. I shoved the letter into the pocket of my jeans.

"Yeah," I lied. "Are you?"

"I'm fine."

There was blood on his t-shirt. I was staring at it.

"India?"

"I'm not good with blood." That, at least, wasn't a lie. "Is she . . . Will she be . . . ?"

"She's badly hurt. And I'm not sure how long she'd been there. No one was here."

"Oh." I felt myself sway. "Oh God."

"I need to get cleaned up." His voice was almost cautious. He still hadn't touched me. There was blood on his hands, too, and his forearms. "But I don't want to leave you."

"I'm okay," I said with more resolve than I'd realised I could muster. "Really."

He frowned but didn't argue. His lips brushed my hair. I waited until he'd gone, until I'd heard his footsteps cross the landing, before I steeled myself to walk out into the hall.

There wasn't as much blood as I'd prepared myself for. A puddle on the bottom step and a smear on the floor that had already mostly been wiped away. I gathered up the spray bottles with shaking hands. The carrier was smashed. I righted the hoover and scrubbed the floor with Dettol. My teeth were chattering by the time I closed the doors of the cleaning cupboard. I scoured my hands in the kitchen sink until they were raw and aching. I could hear the shower running as I took the letter to my room and buried it with the others in the drawer of the bedside table. I sat down on the bed.

The sound of the shower stopped. Seconds stretched into minutes of silence. He came in without a word. Sat down beside me.

His hair was damp, his t-shirt clinging to his back where he wasn't fully dry. He pervaded all of my senses. His warmth, the smell of his shower gel, his bright, worried, beguiling eyes.

How couldn't she see? That the choice she was asking me to make was impossible?

His fingers encircled my wrist, tracing the goosebumps.

"I still can't make sense of you, India." His voice was very soft, his eyes locked on mine. "I try, but I just can't fathom you."

And if he could? If he had any idea?

All at once I had the overwhelming urge to cry. I closed my eyes, so that he wouldn't be able to see me evade him. Because, suddenly, I had the disconcerting feeling that he knew.

"Neither can I," I whispered.

CHAPTER 21: GIVING UP HOPE

The smell of mulled wine saturated the stuffy school hall, along with the packed heat of a hundred anticipant adults squashed into child-sized plastic chairs. A sea of incoherent conversation lapped at my ears as I hovered by the table at the back.

John Maine said Vee was alive. Her sister had come from Mablethorpe. Critical but stable, he said, the line they always fed you in the press when they didn't know which way it would go. He couldn't tell me much more.

I took a hot glass and fixed my gaze on the tablecloth, trying not to think about how much the crimson stains in the white calico looked like blood on writing paper.

I hadn't seen Alicia yet. I was almost glad. I had lost my ability to plaster a smile onto my face.

What's the matter? You think you're losing your mind?

I gripped the glass so hard that it was at risk of shattering. "India."

I started, and nearly tipped the wine down myself. I turned, tearing my gaze away from the tablecloth. Brett Egan's muscular arms were folded across the chest of his close-fitting black t-shirt, and his smiling eyes were narrowed against the glare of the fluorescent lights as he approached.

"What did I say about you turning up everywhere?" His voice was soft, teasing. I blushed.

"Alicia in the concert?" he asked lightly.

I nodded, mute.

"I'm lending them some equipment." He jerked his head towards the adjoining room, where the squawk of a poorly played clarinet was breaking through the ambient conversation. "A recording for the parents. You know."

"Oh. What a great idea." I couldn't muster a smile. I put my glass down on the table.

"It's good to see you, India," Brett said at last. "You look . . . nice."

Oh, crap. I dropped my gaze hastily. Looked back at the wine stains, colour radiating from my cheeks.

"Thanks," I mumbled. "You, um . . . too."

The pause was agonising. I couldn't make myself look back up.

"How's Alex?" Brett's voice was quiet.

I stared fiercely at the empty glass. "Oh. Um . . . good."

"Good." He smiled. Shrugged. I screwed my fingernails into my palms. Brett shook his head.

"Look," he started lightly. "I—"

"I'm . . ." I broke in, and then trailed off. "I mean, I—"

"No, really." Brett's gaze was level. "I'm glad for you, India. I really hope it works out."

"I'm so sorry." I raised my eyes at last, miserable. "About . . . I never meant for . . . to . . ."

The surrounding conversation was fading. People were taking their seats. I swallowed painfully. Brett uncrossed his arms.

"India, stop worrying about it." His fingers brushed my shoulder. "Please. Life goes on." His gaze was surprisingly frank. "You deserve to be happy. I hope it works out. I really do. For both of you."

"Ladies and gentlemen . . ."

We both glanced up.

"Year three and four are very excited to welcome you to their Advent concert. Would you please make your way to your seats?"

"I'd better go." Brett jerked his head towards the doors.

"Yeah," I mumbled.

"Enjoy the concert."

"You too."

Brett smiled, fleetingly. "See you soon, India." He pressed a hand briefly to mine in farewell, and started to move through the crush of people fighting to find their awkwardly small seats. I stood, motionless. The phone suddenly felt like a lead weight in my pocket.

"See you," I whispered.

Brett had reached the door. The crowd sealed behind him in an unswimmable tide. I made a conscious effort to unclench my hands. He turned back suddenly, startling me.

"Just—" For a split second his eyes were on mine, unexpectedly serious. "Just be careful, India."

I stared at him, unnerved. At the flicker of friendly, painful concern in his face.

"Don't let yourself get hurt."

Then he was gone, leaving me staring blindly through the mass of parents.

"I won't," I whispered, to no one.

Alicia's class started to sing. I hastened to a seat, and scanned the rows for her face, but I couldn't see her. The doors at the back of the hall opened and closed softly somewhere behind me. Finally, I located Alicia, hovering anxiously beside the piano, her music book held tightly in both hands.

I smiled at her, but she wasn't looking at me. I glanced over my shoulder, following her gaze to the furthest corner of the hall. To where Alex was standing just inside the door, unsmilingly reassuring, his eyebrows raised encouragingly at her, his hands thrust deep into the pockets of his familiar, faded blue jeans. My heart missed several beats.

"Go on," he mouthed silently.

Alicia bit her lip.

"Go on." He jerked his head. Alicia gulped in a huge breath, and stepped forwards.

"I would like to play . . ." Her voice was breathy and nervous. "'Away in a Manger'."

She sat down on the piano stool. I chanced a look back at the doorway. This time, Alex's gaze was on me, not her, and the darkness in his blue eyes was dangerous and intense. My breath hitched. I watched as he noticed me looking, watched his eyebrows lower tellingly, watched the tiny, seductive smile play briefly on his lips.

The stumbling piano chords broke the spell, and I looked away quickly, back to the piano, where Alicia was concentrating desperately on her hands. I could see her mouthing the words, pink-cheeked and determined. I focused, hard, on not letting myself turn around. Asking me to stay away from him was like asking me not to breathe.

The last few notes drew the piece to an uncertain close, and I let out my breath slowly as applause erupted around me.

"India." Iain Trevers' voice startled me. He was leaning forward from his undersized chair in the row behind. "Is there any news?"

News? I floundered for a moment.

"About your cleaning lady?"

"Oh." I swallowed. What did I think he'd meant? "She's stable, apparently. They wouldn't tell us much."

"Good. That's good." He was nodding.

"We're not going to tell Alicia. She doesn't need to know." About the blood. The paper.

"No, of course not. She played very well." He gestured towards the piano, but she'd gone. "In fact, she plays like a different child, these last few weeks."

He paused, the observation hanging between us. We both knew that he knew. There was a shuffle of movement as two dozen children got to their feet, and Alicia re-joined their ranks.

"Um . . ." I floundered, completely at a loss for what to say. I was saved by the singing. Iain sat back, and I gripped the edges of my chair tightly, too afraid to look round and see if Alex was still there. *I'm warning you again . . .*

It was my fault. It had gone too far. And now I didn't know how to stop it.

Tears of terror stung my eyes as a tunelessly crooned carol ended and the clarinet slaughtered a couple of verses of 'Have Yourself a Merry Little Christmas'.

What could I do? Who would be next?

I blinked, the applause ringing in my ears. Everyone around me was getting to their feet. At the rear of the hall, glasses chinked in proclamation of a second round of mulled wine.

"Iain." Alex's voice made me jump. I stumbled to my feet, the stranglehold of fear tightening around my throat as he reached past me to grasp Iain Trevers' hand. *Stay away . . .*

"India." He inclined his head. His tone of voice was inscrutable.

Iain stood too, and shook Alex's hand.

"Alex! I didn't imagine I'd see *you* here." He let go of Alex's hand and clapped his shoulder instead. His gaze travelled from Alex's emotionless expression to my deliberately averted eyes, then back again. I swallowed.

One of Iain's eyebrows raised a fraction. "Are you—"

"Mr Trevers!"

We were saved. A student in the same uniform as Alicia dashed up behind us.

"Mr Trevers! Sara . . . I mean, Miss Selleridge in the kitchen, wanted to know if . . . oh. Sorry."

"Oh." Iain's smile faded. "Sorry, India, Alex. I think I'd better go."

I nodded, speechless.

Alex shook his head, his eyes alight with something I couldn't name. He didn't touch me. Didn't come any closer. The awkward, respectable two-pace gap between us gaped wide and perilous.

"I didn't know you were coming." I looked up, suddenly remembering that Brett was here somewhere, too.

Alex shrugged. "My father left an answerphone message for you, to say he was going from the hospital straight to Gatwick for my mother. They won't be back until the early hours. So I took my chance."

"Alicia saw you. Do you have any idea how happy she'll be?"

Alex laughed softly. Something in his expression sent a chill through me. He glanced around at the milling parents, familiar and unfamiliar faces.

"Dangerous ground, India McKenzie," he whispered.

His forefinger brushed the back of my wrist. And then he was gone, disappearing adeptly into the shadows.

* * *

My car was covered in a thick layer of ice by the time I emerged into the school drive with Alicia, who had her piano book clutched tightly against her chest.

"India." Alicia scrambled into the car as I scraped holes in the frost on the windscreen. "How many days is it till Christmas?"

I climbed in beside her and we joined the queue to get out of the drive. "How many do you think?" I raised my eyebrows. "If today is the start of Advent?"

"Oh yeah." She nodded gravely. "I didn't think of that. Where's Alex?"

"Um." I hit the indicator, and we managed finally to pull out onto the road towards home. "I don't know. I think he went home already."

"Didn't he come with you?" Alicia looked up at me sideways. I shook my head.

"Is that because of it being a secret?" she whispered, loudly.

I glanced over at her fleetingly as I accelerated out of the thirty limit. She had no idea. *People start to get hurt . . . People that matter . . .*

279

I smiled weakly.

"I think he only came to see your bit," I said.

"Oh." Alicia smiled and looked down, swinging her legs against the edge of the car seat. For a few miles we drove in silence. Alicia drew up her legs, hugging herself in her seat.

"India?" She sounded thoughtful.

"Mm?" I glanced down as she touched my sleeve.

"You know when we get home? Can we watch Netflix?"

I let out my breath, relieved that for a change her question had an easy answer.

"Yeah. I guess so. After you've had your bath."

"A *bath*?" Alicia groaned.

By the time we were home and Alicia had been washed, dried and fed, by Julia's rules it really should have been bedtime. But Alicia was still buoyant. We lined up every candle we could find on the coffee table in the sitting room. We didn't draw the heavy curtains, and the reflected multitude of their tiny flames danced in the glass.

"Indi*aa*."

I looked up from the flames, realising my mind had wandered. Alicia was wielding the remote like a weapon.

"It's not *working*."

She handed it to me, as though there was a chance I might be capable of operating it better than she could. I stabbed at a few buttons.

"The internet must be down."

"Can we have a disc then?" She didn't wait for an answer. There was a crash and clatter of shifting boxes as she vanished into a cupboard behind the TV. I sat down on one of the vast sofas. Moments later she reappeared, a plastic case triumphantly clasped in her hand.

"Look!" She plopped down on the floor in front of the TV and jabbed at the DVD player with her other hand to open it. "I found a Christmas one! *X M A S*. Did you know that stands for Christmas? It was right at the back." She rammed the disc into the player and brought the case to show me the handwritten title. "It looks *really* old. Maybe it's an antique?"

"Er, yeah." I watched her press the buttons. It looked like a home recording. Heaven only knew what was on it.

"Oh." Alicia frowned at the TV, where nothing had happened except a blank blue screen. "It's not working."

I couldn't help feeling relieved.

"Perhaps you should pick a different one? Have you pressed play?"

"Yes. Duh."

"Oh, well—"

I was cut off mid-sentence. The TV flickered from blue to mottled tones of grey and black motion, badly focused and at an angle. To begin with, it was too dim to see. A flash of blurred light crossed the shot. There was a soft crackle, close at hand. The shuffle of movement.

And something else?

The voice was faint, oh so faint, over the hiss of the recording. It halted me, left me immobilised in my seat. I strained my ears to pick it up, a sudden, electrifying chill running down my spine.

Once in royal David's city
Stood a lowly cattle shed

The scene was becoming clearer, the camera light adjusting to the relative darkness of a cathedral nave, lit only by candles. The sound rang ethereally around the lofty stone walls, high, pure and gut-wrenchingly beautiful. The voice of a child.

And as the picture came into focus, I could see him. The choirboy from the portrait. He was young, slight, and nervous. His blue cassock touched the floor, the white surplice a stark contrast to his soft, black-brown hair and the dark, painfully familiar brows that flickered low over his eyes. Strangely intense, breathtaking blue eyes.

The camera shot wavered, then was adjusted in the hand of whoever was holding it, its shuffle and click interrupting the last few words before the rest of the choir began to sing.

Then they started to walk, slowly; I watched Alex lead them, a ghost of Christmas past, biting his lip in concentration. Unsmiling, solemn, and undamaged.

For he is our childhood's pattern
Day by day, like us, he grew.

The camera tried to pan, scanning fleetingly over the body of the choir and the congregation. And for a fraction of a moment, something else caught my eye. A man, in shot for barely a second, a man in a shabby long wool coat that had once been expensive. He was alone, despite the mass of people around him, and he wasn't singing even though the lips of the rest of the congregation moved, now, in unison with the choristers'. And his eyes were piercing; they looked straight through the camera lens, straight into mine.

The camera moved again suddenly, a muffled clatter and another series of clicks. The picture distorted into a hundred tiny squares of mutilated candlelight and cut out.

"Oh no!" Alicia's voice rang out in dismay. "What happened to it?" She shuffled upright on the sofa beside me, and I suddenly became aware of her tugging at my sleeve. "India . . . India! Why are you crying?"

"What?" I wiped my wet cheeks with the heel of my hand, startled. "I'm not." My voice seemed to suggest otherwise. "I'm not crying, Alicia."

The sitting room moved in a haze before my eyes. I blinked hard.

"Don't cry." Alicia was frowning. She climbed into my lap and put her arms around my neck.

For some reason, something made me look up. I felt a ripple of goosebumps and glanced over my shoulder.

Silent, barely more than a shadow, Alex stood in the doorway. Watching, bleakly, from beneath his brows, his face grim. His teeth were gritted, his lips pressed hard together. There was a ringing silence.

Then the sound of his footsteps reverberated on the wooden boards as he turned without a word and walked away.

"Oh . . ." I let out my breath in a rush. The candles were burning low. Alicia's arms were still tight around my neck. I loosened them carefully.

"I think it's bedtime." I got hastily to my feet, fighting back the lump in my throat.

"Oh, *please*." She looked up at me, imploring. "Not *yet*."

I glanced back over my shoulder. The doorway was empty. He had gone.

"Just *five minutes*?" Alicia got up too, fidgeting very un-sleepily.

"You've already had an extra hour," I pointed out. "And a DVD."

"A *really short* one." She was clearly unimpressed.

"Come on." I nodded her towards the door. "Bed."

She rolled her eyes. But she didn't argue. In fact, it was a little too easy to persuade her to help me blow out the candles; worryingly painless getting her up to her room and into bed. She gave me a hug and lay down as I whispered goodnight and closed the door. I pretended not to notice when, as I got halfway down the stairs, her light clicked back on again.

I returned to the sitting room to gather together the candles. I picked up the closest one, tracing my fingers over the dripping, beaded chains where rivulets of smooth wax had melted and solidified.

"Hey."

I started.

Alex took the candle from me, and set it down slowly on the table. He reached for the matches to light it and switched off the lamp.

"I like candlelight." His voice was enigmatic. "It reminds me of the folly."

"Oh." It reminded me of the folly, too.

"Sit down?"

I nodded, and he pulled me down beside him onto the sofa, one hand drifting gently over the knee of my jeans. I stiffened. We were both looking at the candle.

"Jim was in that video," he said at last, so quietly that his voice was barely audible. "He came to watch. He'd been teaching me piano at school for a few months by then. I was nine years old. My parents had never met him. I guess they never even knew he was there. He was so proud."

I frowned, trying to add it up. Or even, trying to work out what it was that still *didn't* add up. Falteringly, I leaned against him, breathing in the enticing smell of his clothes. Alex's lips brushed my forehead.

"It was his idea to apply for a scholarship to the Minster. He said I'd easily get in. I'd been in the choir for a couple of years. He wrote to my parents, and they put the application in. He took me to the audition himself because my parents couldn't. Or wouldn't." He let out a measured breath. "My father wanted me to go to his old school, and my mother was against the whole idea from the moment she came to watch me sing that Christmas. A few days later, they told me that I hadn't got a place and I was going to Embarby. They said Jim had been unfair in raising my hopes."

"But you did get a place." I felt my brows pucker in confusion.

And there, for a moment, he was back. The ghost of Christmas past, a hurt, betrayed little boy behind those immeasurable eyes.

"Yeah." His voice was very quiet. "They lied."

The letter. The one I had found, by accident.

"But why?"

"I don't know. Choir was my mother's idea, to start with. She never really spared the time to come and watch — she liked the idea rather than the commitment — but she didn't mind me going. But all that changed after she came that night."

He was still there. The small, unwanted boy. The dark-haired, bright-eyed chorister sitting right beside me.

"When she told me I was stopping choir, I was heartbroken. I screamed at her. Told her I was running away. That I'd go and live with Jim." He laughed wryly. "It made sense at ten. I took some clothes, my music, and the cricket bat my father had brought me back from Lord's, and I walked out. I got as far as the sheds before she found me. I wanted to take my dog."

The flicker of pain across his face was almost too much to bear. I slipped my arms around him.

"And my . . . my mother . . . it was like she'd gone insane. She was trying to grab my things. She got the bat, and Bess didn't like it; she was jumping up and snarling. And my mother hit her. She didn't stop hitting her until she stopped moving. They blamed me. When Roy got there, everybody said it was me. The vet put her down. To this day, that's what everyone believed. That I'd killed her. The only creature on Earth that loved me."

"You didn't tell anyone?" The disbelief was raw in my words.

"Who would have believed me?" He blinked, as if surprised by the question. Adult Alex was back. "And anyway, I was ten. Traumatised. That was the end, for me. I gave up. I didn't need a mother."

"You went to Jim."

"He was more of a parent than she was."

I nodded.

"I got a call from his solicitor this morning."

Solicitor? What? I glanced up at him, lost.

"I know." He smoothed the frown from my forehead. "I didn't understand, either. I thought there'd been a mistake." He shook his head. "But there wasn't. She apologised. Told me I would have heard from them before, but there'd been some complications. About the will."

The will. Jim's will. But why?

"At first, I didn't quite understand what she was trying to explain. But apparently," Alex paused, his gaze searching mine, "I'm a beneficiary."

"Because you *did* matter to him." I surprised myself with my own ferocity. "Of course you mattered enough."

"The problem is, I don't think he can have had any idea what it's worth." He shook his head slowly. "Since he bought

285

it, the value of property for renovation has gone through the roof. I'm sure he hadn't realised."

"The old school." Realisation was dawning.

"They've valued it at over three hundred and fifty thousand."

"Three hundred and . . ." I was speechless. No wonder Iain Trevers looked haggard.

"And you had no idea?" I managed at last.

"No." Consternation flickered across his face. "Of course I had no idea. I . . ." He trailed off. "Do you have any concept of what this means?

Any concept? *If there was another choice I'd be out. I'd be long gone.* And now there was another choice. I just wasn't sure where that left me.

Silence. I looked back at the candle. Alex did, too, watching it gutter and dance upright in some unfelt draught. Seconds stretched into minutes, the flame lengthened and burned low, the candle liquefying into a pool of molten wax.

"There were times when it crossed my mind," he said, suddenly.

"What?" I looked up sharply. The note in his voice had made me uneasy. "What do you mean?"

Alex's eyes locked with mine. They were the darkest blue I had ever seen.

"What he did. Jim. There were times it crossed my mind. Times, not so long ago, when there didn't seem to be a reason to carry on living."

"Oh." I stared at him, winded. Tightened my fingers through his. Looked at the slow rise and fall of his chest, warm and slightly unsteady. *No.*

But I could remember, vividly. *There's pills for that. Pills that stop you feeling.*

"No secrets." Alex's gaze was level. Infinitely, terrifyingly deep.

"No secrets." I swallowed. The pain lanced through my gut.

You didn't tell . . . did you?

286

My teeth chattered. I let go of his hands to wrap my arms around myself instead, suddenly cold.

"What are your plans for Christmas?" Alex's voice was a whisper. I glanced up, caught off guard by the question.

"I don't know," I mumbled.

"Tell my parents that you're going to your mother's." He caught my face in both of his hands, ran his thumbs over my cheeks. "I spoke to my uncle yesterday." His mouth was close against mine, close enough to kiss. "He won't be at the folly. No one will. He's in the South of France until New Year. We could be alone."

I drank in a deep breath. Alone? At the folly? Undisturbed, for days? If we could. If only we could . . .

Alex's eyes burned into mine. Startlingly, heart-stoppingly blue.

"Say yes."

"I haven't said no to you before," I whispered.

A tiny sound escaped his lips, somewhere between a sigh and a groan. His hands closed around my upper arms; I clutched at the front of his t-shirt, reached desperately for his kiss, breathless, wanting—

"India!"

A square of light fell over us from the open door. We leapt apart, but too late. In the doorway, both Alicia and Tatty Rabbit were poised, staring.

For a moment, I wasn't sure who was more lost for words. I almost tripped as I extracted myself from the sofa. Behind me, Alex shifted sideways.

"I can't sleep," she said.

Silence. I hastily brushed a stray, damp strand of hair from my lips.

"I can't sleep," she repeated plaintively. "And I was scared."

"Alicia . . ." I hurried to her, attempting vainly to sound calm. I reached out and took her hand. "Why didn't you call me?"

"I did." Her lips tightened.

"Oh." I felt my colour rise. "What's the matter? Why were you scared?"

"Of the dark." She looked up at me from under her brows ominously. "I thought there was something there."

"I thought you put the light on." I raised my eyebrows at her, despite my pounding heart. Alicia paused.

"Yes." She recovered her glare quickly. "That's because I was scared."

"That was half an hour ago, Alicia," I pointed out.

"Oh." Alicia chewed her lip.

We stood and regarded each other, at stalemate.

"I don't want to go to bed." She yielded and looked down, glowering at the wooden floor. "I'm not tired."

I watched her, at a loss. Behind me, I heard Alex shift again and stand up.

"Alex!" She moved past me to try her luck with him instead, apparently oblivious to the tension in his folded arms. "Please. I'm not sleepy."

Alex uncrossed his arms slowly. I couldn't even look at him. My face was on fire.

"That's a problem." He crouched down beside his sister, his voice low. "You see, it's nine thirty. *Way* past sleep time."

Alicia faltered under his scrutiny. I had to admit, there was something in his tone that made me nervous, too.

"So," Alex continued. "What do you propose we do about it?"

"Um . . ." Alicia twirled Tatty Rabbit's ear in her hand, suddenly tongue-tied. She looked from me to Alex, and then back again. She shuffled her feet. "Maybe we could . . ."

"No more DVDs," I interjected sternly.

"Maybe we could . . . um . . . play a game?"

"I don't know." I shook my head. "It's very late, Alicia."

I listened to my own voice, weary and cynical. Why was I sticking so pig-headedly to the legacy of Julia Maine's commandments? It was already too late. We'd already broken the rules. Every single one of them.

"Oh, come on. *Please*?" Alicia turned beseeching eyes on me. "Then I'll go to sleep straight away afterwards. Mum'll never know."

"Mm." There was still a treacherous gentleness to Alex's voice. His gaze locked with his sister's. "I guess it would be pretty bad if she knew. But India and I won't tell her, if *you* don't tell her anything. That's a deal."

Alicia's eyes narrowed. "Deal."

"Okay." I broke in from the side-lines, trying to claw back any semblance of control. "But we have to play it in your room. So you can get straight into bed afterwards, no more messing around."

"Cool!" Alicia immediately returned to buoyancy. She grabbed Alex's hand. "Come on! Let's get Monop—"

"Uh-uh." I put my foot down. I saw Alex's eyebrows flicker upwards, and the impatience in his less-than-chaste glance made me blush furiously.

"Something shorter than Monopoly," I said firmly.

* * *

We played snakes and ladders by torchlight, sitting on Alicia's floor. I avoided Alex's eyes resolutely, and failed to throw a single six as he and Alicia navigated their way to the top corner of the board.

"Yess!" Alicia interspersed her yawns with a hiss of triumph as she slid her counter up two rows, counting the rungs of the ladder with her finger. "I've overtaken you!"

Alex straightened his piece, one square behind hers. "You know where snakes and ladders came from, Alicia?" he asked her.

"No. Where?" Alicia pushed the die in my direction, and I promptly threw a one.

"India."

Alicia stared at him. "The country?"

"Yep." He took the die from me, rolling it in his palm for a moment. "You know what it means?"

"No." Alicia watched enviously as he tossed the die and it landed another six.

"Well," Alex moved his piece over hers and along the row with a gentle click. "It's about good and bad. The top of the board is good. It's where you want to be. Do you know what virtues are?"

"Are they kind of . . . being good things? Like being kind?"

"Yeah. That's right." His voice was soft. "Well, ladders are virtues. So they make you get to the top quicker. And snakes . . ."

I had the uncomfortable feeling that he was looking at me.

"Snakes are vices," he told her, inscrutably.

"What are vices?" Alicia breathed.

Alex raised his eyebrows. His voice was a whisper.

"Vices are downfalls, Alicia. Your weaknesses. The things that you want so badly that they make you forget everything you ever learned, so you can have them."

"That's scary." Alicia drew the outline of the biggest snake with her finger. "Oh no!" She eyed his counter with dismay. "You've almost won!"

She hurled the die fervently, almost losing it in the sea of toys on her bedroom floor. A three. I rescued the die and took my turn. Then Alex rolled a final six, and Alicia buried her face in her arms.

"Noo!" she grumbled. "You cheated!"

Alex smiled and folded up the board slowly. "Bed time, Alicia."

"Oh no, I—"

"Remember the deal?" He got to his feet. Alicia closed her mouth, glanced to me for assistance and didn't get any. Alex vanished without another word, leaving me to pull back the covers and steer her into bed.

Alicia slipped her thumb into her mouth as I passed her Tatty Rabbit and perched on the end of the four-poster.

"Hey, Mrs I'm-not-sleepy," I chided her gently. "What was that all about?"

Alicia blinked heavy lids to look up at me. "What?" she asked coyly.

"You know what."

"Oh." She smiled. "Nothing."

"C'mon." I tugged the covers over her and rested a hand on her shoulder. "You've never been scared of the dark."

"No." She snuggled down, stroking Tatty Rabbit's ear against her cheek thoughtfully. "Not really. But I didn't want today to be over."

"Why not?" I smiled too, despite myself.

"Because it was happy," Alicia said simply.

"Oh." I rose to my feet and paused, taking my hand from her shoulder slowly. "Well, in that case I'm glad. You did really well today. With 'Away in a Manger'. I was really proud."

Alicia turned over to face me, folds of duvet rustling around her.

"Was Alex proud, too?"

"Very." I stroked back her hair from her face. "Now, try and get some sleep."

I tiptoed to the door. I heard her squirm and turn over again, and the duvet sink and settle. I waited, listening to her breathing slow down and even out. Despite her protests, she was asleep within minutes.

I closed the door soundlessly and crept across the landing. All the lights were out downstairs. And every nerve in my body was stretched to breaking point.

I went through to my room, switched on the bedside lamp and closed the door. Sat down on the bed and stared at the monotonous walls. I needed to get some pictures. Maybe I should go for landscape paintings, like Alex. Much safer than photos. Much less revealing.

I got up to draw the curtains, and tugged my shirtsleeves down over my hands, suddenly noticing the chill in the air. I had tried, for days, not to be here. Not to let myself stop, stand, wonder. But the thoughts came unbidden, a thousand fragments, none of which fitted together . . . *You think you're losing your mind?*

I gritted my teeth, moved to the bedside table and sat down heavily on the edge of the bed, my fingers lingering on the handle of the drawer. I couldn't make sense of it. Any of it. *Any of it.*

But if I could? What if I *could*?

I watched my own shaky fingers toy with the handle, pulled to it as if magnetically, but I was too afraid to open it. Perhaps that was it. I was too afraid, too afraid to face the truth—

A shadow fell across the bed.

I looked up.

The door had opened without a sound; no knock, no footsteps, no click of the latch, nothing. At once my pulse was racing. And it wasn't fear that made me let go of the drawer.

Alex's eyes were on my face as he closed the door behind him and drew the bolt silently.

"This last hour was hell," he said.

His fingers lingered on the bolt for a second, then slipped free. He took a step towards me, another; I stood up quickly.

"Alex," I whispered.

He took my face in his hands, made me look at him, traced one finger over my cheeks and my lips. I was on fire. Every part of me. Burning like Guy Fawkes in his final moments.

Alex's fingers curled into my hair.

"I don't think I can do it. I can't stop wanting you." His voice was perilously soft. "Someone's going to see."

I thought of the concert. Of the danger in the lock of our gaze across the hot, packed school hall. Of Alicia staring from the sitting-room doorway.

"They'll just see me looking at you and they'll know." Alex's lips brushed my cheek, my throat. He didn't sound regretful; he didn't sound like he cared.

And suddenly I didn't care either. I didn't care about anything except his body against mine, the incendiary pressure of his kiss, the hot invasion of his tongue in my mouth. I caught hold of him tightly, and let my grasp move up his arms.

"*I want you, India McKenzie.*" His murmur against my lips was almost unbearable, his biceps warm and hard beneath my fingers. I gripped harder, pressing deep into his flesh, wondering if he was as immune to the pain as I was immune to the graze of his teeth on my neck, or the pull of his fingers in my hair.

"I want you too," I whispered.

And I did. More than anything in the world I did. And I had done all along. Whatever the truth; whatever was going to happen. No matter what Hope's letters said, or what people would think.

"Alex . . ." My heart was beating hard.

His gaze was on me, smouldering and inescapable.

"What?" he whispered back.

At once my breath was coming unevenly, in heady, shuddering sighs.

"*What?*" His lips were against my ear. His fingers wove more tightly into my hair.

I'd forgotten. Forgotten the Alex from before, bitter, angry. Forgotten just how fine the line was between passion and rage, shadows and flames. Until now, when the distinction became unclear. Between pain and pleasure, darkness and desire. He was pushing me backwards, his downward glance reverent, hungry and breathtaking.

"Alex." I inhaled sharply. But it wasn't a protest.

He smiled.

Then his whole weight pinned me against the side of my bed. He let go of me only for a moment to unbutton my shirt and dispense with it swiftly, to drag down my jeans and reach to click off the light. My hands were unsteady as I succumbed and let him press me into the covers, pulling off his t-shirt over his head. He kicked free of his jeans, and his phone hit the floor with a screen-shattering crack, but he didn't hear. Or if he did, he didn't care.

And then we were in freefall, plunging like the dropped dice. Forgetting everything we'd ever learned. Everything we knew was wrong — or right. He clamped his hand over my

293

mouth, the darkness intensified, peaked; I cried out into his palm and his grip redoubled. And I realised — I didn't want it to be over either. I didn't want today to be over.

"*You. Are. So. Beautiful.*" His hand cradled my cheek.

Then his thumb covered my lips. I saw his teeth grit hard together, heard the breath leave his body—

And then silence. Sudden, resounding silence.

Alex's lips brushed my forehead, my cheeks; he took my face in his hands. Paused, wordless, his eyes searching mine in the darkness. I clutched at him, pushed my fingers through his dark, dishevelled hair, and tried to remember how to breathe.

He lowered me carefully, lay down beside me. I kissed his chest, the taste of salt on his skin. Rested my head on his shoulder, feeling his breathing slow gradually in pace with mine. My bright-eyed chorister. My dark-eyed downfall. My vice.

I couldn't change my mind. It occurred to me, as I listened to the rhythmic racing of his heartbeat, as I wove my fingers through his and held on. *I'm not going to let go of you. Not ever.* And if that meant letting go of something else? There had never been a moment when I had doubted what I'd chosen. Not until—

The ring of the phone cut through the darkness like a knife, echoing off the walls. I jumped. Alex flinched in surprise. I felt him roll over, his warmth shifting as he fumbled with the light-switch.

"Oh, fuck," he groaned, blinded. I blinked hard against the scattered lamplight.

"That's mine. Where is it?" He thrust a hand through his hair, perplexed. The phone rang again, vibrating loudly somewhere on the floorboards. Alex stretched over me to rifle fruitlessly through the pockets of his jeans.

"Oh, fuck it." He leaned over me further, to try and reach under the bed. "Where the fuck's it gone?"

Oh shit.

"Alex—" Something suddenly occurred to me. I struggled to free myself. "Don't—"

"It's okay." He put out a hand against the bedside table, to steady himself. "I've nearly got it. It's here. I can't quite . . . Oh."

The phone stopped ringing; it skidded out from under the side of the bed and across the floor as his hand caught it, coming to an unspectacular halt at the foot of the door.

Alex straightened, his weight lifting abruptly from on top of me. And suddenly my ears were ringing.

"India?" He whispered. "What's . . ."

Hope Bryant, Ridge Farm House, 32 Cedar Walk

He was holding up an envelope. Staring at it, mystified. I paled.

"No . . ." I grabbed his wrist as he leaned over again, tried to stop him. "Wait—"

But it was too late.

The box came free suddenly, sliding from under the bed, a cascade of paper pouring over the floor. Envelopes, letters, notebook pages. Folded, unsealed, unread. All addressed the same.

"No . . ." It escaped my throat unchecked; I sat bolt upright. Tightened my hands around my head. I could hear myself hyperventilating. Overwhelmed by panic.

No, terror.

"Please," I moaned. "No . . ."

"*India?*"

"Don't!" I clutched at his arms again as he bent to scoop them from the floor. "I—"

"These are the letters you wrote." His eyes were fixed on mine, wide with slowly dawning comprehension.

I shook my head wildly. "Alex, I—"

"They are." He was frowning, his brows low over his staring eyes. "Aren't they?"

"Oh God," I inhaled. "Oh God."

"India?" His voice was painfully soft.

Slowly, I nodded.

295

Dear Hope,
I don't know why I always start letters to you that way.

Dear Hope,
I'm back. To finish the letter, like I promised.

Dear Hope . . .

The tears welled over, irrepressible, impossible to deny. How could I deny it? How could I deny her? How could I have tried? A sob rose in my throat; I tried to choke it back and failed miserably.

"Jesus Christ." Alex's arms closed around me tightly. "India, tell me." His voice was raw. "Tell me the truth. This has got to stop. Tell me. About Hope."

"I . . . I can't." I closed my eyes, reeling. Trying to fight back control.

You didn't tell him our secret, did you?

"Tell me!" He grasped both of my wrists and the touch was unbearable. His touch. It was going to break me. I was going to crack under the pressure. And there was nothing I could do to stop it. Not anymore.

"I know she's real. I *know*. I saw the pictures. I know because I heard you cry, India! Every night, for weeks and months, I heard you cry. So you need to tell me. Tell me about her. Who is Hope?"

"My best friend." I managed to choke it out between clamped teeth. "I *did* tell you. I *told* you!"

"No." His gaze was level, inescapable. "No, I don't think you did. Where is she? Tell me *that*. Where is she? What does she do? Do you still see her?"

"No." My voice was strangled. Another sob almost suffocated me. I tried to wriggle free of his hold, to get away, but he wouldn't let me go.

"India." He took my chin in his hand, made me look at him. "Tell me who Hope is. Tell me who she really is."

Who she really is?

I gave up struggling. It was bound to come to this, eventually. All I'd been doing was putting it off.

"Please," I whispered. "Please don't think I'm crazy."

Alex shook his head.

"Please." I met his gaze, despairing. "I had to write. I had to. I didn't have anything else—"

The look in his eyes made me break off. Pain, horror, sympathy. I couldn't bear it.

"No," he breathed. "I don't think you're crazy. How could you imagine that's what I'd think? Don't say that. Don't—"

I pressed a trembling hand to my mouth. "I didn't have anyone else to talk to. I was so afraid. I had to talk to her. I needed her. I just wanted someone . . . someone to . . . to understand . . ."

He took me by the shoulders firmly. "I'm *trying* to understand. I'm trying."

"I . . . I know." I rubbed my forehead, dizzy. "I know."

"India." His voice was terrifyingly quiet. "What happened to Hope?"

"Oh . . ." I exhaled, weak and shuddering. "Oh."

"India?"

"Hope . . ." I pressed my hand harder to my forehead for a moment. "What happened . . . I . . ."

I gripped the edge of the bed with both hands.

"We were never apart. Not since we were seven years old. She was in my class, we slept in the same dormitory, went to the same college. She wasn't just my friend, Alex. She was . . . she was my whole world. We were together the whole time, every day. *Every single day.* We applied to Leeds together, lived together. We did everything together. For fourteen years."

He knew. He already knew. I could see the appalled realisation in his eyes. I couldn't look at him.

"The day after we graduated, we went out. We went out to celebrate. It was late. We were so happy, stupid. We danced for hours. She was like that — she just went and went. She got so drunk. Really, *really* drunk."

"You . . ." Alex's voice was a whisper, sickened. "What happened?"

I stared at the floor, at the phone, at the white paper and my handwriting moving in a haze before my eyes.

"We left the club when it closed . . . and . . . and she walked out in front of a car. She walked out in front of a car and it . . . it didn't even stop . . . It didn't even stop! And . . . and . . ."

I couldn't carry on. I sat, frozen, trying to find the truth, to force it out. The real truth.

Who Hope *really* was.

"I didn't know what to do, Alex! She was . . . she was . . . hurt. Badly. Really badly. I knew it was bad. And I didn't know what to do. I didn't help her! I couldn't help her!"

The tears were dripping onto the sheets, onto the floor between our feet. I was shaking so much that it hurt. My body ached. I wanted it to stop. Wanted so much for it to stop.

"She's . . ." I didn't recognise my own voice. Couldn't listen to it, my own words, the words I had never let myself say. Hear. Accept.

"She's dead. Okay? Hope's dead! She died in July. She never woke up, she never—"

Never opened her eyes. If only I could close my eyes, too. Close them and not open them. If only—

"India." He gripped my arms. "India, it's okay. Tell me. It's okay."

He wouldn't let me go. Just like he'd said. I couldn't close my eyes, I couldn't get away, because he wouldn't let me. I couldn't stop, now. I had to tell him, and I had never told anyone. Not anyone.

"I . . . stayed with her. Three days. Three days in ICU — she didn't look like her. It didn't look like her — she . . . Hope was so beautiful. It should have been me! We were both there, we were both drunk, we were both stupid . . . why did it have to be her? She lived life . . . so much . . . so much *better* than me. How could she . . . ? How could it .

298

. . ? I didn't . . . didn't leave. *I didn't leave* until ten minutes before, ten minutes . . . I went to get a drink. I went to buy a Coke from the fucking vending machine and it was too fizzy. I couldn't even drink it anyway. I couldn't even fucking drink it!"

I could see the horror in his eyes.

"No," he whispered. "Oh, India—"

"Ten minutes!" I clung to him. "Ten fucking minutes! I was gone for ten minutes! Please . . . please don't think I'm crazy, I don't want to be crazy. Please, I—"

"India." His voice was firm. He lifted my chin again gently. "India, you aren't crazy. You're not crazy. How could you . . . how could you go through that and not tell anyone? Why didn't you tell me? You should have *told* me."

"I couldn't! Don't you understand? I couldn't! I—"

"Listen to me." He held my face between his hands. "Hope was a part of you. She always will be. There's nothing wrong with that."

"I'm sorry." I hid my face against the warmth of his chest and tried to stop crying. But I couldn't. My jaw ached, my head throbbed as if it could split in two. "Alex, I'm sorry."

"No. No, don't be sorry. It's not crazy. I promise." His lips were close against my hair. "It's like I said. I want to know. I *need* to know. When I asked you who makes you feel better it was because I want it to be me. I want it to be me."

His arms around me were crushingly tight. There was something reassuring in their vehemence. I clutched at him, trying to hold on, even though reality was spiralling. Escaping me. *You think you're losing your mind . . .*

"I stopped writing," I whispered. "After you told me, about the one thing. I didn't write any more letters."

Alex's smile was poignant. Painful.

"You don't know how much that means to me," he said.

I shook my head.

"Yes, but Alex . . ." My voice cracked. "I—"

"Ssh." He pulled the duvet from the bed and drew it up over my shoulders. I was shivering helplessly. "Ssh. It's okay." He stroked my lips, wiping away the tears. "It's okay, India. I promise."

"No!" I broke across him suddenly, the panic rising in my chest like a storm, swirling and destructive. The room beyond him was out of focus; the sound of my own voice drifted in and out like a badly tuned radio.

"No! It's not okay!" It was a scream, a hopeless sob. The leaden weight of realisation: my own terror. "It'll never be okay! Because I *am* crazy! I *am* crazy! *Because she's started writing back.*"

CHAPTER 22: WHAT FOREVER MEANS

"Alex!"

I stirred and shifted in the warmth. Alex muttered and cast a possessive arm over me, and I let myself slip deeper back into the protective sleeping curve of his body.

It had been midnight when he brought me here, away from my room and the letters, safe amongst the muted harmonics of guitar strings and dusty landscape paintings. As my sobs faded into exhaustion, he kissed my forehead. And for the first time in four months, I had slept without dreams. Until now.

"Alex!"

The voice echoed, dimly, in the periphery of my awareness. I didn't open my eyes. Even closed, they were swollen, smarting like the embers of a fire that had been left to burn itself out. I had a sinking feeling that dawn was already upon us, and that soon I would have to face it, and the inevitable questions that accompanied it.

I'd told him about Hope.

I exhaled into the pillow and opened my eyes.

The sun was only just coming up, a hint of colour that crept in gentle tones at an angle through the Velux, dripping reluctantly onto the crumpled bedcovers and running onto

Alex's bare chest. I was still wearing his t-shirt. I drew in a deep breath.

"Alex! ALEX!"

Before the closeness of the voice could strike home, before I could process what was happening, the door swung wide, throwing harsh electric light in a rectangle over the bed. Alex muttered again and turned over, his arm tightening around me.

"Alex—"

Julia Maine's footsteps stopped abruptly. The piece of paper she had been holding slipped through her fingers.

"*Alex!*"

Her eyes were on me, bulging with incredulity; I was speechless, immobilised by fear.

"*You!* You . . . *you!*"

Alex sat up bolt upright, disorientated. "Wh . . . what . . . ?"

He trailed into silence.

"Oh shit," he breathed. "Oh shit."

"What have you *done?*" The pitch of Julia Maine's voice was rising. "What have you *done?* Get out!" She was looking straight at me. "Get *out!* Out!"

Everything was a blur. I scrambled upright, reeling. Dawn. The voice. Alex . . .

"Now!" Her scream lanced through my head, shattering, sending sharp fragments into my bloodstream. "Get out!"

"No!" In an instant, he was on his feet.

Time twisted, slowed, sped to super-speed. I clutched dazedly at the sheets, blinking hard as their voices panned and came into focus.

"No!" Alex towered over his mother. And, in a single breath, it had returned: all of his darkness, all of his hatred. It was there in his face, in his eyes, furious and menacing. I felt myself cower.

"No! *You* get out! Get the fuck out of my room!"

He paused, and the silence resounded around me. I lurched tremblingly to my feet.

"It's okay," I whispered. "It's okay, Alex. I'm going."

"No." His hand closed around my arm. "No. Don't!"

"Don't stop her!" Julia Maine was barely recognisable. "How dare you! How *dare* you! After everything we've done for you! How could you?!" Her face was white, so distorted with rage that it made me stumble backwards, colliding heavily with the bedframe.

Her pale gaze froze on my face. "I said, *out*," she spat. "Go! Downstairs, and start packing!"

Alex caught me. "No. Don't, India." His low voice suggested danger. "Don't go anywhere."

"You . . . filthy, *deceitful*—"

"Stop it!" Alex snarled. "Get out of my room. Get the fuck out! It's nothing to do with you!"

"It's *everything* to do with me! *Everything* to do with me! In my house. *My* house. Where I pay her to look after *my* child. And you . . . You've got her in your bed like some kind of . . . some kind of *common slut*!"

"How dare you?" Alex raised his hand, and for a terrifying moment, I thought he was going to strike her. But he didn't. His fingers closed around the edge of the door, white-knuckled, crushing. "How dare you speak about her like that?"

"Alex." I caught my breath and tried to disentangle my legs from the sheets. "Alex, don't. I'll go. She's right. I'll go."

"No!" He grabbed me, hard. So hard that I gasped in pain. He loosened his grip instantly.

"No, India. She has no right. She's going to apologise." His whisper was perilous. "Right now. You're going to apologise!" He turned on his mother, with force that made my blood run cold. "Apologise to her!"

"Who do you think you *are*? Don't tell me t—"

"Who do *you* think *you* are?!" His face was half in shadow, and the rage in his eyes was the manifestation of every fear I had ever known. "You have *no right* to speak to her like that! You want to control everyone. But you can't! This is nothing to do with you! *Nothing!*"

My heart lurched as he took a step towards her, the door swinging unsteadily in his hand.

"India has given you more than you will ever know! But maybe you're so blind that you can't even see the change in your own kid! You can't even *see* what she's done for you! For Alicia, for me. You tried to trap her into your miserable life, like it was up to you. To use her, like you use everyone. But she never had to stay here! And you know what? I don't either! Not anymore! You can have your fine with interest at the end of the month. Then there's no fucking debt to repay! Now get out of my room. If you're making her leave, I'm going with her."

"What?" Julia Maine was staring at him in pallid disbelief.

"We're leaving. You told her to pack." Alex grabbed the door handle and started to ease the door closed, forcing his mother from the room. "So get out and let us get on with it."

Julia planted her foot in the door, wedging it open.

"Your father—"

"Oh, I'm sure it won't trouble him too much." Alex's voice was scathing. "You can reassure him we won't be back to bother either of you again."

He pushed against the door with his shoulder, over-whelming her resistance. The rectangle of light narrowed to a slit.

"India?"

My heart turned cold.

Alex faltered. The door rebounded, swinging on its hinges.

"*India?*"

Oh no, no.

Barely thinking, I stumbled past him. Past Julia Maine, and into the doorway. I looked down, at sleep-tousled chest-nut hair and pink pyjamas. At Tatty Rabbit trailing on the floor. Down into Alicia's wide, bewildered eyes.

"Go back to your room, Alicia." Julia Maine's voice was frosty.

304

"No." A frightened sob rose in Alicia's throat. She shook her head. Stared at her mother, round-eyed.

"Now!" Julia snapped.

"No!" Alicia screamed, and the sound pierced me to the core. I started forwards, and then stopped dead as Julia Maine's icy hand shot out and barred my way.

"No. I won't. I won't!" Alicia was gripping the end of the banister with both hands, her bottom lip trembling threateningly. "I heard Alex! I heard him! What does he mean? *What does he mean?* He said you're making her leave! Why did he say you're making her leave! Why did he say that? Why did he—"

"Go. To. Your. Room." Julia was on the stairs in an instant, her steps rapid, clipped, brutal. "Right. Now."

"India!" Alicia ducked under her mother's arm, grabbed at the broken banister rail. "No! What does he mean? What does he mean you're leaving? Why did he say—"

"Now!"

I heard Alicia whimper. And then Alex's fingers closed resolutely around my arm, and the door slammed shut and I was left staring at it, gasping—

"India." He touched my waist gently.

"No. Not this."

Numbly, I shook my head. Crouched down to pick up the sheet of paper from the floor. It was folded into an irregular octagon, all four of its corners turned in and neatly creased around the handwritten message.

2 December

Dear Mrs Maine,

I hope this letter finds you well. Please excuse me writing to you directly. I just wanted to ask when you last checked on the whereabouts of your au pair.

If you can't find her, I suggest that Alex might be able to help you.

Yours sincerely,
Hope Bryant

"India!"

"No!" I batted his hand away blindly, snatched the note out of his reach. For a moment I wavered, winded, trying to comprehend.

"No . . ." My mind was racing. "I . . . I have to go and pack . . ."

"India." His voice was dark with misgiving. "It's from her, isn't it? What do you—"

"I have to go and pack." It came out garbled, the words running together. "Like she said. Go and pack . . ."

"Okay." Alex took a step backwards, breathing hard. He pushed a hand through his hair, perplexed. "Okay. If that's what—"

"Yes." I lurched dizzily for the door, grasped the handle with a hand that was slippery with sweat.

Alex caught it.

"I'll come and find you." His eyes penetrated mine. "Half an hour. I don't need to take much. I'll be half an hour. I just need to make some calls."

I nodded, mute.

"Half an hour," he reiterated.

"Yeah," I choked. Then I turned and fled.

* * *

I descended the stairs, ran across the empty landing. Kicked my bedroom door to behind me and got dressed, trying to stay focused enough not to break down and sob.

Half an hour. Could I be ready in half an hour? Finished? Packed?

Yes. I could.

Ready to walk out and know I wouldn't be able to look back?

I would have to be.

I flung open the wardrobe doors, unsteady and nauseated. Stared silently at the two full cases in the bottom, stacked under the empty ones, at the meagre collection of hanging clothes. Four months. I'd been here for four months, and I'd barely even unpacked. I dragged the cases out, plucking clothes from hangers and thrusting them haphazardly inside. I turned out the contents of the chest of drawers into a pile on the floor, and heaped it into the second suitcase in armfuls, until the case was bulging and I had to stand on the lid to zip it closed.

Rucksack. I glanced around, frantic. I needed my rucksack.

It was downstairs. I heaved the suitcases to one side with shaking hands so that I could get out through the door. It had been wet, after I came back from the folly. I'd hung it up in the utility to dry . . .

I half fell out through the doorway, my arrhythmic footsteps thundering hollowly on the stairs. I could hear shouting from the sitting room. Alicia. My stomach tightened.

I snatched the rucksack from its peg, almost tripping myself up on its dangling straps as I made my way back through to the hall, and stopped dead. The envelope stared up at me from the doormat.

In aeternum

"No!" I hissed.

But the sound of footsteps on the gravel outside changed my mind. I staggered the length of the hall and snatched it up, my gaze falling on the Porsche in the driveway as John Maine's key grated in the lock—

I was up the stairs before the key had finished turning, rucksack and letter crumpled in my arms. I couldn't be there when he came in, when Julia told him. If she hadn't already told him.

"Shit!" Tears stung my eyes as I stumbled into the bedroom, dropping my rucksack into a heap on the floor.

"*Shit!*"

I slumped backwards against the wardrobe, fumbling with the envelope, my hands cold. I didn't even dare to close my eyes, because I knew what I'd see. Blood. Blood, soaking through his t-shirt, smeared across the hall floor. Dripping, pooling in the road. *You think you're losing your mind.*

307

What had I done?

I'd told him. After everything. Despite everything. There was no going back. No hiding it. *I know everything about you, remember. I know . . .*

I unfolded the letter.

You betrayed me, India. You told him about me. Even though you knew how I felt about it. You told him I was dead. Why would you do that to me?

> *So I told, too. No secrets, isn't that what you said?*
> *One day you'll be grateful for this. I've made one last chance for you, India. One last chance to get out. To end it.*
> *It has to end.*

I should never have told him. I had known, the whole time. That I shouldn't. That I *couldn't*. Because now . . . *now—*

The end of everything.

The blood. I couldn't stop thinking about the blood.

I stumbled to the bedside table and flung open its drawer. Snatched them up, the rest of them. Blue biro, bent corners, lined paper.

You know, sometimes, when you lose your mind, people start to get hurt. People that matter.

> *Don't let anyone else get hurt, India.*

I smoothed out the folded corners, one at a time, ironing flat the creases with my hands. I had told him about Hope, but I hadn't shown him. I hadn't shown him this. The rest. What she'd said. How could I? How could I tell him? That *he* was in her letters? That she knew about him, about everything — everything we'd shared? Even the most private, the most secret—

I know you have a lot to tell me about the folly . . .

> *It's like I said before. You need to stay away from Alex.*
> *Stay away from him, or it will end badly, and not just for you.*

"Fuck." My hands fumbled with the pages, frozen and terrified. "Fuck."

I'm your best friend, India. Remember?

The blood.
"No. Hope. *No.* Please . . ."
I couldn't go with him. It hit me, a cold dead weight. This was what it had come down to, all along. *It has to end.*
"Oh God. Oh God . . ." I lurched upright, folding the wad of letters in half in my hand. "*Oh God . . .*"

Yours (Forever),
Hope
PS. Don't forget what forever means.

"India!"
I jumped, violently.
"India!" The small figure had appeared without warning. She darted in through the open door, leaping over the suitcases, half-falling in her haste. Clutched at me, her arms clamped fiercely around my waist.
"Alicia!" I exhaled.
"What . . . what . . ." She was owl-eyed, white-faced. "What's going on? Where . . . where are you *going*?"
"Alicia."
The voice on the landing turned my blood to ice. I looked up. Alicia hugged me tighter.
"That's enough." John Maine's face betrayed no emotion. His voice was cold, clinical. "Let India finish packing."
She shook her head.
"Alicia." He regarded his daughter dispassionately. "Do as you're told."
"No." She quaked against me.
"India has to leave. She won't be looking after you anymore." His voice was frighteningly calm. "Please go back to your room and let her finish packing."

309

"No!" She didn't let go of me. "No! Why?!"

I could feel her starting to sob, her small shoulders shuddering.

"Because—" John started.

"Because of secrets, Alicia." At last I found my voice. I knelt down in front of her and took hold of her shoulders gently. "Because of Alex. And . . . *vices*." I closed my eyes for a fraction of a moment. "You'll understand one day, Alicia. I'm sorry."

She glanced from my face to her father's and then back again, rooted to the spot.

"They . . . they . . ." She stared at me, horrified. "Mum found out. She found out and she's—"

"I'm sorry." I swallowed and got quickly to my feet.

"No!" Alicia's shriek was ear-splitting. At last she had let go of my waist. For a second, she teetered. Then she flew at her father.

"No! No!" She seized the hem of his suit jacket, tearing at it ineffectually. "You can't make her leave! No!"

John Maine caught her fists in his hands and detached her carefully.

"That's enough." Anger was creeping into his voice, a deadly note of wrath that was breaking through the barriers of his control.

"No!" Alicia tried vainly to wrench herself free. "No! If . . . If you make her leave, I'll — I'll never forgive you! I'll run away and *never* come back! I'll—"

"ENOUGH!" His roar made me cringe backwards. Before I could react, he grabbed her full around the waist, lifting her kicking and screaming. I pressed a trembling hand to my mouth as he turned and strode away, her screams receding across the landing, and I heard her bedroom door close.

Half an hour. I looked up at the clock.

I was out of time.

Shit. I started to stuff the remaining belongings into my rucksack, panic ringing in my ears. Half an hour. And I couldn't go with him. I knew I couldn't go with him. It was going to end badly. He'd said so himself. He'd told me . . .

I had to go, now, before he could stop me. Before he came down and took away my rationality, before the passion and the persuasion in his all-pervading blue gaze had the chance to change my mind. It wasn't an option.

Don't let anyone else get hurt . . .

"I have to go." I gasped it to myself, to the empty room, to the peeled-off Blu Tack. What was left? I swept the mess frantically from my dressing table into a carrier bag and shoved it into the last suitcase, ramming the lid closed. *What was left?*

A yellow rose and a silver ring in the bedside drawer.

I halted, pain stabbing in my gut. I stared at them for a moment, sickened. At the dead, dry petals, crumbling into the scuffed wood.

I banged the drawer closed.

It took me two trips to get the cases down the stairs and into the hall. I rifled through the coat stand for my jacket and waterproofs; pushed my feet into my pumps and swept up the rest of my boots and shoes to carry them to the car. I had to go back for the suitcases, two at a time, jamming them into the boot and the rear seats and flinging my handbag in through the passenger door. I needed my rucksack. Just my rucksack, from the foot of the stairs, and it was done.

It was cold, but I was sweating. I leaned against the car for a moment, fighting to catch my breath. Then I strode back to the front door. For the last time. *The last time.*

A sob rose dryly in my throat. I clamped my jaw, fighting it back.

How could it be the last time?

I swayed, my key in the lock, somehow too weak to open the door. How was I going to do this? How was I going to walk out? Not look back? Leave?

Without even seeing his face. The sob escaped, uncontained. I twisted the key sharply, like a knife in a wound. It was silent in the hallway. Strangely, echoingly silent. I stopped dead.

My rucksack had gone.

I wavered beside the stairs, sweat stinging my upper lip. Any moment, and it would be too late. Any moment . . .

"Please."

It was a whimper, cracked, indiscernible. I spun, a chill running through me.

"Please. Don't g-go."

She stepped out from the end of the corridor. Her eyes were brimming with tears, huge, gathering, weighty tears that slipped over unchecked and splashed in huge droplets onto the floorboards. She was hugging my rucksack to her chest like a beloved friend, forlorn and desperate.

"Alicia."

She shook her head, jaw set stubbornly.

"Alicia," I whispered, defeated. "I need my rucksack."

She shook her head again, and another storm of tears welled over, trickling down her nose and cheeks and dripping from her chin. She squeezed the bag tighter.

"N-no." She gulped. "You . . . c-can't."

"Alicia, please . . ." Every muscle in my abdomen was clenched, trying to hold it in, my own tempest of sobs.

"No!" She gritted her teeth. Her nose was running, over her top lip. "No. You c-c-can't." The sobs were shaking her from head to foot, hiccupping and violent. "You c-can't g-go . . . You s-said you wouldn't. Y-you said you'd n-never forget m-m-me . . ."

"Oh, Alicia." I couldn't move. I was frozen, blinking furiously, tears forcing themselves relentlessly from the corners of my eyes and sliding over my cheeks.

"Y-you . . . You make me be able to do things!" Her sobs gathered momentum, juddering and hysterical. "You made -ev-everything happy. You said . . . You, You said that w-when you're sad I-*I* make you feel better! You can't g-*go*! If you go *no one* will make *me* feel better! Please! *Please*!"

Somewhere in the background, I could hear Julia Maine's voice speaking on the phone, sharp and angry. I drew in an unstable breath.

"I'm sorry, Alicia." Suddenly I could move again, and I stumbled to her. I put my arms around her and held her tightly, rested my cheek on the top of her head and breathed in the smell of chamomile and soap from her tangled chestnut hair. "I'm so sorry."

She didn't hear, but I did. The footsteps.

I raised my eyes to John Maine's face.

Without a word, I let her go. Like a traitor, I let him step in and take my place, prising the bag from her hands. He held it out to me. I reached into my pocket for my key. The exchange was silent.

"Goodbye, Alicia," I choked.

John Maine folded his hand around the key.

"NO!" Alicia erupted from behind him. John grabbed her, and she rounded on him.

"I hate you! I HATE YOU!" She struggled wildly, scratching at his unmoving hands with her fingernails. "I'll never forgive you!"

I started to walk. I had to. Because if I didn't, then I wouldn't. I wouldn't be able to make myself. I opened the door. Alicia's heels struck her father viciously in the shins, breaking his grip for a fraction of a second. She ran past me, gasping.

"India. INDIA!"

Then John's fingers closed around her upper arm, dragging her back, so that she couldn't follow me. I stepped out through the door.

"INDIA!"

It crashed closed, and I fell, off-balance, down the steps and onto the gravel, my chest heaving with silent sobs.

I opened the car boot, attempting vainly to wedge my rucksack inside. Gave up, and shoved it onto the passenger seat instead, blundering around the car to rub the harsh remains of last night's frost from the windows.

"Wait!"

The voice rang out across the drive.

I felt myself crumple. Alex's boots skidded loudly on the gravel.

"Wait! What—" He reached me within seconds. His gaze was fixed on my face, wide, appalled. "What . . . what are you *doing*?"

"I'm sorry."

"You're—" He inhaled sharply, his voice black with foreboding. "No . . . "

End it. It has to end.

"I've . . . got to go." It emerged as a sob, a sickening gasp of realisation. I faced him, reeling. "I've got to go."

"No." He shook his head. His hands found mine on the boot-hatch and pulled them roughly away. "Wait a minute. What are you doing? This isn't what—"

The foreboding was in his face, too. I twisted free of his grip and took a step backwards, horribly afraid. Afraid of myself. Of the words that I could hear myself saying.

"I'm leaving, Alex. Alone. I'm—" My voice cracked. "I'm sorry."

"*What?*"

"I . . . we . . . can't do this." Another string of sobs rose forcibly in my chest. I slammed the boot feebly, it didn't latch. Alex caught it.

"What?" His lips were pressed hard together, his eyes locked on mine, dazed and uncomprehending. "No . . . *No!* I told you! I'll go with you. Anywhere! Wherever you want to go."

"Alex . . ." Terror gripped me, choking off my words. "We can't."

"What are you saying?" Something in his face hardened, stubborn, incredulous. He banged the boot violently, breathing hard. "What are you trying to *say*?"

"I . . ." I clutched at my hair with both hands. "Alex, I'm sorry. I can't do it. We can't do it . . ."

"India . . ." He caught my wrists, making me let go. "What are you talking about?! What are you—"

"We can't!" I broke across him, panic ridden.

"Yes, we can!" Suddenly he was shouting. "We *can*! I've already spoken to Iain! The school's going on the market today!

We can go wherever we want to, and never go back. Anywhere you want. Where do you want to go? We can go anywhere!"

For just a split second I couldn't help but see, imagine what it would be like to start again. To be with him forever.

But it wouldn't happen that way.

This will end badly, if you don't stay away from him. It will end badly, and not just for you.

"It's not . . ." I shook my head despairingly. "Not that simple."

"It really is!" The darkness in his face was frightening me. "If you want it enough!"

"I . . ." I pressed a trembling hand to my forehead. "Alex, I can't do it. We can't just disappear without a second thought and honestly believe it would be okay. We kept on fooling ourselves that this could work. But it couldn't! We both knew all along it couldn't! *You* told *me* that! That it would end badly! How can we . . ." I shrank from him, sick and shaking. "I . . ."

"You don't want to." Suddenly, his voice was flat.

"I do!" I dashed the tears from my cheeks hopelessly. "More than anything. But . . ."

"But what?" His brows were low, eyes narrowed; the old, bleak, bitter Alex had returned in less than a heartbeat, and the Alex that I had come to know was gone. Lost, swallowed by the impending, hopeless reality.

"Someone . . . *someone'll get hurt*." My voice was barely audible.

"What?"

I faltered. "I mean . . ." I tried to think sensibly. *When you lose your mind . . .* "What about Alicia?" I whispered. "I can't just . . ."

"You choose her over me?" He stared at me, cold.

"No!" I gasped. "Alex——"

"Then what?" His gaze was hard. "You don't want me?"

"Alex, stop! Don't do this!"

"Just say it," he snarled. "Just say it, if that's what it is. That you don't want to. That you don't want me enough. Say it!"

I clutched at the door, dizzy, nauseated. The tears were choking me. The words. Slowly, I climbed into my car.

"Is that it? All this time, and *that's it*?" He was still staring at me, disbelieving. Agonised. "What *is* this, India? What *was* this?!"

"I—" Any second, and I was going to lose my grip. I was going to crack into pieces. And we would both be destroyed.

"Tell me!" Alex's hands struck the car's bodywork with a resounding crash. "For fuck's sake *tell me*! Make me understand! I don't understand!"

A sob rose in my throat. I tried to shake my head, to choke it back.

"Alex . . ." I whispered.

"*Tell me!*"

The force of it made me recoil. I flinched from him. Alex stopped dead. I saw his eyes widen, saw his breath catch. Saw the muscles clench furiously in his jaw as he bit back whatever it was that he had been going to say. For seconds, minutes, a lifetime, his gaze was on mine, his rage and pain at me taking away every ounce of strength that I had left.

Then I closed the car door. And as I did, something inside me seemed to break, to tear; something that wouldn't mend. His palm was pressed against the window. I looked up at him, one last time, and it was my undoing. The hopelessness in his eyes. The desperation.

I realised, numb, that I couldn't breathe at all.

Just for a moment, I pressed my hand to his, separated by the cold glass. His gaze was on mine, and I couldn't bear it. I couldn't look anymore.

The smash of his fist against the front wing made me jump violently. Then, without another word, he turned and strode away, leaping the wall, disappearing into the mist and the long grass.

Disappearing forever.

PS. Don't forget what forever means.

I clamped one shaking hand to my mouth.

"I don't want you, Alex." I whispered it to the silence. "*I don't want you.* I *love* you. I love you, and that's where it's all gone wrong. I love you."

I was fumbling with the key in the ignition, my hands slipping on the wheel. I made it out of the drive, a hundred yards down the road, before I had to stop. Before the tempest overtook me, relentless, exhausting.

The one thing. One thing—

I slid down in my seat, curled up on myself, my arms folded around the void in my chest, and sobbed. Sobbed until there was nothing left; nothing except pain, and the unbanishable image of his face. My downfall. My weakness. The thing that I wanted so badly that it had made me forget everything I ever learned.

Don't forget me. Promise me that?

The rest of my breath left me: a shuddering, visceral release. And then, bereaved and broken, I closed my eyes, and let the chasm expand enough to swallow me up completely.

CHAPTER 23: CONCRETE

There was barely any petrol in the car. I squinted at the fuel gauge. The morning sky was darkening, coagulating with brooding, inevitable clouds.

I needed to leave. But there was nowhere to go. *You don't have anywhere else.* He was right. I tried desperately to exile his voice from my head. If only he hadn't been right. About everything. *You should keep away. Because this . . . this is going to end badly.*

I had to get rid of his voice. I spun the volume dial of the radio to deafeningly loud and fought open the zip on the top pocket of my rucksack. Fuel. I needed fuel. I fumbled in the pocket for my purse. The Maines had paid me on the first of the month; I should have enough money to—

I froze.

"Please," I whispered. "*Please, not already . . .*"

It couldn't be another one already. Not already. I couldn't bear it. I drew the paper out, quaking.

It was a piece of cartridge paper, folded up on itself, a tiny, bulky rectangle. Not another letter after all. My gut clenched.

Alicia's picture. A tent, an orange fire. It was folded around something; as I opened the paper the rest of the way it fell out, dropping into the foot-well and rolling under the seat. An acorn. It was folded around an acorn.

Alicia. I choked on the new onslaught of tears. Oh, Alicia.

It was too late. I slammed the indicator stalk upwards, glanced over my shoulder and pulled out into the lane. I drove through Rifway with my eyes fixed on the road, nothing else. Stopped in Meresham for fuel. Hit the main road and pressed my foot to the floor.

I found myself driving through city suburbs before I had even registered where I was, the irregular concrete outline of tower blocks and factories jagged on the horizon. The traffic ground to a halt, and I crawled the rest of the way through the half-familiar streets with my foot on the clutch and my teeth gritted. Eventually, the restaurant I had eaten at with Brett flashed past the window, and I picked up a sign for the multi-storey and followed it without thinking.

I parked the car and left it, taking the echoing stairs back down to street level and setting off, directionless and bewildered by the noise of the passing crowds. It was starting to sleet and the air was mercilessly cold; I wrapped my jacket around myself, frozen to the bone.

I was never going to see him again. I walked blindly, gaining pace as I forced my way through the meandering masses of shoppers. Never. I was never going to see him again.

I stopped, suddenly, as the reality struck me. Stared at the fountain in front of me, at the endless churning motion of the water. Never again. I would never see his face, touch his lips, watch his bleak, beautiful, vulnerable smile—

I reached out and gripped the railings, sinking slowly to sit on the stone steps, the growing wind tearing at the canvas signs for the theatre at the top.

What was worse? I had loved Hope. I had loved Hope with everything I was, everything I had been, for fourteen years.

But I loved him more.

I curled up tightly, resting my head on my knees. Sleet was striking the side of my face and running down my neck;

the chill of the stone steps seemed to soak through my clothes and seep upwards through my body.

I loved him more.

Tears squeezed themselves silently from my eyes. I pulled out my phone and looked at it. Nothing. I pushed it back into my pocket with a hand that was numb and clumsy with cold. The pocket with Alicia's acorn. A subdued sob slipped out, and I clamped my teeth harder together.

"You all right, love?"

I glanced up. A man in a hi-vis jacket was picking up litter from the steps. He was looking right at me.

"Yes. Thanks," I gulped.

I stumbled to my feet and beat a hasty retreat from his crooked-toothed scrutiny. I began to walk, through the crowded city centre and out the other side. Kept walking, doubled back, just kept going — walking, not thinking — until the crowds dispersed, until my jacket was soaked through and my hair was stuck to my cheeks.

When you're sad . . . who makes you feel better?

There were decorations in all the streets, Christmas lights: shooting stars, bells, sparkling gaudy red and gold. Noon had come and gone; the sky was starting to grow dark. I couldn't remember ever having been so cold. I pushed my hands deep into my pockets, trying to bend my frozen fingers. I ached with shivering.

Once, Hope and I had—

No. I pushed that thought from my mind, too. I wouldn't replace his face with hers. If I had to choose . . .

I didn't get to choose.

God, I was cold.

I paused, glancing around me as if for the first time. I must have walked the road twice, at least. Everything had taken on an unnerving hint of familiarity. The shops were closing, and there were blisters on both of my heels. I looked down, shivering, at my feet, bare in my battered pumps, at my aching legs and damp jeans.

What was I doing?

Never again.

"Oh . . ." A shuddering breath left me. I couldn't even make my lips shape his name. Maybe I was too cold. Or maybe I just wasn't strong enough.

I want you . . . so much . . .

I needed to get warm.

I pushed open the door of the nearest bar, not letting myself stop to consider it. The light was inviting; a wave of heat washed over me as I stumbled inside. The place was empty. It was only half five. There was one guy behind the bar, blond and not much older than me. I avoided his eye studiously as I pulled out a barstool at a table by the end of the bar and sat down, searching my pockets for my purse and covering Hope's face quickly as I found it.

"What can I get you?"

I glanced up. The barman eyed me up and down, one hand resting lightly on the taps, and it occurred to me that I would have to buy something. Drink? Not a good idea. I couldn't remember the last time I'd eaten. Food? I felt slightly sick.

"Just lemonade," I whispered.

He didn't even have to move; he brought out a glass from under the bar and filled it, the soft hiss and sputter of the pump filling my ears.

"Anything else?"

I hesitated. "Are you serving food?"

He jerked his head to the five-foot-tall menu on the wall behind me. *Food all day.* "Specials are on the chalkboard."

"Oh." I took the drink. "Thanks."

I pretended to read the menu until the silence became awkward. He was waiting.

"Scampi. Thanks." I pushed a note at him across the bar. He punched the order into the till and passed my change back and I went to find a table.

I was glad when he disappeared. I picked at the scratches in the slightly sticky table top. My food came, steaming hot, and I warmed my hands on the plate. The door opened and closed, and a group of students came in, shambling loudly into the far corner by the window, laughing and arguing. A ketchup bottle fell to the floor and cracked. I picked up a piece of scampi and failed to put it in my mouth.

I pushed the food around the plate until it was cold. Got up to use the bathroom, leaving my jacket hung over my chair until I got back. I sat down and pulled it over my knees, took my phone from my pocket and put it face up on the table. No messages. I let my gaze lose focus, the colours of the pictures on the walls moving in a haze. More people came in; food smells pervaded the room and someone switched on some music. I tuned that out too, twisted my hands together in my lap. A church bell somewhere struck seven, and I looked up, confused.

"Are you done with this? Can I get you anything else?" The guy from the bar had come to take away my empty glass and plate. His eyes scanned the rapidly filling room pointedly and then came back to my untouched food.

I glanced over my shoulder at the darkness outside, and turned to him, unduly indignant.

"Yes," I said.

There was a pause. He looked at me, expectant.

Screw a good idea.

"What cider do you have?"

"Draught or bottle?"

"Bottle."

"Apple, pear, mixed fruit?"

"Mixed fruit." I followed him to the bar and shoved the change from earlier back at him. He flipped the lid off the bottle as I sat down, then vanished.

I drank half the drink in one go, the fizz bringing tears to my eyes. It was definitely the fizz. I stabbed at the touch-screen of my phone, lighting it up, and stared at it until it dimmed again.

Then what? You don't want me?

I sniffed.

More than anything. *More than anything.*

322

Someone had turned up the music. The drumbeat invaded my head, thumping and unwelcome.

You realise, if anyone finds out. About this . . .

Fuck. I finished my drink and banged the bottle down harder than I'd meant to. No one noticed. Suddenly, somehow, the place was full. Full of people, talking, laughing, shouting. I got up to order another drink. I hated whisky and I hated Coke. I downed it, still staring at the blank screen of my phone, something new taking root inside me. I clenched my jaw and toyed with my empty glass. How could I have made such a mess of everything?

How could I have been so wrong?

He'd let me go.

I put down the glass abruptly, my eyes not leaving the phone. Despite everything he said, he hadn't followed me. He was gone. Forever, don't forget what forever means. And he'd never said it. He'd beguiled, broken through with the darkness in his eyes. Stormed and raged . . . but he'd never said it. Never said it once.

Well, some people weren't gone forever. *I'm your best friend, India. You know, if there's ever anything you need to talk about, I'm right here.* And some people had said it.

I love you, Hope. And I know you love me too. No matter what . . .

She was writing back. She was writing back, and she just wouldn't stop. She wouldn't stop. I pressed my hands to my ears for a moment, trying to shut out the noise, but it made no difference. The noise was inside, not out. There were no two ways about it. I was losing my mind.

Sambuca. I didn't have to leave my seat to order this time. I gestured across the bar, deaf and mute in the chaos. The bartender winked and nodded, and I paid with the next note in my purse. There were a few more yet. Julia Maine's pay packet. Sod that. Sambuca — I remembered drinking Sambuca with Hope in Leeds. She'd done it like in the films, a rush of perfect flame from her red lips. I'd wimped out and burned my mouth. The effect was the same either way, though. I swallowed it in one.

I wanted her to stop writing back. What would it take? I rooted in my jacket, and then remembered that I'd left everything in the car. The note-rose paper. Rose-note. I blinked and pushed the empty shot glass aside. If I wrote back? Was that all she wanted?

Somehow, I doubted it.

I ordered the next two shots together. Apart from that one time with Hope, I'd never drunk shots in my life. But it was definitely starting to work; it was unfolding like a blanket over me, blissfully warm and impenetrable. Everything was losing its edge. The pain was losing its edge. And I was starting to understand. Why Alex used to do this. Did this. Was probably doing it right now. At least we were doing something together.

What was the time? I couldn't hear church bells anymore. The place was rammed, and the clientele had changed. No one was eating now. Everyone was drinking, like me.

Validated, I ordered a Jagerbomb to find out what it was like. Sipped it carefully, distantly aware of my blossoming incoordination.

There was something secure about the crowded mayhem. I curled my hands around my glass, camouflaged in the disorganisation of students and Saturday-night over-twenty-ones. It must be late. The jeans, jackets and scarves had been replaced by less comprehensive clothing and dangerous shoes. There was a group of girls at the bar, my age, teetering on their heels, drinking sickly cocktails. One of them turned as I watched, and saw me looking. Her eyes travelled disdainfully from my washed-out face to my jeans and shabby pumps, to the rose on my ankle. *Tell me the truth. Tell me.*

"India?"

I leapt out of my skin, clutching at the Jagerbomb in panic. I looked over each of my shoulders, deafened by the noise. The sodding noise. I couldn't hear anything past it.

"India McKenzie!"

Through the chaos, his voice was familiar. I spun on my stool, my gaze refocussing slowly. Brett was approaching through the crowd. He raised his arms to push through, weaving between people, surprise on his face. I narrowed my eyes to see better, watching him come nearer, sharply casual, coolly hot. Brett Egan. I blinked again, bewildered.

"India, it *is* you." He had to shout to make himself heard, sitting down on one of the bar stools next to me. My head was swimming.

Brett paused, his gaze flickering momentarily over the three empty shot glasses and half-finished Jagerbomb.

Silence. I sipped my drink. I hadn't noticed before how disgusting it was. I felt vaguely nauseated. Rose-note. Note-rose? I had never drunk this much in my life. Why did he have to show up now? Of all the places. Of all the times. *Don't be a stranger.* Why the fuck not?

Brett frowned. "Are you okay?" He touched my shoulder lightly.

"Fine," I slurred at him.

He glanced at the glass again, then back at my face, dubious. "How many of those have you had?"

I shrugged, and the glass nearly fell through my fingers. I snatched it and steadied it. Brett stood up. His frown hadn't gone. He reached out and took the drink, and I didn't stop him.

"Do you think maybe that's enough?" he asked gently.

I scowled. "I thought you liked it when I was drunk?" I couldn't quite keep the bitterness out of my voice.

Brett's eyebrows flickered. "Not drunk to the point of needing medical attention."

I slid from the stool to my feet quickly and regretted it. The patterns of the polished floor swirled beneath me. I clutched at the bar for support.

"Why are you here?" I turned on him, suddenly. Brett didn't miss a beat.

"I could ask you the same question." His frown deepened. "India, this time I'm not messing around. Are you here by yourself?"

"Yes." I stared back at him, unsteady. "On purpose. By myself on purpose. And I'm going now, anyway." I pulled my jacket from the stool and struggled into it, fumbling in the pocket for my keys.

Alarm crossed Brett's face. "You're *not* driving. India—"

I looked up at him, scornful.

"No. What do *you* think?" I dangled the keys from my hand, surprised by the tone of my own voice "I'm fucked off my face. I'm going to sleep in my car."

"India—"

"Really." I snatched up my phone and started for the door. My head was pounding. Why was he here? All worried glances and careful touches, and confused recollections of a lost time and a different choice. I was starting to feel disorientated. I opened the door quickly, glad of the blast of bitter air that hit me from outside.

"India." Brett was close behind me. "In all seriousness. I really think I'd better drive you home."

I snorted. "Cambridge is a fucking long way from here."

The door closed behind us, clicking on its latch. He regarded me, puzzled.

"I meant to the Manor."

"*Right*." I began to walk, concentrating on putting foot safely in front of foot. "No thanks."

"India—"

"*No*. Thanks." I stumbled to a halt, suddenly dizzy, putting out a hand to support myself against the wall of the closed shop we were passing. It was very dark. Even the blur of the streetlamps didn't seem to be able to dispel the shadows. And still so noisy. My ears were ringing. I took a half-step forwards and paused, giddy.

"India?" Brett's voice was quiet.

I slid my head against the cold stone wall, gulping in a few deep breaths. Out of nowhere, tears had spilled over, running helplessly down my cheeks and dripping onto the pavement. Sobs rose like a storm in my chest. I tried to swallow them back.

One thing, one moment, that can change everything. That can make it worthwhile waking up, every day . . .

You remember?

If only I could *stop* remembering.

I drank in another shuddering breath, nausea rising abruptly in my throat.

"Crap."

I lurched to my feet.

Brett took a hasty step backwards as I heaved and vomited spectacularly into the road. One of his hands caught hold of my hair, pulling it off my face as I coughed and strained and straightened. I dashed the tears from my cheeks with the back of my hand. He paused, and tugged a bundle of tissues from his jacket pocket.

"Well, that's better," he said dryly. "If that lot had made it into your bloodstream, it probably would have killed you."

I stood still for a moment, gasping, cold sweat prickling my forehead. Brett released my hair. He passed me one of the tissues and stood, waiting for me to recover, folding the corners of the next tissue inwards absently, one at a time, and smoothing the edges with his thumb.

"Come on." He pressed a hand lightly to the middle of my back. "Where's your car?"

"Multi-storey," I gulped. My breath curled in an alcoholic fog in front of my face. I blinked hard, squinting to try and stop the spinning.

This was why I didn't drink like Alex. Fuck. What if I passed out? I groaned under my breath.

"I wish you'd let me take you home, India." Brett's forehead was creased with concern. His hand brushed my shoulder blades, steering me forwards. "You're in no state to be left. And you'll freeze to death in your car."

"No." I gritted my teeth. "Thanks. I'm. Not. Going." I turned to look up at him as we reached the stairs to the car park. "Home. With you."

"No." Brett shook his head. He breathed out slowly. "I guess not. Come on. Where are you parked?"

"Upstairs. Level two. Three. *Two*."

"Two?" He regarded me levelly. "India, give me your keys."

I glared at him. He took the keys from my hand, eyebrows raised.

"You want to take the lift?" He nodded to it. I shook my head.

I had to stop halfway up the stairs, the nausea making a sudden and unwelcome return. I leaned forwards, pressing the palms of my hands to my knees, and my purse dropped from my pocket, falling open on the cold steps. Hope's face stared up at me, smiling, the yellow rose in her hair reflecting the harsh orange multi-storey lights. Another sob rose in my chest.

I'm your best friend, India. I have to warn you . . .

Brett's fingers closed firmly on the purse. He picked it up, his gaze falling on the picture too, just for a moment, before he pushed it back into my pocket.

"Come on." He took me by the elbows, guiding me carefully upright. "That's it."

I began to climb again gingerly, trying to hold myself together, trying to block out the noise. So much noise. I fought the urge to clamp my hands over my ears.

"I wish you'd listened to me, India." Brett's voice was soft, regretful. "I really do."

We reached the top, and I quickened my pace, half running across the deserted car park, desperate to beat the impending, inevitable sickness. Brett matched my strides. It was only as he stopped, suddenly, that I looked up and realised we were already at my car. I heard him unlock the doors; saw the flash of the lights reflected off the grimy walls. Then I retched, bent double, and emptied the rest of the contents of my stomach torrentially over the floor.

His fingers were gentle in my hair. He reached around me to slip a hand into my pocket, locating a band and dragging the sweat-dampened locks back to fasten them off my face. This time, he didn't let go straight away. His touch lingered, cool and refreshing, at the back of my neck.

Brett waited until I managed to stand straight again before he opened the car door. His eyebrows lifted a fraction.

"I take it that it didn't turn out so well with Alex?" he asked, finally.

"Fuck off."

For a disconcerting moment his face separated into two, two pairs of anxiously watching eyes. Then the whole world followed suit and I crashed face first into concrete.

CHAPTER 24: GONE

"India . . . would you come down to the relatives' room?"

"No. No—"

"Do you want someone else to be here? Can we call someone?"

"No. What's happened? Just tell me. Just—"

"Let me close the door. India, Hope's parents are with her. Do you want me to see if one of them will come through?"

"No! Just tell me!"

"India, Hope sustained a significant brain injury when the car hit her. We knew that from the beginning. When we spoke with you and Hope's parents before, we knew it was unlikely that Hope would be able to wake up. In the last few minutes—"

"No. Wait. What . . . what are you saying? What are you say—"

"India, for a little while, Hope's heartbeat has been slowing down. And while you were gone, it stopped."

"No . . . You mean . . ."

"I'm afraid Hope has died, India."

* * *

"Please . . . please."

"What's the matter, India? What's the matter? You think you're losing your mind? Is that the problem?"

"Stop! You can't . . . be. You can't be. Please. Just stop."

'We both know it's a possibility—"

"Shut up! Just SHUT UP! You're not . . . you can't . . ."

"I'm your best friend. I'm just trying to warn you."

'No! You're not! You're—"

"I'm what? I'm what? What are you trying to say? I'm dead, India. Remember? You shouldn't speak ill of the dead."

"No . . ."

"When did you stop trusting me, India? Why did you stop listening? Why have you stopped writing?"

"Leave me alone . . . Oh God, leave me alone . . ."

"I didn't choose this, India. You chose this. Don't you get that? How do you just not get it? It was your fault, India. Vee was your fault. This is your fault. You chose this. I warned you."

"No . . ."

"Someone gets hurt, India—"

* * *

"No!"

I gasped. My head contacted something solid. I couldn't move my legs. I was trapped . . . I flailed, desperate to free my hands, but they were stuck too, numb, paralysed. *Help me.* I appealed to her, even though suddenly I realised I couldn't see her face and hadn't all along, that I must have been alone the whole time. *Help me . . .*

I twisted, and all at once I could move. I jerked and curled sideways. I was so cold. So cold that my whole body ached. My mouth tasted of bile, and my throat was burning.

Water. I needed some water.

I opened my eyes.

Early daylight was streaming through the condensation on the car windows. I had been sleeping with my feet tangled in the pedals, my body contorted in the driver's seat. Vague memories returned all at once. The pungent taste of whisky and Jagermeister, hurling in the road, Brett's worried eyes. Worse, even hazier images of being picked up from the floor

331

beside my car, and lifted gently. Of sobbing into his shoulder as he tied back my hair. Of his cool, careful fingers . . .

"Oh shit." I hauled myself upright, head pounding. "Shit."

I tried the car door. It was locked. Confused, I glanced around. The car windows were misted to opacity, the air chill. And the back window was open an inch, enough — just enough — to fit my keys through.

I strained to reach back, and the headache hit violently, pounding with a vengeance behind my eyes. I clutched at the sides of my seat. It took me a moment to recover enough to retrieve the keys from the foot-well. There was a note, written on the back of an old receipt, punctured on the key ring. I tore it off, blinking hard to try and read the scrawl.

India, please don't drive until you're sober. Here's my number, in case you lost it last time. Call me if you need picking up. Brett 07731 489652

"Ohh." It hit me in the stomach, a kick to the gut, sudden, brutal and breathtaking. I curled around the pain. "Ohh."

I'm leaving, Alex. Alone.

I pushed the key into the ignition and the receipt fell through my fingers as I dragged myself upright.

One thing. One thing . . .

I was gasping, insensible. What happened? What had happened? *What had I done?* I fumbled for the piece of paper, and gave up on it, hanging on the steering wheel for a moment as I tried to regain my balance. I felt so sick. So very sick.

Yeah. That would be about right. I closed my eyes, remembering. Remembering more. Remembering multi-storey lights and Hope's face looking up from the back of my purse. Remembering vomiting on the concrete.

"Oh shit," I repeated.

My jacket smelt like aniseed and spirits. I searched its pockets for my phone fruitlessly, and then found it in the back pocket of my jeans, warm from being slept on. I jabbed erratically at the touchscreen, but nothing happened. It had turned itself off. The battery must have died.

I dropped it into my lap, staring dully at its blank screen. Black, empty. I had forgotten about the void. But it was there, abruptly, yawning wide open inside me. Gaping. I wrapped my arms around it, hugging my chest, and gulped in deep breaths of the stale cold air.

What *had* I done?

I'd done the only thing I *could* do. I leaned across to the passenger seat, moaning under my breath, blinded by the pain in my head. I searched out a lead from the jumble of belongings in my rucksack and plugged the phone into the power socket, turning on the car engine so that the screen came abruptly back to life.

This was the only thing I could do. Put as many of the pieces as I could find back together, and drive back to Cambridge. Angela Warner still had a house on Jesus Green. It was the weekend, so she'd be there. I'd have to go to her. Go, and pray that the Maines hadn't divulged everything: everything that was no longer secret. *What you've done, you and him . . .*

I closed my eyes, trying desperately to blink the images away. Unrelenting fingers, lips. Skin, salt, candlelight . . .

I opened them again. The condensation was melting from the windscreen. I found the water bottle from my handbag and drained it, notched up the heater and wound down the windows. The noise of the city reached me distantly, the clash of horns and screeching brakes. Nine a.m. Best to go, before I had time to think about it too much.

My phone buzzed. I looked down at it slowly, my breath catching in my throat.

Alex?

It was ringing.

I fumbled to pick it up. The Manor. *The Manor?* My hands were suddenly cold.

"Hello?"

I couldn't even sit up straight, constrained by the reach of the lead. I strained sideways, struggling to hear. The line crackled, indistinct.

And then I heard the voice. Julia Maine's voice.

Not Alex.

My throat seemed to have closed completely.

"Hello?"

I couldn't hear what she was saying. The force of it splintered into obscurity. I scrambled sideways in search of a better signal, panic gripping my gut.

". . . 's Alex!"

"Wh-what?" I stammered. The phone wrenched from its lead as I forgot about the flat battery and sat bolt upright, sweat breaking on my upper lip. "I . . . I can't hear you."

"Where's Alex?! Tell me! Now! TELL ME!"

I grabbed the door handle and opened the car door with a clunk.

"I . . . what?" Stars swam in front of my eyes as I lurched upright and swung myself out of the car. I staggered, light-headed.

"I don't know." I could hear the note of fear in my words. "I don't know. Why? What's—"

"Yes, you do!" It was a shriek, hysterical. "You *must* know! Tell me! You, you . . ."

"I don't know!" A tremor ran through me, cold blood, contracted muscles. I took a step away from the car. "Why?"

Something had happened. Something had happened to him. I swayed, darkness encroaching on the edges of my vision.

"Why?!" I could hear an edge of hysteria in my own voice, too. "Because he's taken her! *He's taken her.*"

"What?"

"A—"

Static broke across the line, fracturing her words into a thousand pieces. No. *No!* I stumbled forwards, thrusting the phone forcefully against my ear. It couldn't. It couldn't drop out.

". . . a. I—" The transmission was mutilated. "I . . . of . . . im . . . iss!"

"*What?*" I gripped the phone tightly. "What?"

"Since yesterday! After you left. Gone!" For a moment she was back, yelling, high-pitched and incomprehensible. Then the line scrambled again, breaking apart her words as I clutched at each one in horror.

"Alex. . . . said . . . John told . . . Gone! We haven't seen her since! She's—"

Gone?

Dread dropped into the pit of my stomach like a lead weight.

"No. What? I don't understand." I tried turning up the volume, pressing two buttons at once with my violently shaking thumb. "Who? What? Alicia? Say it again? I don't—"

"Alicia's missing!" Julia Maine's voice came suddenly and sharply back into focus. "Gone!"

"No." I reeled backwards, clutched at the car door for support. "No, no. She can't be. No."

Unthinking, I reached for my right pocket. The acorn, *the acorn.* The piece of paper was crumpled, and the acorn had split from its cup. I pressed it desperately back together in my fingers.

"We haven't seen her since yesterday! Since he left!"

I hate you! I hate you! I'll run away and never come back!

Shit. Oh shit.

"She said she'd run away," I gasped. "She said she'd run away. Oh God."

Where would she have gone? She was seven years old, and it was winter. Dark. Cold.

Seven years old.

No. Oh no, no . . .

"No!" Julia's voice exploded down the line, jarring and high-pitched. "You don't get it, do you?! You don't even understand what you've done! She hasn't run away! You have *no idea.* No idea what you've done!"

What I'd done? My ears were ringing. *What I'd done?*

"He's taken her!"

"What?"

"Alex took her! She disappeared when *he* went! He's taken her! He's taken her, because of you! Because of you . . ."

"No." I shook my head wildly. "That's not possible. No. Alex wouldn't do that. He—"

"Tell that to her father!" Julia's scream was so loud that it distorted on the line, fragmenting. "Tell that to the police! He's taken her! If he's hurt her . . . if he's hurt her—"

I was too afraid to be angry. I let go of the door, reeling. Pressed the phone to my cheek so hard that it hurt.

"No," I choked. "No. You've got it wrong. All wrong. If Alicia's gone with Alex, it's because she chose to. She . . . she said she'd run away. If she's gone anywhere with him, it's because she wanted to."

"He's taken her!" It was a demented repetition, shrill and piercing. "He's taken her!"

"He wouldn't—"

"Then why . . ." Julia's voice rose; rending, tearing. I could barely recognise it, barely make out what she was saying.

"*Then why has he taken John's gun?*"

CHAPTER 25: AT DARK PEAK

The roar of the car engine echoed around the walls, drowning out the other sounds, squealing tyres, the slam of a door, so normal; too normal. Exhaust blew in a low mist around my feet as I clutched at the bonnet, lowering the phone from my ear, her voice still spilling, distant and tinny, from the speaker.

Sometimes, when you lose your mind, people start to get hurt.

I touched the 'end call' icon and let the phone slip from my hand and slide down the bonnet. There was a dent in the front wing from his hand.

People that matter.

I stood, motionless, ice crystallising in my veins. If I'd thought I was afraid before . . .

Alex. *Alex.*

Why has he taken John's gun?

"Alicia." At last I found my voice, and it emerged from my throat strangled. I was speaking to myself. I could feel the passers-by starting to stare. To nudge and mutter. I swiped my phone from the front of the car, lurched back to the driver's seat and slammed the door behind me, staring unblinkingly at the inside of the windscreen.

"Alicia . . ." I clutched the pieces of the acorn together in my hand.

Missing . . . *missing*? But this was nothing to do with Alicia. Nothing to do with Alicia . . .

Dry, heaving sobs erupted in my throat. I clamped my jaw and plugged the phone back in, trying to steady my hand enough to scroll to his number. My fingers kept missing.

Missing. She'd said she'd run away. She *must* have run away. To think anything else . . . to think anything else would be crazy . . .

Losing your mind . . . We both know it's a possibility.

The phone started to ring. It rang and rang and rang. Nothing. Oblivion.

"Alex," I whispered. "Please—"

Nothing.

Oh, God.

I hung up, numb.

She had said she would. If I left. She said she would. But where would she have gone? Where *could* she have gone?

I had to go back.

I rammed the car into reverse.

"Oh God," I exhaled. "Oh God. Please be okay. You have to be okay." I almost ran into a Mercedes as I backed out of the space without looking. "Alicia . . ."

The police would find her. If she'd run they'd find her; they were looking, Julia had said so. She couldn't have gone far. She was seven years old.

Seven years old and alone. All night. In the dark. On the road.

Oh God.

I pressed a trembling hand to my forehead as I queued to get out of the multi-storey. I hadn't paid, had to stop at the row of machines on the way out, the bearded parking attendant glaring at me from the side-lines as I fed my last twenty-pound note into the slot and snatched my release ticket without waiting for change.

It would take me half an hour to get back to Rifway. Sunday morning. There'd be no traffic. People were already looking for her. It was light now; they'd find her. *I'd* find her. I knew her better than anyone. Where she would have gone.

Where *would* she have gone? I pulled out rapidly into a tiny space, weaving between cars to change lanes, my sweating palms slipping on the wheel. The village, the Betton-Worthings' house? No. We would have heard by now. What else? *Camping was the best thing ever. And Alex has made me good at piano. And he did sparklers with me . . .*

Camping. *Camping.* What if . . . what if she hadn't gone anywhere? Like the time she was in the drawing room, the only place no one had thought to look. What if she was still in the grounds?

But Alex wasn't. Was he?

Why has he taken John's gun?

I slammed on the brakes, and the van behind almost ran into the back of me, traffic swerving around both sides of my stationary car, hooting, people swearing.

John's gun.

You're going to be the death of me, India McKenzie . . .

The city rang distantly in my ears, somewhere out of reach. I grabbed the wheel and jerked it sideways, cutting two lanes and swinging across a no-right-turn, my tyres screaming on the tarmac. In front of me, the traffic came to a slow and grinding halt.

"No!" I gripped the wheel with white knuckles. "Fuck's sake!"

The postcode. The postcode was still in the satnav. I stabbed at it wildly. "Turn left."

"I'm trying to turn left!" I hissed at it. "I'm trying!"

Beside me the radio blasted to life without warning. I started, and the car engine stalled as my foot flew off the clutch. I scrabbled to turn the key in the ignition.

". . . travel with Huw. Yes, and big problems this morning on the Manchester Road going west out of the city—"

"No, *no!*" I punched at the satnav with one finger. "No!"

You have no idea, do you? What you do to me . . .

"No, no, no . . ." One more time. One more time I spun the wheel and pressed my foot to the floor. I didn't care how many cameras caught me. I hit forty, fifty, sixty, switching lanes every time someone got in the way. Ten minutes, and I was out of town. Twenty, and hills were building either side of the car, green and dark with foreboding. There was a hard frost lacing the grass verges, decorating the puddles with a sheen of glimmering ice.

I was lost. I had no idea where I was. I pushed down more firmly on the accelerator, ignoring the siren of warning that emanated from my satnav as the speedo crept to eighty on the straight.

The road was getting narrower. Streets and trees and scattered houses gave way to empty moorland. The road to nowhere? I hoped so. The middle of nowhere. I had to find the middle of nowhere. I had to find Alex. I had to find him before anyone else did.

I hung onto the wheel grimly, easing off the gas as the car jolted over the bumps and I saw the glistening threat of ice in the middle of the road.

He wouldn't have taken Alicia. Not against her will. I knew that without a shadow of a doubt. He would never hurt her. He would never . . .

You choose her over me?

Alex! Let him go! Let him go. ALEX!

No. Not ever. *Not ever.* I could see him in front of me, his dark nod, unsmiling reassurance. *Go on.* Scribbled notes on piano music.

He wouldn't. Not ever. Which meant there were only two possibilities. Two completely separate possibilities.

The set of bends came out of nowhere; I took the first one too fast and almost skidded coming out of it. A village flicked past, school signs, shopfronts, the toll of church bells fading behind me.

The first possibility was that Alicia *was* with him; that she was with him, and it wasn't him that had taken John's gun. He didn't have it, and she'd chosen to leave with him, and he'd been stupid enough to let her—

But Alex wasn't stupid.

A sob of terror rose in my throat.

The second?

The second was that Alicia wasn't with him. That she'd run away, like she'd said she would. That right now, even as I sped towards the bleak, black shadow of the hills, they had found her cold and subdued and taken her home, and that . . .

And that Alex had the gun.

There were times it crossed my mind. Times, not so long ago, when there didn't seem to be a reason to carry on living . . .

The road had straightened out, widened. Even the trees were frozen, like spectres either side of my path, rearing up, wind-blasted and bitter. I sped up again, desperation flattening my foot to the floor. Another cluster of civilisation appeared and vanished, barely penetrating my awareness as I raced through an amber light.

There's pills for that if you want them — ask my dad — pills that stop you feeling. Problem is, they don't stop you having fucked up . . .

I overtook two cars, and then had to slam all-on as I nearly wiped myself out on the next bend. I barely noticed the chevrons, the next speed limit, road signs. Until suddenly—

Turn around when possible.

I glanced down at the satnav. What? I'd missed the turn. I must have. I looked back up.

Fuck.

I stood on the brakes; the smell of burning rubber pervaded the car in seconds, acrid in the hot air that still blew from the heater. Everything fell onto the floor, the cases behind me colliding with the back of my seat, my seatbelt clamping across my chest as I swerved to a halt on the frozen grass verge.

Ahead of me gateways broke the hedgerows, lampposts, houses, a church spire in the distance. Another village. My eyes locked on the sign, underneath the sunny-faced 30 limit. The four letters of its name stared back at me.

Hope.

"You've *got* to be kidding me." I killed the engine and undid my seatbelt, leaning forwards, the nausea overwhelming. "No way. No fucking way."

"Turn around when possible."

I swiped out. The screen warped and blurred with a discordant tone of simultaneously pushed buttons. The voice stopped abruptly.

I should get out of the car. I was going to be sick. Maybe it was my driving. Perhaps it was the alcohol.

Or maybe it was her, there, right there, in the car with me. *You think you're losing your mind?*

I pressed my hands to my temples, took a few deep breaths. Sweat was prickling my upper lip and under my arms. A lorry thundered past, making my car shudder, the windows rattling. I yanked my rucksack upright in the footwell, pulled out the wad of folded letters, then stopped.

No. I had to think. Rationally.

I shoved them into my jeans pocket, and plucked my phone from its lead, hands shaking. I would call Alex again, while I was stopped. I would—

"The person you are phoning can't take your call. Please leave a—"

"Shit!" The palm of my hand struck the dashboard stingingly hard. "Shit!" I clutched at my hair, desperately trying to fight back the wave of panic and tears.

I was still wearing my jacket. I struggled out of it, opened the window wide, drinking in the fresh, cold Derbyshire air to try and suppress the imminent sickness. I pushed my hand into its left pocket, remembering the acorn. The picture. Two figures holding hands, an orange campfire, burning like Guy Fawkes . . .

I found the paper, explored it with my fingertips, pulled it out to look. To look at—

Blue biro.

I heaved, dryly. Flung open the door and stumbled into the verge, retching.

Dear India,

I told you I know everything about you.

So, Alex read your letters to me. Did no one tell him that it's rude to open someone else's mail? In fact, in some circumstances, I'm pretty sure it's illegal.

It's really too late for that now, though, isn't it?

I think you'd better hurry up and find him, India. Before it's too late for that, too.

Just a thought.

Love

Hope

Too late for that, too?

"No!" It was a sob. "No. It's not. It's not too late."

There was nothing to be sick with. I leaned forward, hands on my knees, gulping in the fresh air.

I couldn't be far away. The rugged peaks on the horizon were familiar. It couldn't be far at all. And maybe they would both be there. They could both be there. Both okay. Couldn't they?

It wouldn't be long before the Maines remembered, before word got to the estranged uncle, or the police made wide enough enquiries. Someone would know, someone would guess. They'd find him. And if Alicia was with him . . . I had to get there first.

And if she wasn't?

I remembered his hand pressed against the glass. The pain in his eyes. The hopelessness. John's gun. *Why has he taken John's gun . . .*

No. Barely thinking, I got back in and turned the car around. Restarted the satnav, pulled out the way I had come, and let the signpost fade in my rear-view mirror, determined not to look back.

"Turn left."

The flash of the indicator reflected off the icy puddles. The tiny lane had grass growing up the middle of it. A road to nowhere. It twisted, wound, consolidating my nausea. Then suddenly, it emerged onto a main road. A familiar road with craggy ascending hills at either side, the memory of wind, shattering fallen branches. Patches of gorse and fading heather. Wildness stretching into wilderness. Dark Peak.

I stared out of the window at the unforgiving landscape. Miles and miles of emptiness, the wind ravaging new paths across its exposed faces. I hit the indicator and listened to its frenzied tick cut through the silence. Watched the gateway draw into view—

I didn't even stop to put on a coat. The mud was frozen hard as I jumped out and stumbled around my car, twisting my ankles in the icy ruts made by other people's tyres. Started uphill, the ground crisp and unforgiving, jarring my feet as I broke into a laboured jog . . .

His folly.

I stopped dead.

The black Volkswagen was abandoned on one side of the track, hidden from the road by the trees, its rear screen opaque with ice. All of the breath seemed to have left my body. I staggered towards it, gasping.

"Alex?"

The windscreen was frosted too, and ice was sliding slowly down the side windows, starting to melt. I scrubbed at it with my sleeve, and then stopped, numb.

The car was full of paperback books and landscape paintings. Two guitars. A hundred sheets of paper. The heaped disarray of a life torn down.

Tears sprang, terrified, to my eyes.

I recoiled, winded. Lurched to an unsteady run, through the skeletal trees, out into the brunt of the weather. It struck my face, abraded my aching cheeks, its cold assault on my ears savage and deafening. My eyes and nose were streaming as I ran, ran until my lungs burned and my legs almost gave way. Until the folly was in front of me, close enough to touch.

"Alex!" I literally fell up the steps, onto the terrace, the wind-chimes clanging and clashing over my head. "ALEX!"

I stumbled along the icy wooden boards, clutching at the balustrade.

"Alex!" Pain jarred through my fists as they contacted the door, pounding the wood. "Alex, please!"

Nothing. I faltered, wilting. My ears were ringing with the sound of the wind-chimes; I could hear nothing else, nothing at all . . .

"Alex . . ." I ran to the window instead, my hands striking the glass. I could see the wood burner, cold and unlit. The empty sofa, the blankets draped on the back of it where we had left them.

"*Alex, Alex . . .*" I sobbed it, under my breath, staggered back the way I had come. Thundered down the steps and around the mercilessly sloping bank, grasping at the stone wall. The bedroom curtains were open, the room in clear view, the unmade bed — no covers, nothing. There was nothing there, no one had slept there—

"No . . ." I rubbed at my forehead, at my streaming nose, at the stinging torrent of tears that chafed my cheeks in the brutal wind. "Please . . ."

Deserted. It was deserted. But he *had* to be there—

"Alex!" I blundered back onto the terrace, from window to window, hammering against them, panic-stricken. "Alex! Alex please!" I pressed my face against the glass, numb with terror at the thought of what I might find if he *was* there. Because he had to be there. His car was there. And he wasn't answering. *He wasn't answering.*

"ALEX!" It was a scream, shrill and hopeless; I was collapsing in on myself, giving way. I pressed my hands to my knees, fighting to breathe through the tears. Floundering, for a split second, before despair got the better of me and I jogged back to the door, raised my fists to knock one last time—

It opened so suddenly that I almost fell.

"Alex?"

I stumbled.

Too late.

He stood immobilised in the doorway. Completely still. Wordless. And suddenly I didn't know whether my prayers were answered or shattered.

"Oh God," I whispered. "Oh God."

He was staring at me, mute; his dark hair was a mess, standing on end from the agitated thrust of his hand, his jaw clenched, his teeth gritted so hard that seeing it made my head ache. His gaze was excruciating, barely blue anymore; it was hollow, bitter — like the void I had been trying so hard to ignore in my own chest. A new kind of coldness closed around my heart.

"Alex . . ."

Still he didn't speak. His eyes were bleak, barren. They didn't leave mine as, slowly, he shook his head.

"Please—" The word seemed to stick in my throat. I was struggling to make sense. Struggling even to breathe. I could see his fists, clenched too, at his sides. I watched as he released them, with evident effort.

"Oh God, Alex, *please*! It doesn't matter if you hate me, it's—"

"I don't hate you." At last he spoke, so suddenly, so vehemently that I stumbled backwards away from him.

"I don't hate you."

He was motionless, still blocking the doorway. I could see the heavy, sickened rise and fall of his chest, the dark descent of his eyebrows, the disbelief in his eyes.

"Alex— . . ." I couldn't pull it together.

At last, he stepped back. I faltered in the doorway, choking back my sobs.

Alicia wasn't here.

The place was freezing. Unlit, unheated and desolate. At my feet there was a coat, scrunched limply on the floor against the kitchen cupboards. The shape of where he had been sitting was imprinted in its folds, comfortless and flat.

And in the depression lay two carabiners, clipped through one another, still locked.

"Ohh." I gulped. Tried to breathe out again, but couldn't. The tears were a tempest, unstoppable, the sobs impossible to stand against; I crumpled, my hands contacting the coat, its fabric still warm from his body.

"Alex . . . Alicia. *Where's Alicia?*"

It was strangled, indistinct. He didn't seem to hear me.

"You shouldn't have come." His voice was bitter, perilous.

"What?" I could hardly whisper.

"You shouldn't have come." Alex closed the door, letting it bang, abruptly severing the senseless banter of the wind-chimes. "You shouldn't *be* here."

I stared at up him, speechless. Frightened by the conviction in his voice. The blackness.

"You were right to leave." He strode forwards, and then stopped, as if thinking better of it. "You were right not to go with me." He spoke under his breath. "You should get away from here. Now. Go. Get away from here. From me."

"Alex, what?" I hauled myself dizzily upright, the lock of the carabiners cutting into the skin of my palm.

"I mean it, India." His snarl made me flinch away. "You shouldn't have come here. How don't you get it? How do you not see? You evidently don't understand what I'm capable of, or you wouldn't be here!"

"Alex." I took a step forwards and caught his hand although I was petrified by his certainty. By his self-loathing. He froze.

"Don't." He inhaled sharply. I felt every muscle in his arm tense, his body stiffen. "*Don't.*"

"No!" I dashed the tears from my face. "Alex, I—"

"For fuck's sake, India!" He wrenched his hand from mine. "*Go.* Last time I was this fucked up, I nearly landed up in prison. Just go. It's like you said. About someone getting hurt. You'll get hurt."

Don't let anyone get hurt . . .

Something wrenched inside me.

"No!" I caught his arm as he turned away. "*Alex!* I . . . I don't *care* if I *do*! If I do get hurt! I—"

"Please!" He spun back suddenly. "I won't do it! I don't want it to be *me* that hurts you! Please — just leave. It can't be worse than it was last time!" His hands closed in his hair, gripping it painfully, white-knuckled. His right fist was bruised, swollen, tracked with dried blood. I remembered. Remembered the smash of his hand against the front of my car.

"No!" I lowered my voice to a whisper, crushed. "No . . ."

"What do I have to do?" His face twisted. "What do I have to do to change your mind?"

"Nothing." I faced him, trembling. "Nothing will change my mind."

I felt him exhale. and watched, reeling, as he turned away from me.

"Why won't you listen to me?" His voice cracked, and the sound almost destroyed me. I wanted to reach for him, and I couldn't. I couldn't reach him.

"Because love is unconditional, Alex," I told him, very softly.

Agonisingly slowly, he turned back. For a moment he stared at me, lips pressed tightly together. And I suddenly realised that the fierce gleam in his shadowed, anguished eyes was tears.

My tears overflowed, too. In a single stride he reached me, gathering me up tightly in his arms. He leaned his forehead against mine, the muscles in his jaw clenched furiously, his too-bright gaze locked on my face.

"I don't understand." His voice was soft, defeated.

"Don't you?" I whispered.

"You didn't come with me." His teeth were gritted, hard. The words so raw, so painful, that I couldn't breathe.

"I—" I choked. "I couldn't."

The bewilderment, the helplessness in his gaze, was unbearable. I held onto him, trying to rein back control. Failing. The tears were soaking into the front of his damp shirt. My tears, his tears, I couldn't even tell.

"I couldn't. Alex . . . I . . ." I was fumbling in my pocket for them, for the rest of it, the rest of the truth. *You didn't tell him our secret, did you?* I hadn't told him. And now it was too late, too late for any of it, and it had made no difference. Walking away, keeping it from him. It had made no difference at all.

I nearly tore the top sheet; my hands were shaking too much to unfold them. The letters. The warnings. The threats—

"India, what . . ." His voice was unsteady, the frown deepened in his forehead as I pushed them into his hands. "What the fuck?"

Dear India,
    This is just a quick note from me.

Dear India,
    I'm so sorry it's taken me this long to write . . .

Dear India,
    You remember when Alex told you that you should keep away from him? That it would end badly?
    Well, he was right. This will end badly, if you don't stay away from him. It will end badly, and not just for you . . .

    You should have listened to what he said, India, about dangerous ground. And you know it's true.

    Why have you stopped writing to me, India?
    Tell me why you've stopped writing . . .

    You know, sometimes, when you lose your mind, people start to get hurt. People that matter.
    Don't let anyone else get hurt, India.

*It's like I said before. You need to stay away from Alex.
Stay away from him, or it will end badly, and not just for you.*

*I'm your best friend, India. Remember? Forever. In
aeternum. I have to warn you. I already tried, but now I'm
warning you again.*

Stay away from Alex . . .

"Holy fuck," he whispered. "What?" He was staring.
Just staring. "That's sick. Who would do that? Who would
do that?! Some crazy, sick . . ."

"Alex, we have to go back." The panic escaped, washed
over me, an icy breaking wave. "We have to go back to
Rifway. A—"

"I can't."

I looked up sharply. The hardness in his voice stopped
me in my tracks.

"I can't go back there. Not now." Abruptly he moved,
striding past me into the cold sitting room. He reached the
sofa and stopped, resting the letters on the back of it, crushing them in his fingers. "Not ever again."

And suddenly I noticed. The split in his lip. The redness
that contrasted with the shadows around his eyes.

My breath caught in my throat. "Alex?"

"No." He spoke between his teeth. "You don't want to
know."

"Alex, *what*—"

He spun to face me.

"You want the truth?" His face twisted. "You really want
to hear it? You want to know what happened after you left?
They told me, India. After you left, they *told* me the truth.
They told me everything. Told me what they'd kept secret
for twenty-four years. Their dirty fucking secret."

I was wordless, frozen.

Alex's fists clenched.

'He waited until after you'd gone. Waited until I walked
back in, with nothing — without a fucking hope left to my

350

name — and *then* he told me. How it was all a lie. My whole life. How I wasn't his son. *I was never his son.*"

He reached out and clicked on the light, supplementing the watery sunshine with an unforgiving sixty-watt glare that illuminated his face, revealing the tracked remnants of blood and tears that pre-dated today's and throwing the dark rings under his eyes into sharp relief. He was a mess. I stared at him, horrified. Started towards him, but he shook his head. I faltered.

"Maybe you *should* hear it." His gaze darkened, bitter and all-engulfing. "Maybe it's only fair that you know *why* they lied. That they wanted to stop me turning into what my *real* father had been. They tried. They tried and they failed. To stop me becoming what *he* was, the man that dragged my mother into the gutter. Violent, unstable. A man who hurt people . . ."

He put down the letters. Took a step nearer to me. Another, and I could feel him breathing. His hands curled into my hair.

"So you see, there's a reason you should leave." Alex's voice was a whisper, grim and bleakly captivating. I wanted to touch him, but I was too afraid. So afraid.

Because she wasn't here. Alicia wasn't here . . .

"A good reason, India. Because he's right." His fingers tightened, his breathing uneven, an agonising, destructive parody of the way things had been before, the line between passion and rage, flames and shadows. And ruin.

"He's not," I whispered. "He's not—"

"She never wanted me. He told me that, too."

One charcoal sketch of a young, dark-haired chorister . . . No family photographs. Not one. *Supposedly our son.*

I swallowed painfully.

"Alex—"

"It was *him* that made her keep me. *Him*, because he's such a fucking saint that he had to try and save me. And he failed. That's what he told me. That he failed. That despite everything, it's what I am. Screwed-up, dangerous."

He stopped suddenly, and the pause was crushing.

"Well, they have their family now."

"Alex—" A fresh surge of tears stung my eyes. Terror, numb and cutting; anaesthetised but brutally deep, a surgeon's knife.

"They . . . they *don't*. That's what I . . ." I freed myself, took a step back, trying to force it out. To make sense. I wasn't making sense. "Oh God, Alex. You have to go back. *We* have to. Alicia—"

"I told Alicia." He gritted his teeth, pain flickering in his gaze. "She heard it all, anyway. She knows."

I sank onto the edge of the sofa, sick and shaking.

"No," I was shaking my head wildly. "Alex . . . *Alicia . . . You . . . you don't know?*"

"Know what?"

My heart went cold. There was sweat on my upper lip and stinging my palms. An aching silence. I looked up into his eyes, sickened. Terrified.

"You really don't know."

"Know *what?*" A note of fear sounded in his voice. His eyes met mine, dark with dread. "Know what?" He dropped to his knees in front of me, and the sudden movement sent the letters cascading off the back of the sofa, fluttering to the floor, their creased corners catching on one another, a paper trail of despair. "*What are you talking about?*"

I choked. "Alex, she's gone. She disappeared when you did. She disappeared, and so did your father's gun. And everyone thinks you've done it."

CHAPTER 26: JIM EGAN'S LEGACY

The silence was absolute. He was staring at me, speechless, and I was staring back. Outside, the wind had dropped; the air was completely still.

"*What?*" At last he spoke, and the word pierced right through me. I felt myself blanch.

"Your mother . . . She called me, this morning." I wrapped my arms around myself, trying to still the shaking; it was exhausting. "Alicia's been gone since yesterday. Since yesterday . . . she . . ."

"*Fuck.*" Alex rose abruptly. "She said she would." He looked at me, appalled. "She said she'd run away. I heard her." He rubbed his forehead with one trembling hand. "She was screaming . . . she just *kept* screaming. I didn't believe . . . Never thought . . ."

"We've got to find her, Alex." My voice was thick with imminent tears. "We have to go back and help them look." My teeth were chattering. "*We* must be able to find her, if anyone can . . ."

I felt over my pockets, and then realised that I'd left my jacket in the car. The picture, *the picture* . . . And the acorn, *A for Alicia* . . . I blinked fiercely.

353

"Jesus Christ." Alex's hand was still pressed to his forehead. I could see the muscles working furiously in his jaw. "Alicia. Jesus Christ."

The image hit me suddenly. The last night, the snakes and ladders board. Virtues, vices, the roll of a six on the die. The ending move. The final moments, and none of us had known, none of us could ever have realised . . .

"She's seven." He tugged at a fistful of his hair, white-knuckled. "How far can she have gone? She can't have got far." He moved suddenly, pacing from one end of the tiny living space to the other, like a tiger in a cage. "They've probably even picked her up by now." He turned back quickly, his eyes meeting mine. But there was no confidence in his voice.

"Alex, she's been gone all night."

I leapt to my feet, and in an instant everything receded from my vision, dematerialising and spiralling into static. His voice echoed somewhere beyond the range of my perception. I staggered.

"India?" He came back into focus, close beside me. I felt his fingers tighten around my arm.

"Sorry," I mumbled.

It took long seconds for everything else to re-establish itself. The ringing in my ears was beyond loud. I blinked.

"India." His expression was serious as he took in, for the first time, my crumpled clothes and stained shoes. "You haven't slept. Have you been drinking? Where have you—"

"I did sleep." My voice sounded hoarse. I prised myself free of his grip, fighting back the dizziness. Crap. The dizziness. When had it come back, with such a vengeance? Suddenly, my nostrils were filled with the acidic smell of second-hand alcohol. I rubbed my forehead, disorientated. "In my car. Please, Alex . . . we have to—"

"Okay." His voice was level, numbingly calm. His hands closed firmly on my shoulders. "Okay, let's go." He was steering me back towards the door; he stooped on the way to snatch up the coat. I suddenly realised that the carabiners were still in my hand.

"We'll have to take your car. But there's no way you're driving." We were out onto the terrace in a matter of seconds, and he was locking the door. "Give me your keys."

A memory chimed dully in the furthest reaches of my mind. I frowned, trying to place it.

"I left it by the road. The car." I had to run two steps to every one of his strides. He nodded, silent. Dropped back a pace behind me as I broke into a futile uphill jog. The moan of the wind through the skeletal trees was haunting. I shuddered. Alex touched the back of my waist gently.

"It's going to be okay," he said, under his breath. "She'll be okay, India."

"What if she's . . ." I trailed off. "What if she's *not*?"

He shook his head. "She will be. They've . . . maybe they've already found her. You should call them."

Call them. Yes. I scrabbled in my pocket for my phone. Then I stopped.

"Alex . . ." I faltered. "They're looking for *you*. The police are looking for you."

"That's why we're taking your car."

"They'll have guessed." There was a bitter taste in my mouth. "If I'm not back there by now, they'll have guessed I'm with you."

"Yeah." He nodded. "Or they will do soon."

I pushed the phone back into my pocket, trembling.

"Come on." He jerked his head towards my car. I hauled my rucksack into the back, and climbed into the passenger side as he adjusted his seat and turned the key in the ignition. We swerved out onto the road in a stomach-churning U-turn; I braced my hands on the dashboard, light-headed.

"You have water in here somewhere?" He shot me a forbidding sideways glance.

I nodded.

"Then for heaven's sake, drink it." His teeth were gritted. "I can't believe you drove here. I'm fucking lucky you're still alive."

355

The bottle in my handbag was empty, and rolled sullenly on the floor as we accelerated. I fumbled with the catch to the glovebox, remembering the bottle I had bought to break my twenty-pound note when I went to meet Maeve in town. I hadn't opened it since. The door fell open, crashing into my knees.

India

I clutched at the sides of my seat.

"Alex . . ."

He glanced round, caught sight of the note in the glovebox, and stood abruptly on the brake, throwing us both into the dash.

"You'd better read it." The foreboding in his voice terrified me more than the threat of my own comprehension. Our surroundings seemed to have slowed to nonsense; even as Alex changed up a gear and we surged forwards again, everything was in slow motion. I tore open the envelope.

> *Dear India,*
>
> *If only you'd listened to me. If only you'd listened when I warned you. I told you I could help you, but you didn't let me. Maybe you'll listen now.*

There was something stuck to the page.

I unfolded it the rest of the way, my fingernails contacting the edge of the tape that held it there. I heard my own breath in as it reached me. The faint scent of chamomile and soap.

The one soft curling lock of chestnut hair.

> *See you soon, India . . .*
> *With all my love,*
>
> *Hope*

"That's . . ." Alex was hardly looking at the road. "That's . . ."

"Alicia," I choked. "*She's got Alicia.*"

But that wasn't possible. Hope. *Hope.* Hope was dead. She was dead — I'd been there; I'd *seen* it. I'd seen her, touched a hand to her cold, white cheek. *Dead.* I pressed my hands to my temples, trying to shut out the echo of my own voice. *She's got Alicia.* She couldn't. She couldn't have Alicia. It couldn't *be* Hope. None of it. Not even the letters. The letters . . . *this will end badly, and not just for you* . . .

The water bottle rolled out and across my lap and fell into the foot-well with a thud.

"India." Alex's voice was strangely quiet and calm. "It's not Hope. Someone's screwing with you. This is nothing to do with Hope. Or you."

I raised my eyes from her writing to his face, bewildered.

"This is about me." He fixed his gaze straight ahead, out of the windscreen. The colour had drained from his cheeks. "India, all those letters were about *me.*"

The phone buzzed in my pocket, a text message breaking the silence with a tuneless ding. I realised I was too afraid to take it out.

"Whoever . . ." Alex didn't look round. The dread in his voice was enough to destroy me. "Whoever wrote that, *whoever's got her,* has set me up. And they've . . ." His hands were white on the wheel. "They've been planning it for a while."

"Alex, no . . ." I whispered, feeling sick.

"Read the message," he breathed.

I shook my head, rigid with fear.

"Read the message." His jaw was clenched.

I pulled out the phone. Stared numbly at the display.

Hope 12:04

My fingers slipped in their own sweat on the touch-screen as I tapped to open it.

You've finally understood, India. Well done. Now why don't you give the phone to Alex?

"What does it say?" Alex glanced darkly in the mirror and pulled out to overtake. I steadied myself against the dashboard as the phone buzzed again.

Hope 12:06

"I . . ." I couldn't. Couldn't tell him. I clutched at it dizzily.

You need to hurry up if you want to save your little sister Alex. Or maybe I should say your half-sister? You finally found that out, too . . . Congratulations on being the last to know. You'd better not be last this time, otherwise you'll be too late. There's no waiting in this game. And it's your turn Alex. Yours or Alicia's. She knows that, and she's really hoping you'll play. Trust me Alex, you'd better start playing . . .

"Give it to me." He spoke between clenched teeth. As if he'd already read it. I surrendered it to him, powerless. He inhaled sharply. Didn't speak. Didn't give back the phone; held it clamped tightly between his fingers against the steering wheel as we flashed under a railway bridge and merged onto a main road, weaving between lorries to reach the outside lane.

Hurry up . . . I didn't dare to look at the speedo. The traffic we were passing blurred and dwindled. I didn't speak, either; the emptiness became a gulf between us. And finally the landmarks were growing familiar, the hills and bare trees well known, the memorial on the green, the last stretch of muddy road . . . the signpost: *Rifway*. My breath seemed stuck in my throat; I suddenly found myself scouring every passing inch, my eyes combing the verges, ditches, gardens.

"Where are we going?" I turned back to him, stomach lurching. "What are we going to do?"

His mouth was a hard, straight line. "I'm going to drop you at the Manor."

"*What?*"

"You'll be safe there." He didn't look at me. "And the police will want to talk to you."

"We can't tell them . . ." Panic seized me. "We can't tell them! Can we?"

Slowly, Alex shook his head.

"I don't think that would be the best idea."

"Then you're *not* dropping me at the Manor!" I heard the hysterical note in my own voice. "Don't be ridiculous!"

Another mud-splattered signpost flicked past the window as we pulled into the lane, the two storeys of age-dulled grey stone rearing suddenly over us. Sweat broke on my upper lip.

"No! Alex!"

"India," he snapped. "I want you to get out of the car."

"*No!* I—"

"I told you." His voice was dangerously soft. "This is about me. Not you. *I* need to go and find her. That's what they want. And I don't want you to come. They've already got Alicia. Not you. I'm not about to let—"

"I told you." I rounded on him. "No. Either you come with me, or I come with you."

We'd reached the drive. We stopped just outside it, blocking the empty road. Alex was breathing hard.

"Fine," he growled.

Before I had time to process it, gravel was scrunching under the tyres, stones chipping the paintwork as we turned at speed and drew to an abrupt halt in the shadow of the rhododendrons. The silence rang in my ears as Alex turned off the engine and pressed my phone into my hand.

"Come on, then." He punched his seatbelt undone and jerked his head towards the house.

There was an empty patrol car beside the front door. The windows stared blankly at us as we started towards the steps; there was no one in sight. The heavy-pillared porch seemed to weigh down on us from above; I raised my trembling hand to press the bell—

"Alex," I whispered. "What if—"

I felt it before I heard it. His absence. I spun at the sound of the engine starting.

"ALEX!" My scream hurt my throat. "Alex!"

I ran, my feet skidding in the gravel, stones flying everywhere. My hands hit the back of my car. And then he accelerated away, out through the stone gateposts.

"Shit!" I folded forwards, pressed my hands to my knees. Tears of terror stung my eyes. "*Shit . . .*"

Somewhere, through the turmoil, it registered in my mind that the door hadn't opened. No one had answered. I floundered on the gravel, torn, panic winning over rationality. The police . . .

I took a few stumbling steps back towards the house. They needed to know. They needed to know that it wasn't him. That they were looking for the wrong person. That someone else had her, someone else—

I stopped. Looked down, something catching my eye. There, on the gravel, where he'd been standing, there was a piece of paper. Damp. Recently trodden on. Blue biro.

> *This one's for you, Alex.*
>
> *I thought you said you were never coming back. Yet, somehow, I had a feeling that you'd pitch up here.*
>
> *Perhaps you should stop and think for a minute who your loyalty is really to.*
>
> *Don't forget Jim Egan's legacy . . . Remember what was written in his last note? He wanted it to end.*
>
> *Do you want this to end yet, Alex?*

I glanced back at the door. One last, desperate look. If they opened it . . .

No. It was never going to be that way. He'd known that. And he'd gone without me.

I ran out through the gateway and into the road without looking. Where? The note was still in my hand. I slowed to a jog, breathless, sweating. *Jim Egan's legacy.* What did it mean, Jim Egan's legacy?

I gained speed downhill, into the village, slowed again to a gasping walk as I reached the level.

Then I froze. I almost tripped over my own feet as I stopped, horror stabbing in my gut. My body seemed sluggish; it took a lifetime to lift my hand, to hold up the note.

Don't forget Jim Egan's legacy . . . Remember what was written in his last note? He wanted it to end.

He could barely even write his own name . . .

"Alex . . ." I whispered it to the empty air. "Alex, if Jim Egan couldn't write his own name . . . *how did he write a suicide note?*"

"Oh God." Suddenly, I was running again. Suddenly I forgot how tired I was, the burning in my lungs, the way my legs gave out beneath me. My footsteps resounded on the tarmac, echoing off the gravestones and the walls of the church. *School Lane.* I surged to a sprint as the last few hundred yards came into view: an empty road, deserted allotments, the forgotten playpark and abandoned vicarage—

"Alex," I panted. "Alex?"

I'd reached the end of the road. Fields stretched into the distance. The old school was watching me, waiting.

"Alicia?" My whisper was swallowed by the loneliness. "Alex?"

The sound reached my ears, unmistakable and close at hand. I gasped.

Music.

Relief flooded through me. Bemused, out of breath, I strained my ears to listen. *Music.* Familiar and yearning; the quiet phrase was barely audible through the cracked brickwork and boarded-up windows. A run of piano notes that I had heard before; not just heard — felt.

"Alex?" I reached the window in a few quick paces, stood on tiptoe to squint through the gap at the side of the boards. I could barely see at all; I could make out nothing more than his silhouette at the piano, wide shoulders, dark hair dishevelled and standing on end from the thrust of his hand.

The playing started again, the softly spoken piano singing into the dusty silence. Jim Egan's legacy . . . *music*.

"Alex!" Suddenly, I found my sense of urgency. I ran back around the side of the building to the unlocked door, in through the ghostly cloakroom and empty classroom. The old fire door was heavy and stiff; I hurled my full weight against it and it gave suddenly, sending me stumbling into the hall.

"Ale—"

I pulled up short.

Brett turned around slowly, his left hand still lingering on the keys, the last few haunting notes fading in the muted air.

And in his right hand, he held John Maine's newly sawn-off shotgun, levelled calmly at my forehead.

CHAPTER 27: IN AETERNUM

"India." A chilling smile played on his lips. "I'm disappointed. You're alone."

His voice sounded out of focus. I blinked hard. My eyes didn't leave the gun. *The gun.* John Maine's gun. I couldn't speak. Couldn't think.

Brett.

"Where is he? Where's Alex? You were supposed to get him here."

Brett shook his head reproachfully. "I trusted you to do that. Yet here you are, India McKenzie, alone." He paused. "Although . . ." A sudden sharp glint lit his eyes. "If he's looking for *you,* perhaps that's even better."

A stifled noise escaped from my throat.

"You don't look pleased to see me, India." He looked me up and down. "After everything. I'm hurt."

"Alicia . . ." My voice sounded strangled. "Where's—"

The tiniest sound cut me off mid-sentence: a whimper, subdued and terrified. Painfully slowly, I dragged my gaze away from the gun.

Only feet away, but unreachable, she was there. Squatting, frozen, in the bottom of one of the floor-to-ceiling cupboards, curled up on herself beneath the lowest shelf. Her face was swollen, blotched red from her incessantly running tears. Her nose was running too, over her top lip and into her mouth, her bottom lip sucked raw, her fingers blue with cold. Her hands were tied in front of her, cheap blue rope digging cruelly into the soft skin of her wrists.

Rage rose inside me. Panic. Terror.

"Brett. *No*. No . . ." I was shaking my head wildly. Tramlines, night air, softly spoken jokes and teasing glances, orange multi-storey lights, the taste of white wine . . . I swallowed back my bile. "No . . . I . . . I don't understand . . ."

"Neither do I, India." Brett's eyes narrowed. His forefinger traced the outline of the trigger. "*I* don't understand." His stare locked mine. "Alex. Why Alex?"

I couldn't open my mouth to reply. I couldn't move at all. I watched the movement of his finger, smooth and careful.

"Tell me." Brett's voice was hard. "Why? Why Alex? Why does *everyone* always choose . . ."

Behind me, the door rattled in its frame.

"Alex . . ." I whispered.

With a resounding crash, it gave way.

"Alex, no!" I choked. A strange, sick smile broke on Brett's lips.

"Alex Maine." His voice was very soft. "You made it."

Oh God. I could hear my own breathing, rasping and irregular. *Oh God.* I wanted to look round, but I couldn't. Alex was less than a pace away from me. And yet, it might as well have been a world.

"Don't come any closer." Brett hadn't moved. The gun was still aimed carefully right between my eyes. "I *would* shoot her."

I heard the pause in Alex's breathing. He stopped, immobile.

"It would be a fucking shame." Brett glanced from one to the other of us. "But there it is. Really, you're fucked, aren't you? While I have her like this . . ."

He moved his finger, and I flinched. I heard Alex gasp.

"Why don't you move away from her a little bit? That way." Brett jerked his head. "That's it. Where Alicia can see you."

Alicia . . .

"What . . ." Alex's hands were raised dazedly in front of him. "*Brett?*"

A small, not-quite-suppressed, sob escaped from the cupboard. Alex spun to locate the sound; I saw his eyes widen, saw the tremor of rage and horror stiffen his shoulders.

"Oh, shit," he whispered. "Brett. No . . ."

The silence was tangible, throbbing. I saw Alex look up, then looked back at Brett's unmoved, sardonic smile. The two boys from the photo. A mirror image.

"Didn't you get my message? About being too late? You're too late, Alex. It's too late to talk about this."

In a movement so slow as to be almost imperceptible, his finger closed on the trigger.

"Don't—" Alex gasped. His pupils had dilated; his fists clenched, white-knuckled. "Please! Not—"

"No?" Brett raised his eyebrows. He relaxed his finger. "Then *what*, Alex?"

"If it's me you want, then—"

"You for her?" Brett cut across him. "Oh no." He laughed under his breath. "I don't think so. Anyway — who said it was *you* I wanted? *She*'s much more desirable, don't you think?" His gaze flicked over me, through me: *You're drunk, India. And I like it . . .*

"There's something about the way she tastes, isn't there? The way she blushes. But you'd already know that, wouldn't you? How was it? Was it good? Maybe we could compare—"

"No . . ." Alex's appalled gaze travelled from Brett to me, and froze, sickened. "What are you saying?"

"What?" Brett shook his head with a disbelieving smile. "You didn't tell Alex about our little bit of not-so-ancient history, India? I thought you two didn't have secrets."

"India?" I felt him recoil. Felt the agony of his dark eyes on my face.

"No!" I started at Brett, and then stopped, reeling. The gun, *the gun* . . . "*No*! You can't . . . we didn't! We—"

"No." Brett's smile faded. "But I could have. I could have last night . . . Shit, Alex, it would've been so easy. I don't know why I didn't. She was fucking wasted. How much would you have liked *that*? The same night she left you . . ."

"*Don't* . . ." Alex's snarl was perilous. "Don't talk about her like that, don't—"

"Or what? Where were *you* last night, Alex? You weren't there. *I* was there. It was *me* that found her. *Me* that picked her up, held her, touch—"

"Stop!" I sobbed, screamed at him; I wasn't even sure what I was trying to do. "Stop! That's enough! Enough!"

"I don't know if it is, India." Brett's light blue stare met mine. "Enough for who?"

He held my gaze. I was too afraid to speak. Too afraid to look away. Instead I looked at his hand on the gun. At the curve of his fingers, absently smoothing the metal.

"And they all thought that Alex was the messed-up one." Brett shook his head. "I guess you didn't tell them you were writing letters to dead people, huh? And getting them back?"

Suddenly, chillingly, he was laughing. And it hit me. Everything. He knew *everything*. The letters, the pictures. Yellow roses. Octagons. The folded-in corners.

"I bet you didn't tell *her* you were writing letters to dead people, did you?" He jerked his head back over his shoulder, to where Alicia's sobs had risen afresh, shocked and heaving, to obliterate the silence.

"You didn't even tell Alex. Good old screwed-up Alex — almost as screwed-up as you — this world really is full of screwed-up people, isn't it? Not until he fucked it out of you." Brett laughed shortly. "Just like that. So fucking *easy*, Jesus Christ. If I'd have known it was that easy, I'd have—"

"*You* . . . *fucking* . . ."

Before I realised what was happening, Alex flew at him. Alicia screamed.

And then I was moving too, running, dropping to my knees among the dust and debris and split-pins, pulling her out to cuddle her to my chest. Fumbling to undo the ropes as her sobs gained momentum, irrepressible.

"H-he t-told me he was my f-friend. I th-thought he was my f-friend. He w-wasn't a stranger! H-he was Alex's f-friend! In th-the photos! He t-told me s-so!"

They were grappling, brawling, their feet scuffling sideways in the grit; Brett's back hit the piano with a reverberating musical thud, his finger still on the trigger. On the—

"Alex!" I didn't recognise my own shriek. "Don't!"

"He c-came to the Advent c-concert! He s-said he'd m-make you come b-back! I'm s-sorry."

"Alex, no!"

He had Brett by the collar. Pinned against the piano, all that was between them was the shotgun. Stalemate, stalemate, like before, but this time the prize was survival.

"Get back, Alex." Brett's growl was so low it was barely audible. "Get back.

"Alex please, do what he says." I was shivering helplessly. "Please!"

He let go. One backwards step, one. Brett levelled the gun; they faced each other, gasping. I looked up, gathering Alicia tighter into my arms.

"Please," I whispered. "Brett. Alicia . . ."

He didn't reply. His gaze was still fixed on Alex's face.

"Brett, please." I clutched her to me, buried her face against me so that she wouldn't be able to see; see, in every dream for the rest of her life, what this moment had looked like. "This has nothing to do with Alicia. Nothing to—"

"Oh, but it *does*." His voice was very soft. Still, he didn't look round. "More than you realise. More than you realised when you laughed off her imaginary friend. More than you realised when you left her, both of you . . . You didn't believe her when she said she'd run away. No one did. Did they, Alicia? No one except me . . . And as for 'never coming back' . . ."

He shrugged.

Never coming back?

"Well, I seem to remember *that*'s a pledge all three of you made. Like I said. It's too late, Alex. Everyone already thinks you've done it. That you took her. They'll all believe you did it, just like last time . . ."

Last time? I stared, comprehension not quite dawning.

"You know the best part? The best part was that last time *you* believed you'd done it; you were so fucked that you believed it yourself . . . Funny, wasn't it, the way he kept asking you for money . . . when for the first time in your life you didn't have any? I'd followed you, Alex — to the Tube — I saw everything. You never even hit him. You let him go. After you went, I finished it for you. He even thought I *was* you. He thought *I* was *you*. You dropped your jacket when you pinned him. You don't remember, do you? It was right there, he bled all over it when he went down — fuck, Alex, it was perfect. I couldn't even have planned it."

The pictures . . . I could taste bile in my mouth. CCTV, his back to the shot . . .

"You see, everyone knows your past, Alex. Everyone knows. They'll all believe you did it. They already do. And when they find her, they'll find you with her. With the gun . . . Both of you. Killed, with your own father's gun."

Never coming back. No. *Please.* I was whispering it, murmuring, half-witted, not even a prayer. Alicia had stiffened against me. Quiet, too quiet. I felt the tremor run through her, but there was nothing I could do. Nothing.

"Except he's not your father, is he? And that's why you did it; you couldn't stand it, the truth — that they loved her like they *never* loved you."

Alex stumbled another step away. The barrel of the gun was level with his chest. With his heart. Cold sweat had broken on my face. I could taste it.

"No," he breathed. "You know. How could you know? No one knows."

I know everything about you, remember.

Everything.

Slowly, Brett slipped a hand into his pocket. Pulled something out, glinting, something metallic. A key. Shiny and recently cut . . .

"It's been a while since I was welcome in that house." He turned it in his fingers, catching the light. "Since the day John Maine found out who I was. But I didn't stop watching. I never stopped watching . . ."

His gaze flitted over to me, long-lashed, ice-blue. Like the first time, the first night, just lemonade and pick-up lines. *What brings you to the Manor, India?* He'd already known.

"Yeah." His brows lifted. "That's right, India. You, too. I followed you from the Manor, the night we met. I'd seen you arrive, watched you for days. I thought you'd be another way in, another way to get to them — I never meant for you to be involved. Fuck, I actually liked you. You need never have been caught up in it. But you didn't want me, did you? At first, I didn't get it . . . I didn't get it until I found the letter in your bag . . ."

Carluccio's. I was paralysed, unable to respond. My bag. I hadn't had any envelopes . . .

"I always planned to give it back, you know." He shrugged. "I only took it for your phone, to find out what you knew. I was going to give it back, all of it. Until I found that letter . . . Alex, Alex, all about Alex. 'I wish I knew something more about him', 'I can't stop thinking about him . . . ' And it just got worse, didn't it? There were more, in your room. Pages and fucking pages. 'He's the most beautiful person I've ever seen . . . Oh, I wish that I could tell you how happy I am . . . ' And the camping. Every fucking whisper! *This is going to end badly.* Yeah — it fucking was."

Shit. Oh shit.

"I read them, all of them. And that card, the one from your purse, with the newspaper cutting, Jesus fucking Christ. As if you carried it around with you, where you could see it *every day*? That would have been enough to drive *me* crazy. It was exactly what I needed. You were already so fucked up, all I had to do was copy the writing. I got pretty good at it, don't you think?"

Hope. It was nothing to do with Hope. It never had been. My breath was coming in uneven, dizzying sobs.

"But it was you that gave me the *real* idea." A slow smile glimmered on Brett's lips. "When you said you couldn't call me. I don't know why I didn't think of it sooner. The one thing you carried with you everywhere . . ."

Suddenly my ears were ringing. I reached dazedly for my pocket, still not quite able to comprehend, my fingers skating the surface of the shiny black touchscreen.

"Everywhere . . . where it could hear every word. Every confession . . . *Every sweet fucking whisper.*"

Brett laid the key down on the piano with a soft click.

"*You still think this is a good idea?*" he mocked.

I put out a hand to steady myself, my fingers clenching in the grit and dust and flakes of withered paint. Alex was staring in silent disbelief. Brett pulled out his phone. Not lowering the gun, he tapped his thumb on the screen.

The sound made me jump. The rustle of recorded motion, a scuffle, a bang. Heavy, hesitant breathing. Voices, filtering through the hiss of background noise—

"*That . . . was the longest seventy-two hours of my life.*"

"*Oh God, Alex . . .*"

"*Fucking not again . . . Fuck.*"

A scuffle of movement, thundering feet . . .

"*I think you have mail . . . It better be fucking important, I had to sign for it . . . Aren't you going to open it?*"

"*Alex . . . Oh, Alex please. Oh God — Oh God—*"

I raised my eyes slowly, dizzily, to Brett's face.

He sliced his thumb across the screen, cutting the recording off abruptly.

"'Oh, Alex please . . .'" Derision glistened, triumphant, in his cold eyes. "'I want you too . . .'" His voice was acid. "'Say yes.' Oh *yes* . . ."

"No!" Alex lurched forwards, stopped short, his hands tightening in his hair, his knuckles white. Sickened.

"What was it like, Alex? Tell me what it was like. Was she—"

"Stop," Alex snarled. "Stop talking, stop—"

"It sounded pretty fucking good. You want to hear? I saved more—"

"NO!" Alex lunged for him. "NO! I'll . . . I'll—"

"What?" In a flash, he had hold of Alex's collar. And this time he was pulling him closer, closer. "You'll what?"

"Alex . . ." I gasped.

"Tell me, Alex." Brett's voice was treacherously quiet. He pressed the sawn-off barrel under Alex's ribs. "Tell me what you're going to do. Tell India what you're going to do. I think she wants to know."

"I . . ." I couldn't. Couldn't respond. Couldn't make a sound as he jerked him nearer, their eyes exactly on a level, their faces almost touching. The gun was pressed so hard to Alex's chest that it shook; from his body, from Brett's hand — I couldn't even tell.

"I've hated you, Alex . . ." There was a hiss of air between his gritted teeth. "I've hated you . . . for *so* long . . ."

A spasm of panic convulsed me. I wanted to scream. To run. I couldn't do either. All I could do was clutch at Alicia's heaving shoulders, and watch. Watch Brett's mouth against Alex's cheek. Watch his finger on the trigger.

"I didn't even know it." Brett's whisper was harsh. "For years, I didn't even know it. How much I hated you . . . How I should have hated you since the day he moved us here, and made me leave everything . . ." His pale eyes were bright, too bright.

"I was eleven years old. Eleven, Alex. I had a life, friends, a future, and he made me leave it all, made me come here, so he could find out what happened to her. And instead, he found out about *you*. And that was it. Once he did, that was it. It was always you. You were the one that should have been his son. He loved me, but he loved you more. And I never forgave him. I never forgave him."

I gripped Alicia's shoulders tightly, something penetrating my blurred thoughts, razor sharp. Nauseating. The edge of realisation.

"I didn't know. All that time, I didn't know — I didn't even *understand* how much I could hate you. How it was only ever about *you*. He never told me, all those years — it didn't have to be this way; I could have loved you, Alex. I could have been your brother . . ."

"Oh God." I choked into Alicia's hair. "Oh God."

"They didn't realise when you used to spend time with me who I was. That I deserved to be there as much as you did. He never told me. *He never told me.* Only *he* knew, only him. Until one day, your mother met your piano teacher. It was never meant to happen. He'd changed his name, changed everything about himself . . . When you went away, Alex, I think I already knew. I felt like I'd known for a long time. I confronted him and he told me everything. About *our* mother. About *them*."

I heard my own strangled breath in.

Alex hadn't moved. Hadn't spoken. The colour had drained from his face, white, ashen, the circles around his eyes endlessly dark. With comprehension. Realisation. Agony.

A bitter smile spread across Brett's face. "It was obvious. So obvious. I couldn't believe I'd never realised . . . Fuck, Alex, even your fucking *cleaning lady* knew by then. Although she got a bit fucking close to telling. That would have ruined everything."

"No . . ." Alex exhaled forcefully. "Jim. He was—"

"Why was it always you, Alex?" Brett cut across him suddenly. "Why was it *you* that everyone chose? Why not me? Why didn't she take me with her? She left me. In her car. She left me. She said she was coming back, and she never did. It was cold. I was three. Three years old and she locked her fucking car and left me behind. It was eighteen hours before he found me. He had to break the window. I loved her. I wanted her to take me with her. But she chose *you*."

"No." Alex was still shaking his head, numb, disbelieving. "No. He would have told me. Why didn't he tell me . . . Why couldn't he—"

"Because he was a liar, Alex. A coward. He barely put up a fight. He begged me. You know that? He begged me not to hurt him. And I put the rope around his neck . . ."

"No!" Alex wrenched sideways. "No." He was gasping, insensible. "You—"

"I pushed him." The smile still lingered on Brett's lips, chillingly calm. "I pushed him off, and I watched him fall. And I spent a long time thinking about what to do next. What to do about *you*."

Brett looked down. Down at the gun.

Your own father's gun. Except he's not your father, is he?

"I wanted you to *hurt*, Alex, I wanted you to hurt the way you hurt me. I waited and waited, and I watched . . . And I started to realise."

His head snapped back up, his gaze alighting on me instead, on Alicia huddled and shivering, a smudge of tear stains and terrified eyes.

"I started to realise that the way to do it was through *them*. Unbelievable — I always thought you were a heart-less cunt. But for the first time in your life, you cared about someone, really cared. After everything, there was a way to make you see."

It always was. It was always going to come to this. I raised my eyes, Brett's words drowned out by the beat of my pulse in my ears. Forever had never been ours to have. Like Hope; gone before she'd lived. Like Jim Egan, with the rope around his neck. There was no salvage. There were no happy endings. And now . . .

Now?

"I want you to know what it's like to have people taken away from you, Alex." Brett's voice was very soft. "People that matter."

People that matter.

"To know how it feels when someone takes away what's yours, like you took it from me. My mother. My father's love. My inheritance. *Her . . .*"

I choked. Brett withdrew the gun slowly from Alex's ribs. He was pointing it at me, instead. Completely steady. Unfaltering.

"Maybe I'll kill her first, and let you watch."

His eyes met mine.

"Or maybe, *maybe* you first, Alex. And I'll take what I should have had three months ago." His gaze travelled downwards. "That really would bring a whole new meaning to 'over your dead body', wouldn't it?"

He turned back.

"Fuck, you can even *do* it, Alex. *You* can pull the trigger. You can't pretend you haven't wanted to, sometimes."

"No!" Alicia's high-pitched scream jarred through me. "*No!*" She was scrambling to get up. One of her wrists was bleeding; her legs gave out beneath her, and I grabbed her sleeve, panic stealing my voice. *Don't.*

"Alex!" she screamed.

"Alicia . . ." I rasped. "Alicia, stop. It's okay. It's—"

"No! It's n-not!" She twisted desperately. "He's—"

"Alicia, don't—"

"Okay," Alex spoke suddenly. I looked up, the fear a cold knife through my chest.

The end of everything.

"Okay, I'll do it." There was a note of desperation in his voice. His eyes were on Alicia, struggling in my grip. I stared at him, uncomprehending. Numb, as it sank in. What he was about to do.

"You won't gain anything by hurting them, if I do." He turned back to Brett, with such sudden certainty that I let go of Alicia's arm, my breath choked off in my throat. *Alex. No . . .*

"If I do it, you'll have got what you wanted. You could let them g—"

The butt of the gun hit him square in the face.

I gasped.

Alex reeled backwards, dazed, blood welling instantly from his nose and mouth. I watched his fingers snatch behind him for the piano, to save himself, watched them close on empty air as he buckled and fell . . . And suddenly he was on his knees, the barrel biting into his skin as Brett shoved the gun hard against his temple.

"Get down, Alex," he snarled. "Get down."

Blood was running over his chin and dripping into the dust. There was a smear of it across two of the ivory keys, where his hand hadn't quite found purchase. *The first piano I ever played . . .*

"Go on." Brett grabbed his hand. For a split second, their fingers were intertwined. "Do it. Do it in front of them. Put your hand on the gun, Alex."

Alex blinked hard. Achingly slowly, he raised his eyes to my face.

"I'm sorry," he breathed.

And then his arm relaxed, and he let Brett take his hand and guide it to the trigger, let their fists close, together . . . *I could have been your brother . . .* his forefinger sliding under Brett's.

"No." I shook my head wildly. "No, no. No. Not—"

"I love you."

It's strange. The one thing it takes. One thing, one moment, that can change everything.

"*H-h-NO!*" Alicia's shriek splintered the silence. And before I could stop her, before I could even register what was happening, she ran.

Brett spun around.

She had bolted for the fire exit, crashed full weight into the bar; it swung open, slammed back on itself so far that the glass cracked, sending her sprawling on her hands and knees into the playground. And in one, two swift strides Brett was behind her, as she stumbled to her feet and scrambled for the wall, and he raised the gun—

An unrecognisable sound came from Alex's throat, visceral and raw. He launched himself upwards, outside, boots skidding on the loose tarmac.

"No!" I lurched for the door in horror.

And then he grabbed Brett's shirt and pulled him backwards, and I watched in slow motion as he swung, and the full force of his punch sent Brett staggering . . .

"Alex don't!" I screamed. "*Alex*—"

The crack of the shot echoed off the broken playground walls and distant trees.

Then there was silence.

CHAPTER 28: LET GO

His name was still on my lips. Stuck in my throat. I couldn't breathe past it. Couldn't move. I clutched at the doorframe, ears buzzing. Brett was still standing on the other side of the wall, the gun hanging loosely in his hand. Looking down, down at . . .

"*Uhh* . . ." It was stilted, incoherent, a sound that seemed to come from somewhere deep in my abdomen. I let go of the door.

Brett looked up. He was facing the other way. The field was empty.

Empty. It was closing in, realisation, like the blackness at the edges of my vision. Alicia was gone.

Something flashed in front of my eyes. White, glistening. And suddenly, time sped out of half-speed, back to over-sharp clarity; suddenly I could move, my feet beating an unsteady, accelerating drumroll on the tarmac.

"Alex?" I sobbed. "Oh God, Alex . . ."

He could be okay. Couldn't he? He could be okay. Could be—

I stumbled. Stopped.

Oh God.

I could see. I could see him. The muscular curve of his back, his shoulder. One arm, splayed outwards at Brett's feet.

Blood.

Bile scorched my throat. After everything. After everything, I'd forgotten how red blood was.

"Alex," I gasped. "Al—"

Brett turned.

A reflex in my legs and back tried to make me run. An arching, shuddering paroxysm of terror. But I couldn't.

In a blur of movement, he was over the wall. And then he was on top of me, and his hand closed around my throat so hard that my vision receded and my knees buckled, and the weight of his body slammed me into the stonework beside the door with a thud.

"*You let her go*," he hissed. "You fucking let her *get away* . . ."

Oh God. *Oh God.* I could hear myself trying to breathe. Choking, heaving. Blood. His blood, Alex's. It was all that was left, as the world came back into focus. All I could see . . .

"Stop. Looking. At him." Brett spoke between gritted teeth. "*Stop.*"

His fingers tightened, grabbing my jaw, forcing my head backwards.

"Look at *me*. Now."

Cold metal sank into my exposed throat. The gun. John Maine's gun. But I couldn't. I couldn't look away from the blood.

"*Now.*"

He rammed my head back, harder, wrenching my face upwards; I gasped. And then his lips were pressed to mine, merciless, forceful, so violent that I tasted the metallic tang of my own blood. I gagged, bucked, tried to fight him off, but somehow it only made his weight heavier.

Brett broke off abruptly.

"That's it, India." His mouth was close against mine. "Fight me. I like it when you fight me. It reminds me how alive you are, right now."

Another white flash. A flurry of them. Snow. It was snow, falling thick and fast, flying into my face, sticking to his clothes as he pressed the gun to my throat. I was no match for him. I couldn't move, couldn't even kick; his legs pinioned mine against the stone.

"So fucking alive. If only you hadn't chosen him." He let go of my jaw suddenly to trace his fingers downwards instead, over my skin, over the gun. "We wouldn't be here. It wouldn't have been like this."

A shudder ripped through me; I felt the graze of the wall at my back. The door was swinging in the wind, with an erratic, recurrent banging as it struck the masonry.

"I heard everything, India. I heard you with him. I heard you *beg* for him." Suddenly, his hand was on my clothes, tearing, rending, fumbling with my jeans as his other hand thrust the gun harder against my neck, crushing my windpipe. I couldn't swallow, couldn't breathe. A strange noise escaped from my lips: spluttering, suffocated.

"Keep breathing, India." His voice was a snarl. "I need you to be breathing."

Stars were bursting in front of my eyes. I tried, one last futile time, to struggle. Brett's hand yanked down the waistband of my jeans.

"I want you to beg me." It was a whisper. "I want you to beg *me*. I want to hear you beg me not to stop."

Blood. Guy Fawkes. 'Minuet in G'. Red on ivory, so red, I'd forgotten how red. All I could see was red; I forced my eyes open against it, against the pain, trying to remember, to remember—

The snow was so peaceful, a pall of pure white. White with red, like crimson wine stains in calico. I tried to focus on the white instead, but all I could think about was writing paper.

And then, like it was a dream, like I was watching it happen from miles and years away, I saw the first flash of soundless blue light across the snow.

Alicia.

379

I heard the gliding skid of tyres on ice. The noise was coming into focus, the crash of feet and fists against outside doors, splintering wood, breaking glass. Boots on tarmac. Brett's weight lifted abruptly from my aching body.

The dark figures were coming into view. Five, ten of them, shouting instructions, chaos. Closing in.

Brett shoved me and I crumpled.

Then he was running, leaping the playground wall, out into the field beyond, over the frozen earth, kicking up the snow. And I couldn't hear, but I could see, as they started running too. As one of them caught him, and he half fell, stumbled upright, ran into the waiting fluorescent yellow arms. Twisted, broke free, ran again . . .

Stopped.

Achingly slowly, he turned. Stopped to stare at the descending uniformed figures, at the more distant ones with their weapons trained. It only took a second. Only a second for him to raise the gun in his hand and press it deep into the soft flesh under his jaw.

I didn't look. I closed my eyes.

Could be okay . . . Could be . . .

I was waiting. Waiting to realise that he was okay. For Alex to slip his arms around me, for his voice to be against my ear, warm, and real.

You're the one thing, India McKenzie . . .

I waited longer, tears starting to spill over my cheeks, until I couldn't wait anymore. Until, somehow, I was beside him. The snow was starting to settle on his back. He was face down, completely still. Cold. So cold.

I dropped to my knees.

"Alex . . . Alex!" I was fumbling for his arm to find the pulse, because it was there somewhere, it had to be. I knew it had to be.

"Alex, please. Wake up. Please wake up! Come on!" I was pulling at his motionless shoulders, tugging at his clothes blindly, trying to turn him over in the blood-stained snow. Unfamiliar hands closed around my elbows.

"India? Miss McKenzie?"

They were easing me upwards. But I wouldn't get up. Couldn't. I fought against them. They'd take me away from him. They'd take me away—

I wrenched myself free, my voice rising shrilly.

"No! Let me go!" I fell back to the ground beside him. "Let me go. Please! *Please* . . . Help me! Help us!" I was sobbing hopelessly, sobs that rose from deep in my gut, violent and irrepressible. "Please, please . . . Alex . . . come on, Alex . . ."

I stroked his back, his hair, brushing away the snow desperately, clutching at his arm, the pulse, *the pulse* . . .

"Help us!" I was shaking too hard to hold him. "Oh God . . . *Help us*! You've *got* to help us. Please . . . Please. Please—"

"India. We're *here* to help him. You need to let go of him. Let him go."

"No!" I gasped. "No . . ."

I'm not going to let go of you, India. Not ever . . .

One thing.

"Come on, India." A second pair of hands pulled me uncompromisingly to my feet. "You can let go now."

"No!" It was a scream.

I love you.

I heard my breathing accelerate, shallow and ineffectual. And then my knees buckled.

CHAPTER 29: SOMEBODY'S SON

"Adult trauma call, adult trauma call. Trauma team to resus, ETA five minutes. Adult trauma team to resus five minutes."

Feet pounded down the corridor outside his office, punctuating the alarm and crackle of the pagers that had gone off in unison seconds before. John Maine slumped back in his chair and stared at the high-frequency flicker of the computer monitor, eyes blindly scanning the first few lines of the article on his screen for the fourth or fifth time.

What was the point? He reached forward to turn the monitor off, and pushed his glasses up onto his forehead. He should be at home. He knew he should be at home.

But Julia's hysteria was driving him to desperation. The second that her mother had arrived from north London, he'd left. He couldn't be there, with them. Couldn't—

He let his breath out in a rush. He just couldn't.

He was on call, anyway, that's what he'd told them. On call, where he could make a difference. Where he had something to focus on. He could sleep in his office. They would phone him if anything changed. If they found her. *When* they found her.

The truth was, no one would have expected him to be on call. But no one knew. Not yet. They wouldn't until tonight, if they *hadn't* found her, if they hadn't . . . When her face would hit the headlines, and nothing would ever be the same, ever again.

He fixed his gaze on the clock, watching the second hand work its way round. Twenty-four hours. *Twenty-four hours.* What was he supposed to do?

When she was born, she hadn't been breathing. The midwife had snatched her away to the resuscitaire. Julia had been exhausted, semi-conscious. And he'd been helpless, for the first time in his life. He'd stumbled to the resuscitaire, and he'd had no idea what to do. After twenty years as a doctor, he knew nothing about babies. He'd watched them press the mask to her face, watched her tiny chest rise, fall, rise . . . and then she was screaming, outraged, and he'd been dashing away wave after wave of tears as he looked down at her pink, crumpled face. Their salvation.

Gone.

The second hand had made ten, eleven, twelve circuits. He leaned forwards and switched the monitor back on.

The buzz of his mobile on the desk made him jump. He snatched it up.

"Maine."

"John, we need you in resus. We've got a penetrating trauma down here, peri-arrest, looks like a massive haemothorax."

"I'm on my way."

He got quickly to his feet, shrugged off his suit jacket and killed the computer monitor as he left, locking his office behind him.

That was why he was here. Here, he could do something. Here he wasn't helpless.

He let himself out of the department, and took the service lift to the ground floor, swiping himself through the bowels of the hospital and into the back of the emergency department. The set of double doors he was heading for flew open.

"John!"

"Neil." In an instant he was the epitome of calm. He paused outside the doors to pull on a plastic apron. "What's the story?"

"Penetrating chest trauma, GCS eleven when he came in about fifteen minutes ago. Had a needle decompression of presumed pneumothorax at the scene, but they got minimal air. FAST scan of chest shows a big collection. No pericardial fluid. We got a chest drain in and it's drained over three litres of frank blood. He dropped his BP almost right away, GCS now is seven. They're just getting ready to intubate, he's had tranexamic and we're pushing blood and Plasma-Lyte, but the chest tube's still draining blood, he's tachycardic and we're just not getting the BP up . . ."

"Have you prepped theatres?"

"Yep. I've fast bleeped Robertson, too."

"Good. Mechanism?"

"GSW. Came in with police. Pretty horrendous story actually; the other guy was dead at the scene."

"What's his name?"

John pushed the double doors open, and the two of them were confronted instantly by a mass of activity, a folding screen and a swarm of people almost completely obscuring the bed, trolleys of equipment, drip-stands. There was blood on the floor, soaking into an inco-sheet that someone had thrown hastily down to stop them slipping. A pile of clothes was slung to one side, cut through with rip-shears, the contents of their pockets emptied haphazardly onto one of the metal procedure trolleys. For some reason his gaze fell on them. Wallet, phone, keys. So normal.

So familiar—

"*What's his name?*" Suddenly it was a shout; suddenly he was striding forwards, thrusting the screen aside with a crash that sent two of the nurses leaping backwards in alarm.

"*His name!*"

John Maine stopped in his tracks. Put out a hand to steady himself.

"John? Are you all right?"

For a moment he didn't, couldn't reply. The crowd had parted at the head of the bed, giving him his first clear view. The undeniable reality of what was happening, right in front of him.

"Oh no." He reeled a step backwards, not wanting to approach closer, to see, to let the realisation dawn on him. "Oh *God*, no."

"John?"

The voice was distant. His own voice was distant, his own reply, the only words that would enter his mind.

"That's my son."

He clutched at the procedure trolley, his fingers finding the familiar contour of his own house keys.

"*That's my son.*"

"Jesus Christ. John—"

In half a pace he was at the bedside, snatching a stethoscope from the nearest junior.

"How much blood? How much has gone through? How much have you cross matched? Has someone put out the twos for major haemorrhage?"

"John—"

"We need another line! Somebody get another line in! Have we got central access?"

"John! They're doing it. Let them do it. Come on, maybe you should step back . . ."

"Let me see the drain. Where's—"

"*John.*"

"Get me Robertson! Get him down here. I'm not having anyone except him doing this — he'll drop his BP during induction and arrest on us. Call theatres and—"

"John." Neil's voice had lowered carefully. "John, please, let me call someone else. I don't think you—"

"Like hell you're calling someone else! That's my son! *My* son! And we're not waiting for *someone else*! Will someone please do what I say! I want Hartmann's running through another line, stat. Cross match me another six units—"

"Lucy, please go and call Mr Dewar in from home." Neil's voice was measured and gentle. "John, they're doing

385

everything they can do. You know this isn't appropriate. He needs to go to theatre. I'll call Dewar."

"We're not waiting for Dewar!" John rounded on him. Sweat was stinging his forehead, running into his eyes. Suddenly everything was in sharp focus, the colours too bright, the air too dry.

"It'll take Dewar half an hour to get here, and we don't *have* half an hour. This is *my* son. *My son.* And *I'm* taking him to theatre. They can strike me off afterwards. Now get Robertson down here. I'm going to scrub."

"John . . ."

He didn't wait. Even though turning his back was the hardest thing he'd ever done. The corridors, lifts, theatre reception passed in a blur. He couldn't think about his face. The number on the monitor. He punched in a keycode and thrust open the doors in front of him. Changed rapidly, forgetting to empty his pockets, forgetting everything else. *Three litres.* He tried to push away the images, but they were replaced with others, worse ones: a silent child on a bike without stabilisers, a choirboy in a blue cassock. A boy scout, a rifle range . . .

His gun.

John froze.

GSW. His own gun.

Everyone knows you couldn't even fix your own son.

"Jesus Christ." John shoved the changing-room door open again blindly. Rubbed his forehead, his fingers slipping in the sheen of sweat. "Jesus Christ."

The scrub room was in front of him. He could hear the clatter of water pouring into the metal sinks. Smell the betadine. And he couldn't move.

The changing-room door banged closed, locking with a clunk. He didn't look back. Didn't hear.

And somewhere in the heap of discarded clothes, a phone began to ring.

* * *

There was blood in the snow. Trampled, into the slushy melee of footprints and kicked-up mud. Dripped in a mutilated trail to the road. I'd followed it, in reverse. Followed it from the police car, where the woman had left me with a foil blanket, where the blue lights still reflected off the broken hopscotch lines. Left me. I wasn't sure if she was meant to have done that. But I wasn't under arrest. I could go, if I wanted to.

Alicia was safe. They hadn't told me much, but they'd told me that. She was with her mother. They were trying to call John Maine.

And Alex. Alex . . .

It had been so fast. I hadn't even seen his face, before they took him. Just the blood. So much blood. There was blood on my hands, too. His blood.

His blood on my hands.

You're going to be the death of me, India McKenzie. You know that . . .

The field was suddenly deserted. Someone had put up a cordon. I knew that, because I'd ducked under it, blue and white plastic tape that crackled in the wind. The snow was starting to adhere to it, blurring the lines. Swirling flakes were drifting along the playground walls, trying to fill in the footprints. Trying to cover up the blood but it couldn't because there was too much, and it was just too vividly red.

Snow was sticking to my clothes. Strangely, I wasn't cold. I couldn't feel much. Except my hands. I could feel my hands. Burning.

I started to walk, my gaze fixed on the ground. These were my footprints, indented in the mud. That was my scuffed landing beside the crumbled wall. I raised my eyes. *Emergency exit.* The cracked door was still open, creaking as the snow blew in through it onto the parquet floor.

This was my primary school.

I stumbled the last few steps numbly, and pressed my palm to the glass window.

And this . . . this was the first piano I ever played . . .

And for a moment, so real, so agonisingly, brutally real, I could see him. There. His palm against the windowpane, his hand-span spread wide. And I pressed my hand to his, separated by the cold glass . . .

"India."

"No." I shook my head, tears spilling silently over my cheeks. "You're not real."

His eyes were on mine, dark, bright and penetrating, bluer than ever; his lips curved upwards in the tiniest heart-breaking smile—

"No." The word was soundless; the tears were running into my mouth, a bitter salty torrent that choked off my breath. The sobs gripped my chest and held me prisoner, unable to move, unable to exhale, to release, to let go. *Let go . . . Not ever . . .*

And then he was gone; I watched him shift, fade, and all that was left was my reflection. Instead of his hand was the mirror image of my fingertips. A bloody smear on the glass.

"India."

I turned around slowly.

"You can't be here. I'm sorry."

I closed my eyes.

Don't have secrets. I want to know. Everything. I want to know. Because you're the one thing, India McKenzie . . .

The one thing it takes . . . That can make it worthwhile waking up, every day . . .

And without it?

If it wasn't worth waking up?

"I can't," I whispered. "I can't do this again."

* * *

The phone was ringing. Ringing and ringing and ringing. Ringing into oblivion, mute words falling on deaf silence. A dark room. I'd been there before, but I didn't remember. I didn't remember, because the brain doesn't remember nothingness. It remembers the actions, the words, the reality. Not the absence, the spaces in between, the ones that have no way out. No solutions. No answer. Just ringing, and ringing. No end call. No messages.

I counted my breaths and counted them over again. I held my eyes closed against the glare. A dark room, but the relatives' room wasn't dark. It was light, and the brightness was unbearable. My head was pounding, like a heart beating the wrong rhythm. A broken rhythm, intermittently too fast, interrupting the too-slow-tick of time doled out by the wall clock over the door. I'd forgotten what was through the door.

Something else broken. Bodies. Hearts.

The carpet was worn in a line along the middle. I wasn't the first to have fallen through the cracks into this space. This nonsensical non-space. It was a lie, before. I did remember. I did remember. You don't forget oblivion.

The phone was still ringing.

CHAPTER 30: OPEN YOUR EYES

There was already a lift waiting as I reached the lobby. As the doors closed behind me, everything was abruptly muted. I pulled my phone from my pocket, but it had no signal.

The lift slowed and I eased myself upright.

Level four. Mind the doors.

I stumbled out, and along the next corridor, past the glow of a machine selling phone cards, and a set of PVC-covered chairs.

Adult Intensive Care Unit.

I pressed the button outside the double doors and waited. Nothing.

I pressed again, dazed with tiredness.

The intercom crackled into life. "Hello?"

"India McKenzie."

A low buzz accompanied the permissive click of the door unlocking. But before I had the chance to pull it, it opened outwards, a blue uniform mostly obscuring the chaos within. Dimly, my mind registered someone pulling a screen across.

"India." The nurse's voice was gentle. "Would you come down to the relatives' room?"

"No." Suddenly everything was sharp, painfully over-focused. I heard the panic rising in my own throat. "No . . ."

I opened my eyes. The room was in semi-darkness, with just the nightlight glow of the lamp over the bed, angled at the wall. Alex was sleeping. I hadn't meant to sleep, too.

I scrubbed the tears from my clammy face with the back of my hand, taking a few deep, steadying breaths. The dream. The dream was still so real. The picture that had hung on the wall of the relatives' room: a faded print of Van Gogh's *Sunflowers*. Hope's waxen, white face, bruised and swollen almost beyond recognition, the disconnected tube that still stuck out from between her blue, lifeless lips . . .

I hadn't meant to sleep.

I got to my feet to move closer to his bedside, wary of the bubbling, water-filled container that still hung there, connected to the tubing that snaked from underneath the crisp white sheets. Alex stirred, a tiny frown creasing between his dark brows, and muttered something incoherent, one of his arms flinging restlessly out from the covers. With a deep sigh, he turned again, and fell silent.

"Alex?"

The voice made me jump, violently. I hadn't even realised there was anyone else there. But on the other side of the bed, John Maine's exhausted face looked up from the table he had been leaning on, with his head in his arms. He was still dressed in hospital scrubs, a paper-cloth theatre hat screwed up in his pocket. His jaw was rough with grey stubble; the lines in his face seemed to have deepened in just hours.

"I . . . I don't think he's awake," I whispered.

The darkness seemed to buzz before my eyes, filled with soundless static. I swallowed.

"No," John replied at last.

The silence hurt my ears. I looked back at Alex, suddenly too afraid to reach out and touch him, although it was all I had longed to do. Just one more touch. I had prayed for it. For hours. How many hours? In the police car, with my hands covered in blood, his blood, in the relatives' room where I had paced, like in the films, unable to make myself sit on the PVC-covered sofas, waiting for something — anything — a word. A single word. Hours, alone with the policewoman who wouldn't leave, while Julia Maine was with Alicia in children's emergency. Hours and hours. Until he came back from theatre. Until I was here, being ushered through the doors, *Adult ICU*, the doors that I still had nightmares about.

"I went back to my office to call Julia." John achingly hauled himself upright in his chair. "After Alicia was discharged. I must have fallen asleep. How long has he been off the vent?"

"I'm sorry?"

"The ventilator. How long has he been off the ventilator?"

"Since this afternoon. About three."

"Three? Jesus Christ." John seemed to be talking to himself. "Jesus *Christ*!" He turned to me. "What are his gases like?!"

I looked at him blankly.

"His gases!"

"I don't know what you're talking about, John," I pointed out quietly.

"Oh . . ." He exhaled. "No. Of course."

He rubbed his forehead and reached for the chart at the end of the bed, pushing his glasses up through his silver hair as he read it.

"Has he woken up at all?"

I rolled the edge of the sheet between my thumb and finger, studying it. "Sort of. Not really. They said he was. He was coughing. Swallowing, after they took out the breathing tube."

But he hadn't. Had he? He hadn't opened his eyes. Not once.

I just wanted him to open his eyes.

"Jesus Christ." John was still rubbing his face. I'd never seen a man so exhausted.

"Alicia?" My voice sounded desiccated. I wet my dry lips with my tongue.

"She's . . . okay." John nodded. His eyes were on mine, suddenly. He looked different without his glasses. "Or she will be. Thanks to you."

"No." I gritted my teeth. "Thanks to Alex."

392

There was a weighty pause. I sat back down, and we regarded each other, deadlocked, across the plastic table.

The police had taken my phone. After the uniformed officer, there'd been a detective. Questions that I couldn't answer. Statements that I couldn't make. They'd found the software on my phone, a voice-activated app, recording everything and uploading it directly to the cloud. It was true, what he wrote. That he knew everything. It had been with me, every second of every day. Right up to the last moment. The worst thing was realising it must even have recorded that: *I want you to beg me . . . I want to hear you beg me not to stop . . .*

I swallowed.

They'd found my car outside Jim Egan's house. Where Alex had left it. He'd worked it out, that it was Brett. When he came for me, he already knew.

In hindsight, I couldn't comprehend how *I* hadn't known. Hope's letters — it was like the person writing them had been in the room, known everything, heard everything. I couldn't understand how I hadn't suspected.

I let out a shuddering breath.

Maybe we are. All fucked up. Maybe we are.

At last I put out a hand. Let it rest, for a moment, on his arm beneath the sheets, solid and surprisingly warm. And somehow the pain redoubled. I gripped the sheet tightly, fighting not to cry.

I just wanted him to open his eyes. His bright, dark, beautiful, guarded eyes. I just wanted to know that he would, that he could. That he wasn't—

"He told you?"

The question startled me out of my thoughts. I looked up. John's eyes were on the sheets too, on Alex's unconscious form and tiny residual frown.

"About his father?" John's voice was very soft.

"Yes." I cleared my throat.

Another pause. This time, the tension was tangible. I realised I was staring at John Maine's waxen, stubbled face. He exhaled slowly.

"It was three nights before the wedding that Julia told me she was pregnant with Alex."

I froze.

I suddenly realised that I didn't want to hear it from him. The truth that could have changed everything.

"Three nights, and there was no way that he was mine. We had never . . . We'd both agreed to wait until we were married."

John wasn't looking at me. His gaze was fixed on the table, unseeing, vacuous.

"I'd found her a room in a house in Crouch End and was helping her pay the rent. I knew she'd been with someone else, before me." He gave a stilted shrug. There was no emotion in his voice; it was a monotone, quiet and flat. "They met when she was a first-year student. It had all seemed glamorous to her, then. He was older than her, a musician, a pianist. He wasn't good for her; there were drugs, alcohol . . . She lost touch with her family, and when I met her, she was a mess. She'd failed her degree. She was on the verge of losing everything. After we met, she left him — or said she had. She told me it was over. I believed her.

"I thought I was everything she wanted. We'd been together eighteen months, and I never knew. I never knew about the child, the *other* child. Two or three years old, by then, and living with his father. I didn't know. I didn't *know*.

"That night, she confessed what she'd done. She'd never meant to go back to him. He tried to persuade her, but she said it had been a mistake — just a fling, one last fling. That she didn't love him. She swore it." John ground his teeth. "I still had no idea about the child. That she'd been living there, with them, when I thought she was in Crouch End. She expected me to call off the wedding. But I couldn't. I couldn't do it. I loved her, whatever she'd done. I loved her whether or not she loved me. So I married her. I married her out of selfishness. I thought that we could forget. Leave it all behind. I didn't know she was leaving behind a son."

Something inside me quaked.

394

"We moved here. Left London. Cut all ties." John drew himself upright, carefully. Planted his hands on the table in front of him. I couldn't help but notice the slight tremor of his fingers, hastily cut off as he linked his hands.

"She didn't want to keep him. Alex. She wasn't going to keep him."

I swallowed, my eyes on Alex's face. He was still frowning. I moved my hand to brush his cheek instead, flushed, rough, unresponsive. The split in his lip had healed, dry and crusted; I touched it with my thumb. All I could think about was the moment he clicked on the light, the redness contrasting the dark rings around his eyes, the tracked remnants of mucus and tears. The pain. So much pain. Buried, denied.

She never wanted me.

"After everything, somehow, I couldn't stand it. How could she . . . how *could* a life mean so little to her? So he wasn't mine. But I couldn't let her do it. Not when he had every chance to live. I couldn't let her. I wanted to do the right thing. I wanted to be the better person . . ."

I felt faintly nauseated.

"We never told Alex." John grimaced, unfolded and re-folded his hands. I noticed for the first time the gold band on his ring finger, glinting dully in the glow of the nightlight. "We never told a soul. I raised him as mine. *My* son. My dark, beautiful, stormy son who was like me in *no way* whatsoever."

I wrapped my arms around myself slowly, trying to breathe. Trying to blink away the picture of him in the drawing room, his face full of shadows, no smiles. Trying to stop hearing the echoing notes, reverberating, throbbing.

John shook his head. "Even as a child, he was all or nothing: obsession or rage, brilliance or despair. He was so secretive, even then, so dark and closed. I didn't know how to understand him. Perhaps I didn't try."

He pushed his glasses back, one hand pressed against his forehead.

"As the years went on, it started to get more obvious. That it was never me she'd wanted, so much as social status for herself. A surgeon sat much better with her family than a penniless musician — her parents are wealthy, well known in their part of the city. After the wedding, they accepted her again. Once she'd got her degree, regained her status in the old circles, there wasn't much left for us." He shrugged again, flatly.

"When Alicia was born, it was my salvation. Our salvation. Our second chance. Alex was sixteen, and he was able . . . *exceptional*, even. I believed, then, that everything was going to turn out all right. That we'd made the right decision."

John breathed out, hard. I sensed his shoulders droop. He sank back in the chair.

"Alex was ten when we found out about Jim. How long he'd been there, only a matter of miles away, we just didn't know. For all those years, perhaps — without us ever even suspecting. He'd taken a new name, a new identity: the unassuming, reclusive piano teacher — impossible to track down out of school hours, just a quiet voice on an answerphone."

Shit. I stared at my not-quite-steady hands. The rest of the story. The terrible moment of realisation. The ghost in the candlelit cathedral nave. The spectre that wouldn't sleep.

I still felt sick. It was all wrong. All so wrong. Every word, every past lie. I glanced back up at John's face.

"Julia found out. In hindsight, she must have suspected. Eventually, we pinned him down. Finally she met him, and it was every fear realised . . . everything we'd ever dreaded. She pulled Alex out of the school, came to me and told me everything. We thought it was enough. But it wasn't. He was clever. He found his way in. For months, years, he was seeing Alex without us knowing. Him, and his older son — *her* son."

"Brett."

"He was even coming to the house. I didn't know — had no idea — who he was. He was just a friend of Alex's. When I found out . . ."

At last John looked up, and his gaze met mine, earnest. As if he might find validation there. I stared at him in mute disbelief.

"I did the only thing I could do. You've got to understand, India." There was an edge to his words. "It would have destroyed us. Both of us. I raised him as *my* son. *My* son. She was *my* wife. That man wasn't going to take them away from me. I couldn't watch history repeat itself, watch him turn Alex into what *he* had been."

"So you chose to destroy Alex instead?" I couldn't believe I was saying it. "You chose to take away *his* life, his *dream*, all he'd ever cared about?"

"It wasn't like that." John's voice was hard. "You wouldn't see it. But it wasn't. There was no good in it. No future."

"No!" Suddenly I was on my feet, my voice hissing low and forceful between my teeth. "No. Not a future that *you* wanted! But you didn't consider Alex. Or Brett. Not for a second. You can't justify it! Not to me! And *never* to him! What you did was wrong. You took away everything he *was*. His music, his passion. His *life*!"

"*I* just *saved* his life!" John was on his feet, too.

"You're not God!"

"No!" John sat down heavily. The sudden, ringing silence was terrifying. I stood up, quaking.

"No." His voice fell, soft, broken. "No. I'm his dad."

I looked up, horrified, at the crack in the last word. Tears sprang to my eyes.

"Not his father. Not his doctor. His *dad*."

John Maine pulled the glasses from his head. His hands closed tightly on the front of his scrubs, screwing the blue fabric into his fists, his shoulders shuddering with forceful, uncontainable sobs.

And I was sobbing, too.

Well open your eyes, India. We're all fucked up.

Blind, unbreathing, I stumbled to John Maine and folded his shaking hand in mine. I slid my other hand beneath the sheet. Felt for Alex's limp fingers and held them tightly. For seconds, minutes, we stayed like that. Unmoving, unspeaking, a chain of hands endeavouring to span the rift of the last twenty-four years. Of a lifetime so powerful, so frail.

I had to. I had to know. I raised my eyes to John's, unable even to dash away my tears. They ran, unchecked, over my lips and chin. Like fresh air and daylight, like light falling rain.

"Is . . ." I choked. The darkness seemed to swallow my voice. "Is he going to be all right?"

John Maine shook his head.

"I don't know," he whispered. "I don't know."

And I realised that, in a moment, we had plunged into oblivion. Together. *Not his doctor, his dad.* There was no such thing as a blank slate. But you could reach a point where the lines were too blurred to make out, where the marks had washed away to the extent that you couldn't read them – and even if you could, it wouldn't make a difference anyway.

I guess what matters is whether it makes a difference to you.

John Maine's glasses fell from his lap as he got to his feet, his hand slipping from mine. Then he turned his back and strode away, the door closing softly behind him.

All my strength was gone. I slumped against the bed, the tears gliding freely down my face. I curled Alex's fingers in mine, crushing them viciously.

"Please." I blinked fiercely, my mind suffocated by the memory: our intertwined hands, his palm against my palm, his fingertips on mine, spreading my hand-span wide and helpless. His soul spilling in C-minor through the darkness. The E-flat-major memory of our Indian Summer.

"Open your eyes. Please, *please* open your eyes."

A tiny sound broke the silence. A gasp, so slight, so shallow that it might not have been there at all. I froze. Looked down.

Down into blueness, dark, startled and immeasurably deep. Deep enough to drown in. Alex's eyelids fluttered.

"Where do you want to go?" he rasped.

POSTSCRIPT

"Mum?"

"India?"

I freeze. Stare at her face in disbelief. She remembers.

Alex squeezes my hand, and quietly withdraws himself. I hear the door close behind him, and I hesitate, lost for words.

"*Mum?*"

"India. You must be India."

I realise she's holding something. A piece of paper. *India is visiting at 10.*

She looks at the clock.

"India is visiting at ten."

All of the air seems to leave my body as I sit down opposite her. *Wiped, like a video tape from the nineties. She doesn't remember me. She'll never remember.*

"Mum, do you know who I am?"

She frowns, and there's absolute silence. It settles, painfully, over the cheerless festivity of the room.

"You look like a little girl," she says at last. Her voice is hollow. Confused. I notice something else in her hand, too. Curled up in her fist, crushed into a crumpled, glossy ball of faded colours.

"*My* little girl." She squeezes the ball tightly, and then suddenly unwraps her hand. She unfolds it, and it's a photo. She opens it on the table and smooths out the creases. "My little girl. Look. That's my little girl."

She points to the picture with a finger that hasn't really changed in the time it has taken for the rest of her to be erased. It's a picture of a toddler, an impish waif of a child in a swimming costume, with a pointed chin and wispy white-blonde hair, half-silhouetted by the sun at the top of her slide.

I suddenly realise that I remember the slide.

I remember the paddling pool at the bottom, and the woman waiting, open-armed, clothes drenched, and smiling.

My mum smiles.

"*I love her,*" she says.

* * *

It's strange. The passing of time. No measure can ever do it justice, any definition is arbitrary: a second, a minute; there's a whole dimension to it that can't be captured in the falling of a grain of sand, or the mechanised motion of a gear. There are moments that last lifetimes, and lifetimes that last moments.

It is Christmas Eve, and the car park at the crematorium is full. That, in itself, is a tragedy. An affirmation of the latter.

I didn't bring the letter here as an affirmation, although perhaps that's what it is. She wouldn't have wanted me to think about it that way.

It's a long walk through the frosty, grey memorial garden, and we have to take it slowly. Alex isn't showing any weakness, but I've become attuned to the changes in his breathing, the slight irregularities that alert me to whatever he's not admitting. After two days on ICU and two weeks confined to a ward of the patched-up and palliated, he was straining at the leash yesterday, when they finally let him out. And I have the feeling that he's not about to concede defeat. So I adopt an unhurried pace, gazing around at the bare trees, barren borders, bouquets tied up with ribbons of remembrance.

The holly tree is at the far end of the gardens; it has no ribbons or flowers. It is what it is, barely knee height, struggling up through the frozen ground. But its leaves are broad, supple and waxy: spikily, lushly alive, a few red berries clustering proudly on one of its two branches.

I crouch down and use my coat-sleeve to brush the icy bark chippings from on top of the plaque. *Never Give Up Hope*.

I smile, despite myself.

It was Alex's idea to come here. Not mine. His fingers touch the back of my neck lightly, and I look up, surprised. He holds out a lighter.

I take the letter from my pocket. I have to strike the lighter twice, burning my finger, and I hold it up to the corner of the page, watching my writing blacken and curl.

Goodbye, Hope.
With all my love — truly, and always.
India

The flames reach my hand almost instantly, and I have to drop it. I watch the last millimetres of paper scorch and vanish, and the sparks fade on the frozen ground. A breath of wind whispers through the skeletal branches, scattering the ashes for me, over the earth and around the roots of the holly. I rise slowly to my feet. The infinity ring is cold on my middle finger.

"I'm ready," I whisper.

"Me too." Alex's hand closes momentarily around my wrist. Then his fingers work their way downwards to weave possessively through mine. We walk back to the car park in silence. His statement hangs between us; we both know its enormity as we climb into the car and I start the engine. He hasn't been back to the Manor.

We made it to London yesterday, with hours to spare. We left the hospital at eight and drove all morning, ate lunch on the Metropolitan line, and I wandered around Regent's Park while he went to his audition, pale-faced and artlessly unshaven. I drove us back as far as Cambridge last night, where we stayed in separate rooms under the watchful eye of Angela Warner; I finally plucked up the courage to tell her about the Shelgate Unit. And this morning, we went to see my mother.

No secrets.

We join the motorway, and I sink back in the driver's seat, blinded by the brilliant winter sunshine. The frost outside the windows transitions slowly to old snow as we travel north, the fields and trees turning from brown to crisp white around us. Alex leans forwards and fiddles with the radio, then clamps his hands over his ears as a hundred decibels of rock music blast through my car. I leap upright in alarm, and scrabble for the volume, and suddenly, he's laughing. There's a wicked glimmer in his dark blue eyes as he slides his right hand lightly over the leg of my jeans, and I stiffen, breathless.

The snow is still a good couple of inches deep as we approach Rifway, ploughed up in frozen brown drifts at the sides of the road. I wish there was a way to avoid driving through the centre of the village, but there isn't, so I slow into the speed limit, and try not to notice how the atmosphere in the car changes. Someone has hung a new sign outside the White Lion. There are coloured festoon lights along all the shopfronts. Jim Egan's house is for sale.

The last few hundred yards are the hardest. I glance over at him as we pull into the lane, but he still isn't giving much away. Only his white knuckles on the handle of the passenger door belie his self-possession. The shadow of the imposing stone gateway falls across his face. Then we pass through it, and draw to a halt on the drive.

The sun glares brilliantly out from the side of the house, low in the sky, pale and bright. Alex shields his eyes and undoes his seatbelt. I do the same, open my door, and step out onto the crisp gravel. There's a Christmas tree in the front window, a seven-foot monster that twinkles all over with soft white lights. Something moves against the glass, and I squint to make it out.

Alicia's face is pale and ethereal, surrounded by the halo of fairy lights. She halts as she sees me, presses her nose to the glass, then scrubs away the condensation her breath has made. Long tresses of unruly chestnut hair fall over her face as she spins hastily and disappears from sight. Seconds later, the front door opens. The metal latch clatters, wood scrapes on stone.

"India!" She hangs on the door, struggling to slip her feet into her shoes. A smile lights up her whole face. "India!"

She lurches sideways, then disappears again abruptly, the door swinging on its hinges.

Beside me, the passenger door opens. Alex gets out of the car. His gaze is fixed upwards, on the towering grey silhouette of his parents' house. We both pause, and I watch him breathe.

"India!" Alicia reappears suddenly, almost trips on the doorstep in her haste, red coat donned and glowing in the sunshine. "I—"

She stops dead.

Alex has stepped out from behind the car. He pauses a pace behind me, eyes narrowed against the glare.

Alicia's smile has vanished. Her mouth opens, and she takes a huge breath in.

"Alex?" I barely hear her voice, just see her lips move, uncertain.

Then, suddenly, she's running.

"Alex!" she squeals. "ALEX!"

Her weight hits his legs full force, and he stumbles, taken by surprise. Then she throws herself around his waist and hugs him tightly, clutching him as if the world might end. I blink ferociously as Alex hesitates and rests a not-quite-steady hand on the top of her head.

Alicia doesn't let go. She holds onto him fiercely, and briefly he's off-balance.

Then he crouches down and takes her in his arms.

"Alex. Alex . . ." Alicia is sobbing and laughing both at once, her whole body wracked with the force of it. Alex reaches slowly to stroke her chestnut curls.

"Hi to you, too, Alicia," he whispers.

For a moment, there is silence. None of us moves. Tears are dripping from the end of my nose into the gravel and I dash them quickly away.

Finally, he lets her go. Alicia steps back

"I-I was going to show you the lights." She's sniffing and smiling all at once, her face blotchy red, her eyes swollen. She takes Alex's hand in both of hers. "Come on."

I bite my lip as he lets her lead him through the stone archway and around the side of the house. I lag a few steps behind as they cross the courtyard into the garden, watching. Watching them go, watching the colours of the unsmiled smile that plays in his dark-bright eyes, watching Alicia's skipping half-run.

I told her yesterday that I'll have to leave. Properly, this time, and probably forever. I was expecting her to cry, but she didn't. Just held my hand, while I tried my hardest not to remember, *I love you, even if Alex doesn't.* I never did get a chance to say it. Perhaps one day I'll write it. I always was good at writing letters.

I don't know where I'm going to go. Where Alex will go. Not here. The truth is, neither of us has a home. Maybe we don't need one. Maybe we'll find one. Who's to say?

There are two figures in the bay window behind us. Standing apart, and watching, like I am, as Alicia lets go of Alex's hand. She hasn't seen them. I pretend I haven't, either.

She asked me once if I was scared of ghosts. I didn't answer her. I don't think I knew the answer, then. But I know the answer now.

I'm not afraid of ghosts, not these ghosts, the ghosts that run unchecked across the lawns and between the trees. The ghost that the Maines observe, unnoticed, from their hall window: the ghost of Christmas past, a piercing-eyed choirboy with a guarded smile. The ghosts that I see when I close my eyes: two girls in the woods, brunette and blonde, over-excited and riotous, their breath misting between the holly bushes.

Alicia runs to the shed to flick a switch, lighting up one of the tall conifers in a blaze of glory.

"*Look!*" she shouts.

I do.

The smile escapes from Alex's eyes to tug at the corner of his lips. Alicia bounds off again, into the trees, and I'm left staring at him instead. The most beautiful person I've ever seen.

A fresh wave of tears stings my eyes, and I blink them back fiercely. I just have to try not to think about the rest. The yellow rose in a closed drawer. Metal pressed to soft flesh; the final punch-drunk gunshot that startled away the birds, blue biro on writing paper. We both know what dwelling on the past can do to you.

A future would do me just fine, India McKenzie.

I reach out my hand for Alex's, and he takes it without a word. There's nothing to say, anyway. There never really was. He already knows what I'm thinking.

I'm not going to let go of you.

Not ever.

THE END

THE JOFFE BOOKS STORY

We began in 2014 when Jasper agreed to publish his mum's much-rejected romance novel and it became a bestseller.

Since then we've grown into the largest independent publisher in the UK. We're extremely proud to publish some of the very best writers in the world, including Joy Ellis, Faith Martin, Caro Ramsay, Helen Forrester, Simon Brett and Robert Goddard. Everyone at Joffe Books loves reading and we never forget that it all begins with the magic of an author telling a story.

We are proud to publish talented first-time authors, as well as established writers whose books we love introducing to a new generation of readers.

We have been shortlisted for Independent Publisher of the Year at the British Book Awards three times, in 2020, 2021 and 2022, and for the Diversity and Inclusivity Award at the Independent Publishing Awards in 2022.

We built this company with your help, and we love to hear from you, so please email us about absolutely anything bookish at feedback@joffebooks.com

If you want to receive free books every Friday and hear about all our new releases, join our mailing list: www.joffebooks.com/contact

And when you tell your friends about us, just remem-ber: it's pronounced Joffe as in coffee or toffee!